9 +

... writers including ... ... first Australian-born woman novelist and one of the country's earliest women journalists – and Charlotte Barton, the author of the first book for children ever published in Australia.

The spark for *The Starthorn Tree*, Kate's first book for children, came in a particularly vivid dream. "After the birth of my second son, I was exhausted and found myself writing in a strange, exalted state. The book took on a mysterious power." Kate lives with her husband Greg, her three children and a black cat called Shadow in Sydney, Australia.

KATE FORSYTH

WALKER BOOKS

AND SUBSIDIARIES

LONDON · BOSTON · SYDNEY · AUCKLAND

This edition published 2005 by Walker Books Ltd
87 Vauxhall Walk, London SE11 5HJ

2 4 6 8 10 9 7 5 3 1

Text © 2002 Kate Forsyth
Cover illustration © 2005 Paolo D'Altan

This book has been typeset in Palatino

Printed and bound in Great Britain by Bookmarque Ltd, Croydon, Surrey

British Library Cataloguing in Publication Data:
a catalogue record for this book
is available from the British Library

ISBN 1-84428-657-6

www.walkerbooks.co.uk

For my beautiful boys,
Benjamin and Timothy

The tower blazed upon the island like a column of white flame. As soon as Pedrin came over the hill, it struck at his eyes, dazzling him. He blinked away tears, shading his eyes with his hand.

Made entirely of glass, the tower soared high into the sky, so slender it seemed to sway. Even though it was still only half-built, the crystal column was already taller than the Castle of Estelliana, the highest building Pedrin had ever seen. The men labouring to build it were dark against its shining walls, as angular and insignificant as ants.

Pedrin stood gazing at the tower for a long time. Its ethereal beauty both enthralled and troubled him. The people of Estelliana had suffered terribly since the Regent, Lord Zavion, had conceived this precarious pillar of glass. Only the very wealthy could afford glass, for Estelliana was a long way away from the sea and the white sand which was its most precious ingredient. Lord Zavion had imposed heavy taxes to pay for the tower and all those who could not afford the extra cost were forced to labour in the building of it, leaving their fields untilled and their livestock untended.

Many had protested. They had been arrested for their trouble and set to work on the tower without pay, bringing further hardship to their families. The hearthkin of Estelliana, although dirt-poor and bone-thin, had always counted themselves lucky for their count, Zoltan ziv Estaria, had been accounted a fair man, if strict. Since his death, however, everything had changed. The hearthkin of Estelliana were poorer and thinner than ever, and the castle soldiers carried their fusilliers at the ready.

A hard head butted Pedrin behind the knee, breaking his reverie. He smiled and put down his hand to fondle the silky ears of his white nanny-goat, Snowflake. "Yeah, enough woolgathering. Let's get a-going then," he said.

She bleated plaintively and bounded away down the slope, a river of shaggy goats pouring along behind her. Pedrin followed more slowly, his eyes still fixed on the tower. Already its incandescence was fading to an eerie violet glow as the sun sank behind the mountains.

As Pedrin and his flock of goats came down the road towards the town, he lifted his wooden flute to his lips and began to play a merry, lilting tune. All through the fields, the labourers straightened their aching backs and lifted a hand to him in greeting, and the children laid down their seed sacks and came running down the furrows to claim their goats, tethering them to graze in the hedgerows until they had finished their day's work.

"Liah's eyes, you're late tonight!" cried Burkett, the thickset, dusty-haired foreman, leaning on his hoe. "Fall asleep in the meadows, did we?"

"Not likely," Pedrin replied. "Too many hobhenkies around to risk a-taking naps. Had to drive one off not an hour ago. Bold they are, these days."

He tried, not entirely successfully, to keep both a swagger of pride and a quiver of fear out of his voice. Pedrin had never before seen a hobhenky, for the wildkin were usually too afraid of the soldiers to come too close to the castle. Since the frontier patrol had been called back to help in the building of the tower, however, the wildkin had grown increasingly audacious. There were many tales of chickens and pigs stolen from villages as close to Levanna-On-The-Lake as Ardeth, the village only half an hour's walk away, while apparently a grogoyle had flown down to feast on a goat at Lake Sennaval, the town closest to the Perilous Forest. A grogoyle had not been seen in anyone's living memory and there had been much muttering and striking of fingers on the news. Many a village had set up their own guards to drive the wildkin away, despite the hearthkin's weariness after a long day in the fields, for all feared and mistrusted the wildkin and begrudged them even the occasional hen.

"Nah, you're tomfooling us!"

"A hobhenky, this close to Levanna-On-The-Lake?"

"You drove off a hobhenky? Nah!"

"Yeah, I did," Pedrin said. "I peppered him with

rocks until he took off. He was a hulking big feller, as thick as a tree, with the ugliest mug you ever did see and hands as big as this!" He spread out both of his broad, brown hands as if holding a meat platter.

"Nah!" all the men cried out in astonishment.

"Pull t'other one, Pedrin," said a thin, narrow-eyed man called Linton. "A young feller like you? With naught but a slingshot and some pebbles?"

"I did," Pedrin cried, clenching his hands on his flute, his face hot.

"Can't have been too hungry," Linton said dismissively.

"Still, 'twas a brave thing to do," Burkett said, patting Pedrin's shoulder. "Hobhenkies are big trouble."

"Big trouble seeing one so close to town," said another man. "Can't say I heard of one so close for many a long year. Mebbe you'd best tell them up the castle."

Pedrin looked up at the high, grey walls and frowning battlements of the castle, built high on a hill behind the town. It cast a long shadow over the brown fields.

"Mebbe not," he said with a nervous grin and shrug. "Likely to get a thrashing for me trouble. Nah, I'm heading home, gonna get me some fishing."

The men grinned, hefting up their tools, turning back to their labour.

"Good idea," Linton said. "Wish I'd the time to cast a line."

"Hope they're biting," Burkett said. "Give me regards to your ma."

10

"Sure," Pedrin said and whistled to the goats, who had meandered down the road, eating the green young thistles in the ditch or rubbing their backs against the fence-posts. They flocked obediently to his side, scudding white and brown as the river in flood. His flute once more at his lips, Pedrin made his way down the dusty road towards the town.

Levanna-On-The-Lake curved around the base of the hill on which the Castle of Estelliana was built. It was a pretty town, built high within encircling walls. A maze of shops and tall houses surrounded the wide marketplace in the centre of the town, which ran down to the jetties where the barges were loaded and unloaded. Before the town stretched the ever-changing waters of the lake, one day serene and blue, another day moody-dark. In the centre of the lake was the small island where the Regent's tower was being erected, its glass walls reflecting every shift in the lake's mood, the lake itself being a mirror for the sky.

The promontory on which the castle and its town were built thrust out into the lake so that the gleaming sheets of water could be seen from just about every window and door. Watery reflections sparkled on the walls of the twisting streets and alleyways, even when the lake was not in sight. Only the marketplace was built on flat ground. Elsewhere the streets ran up sharply, often broken with uneven steps. Behind the town rose the twelve spires of the castle, all fluttering with white and silver flags.

Few of the townsfolk kept their own goats and so Pedrin did not need to go within the town gates.

Instead he headed down towards the Evenlode, the small herd of goats leaping and running at his heels, his lively music filling the warm evening air. Women came from the small thatched cottages scattered through the river-meadows, wiping their red hands on their aprons and calling a greeting to him as they reclaimed their goats. One gave him a long loaf of fresh bread in payment, another passed him a pile of mended clothes, yet another a small pot of honey.

Thus laden, his steps slowed, until at last he had only two goats still running at his heels, one very quick and nimble and white as snow, the other big and black and shaggy, with long horns and narrow golden eyes. This was Thundercloud, Pedrin's buck, and a bold, bad-tempered billy-goat he was too.

Pedrin lived with his mother and sister in a small cottage built on the banks of the Evenlode, well away from the noise and bustle of the town. Though it had only wooden shutters to close against the weather, it was a pretty place, surrounded by a neat garden of herbs and vegetables and overshadowed by a tall flowering tree. Eyebright and meadowsweet grew wild on its low thatched roof, so that the cottage looked as if it had grown out of the meadow itself.

A small, thin boy was sitting on the front step, a crutch leaning against his knee. His blond hair was neatly tied at the back of his head with a black ribbon, and he was dressed in a fine linen shirt under a long-tailed blue coat. Unlike Pedrin, whose bare feet were hard as the hooves of his goats, Durrik wore black brogues with brass buckles, polished to a high sheen.

He had looked up at the sound of the flute, smiling eagerly. "Liah's eyes, you're late!" he cried. "Whatever kept you?"

"Hobhenky," Pedrin replied briefly. "Tried to take one of the little kids. I drove him off though." His ears turning red, he patted the slingshot and bag of stones that always hung from his belt.

Durrik looked at him admiringly. "A hobhenky! Gruesome! Warn't you scared?"

Pedrin drew a curving line in the dust with his big toe. "Yeah," he admitted. "I would've turned tail and run, but me legs had turned to water. They just folded under me. He were a great brute of a thing, seven or eight feet, mebbe, with yellow teeth and mean, little piggy eyes. He could've crushed me skull with one blow! I was sure Tallis were a-calling me name."

Durrik looked solemn and rather scared at the mention of the moon god Tallis, deity of death and resurrection. Instinctively he struck his right index finger against his left, calling upon Liah, the favoured goddess of all hearthkin, to protect him.

"I'd put me hand down on a big rock and so I just lammed it at him, don't really know why. Stupid, really. He roared and roared and so I had to keep on a-lamming him. He went crashing off, holding his head and a-crying, like. I felt so sick and shaky it took me ages to get up again." Pedrin felt his face growing hot and tense again and looked away, twisting his flute about in his hands.

Durrik made a declamatory gesture with his hands. "O Pedrin the brave, his precious goats did save,

13

lammed a dirty big rock, gave hobhenky a nasty knock, all with a big heave-ho, O!"

"You're such a tomfool, Durrik," Pedrin said without rancour, putting down his hand to help his friend to his feet. Durrik struggled up, leaning heavily on his crutch. His left leg was thin and crooked, the foot turning in at an awkward angle.

"We a-going fishing?" Durrik asked. "Sun's almost gone."

"Fish bite best at dusk," Pedrin said confidently.

He put his head in the door to greet his mother and give her his booty. She was bending over the fire, working a pair of ancient bellows in a vain attempt to blow the sullen embers into vivid, leaping life. She looked up as Pedrin came in and smiled, puffing the damp tendrils of hair away from her hot face.

"Hey, Pedrin. I was a-getting worried. I thought you boys were going to catch us some fish for supper? Mina and me are mighty hungry!"

She was tall for a hearthkin and very thin, with a great mass of brown hair coiled untidily at the nape of her neck. It was always falling out and she was always winding it back again, sticking hairpins in at odd angles to try to keep it up. Her face was finely drawn, almost gaunt, with lines about the eyes that should not have been there – lines of grief and anxiety and weariness. When she smiled, the lines ate up her eyes so that their black snap almost disappeared, but her smile was so wide and warm it did not matter. Her hair was grizzled with grey and her hands were pepper-red, but when Maegeth, the widow of Mortemer

14

Goatherd, smiled, it was easy to see the laughing, carefree girl she had once been.

For the third time Pedrin described his encounter with the hobhenky, though this time he did a better job of keeping his voice level and gave no embellishments about yellow teeth, tree-trunk torsos or meat platter hands. All the laughter disappeared from Maegeth's face and she caught him close. Pedrin patted her awkwardly, feeling the bones in her shoulder.

"Chtatchka blast the Regent and his glassy tower! Has he no eyes, to see the trouble he brings? Oh Pedrin, 'tis not safe for you out in the meadows. I could not bear it if … oh, you mustn't go out again!"

He was stiff with embarrassment and shame, and the desire to press close to her thin, hard frame and let her comfort him. So he pushed her away, saying a little more roughly than he had intended: "Nah, what's a hobhenky or two? I drove him off, didn't I? Can't be a-staying home like a little kid. What would we eat if I did?"

Maegeth's face was very expressive. He saw hurt, a quick recoil into herself, and then the bitter twist of her mouth as she acknowledged the truth of his words. They would indeed starve without the bread and corn and honey and apples Pedrin was paid for minding his neighbours' goats. Maegeth was humiliated by this, and troubled by how hard Pedrin had to work, and pricked with a dull, familiar pain at the reminder of Mortemer's absence, and stabbed with a cruel fear that Pedrin might be lost the same way. All this Pedrin saw in an instant and was sorry, but he could not retrieve the words, nor could he back down, not with Durrik listening to every word and his sister Mina glaring at him through the dark tangle of her hair.

So he said sullenly, "Be too dark to fish soon. If we're t'eat tonight, I'd better go."

She nodded and turned back to the fire, thrusting the poker into the half-charred logs so a burst of sparks flew up the chimney. He realised with a sudden stab of guilt and resentment that he had forgotten to gather her any firewood that morning. He felt shame roll up his body in a slow, hot, heavy wave but he looked down, dug his toe into the dirt of the floor, and said nothing.

"I wanna go a-fishing too," Mina whined. She was a skinny little girl, all hair and legs and mouth, and the bane of Pedrin's life, always tagging around after him and Durrik and trying to crash in on their adventures. Pedrin thought it his duty to keep her very firmly in line, reminding her constantly that she was only a girl and much too young to be allowed far from her mother's skirts.

"Nah, you're not a-coming," Pedrin said. "You'd scare the fish off with all your noise."

"I wanna go too!" Mina began to cry.

"Nah, you're not a-coming!"

Despite himself, Pedrin flicked a look at his mother who said crisply, "Mina, I need you to shell the peas. Pedrin, make sure you get the milking done before you go."

"Of course I will," he said in long-suffering tones.

He was disconcerted when Maegeth's face suddenly relaxed into a smile. She seized a handful of curls, dragged him close and kissed the top of his head.

"That's a good boy," she said. "Hurry along now else you'll be too late to catch a nibble. Mina and me are hungry!"

Pedrin blushed and cast a look at Durrik, who was responding instinctively to Maegeth's smile with one of his own. Pedrin choked back his blush, stuck out his tongue at Mina, who stuck hers out in return, and grabbed Durrik's sleeve, dragging him back into the warm dusk of the garden.

"Mothers!" Pedrin rolled his eyes.

"I like your ma," Durrik said. "I wish I had one like her."

Pedrin cast him a quick look of sympathy. "I s'pose she's not so bad, as far as mothers go. Come help me settle the goats, then we can be on our way – at last!"

He seized hold of Thundercloud's collar, dragging his narrow black head up from the herbs growing along the path. Thundercloud swung his head, trying to take a bite out of Pedrin's leg, but the goatherd skipped nimbly out of reach, dragging the reluctant billy-goat down the path towards the little shed behind the cottage.

Durrik leant down and rubbed Snowflake affectionately between her two back-curving horns. She bleated and rubbed her head against him, and he caught hold of her collar. She was far too well-mannered to need a tussle, following Durrik willingly as he swung forward on his crutch, her bell ringing.

As Pedrin carried heavy buckets of water from the river to fill the goats' trough, Durrik stirred a delicious-smelling mixture of oats, molasses and lucerne chaff for the nanny-goat to eat. He then hung up a bundle of chaff for Thundercloud to nibble, while Pedrin swiftly and expertly milked the nanny-goat. The black billy-goat rolled his golden eyes angrily and tried to take a bite out of Durrik's leg. He could smell Snowflake's molasses and wanted some for himself, but such treats were reserved for the nanny-goat, to keep her milk rich and sweet. Durrik had to scramble back quickly to avoid the billy-goat's sharp yellow teeth, almost losing his footing in the straw. He retreated to the safety of the garden, where the cicadas were beginning to whine.

By the time the milking was done, the sun was almost gone. Pedrin grinned at Durrik. "Let's get moving! I can already smell fried fish for supper."

He grabbed his rod and basket from the bench and the two friends set off through the long grass, Durrik swinging along nimbly with his crutch tucked under one arm.

It was early summer and the days were growing longer and warmer, much to the relief of everyone in the valley. In summer, the twilight lasted for hours, giving the hearthkin time to toil in their own little gardens or see to a few jobs of carpentry about their homes. In the cruel cold of winter, they left their cottages in the dark and returned in the dark, and there was no time for anything before bedtime but a hasty meal huddled by the fire.

The path led them along the banks of the Evenlode. All was quiet. On the far side of the river the young green corn rustled together in the breeze.

"What has a thousand ears but cannot hear?" asked Durrik impishly.

"I don't know. A hobhenky?"

"Nah, of course not."

"Some kind of gibgoblin?"

Durrik snorted with laughter, shaking his head.

"Jumping Jimjinny, I don't know then. What?"

Giggling, Durrik pointed across the river. "A field of corn!"

"Oh!" Pedrin tried not to look foolish. "Ha-ha. Very funny."

"What goes in one ear and out t'other?"

"What then?"

"A bug in a cornfield."

Both boys sniggered and Pedrin gave Durrik a little shove that almost unbalanced him. "Cabbage-head!"

They came round the curve of the river and saw the arches of the Levanna Bridge ahead of them. Along this stretch of riverbank the cottages were clustered close together and the path was smooth and wide, so Pedrin did not need to hold back the long briars of blackberry brambles for his friend.

Over the quaint dusk-song of the frogs, they heard the sound of bitter weeping. Pedrin and Durrik glanced at each other uncomfortably, then looked away, the fair boy digging miserably at the mud with the tip of his crutch. The man who lived in one of these cottages had been killed the day before by a falling sheet of glass. He had been married less than a year and his wife had only recently given birth to a baby. Even that tragedy had not seen work on the crystal tower halted. The men of Estelliana, though shocked and horrified, had all been forced to keep on working while the body had been unceremoniously carted home to his young wife. It would now be laid out in the cottage's one room, all washed and neatly dressed, waiting to be burnt on the funeral pyre in the morning. Durrik's father would lead the funeral procession, ringing his largest, most sombre-sounding bell.

As the town bell-crier, Durrik's father Johan was one of the most respected men in all of Levanna-On-The-Lake. He rang in weddings and funerals, drove away ghosts, boo-bogeys and other mischievous spirits, celebrated the harvest and read all proclamations from the castle and royal court. Every day he rang the change of hours, so that everyone knew when the day began and ended, and he was thus beloved by Marithos, the god of time and numbers.

Consequently the bell-crier was a prosperous man, with a tall house in the main square of Levanna-On-The-Lake, with real glass in its windows and separate rooms for sleeping, eating, cooking, sitting and reading. Pedrin found this quite wonderful, if rather odd. He was always eager to see the bell-crier's treasures – the precious lute that Johan Bell-Crier sometimes let him play; the starkin dancers in a glass globe that swung and bowed to the delicate strains of music when a small silver key was turned; the goblets of

violet glass all embossed with silver; the striped spinning top that sang as it spun; the fat silk coverlets and
rose-embroidered bed-curtains; Durrik's three pairs of
shoes and two long-tailed coats with brass buttons;
the row of gleaming bells, hanging by their handles in
the sitting room; and finally, the shelves of books, their
pages as fragile as an old woman's skin, all marked
with strange runes and symbols that Pedrin longed to
understand.

The boys' footsteps quickened past the sound of
weeping. They came to the bridge, and climbed up to
sit on its railing, their legs dangling into the shadowy
air beneath as they cast their lines into the water. For a
long moment there was silence.

The first fish to leap and fight at the end of Pedrin's line broke the strain that had grown up between them. At last the silverback lay gasping and flapping in their basket and, before they had time to remember the baby left without its father, the widow left penniless, Durrik's line went taut with strain.

He reeled in a huge, dark gaper-mouth and, although he had to throw him back, the murky-green fish being both unpleasant to eat and mildly poisonous, he soon caught another fat silverback.

By the time it was fully dark, they had five firm-fleshed fish in their basket, more than enough for their suppers. Durrik had caught three of them but he said rather diffidently, "Papa and I can't eat them all tonight and it seems a shame not t'eat them when they're fresh. Would you and your ma like one?"

Pedrin was not too proud to accept, knowing that Durrik would have plenty to eat that night even without the fish, while his own supper would be a mere crust of bread and slice of cheese otherwise. He nodded and hefted up the rods and basket, saying, "I'll come say good-even to your pa, since I'm so close."

This time Durrik was the one to be grateful. Apart from the difficulty he would have in trying to carry home his fish, weighed down as he was by his crutch, he was often waylaid and bullied by the rough boys of the town. Although they rarely hurt him badly these days, they humiliated and frightened him, tripping him over, jeering at him, and taking any small coins he had on him. Durrik endured these attacks stoically, rarely responding other than to protect his face with his hands as they stood over him, nudging him with their grubby bare feet and calling him "Pretty Polly" or "Hop-Along Hamlin", or whatever other insult they could dream up out of their murky, muddled, unimaginative minds.

"You'll have to be quick if you want to get out before they close the gates," he said.

Pedrin cast a look up at the sky. The river shone still between its stands of rushes, but the first stars were beginning to prick the sky with light. "We'll run," he said. "I don't want me ma to get in a fret."

Durrik nodded. That was one of the things he liked about Pedrin. It never occurred to the goatherd that Durrik could not go where he went or keep up with whatever pace he set. Since making friends with Pedrin, the crippled boy had climbed trees, pushed his way through hedges, climbed up to the very top of High Tor, and much to Durrik's alarm, been capsized in the river when their homemade raft fell apart.

The boys had been friends from the very first moment they had met, six years earlier when Johan Bell-Crier had first moved to Levanna-On-The-Lake from Zarissa, the capital city of the land the starkin called Ziva and the hearthkin still, in whispers, called Adalheit.

There had been a lot of curiosity about the new bell-crier and his crippled son. None of the hearthkin had ever seen one of their kind so richly dressed, with so many strange and precious belongings. The former bell-crier had been a rough, uneducated man with only one bell. He had died alone and sodden with drink in his one-room lodging above the stables at Levanna-On-The-Lake's only inn, leaving nothing but his tarnished bell, a pile of unpaid bills and a rather mangy cat. Bell-crying was an art passed from father to son and so the town had been worried and apprehensive when their bell-crier had died without any issue. Without a bell-crier, the rites of everyday life could not be properly observed. The unrung dead would be displeased that all honour was not given them at their passing and, without the sound of the death-bell to guide him, Tallis the moon god would not know where to come to shine his radiance and light their path to the afterlife. Angry ghosts would hang about the town, disrupting the peace, breaking crockery, unsettling the hens so they did not lay, curdling the milk, stopping the bread from rising, poisoning the well, bringing nightmares and foul odours, and generally making everyone uncomfortable.

Without a bell-crier to bless the fields, the harvest

would be devoured by locusts or lost to root-rot. The apples would be worm-eaten, the grapes would wither on the vine, the corn would not ripen, the soil would turn sour. Marriages would fail, babies would fret and grow sick, businesses would falter and, without the bells being rung in their honour every feast-day, the gods would grow angry and send flood, fire, disease and disaster.

So Levanna-On-The-Lake was most relieved when Johan and his poor, pale, twisted little son came quietly into town and took up residence in the grandest house on the square. For weeks the gossips speculated about why they had come, and what misfortune had caused the crippling of the boy, and where Johan's wife was, and how much money the bell-crier really had. The young women put on clean aprons and found excuses to linger in the square outside his house. The merchants brought their finest wares to show him, tripling their cost as a matter of course, thinking he was used to city prices. The merchants' wives came to visit, looking about with avid eyes and asking as many questions as they dared. To them all Johan was polite, quiet, reserved, intractable. No one found out anything. After a few months the young women stopped lingering outside the door, the merchants' wives gave up visiting and the merchants accepted with good-natured shrugs that Johan Bell-Crier was no fool.

Seven-year-old Durrik was as polite and reserved as his father. It was to be expected that the children of the town would make him a butt of their mockery, for he spoke in genteel tones, was always neat and clean and well-dressed, and never made any attempt to stand up for himself.

Seven-year-old Pedrin, on the other hand, rarely came to town. Since his father had died the previous summer, he had taken over the job of goatherd and so spent all his days out in the high meadows, climbing the rocks with his friends the goats or lying in the grass, watching the clouds shift shape, and dreaming. Pedrin was happy out in the meadows. He did not have to endure the compassion of their neighbours, or see his mother's strained, anxious eyes. He did not have to think about his father at all if he did not want to.

The only time Pedrin came to town was on market-day, once a month, when he would bring in their cheeses to sell. He and the town kids were enemies as a matter of course. In winter, when the children played ice-hockey on the frozen lake, it was always the townies against the fieldies, and in summer, when the town kids came out into the meadows looking for birds' eggs or flowers, the children who lived along the riverbank would always ambush them, slinging clods of mud at them, or shoving them into the this-tles. It had always been so. Even the grown-ups still acknowledged the natural rivalry, pitting townies against fieldies in contests of skill and strength on feast-days, or taking sides in any dispute over money or women.

Keegan, the leader of the town bullies, was a partic-ular enemy of Pedrin's. He took delight in taunting the goatherd over his father's death, a subject most people found far too delicate to even mention. Mortemer Goatherd had died so horribly that the very thought of him was enough to make most people wince and change colour and look away. Keegan was the sort of boy that liked to make people flinch and blench and, best of all, break down in tears. So Pedrin had spent most of the weeks before market-day practising with his slingshot, determined he was going to get that bastard.

He knew Keegan would not taunt him in the marketplace, in full view of the adults. Keegan liked plenty of space and time for his torments. It would happen in one of the dark, smelly back alleys, or down by the river where the cesspits were. So Pedrin kept his slingshot and heavy bag of stones in his pocket, close to hand, and took care never to be too far away from the sunlit square, filled with laughing, talking crowds and long trestle tables loaded with goods of all kinds.

At last, though, he could not avoid being sent to deliver the cheeses to the homes of those who had bought them. It was late afternoon, and the houses were all casting long shadows. With his arms piled high with round, white cheeses, Pedrin felt very vulnerable indeed. There was no help to it, though, so he made his way along the narrow, twisty streets as cautiously as he could. There was no sign of the bullies and Pedrin began to hope they were all having such a good time torturing some small animal that they had forgotten about him. He hurried back down towards the square, turned a corner, and then came to an abrupt halt.

A small, thin boy was huddled into the side of the alley, clutching a crutch close to his chest. His collar was awry, the knees of his breeches were muddy, and there was a nasty bruise on his cheekbone. Blood trickled from his nose. All round him mobbed the gang of bullies, taunting him, pushing him, trying to kick the crutch away.

Pedrin could probably have sidled away unnoticed, but a sudden surge of hot red anger swept over him. He dropped the last of the cheeses, which rolled away into the gutter, and dragged out his slingshot. Pedrin had got so accurate he could knock a bird out of a tree. He found the thick skulls of the bullies such easy targets they were soon howling and ducking for cover, their arms over their heads. Durrik had ducked down too, dropping his crutch so he could protect his face with both hands. He soon realised none of the stones landed on him, though, and so had looked up rather apprehensively, to see a sturdy boy with tousled brown curls and a freckled snub-nose handing him his crutch.

"You got to stand up to them," the rather grubby, barefoot boy had advised. "They like it if you cower." He had hesitated, looking him over candidly. "Mebbe I can teach you t'use me slingshot?" he had offered.

Durrik never did master the slingshot, but he and Pedrin were the best of friends from that day on. Pedrin taught him to fish, to climb trees, to build a hide from broken branches so they could watch badg-

28

ers, and to drink milk straight from a goat's teat. In return, Durrik told him stories of the gods and the starkin, taught him new songs, and kept him in a quiver of laughter with his tomfoolery. To the rest of the hearthkin, Durrik was a quiet, colourless boy without much gumption and they could not understand Pedrin's attraction. They did not know how quick and funny Durrik really was, nor how much the boys had in common with their love of music and tales of monsters and marvels. When they were alone together by the river or in the high meadows, there was a constant sparkle of talk and laughter between them that was dimmed and shielded into a quiet, complicit glow of glance and grin when they were with others. Only Maegeth really understood the depth of their friendship. She welcomed Durrik to their dark little cottage, fed him milk and stale bread without any embarrassment, and teased him as affectionately as she did her own two tousle-haired, scabby-kneed children.

Now Durrik struggled to his feet, crying, "Race you then!" He set off as fast as he could along the dark path, his crutch swinging back and forth, back and forth.

"Oy! Give me some warning!" Pedrin shouted, breaking into a run, dust flying up from his bare feet.

As he rounded the last curve of the river, panting, he saw the township prickling with lights, the dark castle looming behind. Once the castle would have been bright with lights too, Count Zoltan having been a cheerful and generous man. No golden light streamed from its tall glass windows now, though, and there was no sound of music or laughter.

Pedrin put on an extra burst of speed and raced past Durrik to slap his hand on the dark wood of the gate. "Beat you! Nah nah de nah nah!"

"Only just." Durrik bent over, trying to catch his breath. "You didn't drop the fish, did you?"

Pedrin hastily checked his basket but the five fish still lay within their cool nest of rushes, their pale spotted sides gleaming. "Nah, thank Liah! That big one's a beauty, aren't he? Almost got away about three times but I managed to reel him in."

The two boys made their way through the eastern gate and along the main road to the marketplace. With the gloaming shut out by the tall, thin, crowded houses, the streets were dark, only a few homes hanging lanterns out front to illuminate the way. Pedrin and Durrik passed the gang of bully-boys, lounging about in a dark doorway. Although they called out a few cheerful insults, they did not waylay the pair, being far too wary of Pedrin's slingshot.

Both boys relaxed as they came near the town square, for a warm orange light was cast by lanterns strung high all along the square and the area was filled with people gathered at the inn to drink apple-ale. The mood was grim. Women clustered on the corners, talking in low voices, while the men glowered into their ale-mugs, too exhausted to talk much. Many a surly glance was cast across to the astronomer's tower on its island in the centre of the lake. The crystal tower still glimmered as if it had caught the light of the day within its crystal heart and held it captive there.

The bell-crier's house was one of the tall, white houses lining the high end of the square. Apple trees in pots on either side of the steps sweetened the air with the scent of their blossom.

Just as Pedrin and Durrik were climbing the steps to the front door, it swung open. A man stepped out, a large brass bell in one hand. He was well-dressed in a long green coat with brass buttons and a tricorne hat, with his breeches fastened at the knee with little black rosettes. He was a stout man, with grey hair very neatly secured at the back of his head with a black ribbon. Just now his kindly face looked troubled, a roll of parchment tightly clenched in his other hand.

He saw the boys and gave a little gesture of his hand, so that they stepped back without a word. The stout man raised his bell and began to ring it vigorously. It had a beautiful tone, very deep and strong, that rang out across the town square, drowning the murmur of voices and the clink of ceramic mugs. Everyone stopped and turned to look up at the bell-crier. By the look on his face, Durrik's father was not announcing the birth of a new baby.

"The Regent of Estelliana declares the work on his stargazing tower goes too slowly," the bell-crier announced in his sonorous voice. Although he did not shout, his words rang in every corner of the town square. "The people of Levanna do not work with willing hands or hearts. They dawdle and drag their heels. They sabotage the building, so that glass panes

31

fall and shatter. They mutter against the necessary raising of taxes to pay for the glass-blowing. Many have been seen picking up stones and weighing them in their hands, as if they wish to cast these stones against this tower, this marvel of science and engineering, that is the only hope of saving the young Count of Estelliana's life.

"Do you not understand the starkin do not raise this tower to their glory? In twenty-two days it'll be the summer solstice, when the power of the daystar is at its most potent. Lord Zavion, our illustrious and esteemed Regent, shall seek to harness the daystar's power, to break the curse that holds Zygmunt ziv Estaria, the Count of Estelliana, in this unnatural sleep, closer to death than life. In twenty-two days the Regent's tower must be complete.

"To ensure this is so, the Regent commands, in the name of his young kin the Count of Estelliana, that all males above the age of fifteen must present themselves to the Hall of Mirrors in the morning, to labour for the next twenty-one days and nights in the raising of the tower so that all shall be ready for the summer solstice. Any defiance shall be punished by a fine of five gold crowns, to be paid immediately."

The bell-crier's proclamation had caused a slow, sullen muttering that swelled in volume until it almost drowned out his deep voice. At the last words this sullen mutter burst into a roar of outrage.

"Five crowns! Who among us has five crowns?"

"The old count would never have taken us from the fields at sowing time!"

"How are we to pay the taxes if we can't set the crops a-growing?"

"What are we t'eat come winter?"

"I have orders to fulfil," the coppersmith shouted. "I shall lose me customers if I don't meet their orders!"

"Me boy is sick," one woman cried, wringing her hands. "The Regent doesn't expect him to work when he's a-shaking with fever, surely?"

"The only property I own is the shirt on me back, and he's welcome t'it, ragged and worn as it is!"

At the foot of the steps Pedrin and Durrik glanced at each other in dismay. Both had recently celebrated their fifteenth birthdays.

"There goes our summer," Pedrin said grimly. "Twenty-one days! How is Ma to manage without me?"

The bell-crier had not answered any of the crowd's shouts, carefully holding the clapper of his bell with his big white hand and climbing back up the steps. He said in a firm yet gentle voice, "Get along home, Pedrin. The town's no place for a boy tonight. There'll be trouble now, I warrant you. Come, Durrik. 'Tis not unknown for an angry crowd to take out their displeasure on the bell-crier. We'll keep our doors locked and windows shuttered tonight."

"Do we really have to go work on the tower?" Pedrin said indignantly. "I'm the only man in me family, you know that. Who's to tend the goats or draw the water or gather the firewood if I'm off working for the blasted Regent?"

"I don't know, my boy," the bell-crier replied. "I

shall do my best for us all in the morning but the proclamation from the castle was mighty clear. I fear you shall just have to do your best, like all else here tonight."

With those words he guided his son through the door and closed it smartly behind him. Pedrin heard the key turn in the lock and the bolts being slammed home, then the shutters on one side were crisply pulled closed and locked. He turned to go, aware of the angry murmuring of the crowd behind him, like a hive of bees ready to swarm.

Just then he heard a whisper from the window yet to be shuttered. Durrik was leaning out. "Tomorrow! I'll see you tomorrow at the Hall of Mirrors!"

Then his face disappeared abruptly. The bell-crier pulled the shutters closed and locked them. Only then did Pedrin realise he still had all five fish. He raised a hand involuntarily, and then dropped it, turning and running down into the milling crowd, the basket clasped close to his chest.

3

The next morning saw a long procession winding its way up the hill to the castle. There were two hundred or more hearthkin men and boys, from all the towns and villages up and down the river as well as from Levanna-On-The-Lake. Escorting them were the tall figures of starkin soldiers, all clad in silver armour, their fusilliers thrust out threateningly.

Overhead flew a spearhead of great white birds, their heads and breasts protected with beaten silver, ornate saddles upon their backs. Seated astride the sisikas were starkin lords carrying long-range fusilliers, with glass tanks of high-octane fuel strapped to their backs. The air was filled with the sound of the birds' harsh screeching and the beating of their immense wings. As they swooped low over the road, their shadows darkening the sun, the hearthkin all ducked involuntarily. The sisikas shrieked with mocking laughter.

Most of the hearthkin were pale and red-eyed, having sat up half the night drinking apple-ale and

35

declaring that nothing could make them go up to the castle in the morn. Their bravado had drained away with the darkness, for the dawn had brought a battalion of hard-eyed soldiers in helmets and breast-plates, their fusilliers at the ready. It had been many a long year since a fusillier was last fired in Estelliana, but the hearthkin had long memories. Even the youngest child knew bolts of blue lightning zigzagged from the little black mouths of fusilliers, sizzling you where you stood till nothing was left but a smoking pile of ashes. It gave them an almost pleasurable shiver of horror to hear the tales of the first great battle with the starkin, when six hundred men and women were incinerated mid-charge, leaving behind a wasteland of dust and cinders.

It may have been a long time since the starkin had felt a need to fire their fusilliers in Estelliana, but all knew that it was only three years since the king had ordered his battalions to fire upon a rabble of hearthkin attempting to march upon Zarissa. One hundred and sixty-four men, women and children had been incinerated that day, their remains drifting away in the wind. None of the men and boys of Estelliana doubted that Lord Zavion would be any less ruthless than his cousin, the king. Even the youngest of the boys was grim-faced and silent.

Johan walked at the head of the procession, carrying the largest of his bells, the one with the deepest and most authoritative voice. Pedrin and Durrik followed close behind, the crippled boy finding it difficult to manage his crutch on the worn cobblestones. As they walked into the shadow of the castle walls, Pedrin glanced back down the hill, to where the wives and mothers of Levanna-On-The-Lake stood white and rigid with anxiety. He could see the tall, spare figure of his mother, Mina pressed close to her side, and raised a hand. She waved back wildly and Mina waved too, jumping up and down, one hand twined in her mother's apron. Then he was pushed forward roughly by one of the soldiers, passing under the sharp, downcurving spikes of the portcullis.

The hearthkin all filed in through a long, cold, stone tunnel and into the castle courtyard within. Ahead soared the tall towers and pointed roofs of the castle, with the lower buildings extending on either side like embracing arms. On one side was the kitchen wing and servants' quarters, on the other the stables, kennels and guards' quarters.

"Jumping Jimjinny, look at this place!" Pedrin cried.

"'Tis beautiful," Durrik said in a stifled voice.

Pedrin looked at him quickly. There was an expression of wistful longing on his face, overshadowed by something darker, a bitter envy or unhappiness. Pedrin had never seen Durrik look so sombre and it made him uneasy.

"I wouldn't want to be the one having to clean it," he said pragmatically. Pedrin thought of how hard his mother laboured to keep the two small rooms of their cottage spick and span, with two children tracking in river mud and goat hairs all day. "It'd be mighty fine for hide-and-seek, though! You could be seeking for a week and still not find me! I bet it has secret passages."

37

"And dungeons," Durrik said with a little shudder.

In the centre of the courtyard was a wide pool, encircled by a stone ledge. A great tree raised a puzzle of black thorny branches against the blue arc of sky above. The water at its foot reflected the intricate pattern of its thorns, bare now of any leaf or flower. The tree looked as if it was forged of iron, not wood, shaped like some cruel weapon of war. The bareness of its branches was uncanny, when all the trees out in the countryside were bright and green with the first leaves of summer.

Pedrin and Durrik glanced at the starthorn tree uneasily and quickly looked away. It was said the starkin had brought the seeds of the tree with them from their own world and the tree still bloomed and fruited in response to the seasons of that world. In summer it was as bare as if feeling the first frosts of winter. In autumn its thorns were hung with great clusters of sweet-scented, snowy-white blossom. In winter great globes of golden fruit hung heavy on its leafy branches, even though the pond at its foot was white with ice and snow. This fruit was called the star-apple for, when sliced in half, its core showed the perfect shape of a six-pointed star. It was said one bite of the star-apple made you feel more alive than ever before. Three bites would keep you dancing all night. If you ate a whole star-apple, you would dance until you died.

The procession of hearthkin passed by the tree and climbed the wide sweep of stairs into the Hall of Mirrors. At once Pedrin blinked and rubbed his eyes with one hand. He had never before been within the great hall of the castle and, although he had heard it described many times, he was still not prepared for its splendour.

"Jumping Jimjinny!" he cried.

The hall was very long and very high. Instead of a ceiling it had a great dome of cut crystal that caught the light and refracted it around the room in arcs of rainbows. Huge windows lined the room, and the walls in between were covered with mirrors. Everywhere Pedrin looked he saw himself reflected back, many times over.

Pedrin had never looked in a mirror before. The hearthkin could not afford such idle luxuries. He gazed and gazed, and felt a little prickle of embarrassment at the back of his neck. He had never before realised what a grubby, shabby figure he made in his rough clothes and bare feet, with his shaggy mop of brown hair. He tugged at his tunic self-consciously and then realised that all the men around him were smoothing down their hair, fingering their tangled beards, dusting off their clothes. He made a face at Durrik, who was staring at his own thin, twisted form unhappily, and reluctantly his friend smiled back. It occurred to Pedrin that even Durrik looked plain and shabby in the shining world of the mirror, and he was a boy often teased for his girlish good looks.

"Don't think much of mirrors," he whispered. "Who wants to know what they look like anyways?"

There were no seats so the hearthkin gathered together in a great crowd below the dais, shifting uncomfortably from foot to foot. Few had ever been in the Hall of Mirrors before, such privileges being reserved for the reeve, the constable, the guild-masters and the more affluent of the merchants. It was very disconcerting to see your face everywhere you looked.

A silvery flourish of trumpets made them all look up. A herald held open the great doors at the end of the hall and a procession of starkin slowly glided up the aisle. Grandly dressed in pale shimmering silks that swept the floor behind them, the starkin were all very tall and slender, with high-boned aristocratic faces. The men wore their golden hair in long smooth curls and were clean-shaven, so that they looked like young boys. Their robes were as ornately decorated as the women's, with long sleeves all embroidered with silver thread and diamonds. Only the women's head-dresses marked them differently. Most were very high and conical, made of silver filigree with long trailing veils of gauze. Their cornsilk hair had been coiled and plaited within to form a high cone that gleamed within the scrolls and arabesques of their silver cornets.

The starkin moved as slowly and gracefully as swans gliding across a lake. Their carriage was very tall and proud, their heads held high, their hands folded at their breast. All had long nails painted in shimmering silver or violet or blue. The nails of a few were even longer than their fingers, and Pedrin knew these were the most noble. It was a sign of high birth and prestige to be able to grow your fingernails so long. It meant you never had to brush your own hair, button your own clothes, or cut up your own meals, let alone scrub a floor or labour in the fields.

In the centre of the procession walked the dowager countess and her daughter, dressed all in dark wine-red. The colour was shocking amidst all that white and silver and amethyst. The dowager countess's headdress was made of iron filigree, very black against the coils of pale golden hair. Her beautiful pale face was haggard with grief, her eyelids all swollen from weeping. Although her fingernails were so long they looked like ten slim rapiers, they were without colour and very white against the rich hue of her gown.

Her daughter was a slim, pale-faced girl with downcast eyes. Although she would have been the same age as Pedrin and Durrik, she was much taller. Her hair was unbound, as befitted her age, and flowed down her back to the floor in smooth shining ripples of pale gold. She had the same high-boned beauty as her mother, though softened and rounded still with youth. Pedrin could not help staring at her as she passed by, and when the starkin were all seated on their glass and velvet chairs, his eyes again sought her out.

"That's Lady Ginerva, the dowager countess, there in the red," Johan whispered. "That's the starkin's colour of mourning, you know. And that's the count's young sister, Lady Lisandre."

"Which one's the Regent?" Durrik asked.

His father nodded at the man seated on the dowager countess's right. He was even taller and more handsome than the rest of the starkin, and was dressed in white silk embroidered all over with strange symbols in silver thread. On his right hand he wore a great spherical diamond which glittered with sharp rainbow fire. A smile lingered on his finely cut lips but his light blue eyes looked cold and disdainful.

The herald stood at the front of the dais and Durrik's father moved through the crowd to stand at the foot of the steps. Most of the hearthkin had only a rudimentary knowledge of the starkin's elaborate, lilting language and it was the bell-crier's job to translate for those who may not understand. Few of the starkin could speak the hearthkin's language, of course.

Although Pedrin was nothing but a goatherd and had never had anything to do with the castle or its noble inhabitants, he could understand the herald quite well, having badgered Durrik to teach him what he knew of Ziverian, the starkin's language. Pedrin had a deep love of music and most of the most beautiful songs sung by the minstrels were written in Ziverian.

The two boys had spent many a long, dark winter's day with the bell-crier in his music-room, learning to play his beautiful, deep-bellied lute, his zither, his clavichord, his flute and his sweet-voiced silver piccolo. Johan had once been a musician at the royal court in Zarissa, playing to the king himself and teaching music to the prince and princesses. Pedrin was fascinated and envious. He could not understand why Johan had left the glittering life of the Zarissan court to come all the way out to Estelliana, at the very back of beyond. As curious and tactless as one of his goats, Pedrin had of course asked why. Johan had just smiled rather sadly and replied in his quiet way, "It seemed best."

Johan had a wonderful, deep, strong voice and knew hundreds of songs, from sweet love laments to stirring war marches. He taught them all to Pedrin, who was tense and quivering with eagerness at this new world opening up before him. The hearthkin liked a jolly tune to dance to on feast-days, but otherwise were not much interested in music. Before meeting the bell-crier, Pedrin had only known that the heart-piercingly sweet song of the nightingale made him stand still, shivering, some unnamable yearning rising up till it threatened to engulf him. It made the hairs stand up on his arms, a tingle run up his spine, his jaw ache with tension. He tried his best to whistle its song, as he mimicked all the birds of the forest. Always his skill failed his intentions so that he was filled with frustration that made him glower and grunt and punch out at the other boys.

All this rage dissipated once Johan began to teach him music. It was worth spending hours whittling bits of wood until he managed to make himself his own little flute. It was worth struggling with the difficult cadences of Ziverian to learn to sing the gorgeous, thrilling songs of the starkin.

So, although Pedrin could only speak stumblingly and with a truly atrocious accent, he could understand most of what the herald proclaimed. Listening to first the herald and then the bell-crier, Pedrin was struck forcibly by Johan's tact. Where the herald demanded, in the most arrogant and supercilious way possible, the bell-crier requested, with many soft words and expressions of regret.

It did little good, however. Even though the hearthkin were cowed by the beauty and magnificence of the starkin, and unnerved and ashamed of their own rough, dirty reflections, their sullen anger still broke through in low growls and mutters of dissatisfaction.

Twenty-one days until the summer solstice, twenty-one days in which much of the hard labour of the year was done. If the seeds were not sown before the ground was baked hard by the sun, there would be no crops to harvest in the autumn. If the vines were not tended, they would wither and die. If the livestock was not fed and watered, the animals would grow thin and sick, and be unable to pull the wagons and ploughs, or produce milk or meat or wool. If the hay was not cut, it would be ruined by rain. The whole economy of Estelliana was threatened and it was the hearthkin who would suffer, not the starkin with their jewels and silks, their treasuries and storerooms stuffed full of the hearthkin's taxes.

The bell-crier tried his best. He presented the hearthkin's case with much courtesy and rational argument. He pointed to the consequences of taking every man and boy in the county away from their work and begged that the levy be reduced in some way. "We're all ready and willing to labour in your service, milord, but to do as you have requested means famine come winter. May we not design a roster system where each man gives up three days in seven?"

Lord Zavion looked bored. He ate a sweetmeat and gestured to his page to fan him with the great bunch of white sisika feathers he held.

The bell-crier then appealed to the dowager countess to plead their cause with the Regent. Lady Ginerva's eyes were closed, her head laid back against the velvet cushion of her chair. She did not seem to listen. Her lady-in-waiting leant forward and whispered in her ear. The dowager countess opened her eyes, wincing at the sight of the rough, brown, bearded men all crowded together at the foot of the dais. She inclined her head wearily, and closed her eyes again. The lady-in-waiting stepped back and gave a quick order to one of the servants.

There was another flourish of trumpets. Again the great doors at the end of the hall were flung open and the hearthkin all swung round, fear and belligerence mingled on their bearded faces. No one had missed the significance of the soldiers lined up along both sides of the hall, or that they had all been asked to surrender their eating-knives and tools before entering the castle.

It was not more soldiers marching through the mirrored doors, however. Slowly, gravely, came a small retinue of starkin, led by the court minstrel playing a sombre tune on his lute. In their midst was a canopied litter, carried on the burly shoulders of six men. Embroidered with silver thread upon the white satin curtains and coverlet were the arms of the Estaria family, a white swan resting upon the white blossoms of the starthorn tree, an arc of seven silver stars above.

Lying upon the litter was a boy of fifteen years, his eyes closed. His thin, high-boned face was framed by smooth fair curls. His hands were folded upon his breast, his body covered with a satin quilt. Upon his long fingers were rings of amethysts and diamonds. More jewels glittered at his throat. His skin was as white as if he had been carved from marble.

The hearthkin all drew back, staring.

"He's so cold," Durrik whispered. "He looks as if he's dead."

"There lies the Count of Estelliana, your lord and master," the herald cried. "For six months he has lain there, barely breathing. He has not spoken. He has not lifted a finger. He has not sighed.

"Is your countess to lose both husband and son in the same season? Zygmunt ziv Estaria has lived here all his life, and his family has ruled you for two centuries. His father was a good and generous man and always treated you justly.

"Is this how you repay his justice, by refusing to help build the tower of stars that is his son's only hope of salvation? Do you condemn this young lord to death, because of your stubborn pride and recalcitrance? Better that you all die in the service of your lord!"

The litter had been laid on the dais, so that the men and boys of Estelliana were all level with the figure of the sleeping boy, able to see the occasional twitch of his eyelid, the barely discernible rise of his chest. No one spoke or moved.

Lord Zavion yawned behind his ring-laden hand and then made a languid gesture. The soldiers all stepped forward, levelling their fusilliers. Involuntarily the hearthkin all huddled together, looking from side to side with fear and anger. The Regent made another wearied gesture and the soldiers cocked their weapons. For a moment it seemed as if the hearthkin would resist, despite the fusilliers ranged against them. Then there was a soft sigh, a slumping of shoulders, a fatalistic acceptance of their powerlessness. The Regent must be obeyed. The tower of stars must be built.

Briony sat in the shadows, the spinning-wheel turning swiftly before her, the twisting thread held lightly between her fingers. Her foot worked the treadle rhythmically, without need for any thought on her part. She was free to watch the women sitting all around the solar and listen to their low-voiced conversations, or to gaze out the window and dream.

Lady Ginerva sat in a cushioned chair by the fire. One long white hand hung limply, the other rested on her lap. Her eyes were closed. Beside her sat Lady Donella, her cousin and chief lady-in-waiting, working on her embroidery. Occasionally she looked sharply about the solar to make sure that no one else was dawdling over their work. Nearby stood a young page with a tray loaded with fine crystal glasses and a decanter of wine.

Most of the women clustered about the dowager countess's sitting room were starkin, and so magnificently robed in rich silks and satins decorated with jewels and lace, their fair hair elaborately coiled and twisted on top of their heads. It was the task of all the court ladies to help spin and weave the cloth for the household, and to help with the mending and dressmaking. Their long pointed nails and fine clothes made it difficult for the ladies-in-waiting to give any practical help, however, and so much of the heavy work fell to the few spinners, seamstresses and weavers employed for that purpose.

Although Briony had spun and woven the shimmering silk worn by all of the court ladies, she herself was dressed in a loose brown dress, under a drab pinafore, with a black kerchief bound tightly about her head, hiding all her hair. She felt no envy or resentment, however. She was glad to have clothes that were not in rags. She had been living in the Castle of Estelliana for almost six months and had not once been hungry or cold or frightened. She had been able to watch the snow whirling down from behind thick panes of glass, instead of floundering through it in search of shelter. She slept in a warm, soft bed instead of under a hedge or inside a hollow tree. She ate her fill twice a day, with the occasional luxury of roasted meats to vary her diet.

Briony did not know who her parents were or where she had been born. She had been a foundling child, raised by an old hedge-witch in the shadow of the Perilous Forest. Oreal had been bent, wizened, sharp-eyed and sharp-eared, cruel and cunning as a fox. Her witchery was a patchwork of spells and simples, charms and curses. She boiled the roots of hollyhocks in wine and gave it to children to kill intestinal worms. She mixed her own urine with grave-dust and nightshade to poison those she distrusted, and her love philtres contained dead queen-bees and the sundered heart of a rose. She told new mothers not to wash their baby's hands for a year else they would never grow rich. A double-yolked egg was just one of many omens of death, and she taught Briony to never, ever step on anyone's shadow.

Despite her eccentricities Oreal's magic was strong and powerful. Many a hearthkin came tap-tapping at her door, a hood drawn close about their face, seeking some cure or potion. It was dangerous these days to seek out one of the Crafty, and Oreal and the little foundling moved house many times, often packing up in the middle of the night with the red flicker of fire coming up the lane. Oreal taught Briony to be quiet, to be fearful, to hide her true nature like a moth camouflaging itself with the grey texture of bark.

Then, when Briony was six, Oreal died. For once the hedge-witch was not quick enough to move before six starkin soldiers with loathing in their eyes came knocking on her door. Briony only had time to crawl under the kitchen table, the ragdoll Oreal had made her clutched in her arms. Concealed beneath the hanging folds of tablecloth she crouched, unable to see anything, able to hear everything, the ragdoll crammed in her mouth.

The soldiers did not take long, trampling back out into the frosty night only a few scant minutes after they had smashed down the door. Briony did not move for a very long time, however, except for the occasional sharp heave of her chest and the incessant quivering of her limbs.

It was not until a pale finger of sunlight probed under the edge of the tablecloth and touched her foot that Briony at last moved. Slowly, stiffly, carefully, she crept out from under the table, cast one quick, timorous glance at Oreal, lying askew against the wall, and then looked no more. Moving like a sleepwalker, the little girl gathered together all the food in the house and shoved it into a sack, along with Oreal's shabby, dog-eared book of spells and recipes, and whatever charms, simples and evil-smelling potions she could find.

Finally, she picked up Oreal's grey shawl and wrapped it close about her shivering body. The shawl smelt sharply of smoke and rosemary and woodbetony, which the hedge-witch had mixed with mead for her wheezy chest, and cut through Briony's daze like scissors through paper. She had to sit, her face buried in the shawl, trying hard not to cry. Once she began to cry, Briony knew, she would find it hard to stop.

At last she managed to swallow the burning ember that seemed to have lodged in her throat, and got up again, tucking her ragdoll under her arm and shouldering the heavy sack. She still could not look at Oreal but she managed to straighten the old witch's dress without touching her cold, grey skin. She waited until she was sure the forest outside was free of watchers, before slowly creeping out the door and down the path, being careful to put her small feet in the big, deep footprints left by the soldiers, so that no one could follow her trail.

Briony spent the next six years wandering about the countryside, spinning or sewing for anyone who would toss her a hunk of bread or a copper coin. In the woods and hedgerows that were her usual bed, she came to know the ways of all the other spinning creatures, spiders and silkworms, moths and butterflies. She gathered their silks and delicate filaments of wild flax and dandelion seeds, and wove them into shimmering cloth. She learnt which flowers and berries yielded lasting colour and dyed her fabrics in all the shades of the rainbow. She learnt to make lace, taking her designs from snowflakes and cobwebs and frostflowers.

Gradually Briony's fame had spread. The great cloth-merchants began to seek her out in the marketplaces. At last Lady Donella, who loved luxury in all its forms, sent a messenger to find her and bring her to the Castle of Estelliana. Briony had been there ever since.

At first she had been content. Since Count Zoltan had died, however, the castle had been an unhappy place, full of whispers and sideways glances and the distant sound of sobbing. No one knew what had happened. The count had ridden out gaily one crisp winter's morning, with his huntsmen and hounds, his grey destrier and his falcon, his young son and heir by his side. The sky had been clear, no storm clouds or rumbling of thunder to presage disaster.

They had ridden out in search of gibberhog, one

having been sighted near the edge of the Perilous Forest some days earlier. No one expected the hunt to be easy, gibberhogs being fierce and cunning prey, and so it had been several days before the first shadow of anxiety had touched the countess's beautiful face.

At last a search party had been sent out, all riding upon the swift, white-winged sisikas. Able to soar high into the skies, the sisikas had reached the forest quickly. The hunting party's camp was found a few days later, the searchers led to the camp by the mournful howling of the count's great mastiff.

They were all dead, the count, his knights, his squire, the falconer and huntsmen, the dog-boys and the trackers. Their bodies lay in the snow about the ashes of a great fire, the remains of a feast scattered about them, their goblets fallen from their lifeless hands. The count's mastiff lay at the feet of the dead lord, savage with grief and hunger. The searchers had had to shoot him before they could approach the grim scene. Only the count's young son was still alive, though he was so cold and still all thought he was dead too, until one noticed the faint flicker of his eyelids.

At first the dowager countess had been maddened with her grief. Lady Ginerva no longer wept or raged or smashed vases, however. These last few months, she roused only long enough to drink more of the cordial the chief lady-in-waiting had distilled to help deaden her grief. Sometimes she seemed no more alive than her son.

The door swung open, crashing into the wall

behind. Everyone looked up, frowning in disapproval, as Lady Lisandre hurried in, the smooth pale ripples of her hair disordered, her skirt caught up in one hand to show red shoes with very high heels. It was hard to hurry in trailing skirts and high heels and so Lisandre stumbled and almost fell, before flinging herself down at her mother's feet and seizing the limply hanging hand. "Mama!" she cried. "The tower is finally finished! They have just brought the news. Oh, do you think it will work? Will Lord Zavion really be able to awaken Ziggy?" She shook her mother's hand vigorously. The dowager countess's swollen lids did not open.

Lady Donella rose gracefully to her feet. "Lisandre, your mother is resting! You should not run and shout in her ear like some wild hoyden."

Lisandre ignored her. "Mama! Do you not hear me?"

Again Lady Donella reproved her, bending to take her arm and draw her away. Lisandre shook her off, calling her mother loudly and shaking her shoulder. Lady Ginerva's eyes opened and she looked at her daughter dazedly. "Lisandre? Did you speak? What is it?"

Rapidly Lisandre repeated her words. Lady Ginerva's mouth twisted, tears welling up in her eyes. "Oh, by the stars, let Lord Zavion prevail!" she whispered. "If Ziggy should die … oh, I could not bear it!"

Lady Donella drew Lisandre away. "If anyone can wake Count Zygmunt from this unnatural slumber, it is Lord Zavion. Is he not one of the starborn himself, and trained at the university of Zarissa? Come, Lisandre, you should not grieve your mother with doubts or disturb her with such impetuous and indelicate behaviour. The sister of the Count of Estelliana should always behave with grace and dignity."

She was a graceful figure herself, Lady Donella. Although not one of the starborn herself, her patrician beauty had, like her cousin Ginerva, won her a marriage with one of the offshoots of the royal family. Lady Ginerva had been lucky enough to marry a lord in the prime of his youth and strength, although one that lived a long way away from the royal court at Zarissa. Lady Donella's husband had been old and fat and stricken with gout, however, with five children from an earlier marriage. Upon his death seven months earlier, his great castle and expansive lands had been inherited by the eldest son who, being twelve years older than his stepmother, had never felt anything but dislike for her. Lady Donella had been forced to seek a home among her relatives and had gratefully accepted her cousin's invitation to become her chief lady-in-waiting. She showed no chagrin at her abrupt change in status, being always sweet-voiced and charming, but Briony, watching from the shadows, thought she must have found it difficult.

Lisandre had submitted to Lady Donella's firm guiding hand, though she cast an unhappy glance back at the drooping figure of her mother. The lady-in-waiting pulled Lisandre's embroidery frame forward, saying with a rueful laugh, "Oh, Lisandre, look at the size of your stitches! Come, this must all be unpicked and done again. A lady's stitches should be invisible!"

Sulkily Lisandre did as she was told, as Lady Donella beckoned the pageboy forward and poured a glass of deep red liquid from a small bottle she carried in her reticule. She then bent over the dowager countess, coaxing her to drink a little. Listlessly Lady Ginerva sipped from the goblet. The cordial brought no colour to her cheeks, however. She was as limp as Briony's ragdoll.

There was a discreet knock on the door.

"Enter!" Lady Donella called.

Lord Zavion came in, smiling. At the sight of him the ladies-in-waiting all fluttered and preened like songbirds in a cage. Even the head weaver, Brianna, a large, plain hearthkin woman of immense common-sense, was unable to help putting up one hand to make sure her black kerchief was tied neatly. Only Briony shrank further back into the shadows, her eyes dropping to her spinning-wheel.

Lord Zavion bowed low over the dowager countess's hand. She smiled at him, showing the most life she had all evening. "My daughter tells me your tower is finished at last, my lord. That is joyful tidings indeed."

Lord Zavion cast Lisandre a look of dislike, which she returned in full measure. "I was hoping to please you with the news myself, gentle lady," he said, "but I see that privilege has been denied me."

The dowager countess smiled faintly and he sat down opposite her, gesturing to the page to pour him some wine. He caught a glimpse of himself in the mirror opposite and rearranged his long blond curls before sipping his wine, his eyes still fixed upon himself.

"Yes, all is done and just in time," he said. "Indeed those hearthkin are slow and stupid! We have had to whip them to make them work fast enough, and two precious panes of glass were broken just this week! If they were not so bovine, I would swear it was done to vex me."

"Even oxen would be tired and clumsy after twenty-one days without sleep," Lisandre said. Briony smiled to herself. Even though she knew Lisandre spoke more from a desire to irritate Lord Zavion than from any real concern for the hearthkin, Briony always loved to see any evidence of sympathy in her, for such awareness was so rare among the starkin. She always secretly enjoyed Lisandre's audacity too. Briony wished she had the courage to talk back to the Regent, to challenge his authority and undermine his complacency, but she would never have dared, even if she had been a starkin princess herself. And Lisandre was as much within the Regent's power as Briony was, for in the starkin culture, women had no rights whatsoever, no matter how nobly born.

It was this audacity, this rebelliousness, that drew Briony to Lisandre. When Briony had first come to the castle, she had felt very odd and out of place, like a cuckoo bird in a nest of baby hummingbirds. She had never before seen such a grand place, let alone lived in one, and her natural awe of the starkin was honed to a very real fear that they would somehow discover that she had been raised and taught by one of the Crafty. She had seen with her own eyes what the starkin did to those who dared follow the Craft.

If Briony had been brave enough she would have ignored Lady Donella's order, slipping away in the night. She knew how strange it would have seemed, though, to decline an offer so advantageous to herself, and how dangerous it could be to thwart one of the starkin. So she had come to the Castle of Estelliana as bid, all her apprehension and homesickness tightly locked away, hidden beneath her grey moth camouflage. Briony was so very quiet, meek and biddable, so very dull, she was virtually invisible. Most of the starkin did not even notice that there was a new seamstress and those that did forgot her the very next instant.

Lord Zoltan, of course, knew that she was there because he paid her wages. The first time he saw her, sitting so quietly in her corner, her face bent over her sewing, he stopped and asked her how she was settling in, and said he hoped she would be happy at the Castle of Estelliana. To Briony's surprise, he had spoken in the language of the hearthkin, which they called Adalheid. She hid her amazement, answering colourlessly that she was sure she would be. He had nodded and moved away, never paying her any notice again. She had been secretly impressed with his kindness, however, and had softened her adamantine loathing of the starkin, just a little. After a month observing him about the castle, instructing the servants, sitting in judgement over the courts of law, listening to the reports of the town reeve and constable, and arbitrating disagreements between guilds, she had had to admit to herself that not all starkin were cruel, loathsome beings without mercy or compassion. He was never soft, the old count, but he had been fair.

The only other starkin to have paid Briony any attention was Lisandre.

Pampered, indulged, her every need and desire fulfilled by a throng of servants, Lisandre was like a gaudy-winged butterfly, dancing about the court with a swish of silken skirts, a tippety-tap-tap of jewel-studded heels, a trill of merry laughter. Briony was quite prepared to hate her, but found herself fascinated by her luminous vitality. In a court where all affected a languid pose of boredom, Lisandre's vivacity, her transparency, were striking. Lisandre never felt any need to hide how she felt. When she was happy, she sang and danced and embraced her servants. When she was grieved, she sobbed so heartbrokenly that even the lowliest dog-boy sniffled in sympathy, and everyone sought to please her with little gifts and sweetmeats. When she was angry, she flung vases and pounded her pillow with her fists. Briony envied Lisandre the luxury of self-expression even more than she did her beauty, her wealth, her privilege.

Lisandre had noticed Briony her very first day at the castle, and had smiled at her, surprising Briony into a smile in response. It was winter and the starkin ladies were all reclining by the fire, picking desultorily at a plate of little cakes and moaning about the horrid weather. Lisandre was wandering about, restless and bored, alternatively running to the window to see if the snow had stopped falling, demanding her mother explain why she was not permitted to go hunting like her brother, and annoying Lady Donella by teasing a kitten with a tangled skein of embroidery silk. The chief lady-in-waiting was always sweet and charming, but the flash of steel in her eyes, the poisoned barb in her voice, would have frightened Briony and extracted instant obedience. Lisandre only laughed, though, and kept on teasing the kitten.

She soon tired of the game, however, and looked about for something else to relieve her tedium. It was then she noticed Briony and smiled at her. When the drab little seamstress smiled back, she came dancing up and perched on the arm of the chair next to Briony's, exclaiming over the delicacy of the lace she was making.

"How clever you are!" she had cried, speaking rather stumblingly in Adalheid. Briony marvelled to hear the faltering phrases coming from the mouth of a starkin princess, and wondered how she knew the language. The Castle of Estelliana was a long way from Zarissa, however, and Lisandre had grown up surrounded by hearthkin servants. Her father might even have encouraged her to learn it, though Briony thought this unlikely, given the attitude of starkin lords towards educating their womenfolk.

"It looks just like a snowflake," Lisandre continued laboriously. "I would be afraid it would melt were I to wear that on my sleeve."

"Thank you," Briony had said, as tonelessly as she could, and speaking in Ziverian.

Lisandre gave a smile of relief and slipped back into her own language. "You are newly come to the castle, are you not? I hope the other servants are not too formidable. It must be perplexing, finding yourself in a new place with so many new faces. I do not think I would like it at all."

"Everyone has been very kind."

"I am glad of that," Lisandre said, a little less buoyantly. She asked Briony a few questions about her life but received only monosyllables, all in a colourless voice, with eyes downcast. After a while Lisandre, bored, had got up and flitted away, as pretty and careless as any butterfly.

The death of her father had quenched all Lisandre's vivid animation. Her grief had been consuming, a violent torrent of emotion that left her exhausted, blind and mute as a newborn kitten. When at last she began to look beyond her own sorrow and bewilderment, it was to find her life and liberty controlled by Lord Zavion, a man she instinctively disliked and mistrusted. Her rage and resentment were as intense as her grief had been. Lisandre had never before realised how dependent she was upon her father and brother. Starkin women were not permitted to own property, to earn an income or manage a business, or to choose whom they married. They were as much their father or husband's property as a dog or horse or hearthkin serf. Lisandre had never given much thought to this before, being her father's darling and her brother's best friend. Now she had lost both at one stroke and she struggled desperately against the authority of the Regent, heedless of the consequences.

If Lisandre had been as meek and demure as Briony, Lord Zavion would have paid her no heed and she could have gone much her own way, for some time at least. If she had used her wit and wiles like Lady Donella, she could well have charmed him into indulging and pampering her like her father once had. Lisandre scorned to cozen him, however. She argued with him, disobeyed his every command and did everything she could to prick him and provoke him. Watching from her corner, Briony had a sudden insight into her character. She no longer saw Lisandre as a bright-winged butterfly, living out a brief, heedless life, but instead as a pupa within a chrysalis, struggling to break free. All Briony's sympathy was quickened into life and so, although she could do nothing to help Lisandre, she watched and listened with intent interest, aching and troubled on her behalf.

Now the Regent looked at Lisandre with annoyance, saying rather waspishly, "My dear child! We are not stupid ourselves. Of course the serfs were permitted to sleep … occasionally."

Lady Ginerva looked up at that. "Only occasionally? My lord!"

He frowned. "They were treated well enough, I promise you, gentle lady. We gave them food and some sacks to sleep on and if any of them fainted we let them rest in the shade and gave them some water."

Lady Ginerva looked distressed. "But, my lord, you

promised me they would be treated well, and properly compensated for their labour."

Lady Donella rose and bent over the dowager countess, patting her hand. "Oh, such a sweet and gentle lady you are, to be thinking of those peasants in the midst of all your grief and heartbreak! Do not fear. Lord Zavion is the kindest and most considerate of men and your serfs are strong and healthy with the good life you have given them. And the tower is now finished. They will be able to rest for as long as they like now."

"Except for all the work that needs to be done in the fields," Lisandre muttered.

Lord Zavion raised his voice so that his words drowned hers out. "All finished except for the fitting of the magnifying lenses and that I dared not do by the light of mere lanterns. It has taken weeks for the master glass-blower to perfect them as it is! We shall begin work again at dawn and all shall be ready by noon, when the powers of the daystar are at their height. So you see! Your serfs shall have at least five hours' rest tonight."

Lady Ginerva clasped her thin hands together in her lap. "Are you sure, my lord, that the ritual shall work as you expect? Will my darling son truly wake from this cursed sleep?"

Lord Zavion laid one of his hands over hers. His long fingernails glittered silver. "So I truly believe, gentle lady," he said, his deep, melodious voice throbbing with sincerity. "The tower of stars has the ability to harness immense power and the daystar, the source

63

of all light and life and energy, will be as close as it ever comes to this world. I shall be able to direct all that light and energy into the body of your son. If that does not wake him, nothing will!"

"Unless it kills him," Lisandre said.

Lady Ginerva recoiled with a little cry.

"Horrid child!" Lady Donella cried. "You must not upset your mother so! How can you say such a thing?"

"Why do you not leave the magework to the mage, my child?" Zavion said, his smile rather strained. "I assure you I understand the powers of the daystar much better than you do."

Lisandre opened her mouth to argue but Lady Donella laid an imperative hand upon her arm.

"Lisandre, you must learn not to interrupt when your elders are speaking, else you shall have to go back to the nursery," she said coldly. "Indeed, I think thirteen is too young to be allowed to sit with the adults and listen to their counsel. Certainly you do not show any sign of maturity!"

"But—" Lisandre began hotly.

"There is no need for you to fear for your brother, my dear," Lord Zavion said, showing his teeth.

"But we do not even know *why* Ziggy sleeps like that!" Lisandre shouted, her cheeks colouring vividly. "Should we not try and find out what happened to him and Papa?"

Lady Ginerva said miserably, "Oh, Lise…"

Lady Donella had her hands to her ears. "What a noise! Lisandre! Have you not been taught a lady never shouts? You must try and remember to always address your elders with proper respect. By the heavens! Such a wild, noisy child you are."

"I am not!"

"Oh, I know it's not really your fault, Lisandre. You have lived here at the back of beyond all your life, surrounded by serfs and peasants, with so few companions of your own age and standing. It's no wonder you behave like a hoyden."

"I am not a hoyden!"

"Donella..." protested the dowager countess.

"I'm sorry, Lisandre, my dear. Of course you are not a hoyden. Are you not one of the starborn, related by blood to the king himself? I just mean that such boisterous behaviour is not what one expects to find among the Ziv. We, who know and love you, understand that you just get a little carried away sometimes. Such impulsiveness and outspokenness would be frowned on at the king's court, of course."

The dowager countess looked troubled. Lisandre scowled and bit her lip.

"I am sorry to have to keep on reprimanding you, Lisandre," Lady Donella said with a winning smile. "It is just that I know you shall have to be presented at court in only a few years' time and I do not wish you to be snubbed or ostracised. You are not a little girl any more, you know."

"Five minutes ago you said I was!"

Lady Ginerva sighed and shaded her eyes with her hand. "Lise, please!" she moaned.

"Much as I dislike appearing to criticise you, dear

lady, I cannot help but feel your daughter should have been sent to boarding school in the capital city, like other young ladies of her class," Lord Zavion said, seizing Lady Ginerva's other hand and caressing it unctuously. "She is badly in need of a firm guiding hand, I feel. And, may I say, at school she would have the chance to make friends with young ladies from the very best families and perhaps, who knows, to come to the attention of their parents. It is never too soon to begin laying the foundation of a suitable marriage, as I am sure I do not need to remind you, my dear lady."

"Ziggy's all the friend I need," Lisandre cried, perilously close to tears. "I won't go to boarding school, I won't, I won't!"

"That's enough, Lise," the dowager countess said faintly, shading her eyes. "It is very late, I think it's time you went to bed. I know these past few months have been unhappy ones but there is no excuse for rudeness."

Lisandre gave an angry sob and the dowager countess sighed and looked up. "By tomorrow afternoon all will be well and we can forget this little scene ever happened," she said wearily. "Come, kiss me good night." As Lisandre obediently leant forward and kissed her on the cheek, she said, "Starry dreams, darling. I will see you in the morning."

Lisandre murmured something and went out of the room unhappily, her mother closing her eyes once more within the shelter of her hand.

Pedrin was roughly shaken awake. He rubbed his bleary eyes, conscious at once of the aches and pains of his body and the sting of whip cuts on his shoulders.

The overseer was kicking a man opposite to his feet, his whip coiled in his huge hand. Beside Pedrin, Durrik still slept. Pedrin shook him gently.

"Cursed is the son of light!" Durrik shouted. "Cursed the tower shining bright!"

The overseer spun on his heel, his whip uncoiling. "What did that gander-leg say?"

"Naught!" Pedrin shook Durrik more vigorously. "He's asleep. He's a-dreaming, that's all. The light shone in his eyes."

The overseer stared at them through narrowed eyes, and Pedrin gazed back with a look of wide-eyed innocence until at last the burly-shouldered man turned away, grunting. Durrik tried to sit up and cried aloud in pain, cringing back down onto his pile of dirty old sacks.

"You got t'stop talking in your sleep!" Pedrin hissed, with one eye on the overseer's broad back. "I would've thought you'd had enough of that gibgoblin's whip to last a lifetime."

"Was I talking in my sleep again? What did I say?"

"The same sort of stuff you've been a-gabbling all month. Curses and lights shining bright and six together shall prevail. Frankly, I'll be glad when I don't have to sleep next to you any more. You're about as restful as a bed louse, a-tossing and a-turning and a-shrieking out in your sleep all the time."

"I'm sorry."

"I s'pose you can't really help it," Pedrin said gruffly. "How's your back?"

"Sore," Durrik replied, and struggled up onto one elbow with a wince of pain.

"Mebbe we'll see Ma today," Pedrin said, his voice rising in hope. "She'll know what to do for your back. Oh, thank Liah 'tis the summer solstice today. This has been the longest month of me life."

"Mine too," Durrik said.

Pedrin put down one hand and hauled Durrik to his feet. "I can't wait to leave this stinking hot cesspit and get back out on the hills with the goats and enjoy what's left of the summer." He looked around him with dissatisfaction.

Overhead arched the cavernous roof of the warehouse, already thick with fumes that stung the eyes. The only light came from the furnaces that glowed red-hot and hungry, and the orange flare of molten glass being poured onto a pool of seething liquid metal. It hissed and sizzled, sending off thick clouds of black smoke, but slowly settled to float upon the surface. Eventually it would cool into smooth, flat panes of glass. On either side skinny, wan-faced men were rolling great blobs of glass or blowing down a long, thin metal tube so that the molten glass hanging from its end billowed out into new shapes. The master glass-blower himself was twisting the hot, glowing, liquid glass with a few delicate tools, creating a sculpture of a man astride a sisika, holding a glass fusillier over his shoulder. Another such sculpture already stood to one side, the transparent wings of the bird amazingly lifelike.

This dark, fetid warehouse had been Pedrin and Durrik's home for twenty-one long days. They had not seen the sun or tasted fresh air or smelt anything but burning silica and soda and lime in all that time. They had been allowed only a few minutes to eat a very scrappy meal twice a day, and had not slept for more than four hours straight in all that time. Their eyes were red-rimmed and weeping from the acrid smoke, their skin black with char.

Worse than the physical discomfort was the psychic distress both boys felt, separated from all that was safe and familiar, wracked with anxiety about their families, made to feel their powerlessness more acutely than ever before.

Pedrin had always spat in the dust when talking about the starkin, same as any other hearthkin man. He spoke of them with derision if he spoke of them at all. Called them air-dreamers, or dandyprats, as he had heard them called all his life. "I'd like to see *them* pull a plough," he would say with scorn. Yet his contempt had been artificial, constructed from the half-understood conversations and attitudes of his elders, and very much tempered by an unsophisticated admiration for their grace, their beauty, their sinister weapons.

Now Pedrin felt his contempt in every nerve and pulse of his body. He was sick with hatred and bewilderment. The starkin had the right to condemn Pedrin and his family to slavery and starvation. Their guards could whip Durrik's back raw and bloody for stumbling in weariness, his youth and frailty invoking no pity. They could, if they wished, turn every one of the hearthkin into dust and ashes, without fear of retribution or punishment. And for what? A mere folly of glass, a fabrication of sand and air.

With the sour bile of hatred in his stomach and throat every minute of every day, Pedrin found it hard to chew and swallow even when food was offered to him, and he lay awake at night planning petty acts of revenge and great acts of rebellion. To his distress, he saw the same forces acting on Durrik, leaching all the wit and merriment out of him and turning him into a dazed and feeble puppet, moving jerkily at the will of the overseer.

Their misery had sharpened to a point of true acuteness the day before, when an exhausted Durrik had stumbled to his knees while carrying a heavy bucket of coal up to the furnace. Two men carrying a wide sheet of glass had not seen him in the gloom, and tripped. The glass had slipped from their hands and smashed into smithereens on the metal grating. One of the men had blundered backwards to avoid the flying shards of glass. He had slammed into the railing and overbalanced, falling down with a wailing scream and landing with a sinister crack on the floor far below. He had not moved again. Durrik had stood mesmerised at the railing, watching as the overseer knelt over the body, examining him with a grim and angry face before calling for a stretcher to carry the dead man home to his family.

Durrik had been whipped harder and longer than ever before. Pedrin had been unable to watch, hiding his face in his hands as he listened to the crack, crack, crack of the whip and Durrik's little involuntary whimpers. Pedrin thought the overseer might have beaten Durrik to death if the master glass-blower had not stopped him, saying with weary disgust, "No need t'kill him, man, we're going to need all the hands we can get to replace that glass."

That night Pedrin had gingerly tended Durrik's back with water and vinegar, the crippled boy unable to control the sobs shuddering through his thin body. "It warn't your fault," Pedrin whispered, his tongue thick and unwieldy with the inadequacy of his reassurance.

"Who's ... then?" Durrik had muttered in return, his head buried in his arm.

"Those blasted starkin!" Pedrin said with passion. "'Tis their fault, to work us till we drop. 'Tis that Lord Regent's fault. He probably set it up on purpose, wanting a blood sacrifice for the gods."

Durrik shook his head, his breath catching. "Nah, that ... can't be it. The starkin don't believe in the gods."

"Not believe in the gods!" Pedrin had scoffed.

"Well, they don't. The starkin believe the gods are naught but superstitious rubbish."

Pedrin had hastily struck his right index finger along his left in an instinctive call for Liah's protection. "Not believe in the gods? What do you mean?"

"The starkin have the world all measured up and weighed and accounted for. They think everything can be understood with science and controlled by technology." Durrik's voice was weary.

"Then why don't they use their technology to go home?" Pedrin said acerbically.

Durrik had shrugged, wincing at the pain the movement caused him. "Only Liah herself could know that. I think they've forgotten the way. Or mebbe their technology doesn't work here. I don't know."

It made Pedrin profoundly uneasy. If the starkin did not believe in the gods, let alone revere them, how could the gods allow them to live? Not only did the starkin survive the disdain of the gods, they ruled with such utter and luxurious certainty. It made Pedrin wonder, for the very first time, if the gods still watched. That dissonance was enough to make him say, with true sincerity, "I wish they'd never come."

The tales of the starkin's coming were often told around the hearth and the feast-fire, along with the stories of Tessula, the god of breath; Imala the Shape-

Giver, the goddess of the earth; their daughters Lullalita, Liah and Taramis, the goddesses of water, fire and the rainbow, the bridge between the worlds; and their sons Chtatchka the Earth-Shaker, Tallis of the Cold Embrace, Marithos the Counter, and Jerimy Two-Face, the trickster god, called Jimjinny because he liked to disguise himself as a goose-girl nearly as often as he posed as a goatherd. The stories of the nine great gods and ninety-nine lesser ones provided enough material to keep the tale-tellers talking all winter but, because the young hearthkin children saw the proof of the starkin about them every day, they clamoured often for the tales of their coming.

The starkin fell out of the sky like dying stars, the tale-tellers said, crashing to earth with streaming tails of pure, cold radiance. At first the hearthkin and the wildkin had thought them gods come to walk upon the earth, and had been eager with gifts and homage. Soon it was clear they were not gods, though, so indifferent and greedy were these strangers from the sky. Then the hearthkin and wildkin had sought to withdraw their obeisance but the starkin had been angry. It was then that they showed the true purpose of the long silver tools they always carried upon their backs. With the power of lightning at their fingertips and the power of ruthlessness in their hearts, the starkin had soon triumphed, leaving only a scatter of ashes behind them.

Johan had once said the hearthkin and the wildkin could, perhaps, have defeated the starkin and driven them back into the sky if they had been able to set

73

aside their differences and join forces. The hearthkin and wildkin had never lived together comfortably, however. There was too much distrust and suspicion, too many old misunderstandings. Besides, Johan said, the wildkin had no council, no guild, no reeve nor constable. They lived like animals, going their own way, without law or principles. It was inconceivable that they would have submitted to the discipline of an armed force. The only people who could perhaps have persuaded the more intelligent and ferocious of the wildkin to join forces with the hearthkin were the Crafty, and they too were wild and unruly, their only law their own will.

So the starkin had built their cities and their castles, driven the Old Ones and the Crafty into the wild lands, subjugated the hearthkin and made for themselves a life of ease and comfort. They never lost their longing for their homeland, however. Their minstrels sang wistfully of Zivhayr, its crystal halls and shining towers, its diamond-bright seas and perfumed breezes. It was always warm in Zivhayr, they sang. There were no storms, no sadness, in Zivhayr.

Gradually, as the centuries passed, the hearthkin grew used to their servitude, the wildkin grew wilder and rarer, and the starkin gave up dreaming of Zivhayr. Almost.

"Anyways," Durrik had continued, after a long silence when the two boys were preoccupied with their own thoughts, "I do know the lord astronomer wouldn't have broken a pane of his beloved glass just to have a little blood split. If he really believed the

74

gods wanted a sacrifice, he would've had a couple of goats killed. Or if it had to be hearthkin, he'd just have ordered one of his men t'cut a throat with a dagger. He wouldn't have sacrificed the glass too!"

Pedrin had to concede Durrik had a point. Still, he and all the other hearthkin had conceived a deep suspicion and hatred of Lord Zavion and believed him capable of just about any infamy, including murder. It was whispered the Regent had arranged for the death of the old count himself, and was somehow responsible for the cursed sleep of the young count. He would be the next to die, frizzled to a cinder on the crystal altar built in the heart of the tower. Everyone knew Lord Zavion was cousin to the king himself, as he had been to Count Zoltan. No one doubted he would be named heir if Count Zygmunt was to die before his time. All knew the Regent was a cold, proud, ambitious man. Was it so hard to believe he was the secret hand behind this curse that kept their young count in this unnatural sleep, as still and cold as if he were already dead?

With all these suspicions swirling around the glassworks, as thick and foul-smelling as the smoke from the furnaces, the mood among the hearthkin was ugly indeed. It was a slow, sullen anger, however. Apart from anything else, the hearthkin were weary indeed, so tired they could barely plod about their work, let alone plan an insurrection.

The guards were harsher than ever this morning, as if punishing all the workers in the glassworks for the breaking of the window pane. Sore, miserable and aching all over, the boys stumbled to obey their orders, the back of Durrik's shirt stained with ugly brown lines. He looked sick, with blue shadows under his eyes. To Pedrin's dismay, he was muttering under his breath again. Pedrin nudged him, aware of the overseer's eyes upon them, but Durrik paid no heed, mumbling: "Cursed ... the people lost in ... the night..."

Pedrin hustled him away, whispering under his breath, "Durrik, are you all right?" but his friend only looked at him with dazed eyes and, after a moment, nodded.

By the time the birds were warbling, the final work was finished. The intricately cut and polished lenses were being loaded onto the barges, the huge sculptures of starkin lords upon their giant birds were being trundled down to the lake on a heavy wagon pulled by ten burly hearthkin, and the master glassblower was giving one enormous convex lens a final, anxious polish with his handkerchief.

All of the hearthkin were required to help in the final frantic work on the crystal tower, and so Pedrin and Durrik were among those harried out of the glassworks and down to the jetties by the overseer. The cool air that swept over their faces as they stepped outside almost made them swoon, the pearly dawn light stabbing their eyes so that they covered their faces with their hands. Both Pedrin and Durrik found themselves taking deep swallows of air as if it was the most delicious apple-ale. Never had air tasted so cool, so sweet, so intoxicating.

The overseer stood at the jetty, his whip coiled in

the ham-sized hand resting on his hip. Pedrin felt Durrik falter and said to him urgently, "Jumping Jimjinny, Durrik, now's not the time to be a-worrying about getting on a boat. He'll drown you himself if you make a fuss."

Durrik had had an intense fear of the river ever since the time their raft had capsized and he had almost drowned. If Pedrin had not been such a strong swimmer he would have drowned, for the crippled boy did not have enough strength in his legs to keep himself afloat. Ever since he had refused to try rafting again, and would not even go out on the flower-decked barges during the festival in honour of Lullalita.

Now his footsteps dragged, and the closer they came to the boat the more he hung back, so that Pedrin had to grip his arm quite hard and practically drag him the last few steps. The overseer narrowed his eyes and uncoiled his whip, swinging it longingly, and Durrik came down the steps and into the boat in a rush. He huddled at the very bottom and would not look out at the shifting, gleaming water running so silkily under the prow, though Pedrin leant over the side and let his fingers dangle with great pleasure.

The walk up the hill to the astronomer's tower made Pedrin's legs tremble and his breath grow short. Only a month ago he had leapt as nimbly and tire-lessly up the tors as Thundercloud did. He wondered with a pang how his goats were, and how his mother had managed without him, and stumbled as his vision swam.

"Steady there, my boy," came a deep, familiar voice. The bell-crier came up beside them, dropping one big hand on each boy's shoulder. For the first time ever Pedrin saw his friend's father looking dishevelled, his hair falling out of its black ribbon, his shirt grubby and unbuttoned at the throat, his chin unshaven. Johan examined their faces closely, frowning a little at their pallor. "How have you been these past few weeks? Have they treated you well?"

"They whipped Durrik, whipped him bad," Pedrin said urgently. "Look at his back."

Johan lifted the bloodstained shirt and examined the torn and lacerated skin with his lips thinning. "What possible excuse did they have for such barbarity!" he cried. "I shall complain to the overseer."

"He'd laugh in your face," Durrik said wearily.

"Or spit in it," Pedrin said.

Johan's face was haggard with distress. "I can't believe they'd do this to a young boy! What cruelty! Oh, Durrik, my boy, I'm so sorry, so very sorry. Just as soon as we are released from our service, I shall get you home and to bed. 'Tis a wonder you can walk."

"I can't really," Durrik said with a wan attempt at a smile. "If it warn't for Pedrin, I'd fall right over."

Johan went on exclaiming and shaking his head. Durrik was both relieved to be able to lean on his father's strong arm and uncomfortable that he should be the cause of so much fuss. Durrik hated to be reminded of his own feebleness.

Knowing this and wanting to distract the bell-

78

crier's attention, Pedrin said rather plaintively, "Got aught to eat? We're starving!"

Johan frowned and smiled, all at once. "You do look like you need a good feed," he said, slipping his hand into his pocket and drawing out a slice of cheese-and-onion pie. "Get this into you."

"Yippee!" Pedrin cried, grabbing it and breaking it in half. The two heads, one curly and brown, the other with fine hair that stuck straight up like a duckling's down, bent over his hand as the friends carefully examined the two halves and negotiated their division.

"They fed you badly?" Johan asked as the slices of pie swiftly disappeared.

"Pig's swill," Pedrin said succinctly through a mouthful of crumbs. "I've been dreaming of egg-and-bacon pie every night. 'Tis been torture."

"I dreamt of roast pork with crackling and apple chutney," Durrik said dreamily. "And apricot turnovers."

"Blackberry tart with cream," Pedrin said emphatically.

"Mushroom omelette," Durrik said longingly.

"Enough, you're making my mouth water! Never fear. If I know your ma, Pedrin, she'll have brought all your favourite food. She knows what you're like."

"Will she be here?" Pedrin looked about him eagerly.

"The whole town will be here, I daresay the whole valley. 'Tis not just the folk of Levanna-On-The-Lake who have been made to labour on this folly, but the men and boys of every town, village and hamlet in all of Estelliana. Let us pray to the nine great gods and the ninety-nine lesser ones that this experiment of the Regent revives our count!"

6

♦ ♦ ♦

*U*p close the height and brilliance of the tower was even more awe-inspiring than when seen from the shore. The bright radiance of the dawn sky was reflected in the sheer glass walls, which soared twelve storeys high. The tower seemed to defy the laws of air and earth, so that the men clustered on the ground cringed down as they worked, expecting the whole fragile edifice to come smashing down.

At the apex of the tower was a chamber open to the elements, the walls held aloft only by delicate pillars and arches of spun glass. Here a bird could fly straight through the tower and emerge on the far side, while a handspan lower they would crash into the walls and break their necks. Indeed, the ground below the tower was littered with small, limp, feathered bodies with twisted necks and opaque eyes, those birds that had mistaken an impenetrable pane of glass for guileless air.

Above the chamber soared an immensely tall, narrow spire of cut glass, its facets flashing and sparkling like a crown of diamonds. Light could be channelled down this precisely wrought conduit, through a series of concave and convex lenses, and down to the very heart of the tower. Through these lenses, Lord Zavion could see far into the heavens, watching the stately dance of stars and comets and planets amidst swirls of fiery dust and echoing funnels of emptiness. He could read the cryptic messages the stars wrote upon the night skies, he could search for Zivhayr, the lost home of the starkin, he could funnel the immense power and energy of the daystar for his own obscure uses. This slim column of shining crystal was more than just a thing of incomprehensible beauty. It was an instrument of power.

An hour before noon the tower was at last complete and perfect. The hearthkin were allowed to hurry away from its strange lucid shadow and rest under the trees. Families were reunited, old friends greeted. Bread, cheese and cold bacon were handed round generously, and mugs full of cool, frothy apple-ale. The bearded faces split in smiles for the first time in a month. Dour jokes were tossed about. A few fell asleep, their handkerchiefs fluttering gently over their faces. Most sat and drank and chatted, the completion of the tower lifting a dark and galling load from their shoulders. For the first time they began to talk about the harvest, to worry if the weather might break before they got the hay in, to question their wives and daughters about the state of the fields and the vineyards.

Pedrin had searched the crowd eagerly for any sign of his mother and little sister, though when he saw them he greeted them laconically, submitting to his mother's embrace and rubbing his cheek where she kissed him.

Maegeth was horrified by Durrik's back and made him lie down on his stomach in the shade so she could rub some healing ointment on the welts. "I went one night to Naoma's hideyhole and gave her some cheese and honey in return for all the good stuff she could give me," Maegeth told Johan rather grimly. "I knew I'd be a-needing it."

"You should have more of a care for yourself," Johan said with a troubled face. "'Tis only a matter of time before the starkin learn where that witch has hidden herself. You do not want to be caught visiting one of the Crafty."

"Nah," Maegeth said rather defensively. "But if I hadn't gone, I wouldn't have the stuff to put on Durrik's back and, indeed, Naoma knows her healing arts. Durrik's back won't hurt him now and it'll heal quickly."

"'Tis stopped hurting, Papa," Durrik said, quick to defend Maegeth.

His father patted him gently, saying, "That's good, my boy. It was worth the risk, though I could be wishing it was me that had run it and not Maegeth."

"You always think the best of the starkin," Maegeth said, softening the rebuke with one of her flashing smiles. "I knew the boys would come back with cuts and bruises, at the very best. And hungry too, of course! Look what Mina and I have brought for you!"

She drew forward a big basket covered with a damp

white cloth, uncovering it with a flourish. Pedrin began to pull things out with little glad cries. "Blackberry pie. Ma, you're the best! And Durrik, look. Mushroom omelette!"

They all sat down to enjoy their picnic, the boys beginning to chatter more naturally as they told Maegeth all about the glassworks. She grew pale and fierce as they described how the overseer's whip would lash them at the slightest word or look, but said very little about it. Instead, she entertained them with stories about what the women of the fields had been doing while their men were labouring for the starkin.

"Miryam couldn't manage the work of the mill alone," she said, smiling in remembrance, "so we had a day where all we women came along to help out, but we could not be a-figuring how to get the mill-wheel turning. We stood around for an hour before someone thought to open the sluice!"

Pedrin ate and listened, grinning every now and again, his love for his mother rising up so strong in him he could not have spoken a word. She was so dear and familiar with her worn, narrow face and the great mass of untidy brown hair half-falling out of its bun and her big, wide, flashing smile, and her refusal to give Johan the respect he was used to, so that he was half-embarrassed, half-charmed, as usual.

When at last he could eat no more, Pedrin rolled over and began to sternly question his little sister about his goats. "If Snowflake has lost her milk, I'll bury you up to your neck in an ants' nest," he said threateningly.

"You'd have to catch me first," Mina said, sticking out her tongue. He swiped at her and she darted away, squealing, but Pedrin was too tired and too comfortable to bother chasing her. Soon she crept back and nestled in by his side, telling him with great pride how she had looked after the whole flock of goats, all by herself.

"Ma wouldn't let me take them up the hill, though," she said rather sorrowfully. "I had to graze them in our own meadow. Thundercloud warn't pleased."

"I bet he warn't. Did he bite you?"

"Couldn't catch me," Mina said with a grin. "Though he tried."

"He would've bitten you if he'd wanted to," Pedrin said. "He just knew you'd taste awful."

"I wouldn't!"

"Yes, you would. Like off meat. Thundercloud's too smart to take a bite of you."

"He is not! I would not!"

"Urrrgh, you would. Rank."

She pummelled him, and he pinned her down with one arm, chatting to Durrik and ignoring her squeals and kicks and bites. After a while, when her squeals of laughter were beginning to turn tearful, he looked at her in mock-surprise, saying, "Oh, you still here? I thought 'twas a mosquito a-buzzing around and a-bothering me. Off you go then. Go buzz in someone else's ear."

"I hate you," she flashed and went running off, all long skinny legs and tangled hair. He grinned at Durrik and ate another little honey cake.

The sun crept higher. The tranquil waters of the lake parted and curled white before the high carved prows of the starkin's boats. The murmur of conversation died away. All raised themselves on their elbows or sat up to watch the boats cross the lake, their faces sullen once more.

It was almost noon.

Slowly the long procession of starkin glided up the new white road to the tower built on the crest of the hill. They did not glance at the hearthkin, who had all scrambled to their feet and taken off their hats. They did not stare up at the tower, though it dominated the day like a searing column of white flame. Their hands were clasped at their breasts, their long robes riffled the dust, their grave eyes were bent upon the path.

Pedrin did not have to search hard to find the tall figure of the dowager countess's daughter. Dressed in sweeping robes the colour of old blood, Lady Lisandre walked beside the litter which carried the sleeping figure of the young count, her brother. She looked as if she had been crying. She was the sort of girl that tearstains suited.

A small sigh from Durrik made Pedrin glance at his friend. He was staring at the starkin girl with a look of such rapt adoration on his face that Pedrin was moved to elbow him sharply in the side. "Shut your mouth," he whispered. "You're a-drooling!"

Durrik flushed red and put up his hand to wipe his mouth. Finding it dry, he flashed a furious, embarrassed look at Pedrin and turned away.

Silently the hearthkin followed the starkin past the

statues with their upraised glass spears, through the deep shadowy archway and into the heart of the crystal tower.

It was like being entombed in ice. Although they could see out, the world beyond was cold and blue and remote. The glass walls soared up all around them, casting an eerie shadow on their faces. In the very centre of the vast chamber was a wide circle of silver, where astrological symbols danced and leapt and galloped and splashed. In the centre of this circle the unconscious boy had been laid.

Pedrin and Durrik were at the very forefront of the crowd, who had parted ranks to allow the stout figure of the bell-crier through. The two boys had simply followed in his wake and so had an excellent view of the circle. Lord Zavion stood at a high lectern, his hands resting upon a panel of polished steel and stained glass. On the far side sat the dowager countess and the starkin court. The dowager countess looked ghastly. She was even thinner than before and in the bluish dimness her skin was sickly green. Her gown looked black.

Durrik hunched his shoulders. "I don't like this place. It makes me feel sick."

"Why should it?" Pedrin replied practically. "'Tis just a tower. You must've eaten too much blackberry pie."

"I didn't!"

"For such a skinny kid, you eat an awful lot. Must've hollow legs."

"I was hungry."

"So was I. And Ma's pie is mighty good."

Lord Zavion raised his hands dramatically. Silence fell. "The daystar reaches the apex of the sky, the apex of its powers. I, Lord Zavion, shall draw upon the powers of the daystar, source of all light and life and energy, and awaken the young count, trapped in this unnatural sleep. Watch and marvel!"

The crowd of hearthkin shifted and murmured. Pedrin leant forward, wiping his clammy hands on his tunic. Lord Zavion made a sweeping gesture with his right hand, then slowly, delicately, manipulated one of the levers. With a grating noise the spire slowly rotated and then opened out like the petals of a daisy.

A great shaft of white light struck down from above. It shone upon the young count, blanching all colour from his face. The sun was directly overhead, so bright none could look up at it. Everyone was hot and sticky. The attendants of the starkin ladies fanned them with enormous white fans of sisika feathers.

Lord Zavion shook back his long embroidered sleeves, then gently nudged another of the levers. The circle of light narrowed until the young count was impaled upon its bright pin. Everyone held their breath. The court astronomer raised his hands and then, with theatrical slowness, pressed a button.

A flash of blue light dazzled their eyes. There was a reek of smoke. The limp form on the pallet arched upwards for a few seconds, then collapsed back. One hand hung limply. His eyelids twitched.

There was a sharp exhalation of breath from the dowager countess. Lady Lisandre sat forward, her hands gripped together anxiously. The court physician bent over the boy then stepped back, shaking his head. A low growl from the crowd, a restless surge forward. Durrik made a small piteous sound in his throat. His face was white, his teeth gripping his lip.

Lord Zavion frowned and pushed the button again, this time not lifting his finger away.

Another shock of lightning. The young count's back arched, only his head and heels remaining in contact with the pallet. There was a horrible sizzling sound. His fair hair all stood on end. Smoke curled from his fingertips.

"Stop it!" Lady Lisandre cried. She leapt to her feet, wrenching her shoulder free of the restraining grip of the chief lady-in-waiting and diving into the circle of searing, dazzling light, trying to reach her brother. Immediately her whole body stiffened. Her eyes and her mouth opened wide. For a moment she was frozen mid-step, her arm flung forward, then she screamed, a terrible high thin sound that echoed around the shadowy chamber. Her knees buckled, she fell to the ground, arms over her head, still screaming.

"No!" the dowager countess cried. She too leapt to her feet, only to fall in a faint, her blood-red skirts crushed beneath her. Lord Zavion hurriedly lifted his finger from the button but still the blue, sizzling light poured down, the two children trapped within jerking and twitching horribly.

"Stop it!" Durrik cried. He scrambled forward, his crutch clattering on the glass floor as he threw himself down beside the sobbing, writhing Lisandre. As the hissing blue-white light closed about his body, his mouth twisted in a grotesque shriek of pain, his eyes rolled back in his head, his heels rattled the floor.

"Out, out!" Lord Zavion screamed. "You will overload the mechanism!"

Smoke wreathed up from the clothes of the three children, who were now all arched away from the floor, jerking about as wildly as fish flapping in the bottom of a boat.

Although everything happened in just a few swift seconds, Pedrin felt time buckle and stretch so it seemed as if everything happened very, very slowly. He had surged forward, trying to stop Durrik, his fingers just failing to close upon the cloth of his shirt. He heard a long wail wrenched from his throat. His eyes darted, from the three children jerking like broken marionettes in the circle of blazing, hissing blue light, to the heap of red cloth that was the dowager countess, to the avid, frightened, gloating face of her lady-in-waiting, the horrified faces of the other starkin and their servants, the terrified face of Lord Zavion, pounding the lectern, dragging at the levers, and then, flicking as quick as a whip, Pedrin's gaze followed the Regent's frenzied glance up at the long funnel of light, magnified one-hundred-thousand-fold through the curved lenses of glass and into this bolt of frizzling, sizzling incandescence.

With no apparent hesitation, Pedrin thrust his hand within his bag of stones, dragged his slingshot out of his belt, and aimed straight above his head. His pebble spun high into the air, cracked against the curved glass lens above them, and smashed it.

A hail of glass bombarded them. People screamed as sharp slivers sliced into their bare flesh. Everywhere people ducked down, hiding their faces, as glass rattled the floor, pinging off to score hundreds of little cuts on arms, hands, legs. The blue bolt of lightning vanished, leaving only that bright spotlight, all dazed and drifting with smoke. The three children within collapsed limply.

Lisandre moaned and curled onto her side. Beside her Durrik lay still, his arms about his head. Then slowly he lifted his face. Blood slid down from his mouth. He pointed one shaking finger at Lord Zavion and cried:

"Cursed is the son of light,
Cursed the tower shining bright,
Cursed the land withering in its blight,
Cursed the people, lost in its night."

There was a shocked silence. Lord Zavion lifted his rage-contorted face from the shelter of his silken sleeves. Blood crept in a small, snaking rivulet down one prominent cheekbone. "How dare you! Guards, seize the traitor! Kill him!"

Durrik struggled to his feet, cutting his hand as he used it to lever himself upright. Blood dripped from his palm but he did not seem to notice. He looked very small and frail, standing there alone in the circle of light. His eyes were like pits of darkness, the pupils so greatly dilated none of the blue could be seen. Again he spoke, and although he was only a boy, his words rang in every corner of the great glass chamber.

"Under winter's cold shroud, the son of light lies
Though the summer sun burns high in the skies.
With the last petal of the starthorn tree
His wandering spirit shall at last slip free,
Nothing can save him from this bitter curse,
But the turning of time itself inverse.
If those long apart can together be spun
Six separate threads woven into one,
Two seeking destiny in heaven's countless eyes,
Two of the old blood, children of the wise,
Two iron-bound, that tend the hearth's red heat,
Six brought together can the cruel bane defeat."

There was a moment's incredulous silence. Durrik's voice and manner had been so commanding that none had sought to stop him, not even the Regent, who was livid with rage and consternation. The soldiers stood with their weapons half-cocked, an expression of fear and awe on their faces. As one, the hearthkin struck their right index finger along their left, murmuring the names of their gods. The sight and sound enraged Lord Zavion further. He pointed one shaking finger at Durrik and screamed, "Seize him! Seize them all. The hearthkin shall pay for this!"

7

$\blacktriangle$ $\blacktriangle$ $\blacktriangle$

Pedrin darted forward, seized Durrik by the arm and dragged him towards the great doorway. The shards of glass cut his bare feet cruelly but he did not stop.

A guard tried to seize them and Pedrin slung a stone at him that caught him full in the forehead. He dropped heavily. Other guards were closing in on them, but with a deep growl and mutter, the hearthkin moved to hold them back. A cautious, deliberate people, the hearthkin were slow to anger but terrible once roused. Now they grappled with the guards, seizing them with their great brawny arms, tripping them over with a well-aimed foot or knocking them down from behind. Pedrin was able to haul along his dazed and frightened friend without interference, while the starkin drew back, trying not to show their alarm, and Lord Zavion shrieked cruel imprecations.

There was a loud clang just behind them. Pedrin spun on his heels, in time to see Johan knocking down a guard with his heavy brass bell. "Run, boys!" he cried. "Run! You must not let them catch you."

Then he was seized from behind by two guards, struggling to drag him down. "Here, Durrik!" the bell-crier shouted. He managed to free one arm and threw his bell towards his son. It tumbled over and over, clanging dolefully, and Durrik caught it in reflex. "Get away from here!" the bell-crier shouted. "Hide out in the forest or on the mountain. Have a care…" His last words were swallowed as two burly soldiers buried him beneath their bodies. Durrik sobbed aloud, straining over his shoulder to see as Pedrin dragged him away.

The soldiers dared not fire their weapons inside the crystal tower, in case the brittle, translucent walls came crashing down. So they used their butts to beat down the hearthkin. Pedrin felt his stomach clench in sympathy and guilt, but he dared not stop. With Durrik stumbling along behind, he ran at full pelt out through the entry tunnel and into the brightness of the day.

Their eyes were so dazzled they could not see but they did not pause, scrambling and slipping down the hill towards the boats. Pedrin heard a loud bang and saw a flash of bright light. He glanced back and saw starkin soldiers levelling their fusilliers at him. He thought he had been running as fast as he could before but his stride suddenly lengthened, the world flashing past in a roar and a blur. Durrik fell and Pedrin dragged him up again.

There was a shout and another loud bang. Pedrin wondered with strange clarity what it would feel like to be incinerated. Would he feel his skin, his flesh, his bones implode into a white sheet of agony? Or would it be so quick he would feel nothing but a momentary surprise?

He saw a tree beside the path leap into flame. Instinctively he bounded away, a hot wind scorching his arm. For a second the black skeleton of the tree stood within its halo of flame-blossoms and then it slowly dissolved into ashes that choked his throat. Beside him Durrik was sobbing as he lurched along. Inexorably Pedrin dragged him on. His lungs were labouring, his cut and bloodied feet were smarting cruelly, he had a stitch in his side like a spear, but gravity was pulling them down the slope, they could not have stopped if they tried.

There was a guard lounging by the boat. He leapt up with a curse, fumbling for his fusillier, but Pedrin put his head down and charged, butting the guard hard in the stomach so that he fell with an *oof!* of expelled air. Then they were clambering over the side of the boat, the bell in Durrik's hand jangling loudly. Fire arced towards them. Pedrin flung himself flat, dragging his friend down with him. The fire hissed into the water and was extinguished. Pedrin was able to push the barge away from the shore, poling as hard as he could. More fire spat at them, but they were out of range, shooting out across the water.

All was tranquil on the lake. The water rose in silken translucent curves on either side of the prow, creamed behind them in a widening triangle of foam. Pedrin struggled to catch his breath.

"Tessula's tears, what happened back there?"

Durrik shook his head. His face was very white under the smudges of dirt, and the blood from his bitten tongue was crusting hard on his chin and shirt.

"Jumping Jimjinny, Durrik, what were you a-thinking? You can't go a-telling the Regent his tower is cursed! You've started a riot. What was it all about?"

Durrik shook his head.

"What do you mean, you don't know? You must know! You can't have made up all that stuff on the spur of the moment. You've been a-muttering about it for weeks. And now look at the pot of trouble we're in!"

"I'm sorry," Durrik said miserably. "Really, I don't know where it all came from. It just sort of … came."

"But you're always making up riddles and rhymes," Pedrin said impatiently. "Though I can't see the joke in this one!"

"Really, I don't know," Durrik said insistently. He swallowed hard, rubbing at his eyes with the back of a very grubby hand. "You think I'd dare get up and ask riddles of the Regent? He scares me silly."

"Silly as a merry mummer," Pedrin said in disgust.

There was a short silence, during which Durrik swallowed his sniffles gamely and the goatherd poled along, frowning. Behind them a fleet of small boats and barges was hurrying along in pursuit, and Pedrin was sweating and panting as he sent their own little boat flying across the lake's surface.

Durrik looked up at him. "I'm sorry," he said again, his voice quavering a little.

"Well, that doesn't do us much good now," Pedrin snapped. "You've told everyone Lord Zavion's precious tower is cursed and I've smashed his precious lens, and now the whole bleeding guard is on our tail. We'll worry about what it all means later. Let's find somewhere to hide first!"

He drove the prow into the muddy bank and harassed the tired and miserable Durrik out of the boat and down the path, the crippled boy leaning heavily on his friend's shoulder. They heard the smack of oars on water and grunts of exertion behind them, then the thud of wood on earth, and both boys broke into a stumbling run once more.

They reached the shelter of the trees only a few hundred yards ahead of their pursuers. Luckily Pedrin had grown up in the meadow behind this wood, and he knew every tree and bush and rabbit hole, while the guards were in unknown territory. It took only a few seconds of panicked indecision, panting, clutching each other, glancing about wildly and hissing at each other before they half-crawled through the undergrowth and clutched at the tree in which they had built their treehouse the previous summer.

Pedrin gave Durrik a leg-up, whispering angrily, "Jumping Jimjinny, Durrik, muffle that bell! If they hear you a-clanging they'll catch us for sure."

Obediently Durrik wrapped the bell up in his cravat and shoved it in his pocket, where it made an unsightly bulge. Slowly, carefully, he crept higher and higher into the tree, reaching at last a narrow platform of old planks nailed rather haphazardly between two broad branches. He and Pedrin had sheltered here many a time from Mina and her giggling friends, or from a pack of townies looking for sport. From below, nothing could be seen but a shifting puzzle of green leaves.

Durrik pulled himself into the very centre of the platform, then took the bell out of his pocket so he could sit, his arms wrapped tightly round his legs to stop them shaking. A few seconds later Pedrin's dirty, freckled face appeared, scowling.

"They're a-beating every bush mighty thoroughly," he whispered. "We got away just in time."

They sat still, trying to control their breathing, which sounded very loud and rough in the silence. Very cautiously Pedrin peered over the edge of the platform. Below was a squad of starkin soldiers, their silver armour glinting in the sunlight. They were searching under every bush and inside every hollow log, using their fusilliers to push aside the branches. With them was a thickset man dressed in shabby leather, his skin the same colour and texture as his boots, his abundant beard heavily grizzled with grey. Pedrin felt a sickening drop of his stomach. He knew that man. It was Adken, the new chief huntsman up at the castle, a man renowned for tracking game in any conditions. Pedrin let his head droop down onto his hands. He waited to be discovered.

After a while, when nothing happened, he looked over the edge again. Adken was standing at the foot of the tree in which they hid, his big rough hand leaning on the smooth bole. He was shaking his grizzled head, shrugging a little. The starkin soldiers stood around, conferring, then their leader uttered a sharp order and they went marching off towards the river. Adken stood for a moment, looking about him, and Pedrin held as still as he could, wishing he could quieten the painful beating of his heart. Then the huntsman lifted his hand away from the tree trunk, rubbed it ruminatively against his breeches, and strolled after the soldiers, his leathery face as impassive as ever.

Pedrin found he could breathe again. He laid his head back down on his arms and tried to swallow the sob of relief in his throat. When he finally looked up it was to see Durrik rubbing at his eyes furiously with his fists. Neither boy said a word. Below all was quiet. Lizards sunned themselves on a rock, birds hopped about, pecking at the grass. Unable to look at Durrik in case his friend saw his own reddened, inflamed eyes, Pedrin got up and leant along an outflung branch, shading his eyes as he looked across the lake towards the crystal tower.

"Liah's eyes," he whispered.

"What?"

"The soldiers have taken them all prisoner, every single one. They're a-marching them up to the castle."

Durrik wriggled up beside him so he could see too. Together the two boys watched in mounting horror and dismay as a long line of hearthkin was pushed and prodded up the dusty road. Although they were too far away to see faces, it was clear many among their kindred were hurt, for they limped and shuffled, some with arms tied up in makeshift slings or with their heads bound with bandages. The boys watched in silence, feeling young and helpless and calamitously guilty.

"Well, we're in a fine pickle now," Pedrin whispered at last. "What do you suggest we do, riddler?"

Durrik shook his head.

"No funny jokes now? No fancy rhymes?"

"Don't be angry, Pedrin," the crippled boy whispered. "Really, I didn't mean to cause so much trouble. It just sort of … burst out of me."

Pedrin sighed. "Well, what's done is done. We'll just have to figure out what to do now." He lay still, frowning, his chin resting on his fists, his jaw set grimly.

In just a few minutes the whole world had turned topsy-turvy, giving Pedrin a sick, giddy feeling. He could hardly believe what had happened. How could he be on the run, pursued by starkin soldiers, the focus of Lord Zavion's cold white fury? Ten minutes ago the Regent had not even known he existed. Now he was baying for his blood, and everyone that Pedrin knew and loved, everyone who could have helped them, was under arrest. Pedrin was essentially a practical boy, though, and so he pushed down his shock and fear, busying his brain in thinking about what to do.

"Can you remember what you said?" he asked at last.

Durrik nodded. As Pedrin well knew, often to his cost, Durrik's memory was remarkable. In a low, unhappy voice he repeated once again the strange rhyme that had been troubling his dreams for weeks.

"Well, the first bit's not so hard," Pedrin said at last. "The shroud and 'the son of light', that has to mean Count Zygmunt. And it means he's going to die by the time the last starthorn blossom falls, which means by wintertime. Jumping Jimjinny, but the next bit makes no sense at all. Naught can save him 'but the turning of time itself inverse'. What's that supposed to mean?"

"'Inverse' means back to front or inside out," Durrik said.

"Which basically means it can't be done." Pedrin savagely stripped a twig of its leaves. "You can't turn time back. So the count's going to die and Lord Zavion will rule and we're in for the chop. Great."

"But what about the last bit? It says 'Six brought together can the cruel bane defeat.' Surely that means the curse can be broken, if six people get together and break it?"

"Yeah, but all that stuff before it was just like 'the turning of time itself inverse' bit. A whole lot of gobbledygook! 'Tis like saying the count can be saved when hens grow teeth. In other words, never."

Durrik sighed. There was a long silence. Pedrin stripped a few more twigs bare, then sat up, rubbed his curly head roughly, and said, "Oh, well. 'Tis scrambling me brains trying to figure it out and meanwhile we're like partridges in a wood waiting to be netted. Looks like we're outlaws now, willy-nilly, so we'd best try and find ourselves somewhere safe to hide out while we figure what to do."

"But where?"

"Well, where do outlaws and rebels always hide out? In the Perilous Forest, of course." He swung down from the lowest branch, wincing as he landed on his feet, still bleeding from myriad small cuts and gashes, then turned to look up at Durrik, whose frightened white face peered down at him from its halo of leaves. "What's wrong?"

"The Perilous Forest? We can't go in there. 'Tis full of hobhenkies and gibgoblins and boo-bogeys…"

"And outlaws," Pedrin said, with false cheerfulness. "Diamond Joe and his men have lived there for years, it can't be that dangerous."

"Which is why they call it the Perilous Forest."

"Well, you got a better idea? We could always turn ourselves in, of course. Though Lord Zavion looked like he was ready to have you spitted and roasted over a slow fire, and he'd probably have me carved up for sweetbreads. If we go and join the outlaws, mebbe we can persuade them to rescue your pa and me ma. You know Diamond Joe is meant to be stirring up rebellion against the starkin. Mebbe the rest of Estelliana will join him once we tell them everything Lord Zavion's done."

Pedrin's eyes began to shine as he imagined himself leading a charge against the castle, rescuing his mother and the other hearthkin, and overthrowing the Regent. Then he saw Durrik's pale, strained face and some of the glow faded. "At the very least we should lie low and wait for things to blow over a bit," he said practically. "Your pa will sort everything out for us, don't you worry."

"Except they've arrested him too," Durrik said dolefully. "They arrested everyone!"

"They'll have to let them go," Pedrin said comfortingly. "*They* had naught to do with it!"

Durrik sighed and slid down the tree, landing awkwardly with his crippled leg giving way beneath him. He would have fallen had Pedrin's hand not been there to support him. "I've lost my crutch," he said sadly.

Pedrin helped him sit down, Durrik rubbing at his withered leg as if it pained him, then looked about for a stick or branch his friend could use as a crutch. It was then that he saw a brown smear on the smooth grey trunk of the tree, just where Adken had rested his hand. Pedrin looked closer and realised with a little jump of his pulse that it was a smudge of his own blood, smeared on the bark from his cut feet when he had climbed the tree. The huntsman had hidden it from the starkin soldiers.

The knowledge that the chief huntsman had deliberately deceived the soldiers so they could escape gave Pedrin a sudden surge of hope and courage. He looked about him, then bent and seized a branch with a crook in one end that Durrik could tuck under his arm. He bent it over his knee, breaking it to size. "Come on! Quick sticks, slow-worm."

They made their halting way through the warm shadows of the wood, keeping as low and quiet as possible. The wood petered out not far from Pedrin's home and the goatherd was not surprised to see two soldiers on guard outside the little cottage. "We're going to need some stuff," Pedrin said, frowning. "Some grub and me fishing line and a couple of blankets. Not to mention the goats."

"The goats?"

"I can't leave them there," Pedrin replied curtly. "Ma and Mina have been arrested, remember? What if they don't get out today or even tomorrow? Who'll feed the goats? And Snowflake must already be bursting. She'll need to be milked."

"But how are we meant to get them, with soldiers everywhere?"

"I don't know," Pedrin said. "I'll have to figure summat out. Mebbe they'll give up and go home in a while. Let's wait and see what happens."

But the boys waited till the sun was almost gone, getting increasingly miserable and uncomfortable as the soldiers lounged about, playing dice and drinking from a leather-bound bottle. While they had been in motion, the boys had not had time to think about what had happened in the crystal tower. Now they had nothing but time, and the thoughts were enough to make them sick and green.

"I can't stand it any more," Pedrin cried at last, crawling out from beneath the bush and dusting himself off. "Snowflake's gonna start a-bleating the whole house down if someone doesn't milk her soon. I've got to go get her."

"What you going to do?" Durrik asked in a rather shaky voice.

"You just dig in under this bush and keep quiet," Pedrin said. "I'll get them out, don't you worry." He tried unsuccessfully to keep his voice free of its own quiver.

Durrik merely nodded and obeyed, and the goatherd dragged a few brambles across the bush to help keep him hidden. Then Pedrin set off on his belly through the meadow, occasionally lying in silence to listen with every muscle in his body trembling with strain. The sun beat down on his head, and insects chirped and buzzed with maddening cheerfulness. He came to the low hedge along the far side of the cottage, crept along in its shade and swarmed up the big tree that shaded the house and shed.

Pedrin crouched in its shelter for quite a while, his heart hammering so loud he was sure the soldiers must hear it. At last its thudding slowed and he was able to take a few deep breaths and steady himself. Slowly he lowered himself onto the roof. The thatch rustled and he froze, sick with apprehension. The soldiers lounging outside his front door were absorbed in their game, however, and did not hear. Very carefully, Pedrin dragged aside handfuls of the dry straw and wriggled through the gap he made, landing with a soft thump on the beams of the attic below.

Once inside the house he moved with greater confidence, knowing every dip and hollow of the earthen floor, the position of every piece of rough-hewn furniture. It was dim inside but he did not need light to move around quietly, having sneaked out to go badger-watching more nights than he could remember.

It was hard to know what to take, though, and

Pedrin spent a lot of time frowning and biting his knuckle. He had a heavy, cold feeling in the pit of his stomach, as if it might be a very long time before he again saw this dark little room, with the one big bed in the cupboard and the smoke-blackened fireplace. In the end he took just about everything that was in the larder, knowing his mother would forgive him.

There was a big wheel of cheese, a loaf of bread, a string of smoked fish and a great hank of streaky bacon, a ceramic pot of honey, a bag of flour and another of yeast, a handful of dirty potatoes with green sprouting from the top, some dried apples and a cotton bag full of raisins, and some cheese curds hung up above a bowl to catch the whey. He drank the whey to quieten the nervous rumbling of his stomach, then filled the bowl with the wet bag of curds. Even though it would take three or more months for the curds to ripen into cheese, Pedrin was too well-trained to waste it.

Pedrin stuffed it all into a pair of small saddlebags, loading a tin pail with the rest which he hung from one of the saddlebags. He then seized the blankets from the bed and rolled them up tightly, tying one to each saddlebag with some rope.

After some thought, he added a handful of thick tallow candles, his tinder and flint, a bread pan, a small frying pan and a toasting-fork, then grabbed his fishing knife, and a small whetting stone. Hanging from hooks on the back of the door were their winter capes, shiny and smooth with fat to keep out rain and snow. Wincing at every scuff of his sore feet on the ground,

Pedrin made his way as quietly as he could to the door and very carefully took down the two smaller capes. One of the buckles clanked a little and once again he stood stock still, his heart banging in his ears till he thought he might faint. The soldiers did not hear, though, talking and laughing just on the other side of the door. Heady with relief, Pedrin backed away from the door, rolled up the capes tightly and attached them next to the blankets.

He stood for a while, running over what he had gathered, sure that he had forgotten something important. He could think of nothing, his mind completely blank. So he gave a little shrug, shouldered the heavy saddlebags, and climbed back up into the rafters, creeping as quietly as he could back along the beams and let himself down into the shed, which was built under the same thatched roof as the rest of the house.

Snowflake bleated happily to see him, and even Thundercloud gave a huffy sort of grunt and rolled one bad-tempered eye his way. Pedrin quietened them swiftly, hanging the saddlebags over Snowflake's slim back and buckling them beneath her, the tin pail clanking on one side. Thundercloud was much bigger and stronger than the nanny-goat, but he would never submit to the indignity of carrying a load and so Pedrin merely unclasped his bell from his collar.

Pedrin had no idea how he and the two goats were going to sneak past the guards but as it happened he had no chance to even try to conceal himself. Thundercloud was so incensed at being locked up all afternoon that as soon as Pedrin's hand left his collar, he shouldered him aside and stalked out into the garden. Pedrin dared not call him or whistle him and could only watch, needle-sharp anxiety twisting in his stomach.

The guards jerked upright when they saw the big black billy-goat come round the corner. Thundercloud saw them at the same moment and his narrow golden eyes gleamed. He was very displeased to have been left locked up in the stalls for so long and was eager to take his vexation out on someone. If those men were foolish enough to stand between him and the sweet grass of the meadow, they would soon see how sharp his horns were!

The soldiers were foolish enough. With a shout they ran to intercept the big black billy-goat. Thundercloud lifted his lip, lowered his head, and charged. His horns were very sharp indeed, and the shoulders behind powerful. Both men were tossed down with little ceremony and the goats ran over them and out into the meadow, Pedrin exultant at their heels. By the time the soldiers picked themselves up again, bruised and aching, the goatherd and the two goats had disappeared into the trees.

8

The flame kindled in a scatter of hissing sparks, casting a fretful glow upon the faces of the two tired, hungry boys.

"Are you sure no one will see the fire?" Durrik hunched close over the flames, his shirt folded up over his shoulders so it would not stick to the ointment Pedrin had just slathered over the half-healed welts on his back.

"Sure I'm sure," Pedrin lied, feeding the flames a branch of dry leaves. The flames sank for a moment, then blazed higher, red-bright. Pedrin did not look at his friend, busying himself laying slices of bacon in his frying-pan and impaling rounds of newly baked bread and cheese upon the toasting-fork.

Durrik flinched as the wind rattled the branches of the forest looming behind them. Somewhere a night bird moaned. Although they had been on the run for three days now and had slept each night outside, still the boys couldn't help a shiver at the sound. The darkness seemed very vast and unfriendly when there was no warm, familiar house to go home to.

Three days of being hunted through the country-side, three days with their nerves constantly stretched to breaking point. Both boys were surprised and frightened by the intensity of the search undertaken by the castle guards. Bands of soldiers had scoured the countryside on both sides of the river while precise spearheads of white-winged sisikas had soared through the sky all through the long, scrambling, running, hiding days. Neither Pedrin nor Durrik had ever expected Lord Zavion to order out the regiment of sisika riders. Only the most noble of the starkin were permitted to ride the great white birds, and the regiment was only convoked in times of dire need. The Regent must be very angry indeed.

Somehow, though, the boys had evaded capture. Once a soldier had put his boot down upon Pedrin's hand as he lay concealed in the mud and rushes by the side of the river, but Pedrin had not cried out and at last the soldier had moved away, leaving Pedrin's hand sore and bruised. Another time a band of soldiers had sat down to eat their lunch under the very tree where the two boys lay concealed in the branches, too afraid to even breathe.

The Perilous Forest was very close, now, though. Tier upon tier of dark towering trees stood close behind their campfire, reaching to the very flanks of the mountains. The trees rustled and whispered in the dusk breeze, and every now and again they heard the strange wailing cry of some unknown beast. The boys could have sought shelter in the forest but had baulked at entering in the gloom of dusk, making camp right at its verge instead. No matter how frightened they were of the soldiers, they were more frightened of the Perilous Forest at night.

"What was that noise?" Durrik's head whipped round.

"Just some animal," Pedrin comforted, passing him a slice of bread and bacon and toasted cheese.

"It sounded like someone a-creeping up on us." Durrik's voice was tremulous.

"Thundercloud would warn us if it was," Pedrin said, indicating the contentedly grazing goats with a wave of his greasy sandwich.

Just then a twig snapped loudly. Both Snowflake and Thundercloud lifted their heads and stared into the bushes, and the boys followed their gaze, tense as wound-up toys. Pedrin's hand groped for his fishing knife, and Durrik sat up, clutching his father's bell close to his chest.

"Don't be a-feared." A light little voice spoke from the shadows. "I'm sorry to make you jump – 'tis just we saw your fire and smelt your food – and we're so very hungry." The last words came out piteously.

A small girl stepped nervously out of the darkness. In the shifting light of the flames it was hard to see much of her face, but her very smallness and nervousness disarmed the boys.

Pedrin lowered his knife. "Who are you? What do you want?"

"Please … I'm sorry – 'tis just we're so hungry, and your bacon smelt so good. Please … couldn't we buy

111

some from you? Me mistress can pay."

"Your mistress?" Pedrin scanned the bushes all around suspiciously. He could see nothing but the soft wavering of dark leaves.

"Yeah. She's not far."

"Who else is there? What are you doing here?"

"There's no one else, I swear. We're all by our lonesome. Please, there's no need for you to be a-feared of us. Indeed, 'tis us that should be a-feared of you, two big strong boys like you. If we warn't so hungry we'd never have dared disturb you." She spoke in fits and bursts and they could see how her hands clenched and twisted in the dark stuff of her gown.

Pedrin and Durrik exchanged quick glances. They did not have much food left themselves, but neither did they have any money. It could be useful to have a few coppers with which to barter. So Pedrin agreed gruffly and the girl melted back into the shadows.

She was gone a long time, so long the boys began to think she did not mean to return. Then Thundercloud lifted his head, staring into the darkness with narrow eyes. Uttering a low guttural warning in his throat, he bounded forward, his horns low. Snowflake bleated in fright and pressed close to Pedrin's side. He jumped up, ignoring the pain in his tender feet, his fishing knife clenched in his hand. Durrik struggled up too, clutching his father's bell with both hands.

Suddenly the darkness was split by a blaze of light. The boys both gave a little gasp and jump. Slowly the light came towards them, throwing all the intricate filigree of leaf and branch into sharp relief. Dazzled, all they could see were two dark figures coming slowly, awkwardly, through the bushes. One was little and thin, the young girl they had spoken to before. The other was much taller and leant heavily on the girl's shoulder, moving with the slow painfulness of the very old. It was impossible to see anything of her face and figure, for she was all muffled up in a long cloak and hood. In her hand she carried the source of the light, a bright sphere of blazing white.

Thundercloud charged them and both shrieked and cringed back. "We aren't meaning no harm!" the little girl cried. "Call back your billy-goat, we aren't meaning no harm."

"Turn off the light!" To his dismay, Pedrin's voice shook. Was this some mighty enchantress, to so carry light in her hand? Did she mean to cast a spell on them, enslaving them with her powers? And even if her little servant girl spoke the truth and the enchantress meant them no harm, what of those that might see the light and come to investigate? It was not just the soldiers whose attention Pedrin feared to attract, but the many strange wild creatures that inhabited the Perilous Forest. He controlled his voice with an effort, saying sharply, "Do you wish t'alert every living thing for miles that we're here? Turn it off!"

The girl spoke swiftly and softly to the tall figure. The light died, plunging them all into darkness again.

"I'm sorry," the girl said. "Me mistress is a-feared of the dark."

"At least in the darkness we can't be seen," Pedrin

said roughly. "A light like that will be a-rousing every man and beast for miles. Do you want to bring the starkin soldiers down upon us?"

Even as he spoke he wished he could bite the words back, but it was too late, the words had escaped him. He went on hurriedly, "And we're close to the Perilous Forest here, too close to be drawing attention. There are many strange and savage beasts in the Perilous Forest."

"None more strange and savage than those which walk the streets of towns," the girl said rather oddly, dropping the sack she carried by the fire. Solicitously she helped the tall cloaked figure lower herself painfully to the ground. "Please, can we have some food now? Me mistress can pay."

Casting a scared, suspicious look at the shrouded figure lying on the opposite side of the fire, Pedrin hurriedly cooked up some more rounds of toasted cheese and bacon. The two strangers ate ravenously. Then, jewels flashing on her fingers, the tall silent one tossed a handful of coins at Pedrin. He was unable to catch them all and had to scrabble in the dust to gather them up, colour rising angrily in his cheeks. The value of the coins made his eyes widen, however, and he stowed them away in his pocket with some excitement, never having seen so much money in all of his life. There was even a silver crown among them!

"Can we rest by your fire?" the girl asked rather tremulously. "We're too tired to walk any further."

"Of course," Pedrin said, stirring his fingers in his pockets so he could hear the jingle of the coins. "You needn't be a-feared. The goats'll wake us if anyone comes near."

"How can you be so sure?" she asked quietly. "Many a goat has been stolen away from the herd in the dead of night."

"Not a herd guarded by Thundercloud," Pedrin retorted stoutly.

The girl looked uncertainly at the big black billy-goat, who narrowed his eyes at her, shaking his horns menacingly. "He does look fierce," she said.

"His horns are very sharp," Pedrin said, "and he does not much like strangers."

"I see." She sounded rather sad. "Well, I hope he doesn't mind us sharing your campfire, for me legs ache and me head is so heavy I can hardly hold it up any more." She yawned so wide her jaws cracked.

"Have you travelled far?" Durrik asked curiously.

"Far enough," she answered with a sigh. She wrapped a thin, grey shawl about her and curled up on the far side of the fire, a raggedy doll cuddled close to her cheek. Pedrin exchanged a frowning glance with Durrik, who gave a little shrug, then Pedrin stood abruptly and covered the little girl with his blanket. He and Durrik would take turns to keep watch this night, he decided, and it would be easier to stay awake if the watcher was cold.

Pedrin was hunched miserably by the fire as the sun rose, having won the last watch with a toss of his new silver coin. He yawned and stretched and glanced across the fire to examine their night visitors by the light of the day. His breath caught in surprise.

The small one was much as she had seemed in the darkness of the night – a thin child of maybe eleven or twelve, her face pale and pointed beneath a black kerchief bound tightly about her head. She was dressed in a rough brown dress and pinafore, and cuddled an old ragdoll in her arms.

The cloak had fallen away from the face of the tall one, revealing long, smooth ripples of pale golden hair, a round cheek all flushed with sleep and a white brow unmarred by a single line. No old crone this, no mighty enchantress. She was nothing but a girl, no older than Pedrin himself.

Pedrin felt he knew that line of brow and cheek, the colour of that hair. He rose a little on his knees to see better and sucked in his breath with amazement. He had not been mistaken. It was Lady Lisandre who slept so peacefully by his campfire.

He must have made some sound for she stirred again and sighed, and brought her hands up to her cheek. He saw she clutched something close, something which glittered between her fingers. Before he could see more her eyes opened, staring straight into his.

Pedrin blushed scarlet. He sat back on his heels, feeling his hands too big, his collar too tight. She flushed too, and sat up abruptly, saying very coldly, "You dare to ogle me while I sleep, sirrah? What kind of ill-mannered lout may you be?"

Even if Pedrin did not understand the rudiments of Ziverian, he would have understood her meaning from her tone, which was full of contemptuous dis-

116

dain. He tried to stammer some sort of apology, but his never perfect command of the starkin language deserted him, so that only strangled sounds issued from his lips. She paid him no heed, thrusting the glittering thing she held deep into the pocket of her purple velvet cloak and shaking awake the dark-haired girl with an imperious hand.

"I pray thee, Briony, tell that imbecilic oaf to stop staring at me, and prepare me some repast to break my fast," she ordered. "It does not please me to be ogled by peasantry. Is the goat-boy lacking in wits as well as manners, do you think, the way he stares and stammers?"

"Nay, milady, that is, I don't know," the girl said in some bewilderment, sleep still heavy upon her.

"Tell him to lower his eyes and act with proper respect, else I shall have him whipped!"

"But, milady, who'd whip him?" As Lisandre's eyes narrowed in anger, the girl said rather hastily, "Aye, milady, of course. I'll tell him." She turned to Pedrin and said rather diffidently, in the familiar language of the hearthkin, "I'm sorry, but—"

"No need to tell me aught," Pedrin said sullenly. "I heard her."

"You speak Ziverian?"

"Uh-uh." Pedrin felt no need to explain the limits of his knowledge.

"Oh, well then … I'm sorry. She doesn't mean to be rude. 'Tis just the starkin way. You mustn't look at her directly, you know, she's one of the Ziv."

"What are you saying? I was not rude!" Lisandre

cried. "I am near faint with hunger, Briony. Does the goat-boy mean to serve me any time this morn? Though on closer reflection I do not wish him to handle any food that I must then consume. Have you seen how black are his nails? You must cook for me, Briony. Scrub out all the pans and plates first. And tell those repulsive boys not to stand anywhere near me. I am sure their reek is enough to make me ill."

All Pedrin's discomposure had turned to sullen rage but he said nothing, turning aside and kicking the charred log back into life. Snowflake bleated and butted him with her nose. He dug out his bucket and sat beside her, leaning his hot forehead against her flank and squeezing out his anger with her milk. To his chagrin he noticed his nails were black and his hands very grubby indeed. He decided he must have a bit of a scrub in the stream before they set off on their journey again. He suddenly remembered he had not thought to pack any soap or a comb, and felt his discomfiture grow.

By the time the bucket was filled with frothy milk, Durrik had wakened and was sitting up in his blanket, his yellow hair all ruffled like a duckling's down, his blue eyes bright with excitement.

"Liah's eyes, do you see who that is?" Durrik whispered. "'Tis Lady Lisandre! What's she a-doing here, you reckon?"

"I don't know and I don't care. The sooner she goes on her way the better."

Durrik's eyes widened in surprise. "Why so rude, Pedrin? Do you fear she'll betray us to the soldiers? I can't think what she's a-doing here, so far from Levanna-On-The-Lake, and with only one little girl to serve her."

"Whatever the reason, the faster we leave her behind, the safer we'll be," Pedrin said shortly. "T'other starkin can't be too far away. Let's be a-packing now and on our way."

Durrik did as he was told, though his efforts were hampered by the fact that he never took his eyes off Lisandre, delicately dabbing the corners of her mouth with a cloth while Briony searched through her sack. She found a little pot plugged with a cork, then knelt before Lisandre, saying humbly, "Let me look at your blisters, milady."

Lisandre stared haughtily at Pedrin until he blushed and dropped his eyes, then stretched out one foot from under the folds of the purple velvet cloak. It was shod in a high-heeled slipper of red satin with an enormous buckle of rubies. More rubies flashed in the spindly heel, which was at last three inches high. As Briony gently removed the slipper, the starkin girl winced in pain and caught her breath. The skin of her foot was marred with huge red blisters on the heel and toes.

Briony took the bare foot upon her lap and bathed it carefully, then rubbed some salve into the red-raw welts.

"No wonder your feet pained you so much, milady," she said, tending the other foot. "You won't be able to wear your shoes today."

"But I cannot walk barefoot," the starkin girl cried.

"You know I removed my shoes yesterday and could not walk one step for the stones and thistles."

Briony reached up and unknotted the black kerchief bound about her head. A thick brown plait fell down, its unbound end as curly as a corkscrew. More curls sprang about her face and she pushed them back with one hand, then tore the kerchief in two. "I'll wrap your feet, milady. 'Twill help a little, at least till your feet toughen up."

Lisandre sighed. "I suppose it must do. I simply cannot bear to put my shoes on again, they hurt my feet so grievously."

"I'm not surprised," Pedrin muttered.

She heard him and turned his way, flushing. "What did the goat-boy say?" she demanded.

"I'm not surprised," Pedrin repeated, in Ziverian this time and loudly. "What foolish shoes to wear in the rough!"

Lisandre flushed even redder but did not deign to reply, turning away with her nose in the air.

"I beg your pardon, milady, but perhaps you would care to wear my shoes?" Durrik said with a low bow, indicating his brogues with a courtly wave. "They are of very soft leather and would protect your feet far better than mere cloth."

Lisandre had not until this moment spared Durrik so much as a glance, but at the sound of his flawless Ziverian she looked up at him in surprise. Her eyes widened in instant recognition.

"Are you not the boy who leapt into Lord Zavion's circle of power the day of the summer solstice?" she asked. "The one who prophesised my brother's death?"

Durrik blushed. "Aye, milady. Though I thought it was his salvation I spoke of, not his death."

"But all that nonsensical poetry you quoted, about time turned inverse – all that is an impossibility. It means naught, surely?"

"I don't know, milady. I don't understand what it means. I don't know where the words came from. They just came."

Lisandre gave a little snort of disbelief. "Fiddlefaddles will not save my brother," she said firmly. "You are as bad as Lord Zavion with his crystal towers and mage sophistry. What did he do but sizzle my brother's brains and mine, and send my mother into a fit of vapours that I fear she will not recover from easily." She held out her hand imperiously. "I will take your shoes. If I am to save my brother, I shall need to be able to walk."

"What do you mean, if you are to save your brother?" Pedrin asked suspiciously. "What do you do here, so far from Levanna-On-The-Lake?"

"Who are you, sirrah, to question what I do?" she asked haughtily, drawing her stockings up over her bandaged feet and gingerly thrusting them into Durrik's brogues.

Pedrin coloured deeply once again but stood his ground sturdily, his arms crossed over his chest. He was just thinking what to say when Snowflake gave a bleat of warning. Thundercloud was pawing the ground, his horned head lowered, his golden eyes narrowed. Durrik pointed up into the sky, his voice rising into a squeak. "Look! Sisikas!"

They all saw a flock of the great white birds flying swiftly towards them, starkin lords mounted upon their backs. Pedrin bent and grabbed the saddlebags, crying angrily, "See, I knew she'd bring the soldiers down on us. Run, Durrik!"

"Do you think the soldiers pursue you?" Lisandre said regally, holding out one hand for Briony to assist her to her feet. "A couple of grubby goat-boys? You are mistaken. It is me they pursue. You may rest here in peace. They will not disturb *you*. I, however, must flee, and quickly. Come, Briony! Let us run."

And with those disdainful words, the starkin girl broke into a most undignified stumbling run, her faithful maid doing her best to help her. Pedrin and Durrik exchanged one incredulous glance then ran after them, as the shadow of enormous wings fell upon them.

9

◆ ◆ ◆

Aaaark! Aaaark!

The sisikas' screech filled the air. Pedrin dived forward, rolling under the shelter of an enormous spreading thorn tree. Ahead of him he saw a flash of red silk as Lisandre crawled forward on her hands and knees, her long veil of hair hampering every movement. Then he heard Durrik shriek and looked back. A sisika had seized Durrik's shirt in his black talons. Just as the bird spread its immense wings to rise again, Thundercloud charged forward, horns lowered. The billy-goat slammed into the side of the bird, knocking it off-balance. Involuntarily the sisika released its grip and Durrik was able to crawl under the thorny branches, his face white under the grime.

"Hurry!" Pedrin cried.

Durrik scrambled forward, leaning heavily on his crutch. The back of his coat was torn into rags. They heard the frustrated screech of the sisikas as they soared and plunged about the perimeter of the forest, unable to find a gap in the canopy to allow their great bodies in.

"Find a place to land and follow on foot!" ordered one of the starkin lords. There was a great whoosh as the sisikas spread their wings and soared back towards the clearing. The boys scrambled forward, protecting their faces from the thorns with their arms.

Suddenly there was a scream of pain.

"Lady Lisandre – she's caught!" Durrik cried.

Pedrin glanced back and saw the starkin girl was struggling to disentangle great snarls of silvery-fair hair from the thorns. Briony was trying to help her, but Lisandre was caught as surely as a fly in a spider's web, every movement causing her to sob in pain. He hesitated, then, seeing Durrik turn back, drew his knife and plunged past his friend. Slash, slash, slash, went his knife. Down, down, down fell long tendrils of cornsilk hair. Lisandre fell to her knees, one hand going up to her head.

"My hair!"

"Run, you cabbage-head!" Pedrin cried.

Weeping, she obeyed, stumbling forward as fast as she could in her long skirts and throbbing feet. Briony cast one scared glance back then ran beside her, the two boys close behind. They went through the forest in a mad scramble, leaving scraps of torn cloth and skin and broken branches behind them. The ground was slippery and uneven with mossy rocks, fallen logs, ferns great and small, and the thick writhing roots of immensely tall trees that soared hundreds of metres into the sky, their branches intermingling with wisps of mist. It was cool and shadowy under that green canopy, the air so clean it seemed to pierce them to the very marrow of their bones. When they came at last to a panting, skidding halt in the shelter of a great pile of boulders, their breath hurt their lungs.

All was quiet. Birdsong and trickling water and the whisper of leaves. Their thudding hearts. Their rasping breath. Hiccuping sobs from Lisandre.

"My ... hair," she wept. "You imbecilic oaf, you cut my hair!"

Pedrin was taken aback. "But the soldiers would've caught you if I hadn't."

"A lady of the Ziv must never cut her hair!" Lisandre cried. She tugged at the short jagged spikes of her hair, distraught. "Oh, comets and stardust, what must I look like?"

"Mighty ghastly," Pedrin admitted unhappily. "It'll grow back, though."

Lisandre held out an imperious hand and Briony dug out an ornate silver mirror from her sack, passing it quickly to her mistress, who examined herself anxiously.

"Thirteen years it took to grow so long," Lisandre snapped. "It was washed in chamomile water every day and brushed two hundred times morn and even."

"Jumping Jimjinny, your arms must've ached."

"I did not brush it myself, you fatuous fool."

"Don't call me a fool!" Pedrin scowled. "I'm the one that saved you from the soldiers, remember?"

Lisandre struggled briefly with herself. "Well, for that I do thank you," she said at last, ungraciously. "Though did you have to cut my hair to do so?"

"Yeah, I did," Pedrin snapped. "'Tis only hair, not

worth a-weeping Lullalita's tears over."

Although Lisandre did not recognise the name of the goddess of water and grief and lost causes, Pedrin's tone stung and she flushed and looked away. Apart from the haughty expression, she did not look much like the proud lady the boys had so admired in the Hall of Mirrors, with her fair hair sticking up like a scarecrow's and her face all dirty.

"Do you think the soldiers will follow us?" Durrik whispered, looking about him nervously.

"Of course they will follow us," Lisandre snapped. "Am I not the second cousin, once removed, of the king himself? And much as Lord Zavion would like me to just disappear, he cannot take the risk that I may find out something about my father's death. He will not be able to rest easy until he knows I am safely packed off to boarding school, where I can do nothing to help my brother." Her voice had risen throughout her speech. At the very end it quavered and broke, and she bit her lip and turned away again to stare off into the forest.

Briony took her hand and led her down the rocks, saying over her shoulder, "Come, we'd best get a-moving again. And this time, try not to leave such a trail. Milady's right. They'll be a-following quick behind us."

For some time they walked in silence, the goats trotting on either side of Briony who had somehow assumed the lead. She was swift and nimble over the rocks and tree-roots, so that even Pedrin had to scramble to keep up. Dressed all in brown like the trees, she

126

seemed to merge right into the woods, and it was only the flash of Snowflake's white tail that kept Pedrin on the right track. Behind him, Lisandre struggled on with her long, trailing skirts hampering her every step. Even Durrik had to stop often to wait for her and he found it very hard going with his withered leg and makeshift crutch. Before long he was rubbing his leg every time he paused, his blue eyes shadowed with pain.

At first Pedrin was so busy expecting trouble he did not much notice where they were. With his slingshot in one hand and a smooth rock in the other, he scanned the forest about them anxiously, expecting a horde of hobhenkies to swoop down upon them any moment. After a while his nervous strain relaxed a little, unable to sustain such intensity for too long. Pedrin was able to think over what had happened and begin to wonder what lay ahead.

"Hold your horses!" he called to Briony, whose thin brown form was flitting silently ahead of him through the trees. "Hadn't we better think about where we're a-going? We don't want to get lost in the Perilous Forest, of all places!"

Briony looked back at him. "I'm a-heading down the river," she said. "I'm sorry, I thought you realised."

Pedrin dug his bare toe into the deep mulch of leaves. "Why the river?" he said gruffly. "And how do you know where it is?"

"The Evenlode was to our south last night, it won't have moved overnight," she answered gently. "And I

127

go to the river because milady's father was found there. She wishes to see the place for herself. I promised I'd lead her there."

"But why?"

She looked past him to Lisandre, who limped up behind them, her face pale under all the dirt. "The least I can do is *try* and find out what happened." Lisandre's voice shook. "Lord Zavion has not even tried to find out why or how my father and all his men died so strangely. They just put it down to wildkin, or perilous beasts, or even to outlaws, though my father came home with all his jewels and weapons intact. But none of it makes any sense. There were no wounds on the men, and no sign of any battle. It was as if they all just fell asleep and died in their sleep, all but Ziggy, who might as well have died for all the signs of life he shows." Now there were tears on her face as well as in her voice. She sat down on a tree-root, wiping her face defiantly.

"But what do you mean to do?" Durrik asked, his voice soft with sympathy. "What do you do here, all by yourself in the Perilous Forest?"

"Lord Zavion was very angry that I had spoilt his experiment," Lisandre said. Her voice had steadied. "He fears the king will believe the rumours that he was trying to kill Ziggy so he can rule Estelliana. He said I was to be sent off to the Zephyr Academy for Ladies of the Ziv first thing in the morning. In the meantime, I was sent to bed without any supper. I was very upset." She coloured delicately. "They would not let me see my mother or Ziggy. Lady Donella said I'd disgraced myself and my blood – they locked me in my room."

"I decided I had to run away but could not see how in the stars it was to be done. My bedchamber is on the sixth floor and there were guards at my door. Then Briony appeared at my window. She had brought me her own dinner, such as it was."

"It warn't naught but some old bread and cheese," Briony said apologetically. "I knew milady would be hungry. She'd eaten naught all day."

"If her room is on the sixth floor, how did you get to her window?" Pedrin asked incredulously, knowing how sheer were the walls of the castle.

"I spun a rope," Briony answered. "I'm a spinner and seamstress at the castle. Or at least I was."

"When I beheld what Briony had done, I commanded her to spin me a rope long enough to reach the ground," Lisandre said. "She did not wish to, but in the end I prevailed. We climbed down the rope and went and hid on one of the river barges. In the morning it sailed upriver. They moored at Lake Sennaval, just near the edge of the forest. We waited until it was dark and then we climbed down and tried to make our way surreptitiously into the forest. We were seen escaping the boat, however, and the alarm was called. The soldiers have been pursuing us ever since."

"We ran and we hid and we ran again, but me poor lady could hardly walk a step for the pain in her feet," Briony said in her soft, shy voice. "And we were so very hungry! We hadn't eaten since we left the castle. So when we saw your campfire ... I came to see who it was and mebbe beg some food. When I saw you, I recognised you and knew you wouldn't betray us to the soldiers."

Pedrin and Durrik were both shaking their heads in disbelief. "But why on earth would you run away from the castle? What could *you* do to wake the count up?" Although Pedrin did not mean to be rude, his tone was coloured by his contempt for someone who went running through the countryside in three-inch, ruby-studded heels and who had to have their hair brushed for them by someone else.

Lisandre glared at him. "I do not know yet. I thought if I could only find where it all happened, there might be some clue, something to tell me what happened. Twenty men could not be easily felled without leaving some sign ... and if I can find no clue, well then, Briony tells me there is a witch who dwells here within the Perilous Forest who has a pool where one can perceive what is hidden or unknown. If I must, I will go to this witch and command her to look within this pool and see the truth of what befell my father."

Her cheek was now white where before it had been suffused with red, but she spoke steadily, with clenched knuckle and jaw. Pedrin was impressed despite himself.

"Do you mean the Erlrune of Evenlinn?" Durrik whispered, casting a quick glance around him. "You'd dare approach the Erlrune?"

"What else can I do? If your predictions are right, my brother has only a few more months in which to live – and Lord Zavion has already been granted the Regency of Estelliana by the king. Once Ziggy dies, Lord Zavion will be count and my mother and I will be dispossessed. We have lived at Levanna-On-The-Lake all our lives, I do not wish to live anywhere else."

Although Pedrin knew that starkin women were totally dependent upon their menfolk, he was puzzled by her vehemence. "But surely Lord Zavion wouldn't throw you out into the streets?"

"No, probably not," she admitted. "He would send me away to some loathsome academy for fine young ladies, though, would he not? And you should see how he fawns over my mother. I know he plans to woo her and wed her, and then he would be my step-father and that I could not bear! I know everyone else thinks he is so handsome and charming, but I do not. I think he is cruel and cold-hearted and I am sure he has had something to do with my father's death and this unnatural sleep of my brother's. I just need to find some proof."

"But to seek out the Erlrune of Evenlinn!" Durrik's eyes were wide with admiration. "Aren't you a-feared?"

"Why should I be afraid?" Lisandre said. "I am of the Ziv. She would not dare harm me."

Briony and Pedrin's eyes met in involuntary dis-may.

"You see why I had t'come with her," the dark-haired girl said. "Milady has no idea how perilous the Perilous Forest really is."

"And you do?"

Briony nodded. "I spent the first half of my life a-living on the verge of the forest. I was raised by one of the Crafty, you see. She knew more about the wildkin than anyone and she taught me what she could. It was from her I learnt about the Erlrune. Lady Lisandre insisted she meant to set off to the Perilous Forest, willy-nilly, and I knew she wouldn't make it very far by herself."

Pedrin frowned. "The two of you have about as much sense as a couple of hens," he said rudely. "Look at you, you're skinny as a broom-handle. What would you do if you came across a gibgoblin?"

"Run," Briony said. "As fast as I could. Though that's one reason why I plan to stay near the river. Gibgoblins don't much like water."

"What about the lake-lorelei then? Or river-roans, for that matter? You think you could outrun a river-roan, and her ladyship mincing about in three-inch heels? Jumping Jimjinny, what a couple of cabbage-heads!"

She blushed and dropped her eyes.

Pedrin hefted his pouch of stones. "Lucky you ran into us," he said. "Else you could really have found yourselves in a pot of trouble."

"You'll come with us then?" Briony gripped her hands together anxiously. He noticed for the first time that her eyes were as green as the summer-bright leaves.

"Well, we don't really have any other plans," he replied gruffly, feeling his neck getting hot.

"I thank you," Lisandre said regally. "Your offer of

assistance is most gratefully accepted – though I really must insist that you wash if you wish to serve me."

Colour burnt up his face to the very tips of his ears. Pedrin was trying to think of some suitably blistering retort when Durrik stepped forward, bowing so low his hat swept the ground.

"We're at your service, milady," he said adoringly.

In single file the children made their way through the trees, scrambling over roots and boulders and slipping occasionally in the slick mud. The mist had gathered close about the branches, rattling leaves with an occasional gust of rain. The children jerked around every time, their pupils dilated with fear. Pedrin's hand was clenched so tightly on his slingshot, his fingers were white and cramped.

The goats were uneasy too. Thundercloud bounded around madly, his eyes narrowed so sharply none of their golden gleam could be seen. He leapt from a high mound of grey boulders down into a fern-shrouded gully, back onto the path, and then up onto a tree-root, where he stood, his narrow head raised to sniff the wind. Snowflake ran close to Durrik's side, letting the crippled boy lean on her back so he could get along faster.

A gust of wind roared down the gully, blowing back Briony's curls and ruffling Lisandre's silken skirts. A volley of seedpods suddenly blew down from the trees, making Pedrin swear and duck, his arms over his head. There was a trill of mocking laughter.

Pedrin's head snapped around. "What was that?"

"Just the wind?" the starkin princess said nervously.

"That warn't no wind," Pedrin said scornfully. "Someone's a-lamming us with pebbles." He looked around suspiciously, torn between affront and fear.

There was another rattle as seedpods showered down upon their heads. Lisandre screamed and ducked down, her head buried into her arms.

"Look, look!" Durrik cried, pointing up into the canopy.

Pedrin stared, one hand automatically fitting a stone into his slingshot. For a moment he saw nothing but the wild lashing of branches in the wind, then he heard another trill of laughter, right behind him. He spun around, craning his neck, and saw the treetops were filled with tall, slim, agile figures, all swinging nimbly from branch to vine to branch, some leaping incredible distances to catch a mere twig with one hand. They were so high and so quick it was hard to get more than an impression, but they were easily as tall as himself and dressed all in leaves.

"Wood-sprites," Briony whispered, crouching down so she was hidden by a bush. "They won't hurt us, not unless we've summat they're a-wanting. Keep quiet and still and they might let us be."

With shaking hands Durrik fumbled in his pocket for his bell. As he began to unwrap it from his crumpled cravat, it clanged softly. Briony said hurriedly, "Is that a bell? Put it away, Durrik, unless you want to lose it! They're not boo-bogeys to be frightened away by bell-ringing. 'Tis just the sort of thing they love, summat bright and shiny that makes a noise. Put it away."

Durrik obeyed quickly and they all crouched down, gazing fearfully up at the wood-sprites as they leapt and swung through the trees, calling to each other with high, sweet voices like birds.

Thundercloud bleated a loud challenge, and a group of wood-sprites came swarming down through the branches to pepper the billy-goat with seedpods plucked from the trees. One hung upside down from long, prehensile toes to tickle his nose with a leafy twig. Thundercloud charged, and the wood-sprite swung gracefully out of his reach, laughing.

He was a tall, slim, brown figure, with tousled curls all matted with leaves into wild elflocks that stuck out all over his head. His face was triangular with narrow, pointed ears, slanted hazel-green eyes and a wicked grin. His torso was very smooth and muscular, and he wore a short robe of green leaves so tightly sewn together it looked like living chain-mail. His bare limbs were very long and supple, his fingers and toes longer than the palm of his hand or sole of his foot.

As Thundercloud wheeled and charged again, bleating with fury, the wildkin somersaulted with incredible speed through the branches and landed on his feet right beside Pedrin. He grinned at the cowering goat-boy, showing white pointed teeth, and snatched at the knife strapped to Pedrin's belt.

Pedrin slapped his hand away. "Get outta here!"

The wildkin tugged again but the knife was secure within its sheath and did not come loose. The wildkin gave a snarl of frustration, making Pedrin cringe back into the ground. As swift and supple as a deer, the wildkin leapt past him and seized Lisandre's delicate necklace of diamonds in his hand. She screamed and slapped him. He slapped her back, so hard she fell to the ground. As she fell, the wildkin dragged the glittering necklace over her head, scratching her cheek and tearing the lobe of her ear. As Lisandre sobbed with pain, holding her ear, he vaulted over a mossy log and high into the trees, trilling with triumph, the long chain of diamonds in his hand catching the light like a fall of water.

"They'll all be a-coming for us now," Briony whispered. "If we're not careful they'll steal everything. Let's run and see if we can't be a-shaking them off. They're easily bored, wood-sprites."

She helped pull the sobbing Lisandre to her feet and began to run up the path, the starkin princess floundering along behind her, hampered by her heavy skirts. Pedrin and Durrik ran too, the crippled boy doing the best he could with his makeshift crutch. Wood-sprites swung through the trees after them, calling and jeering. One deftly swiped Durrik's crutch away from him so he fell headlong. Another seized Lisandre's skirt and tripped her up, hanging upside down from a branch so he could try to steal her bracelet. Pedrin dropped to one knee beside Durrik and swung his slingshot above his head. As his first stone found its mark, the wood-sprite yelped and bounded away. Pedrin sent stone after stone whizzing up into the canopy and although many of the wood-sprites threw down hard green fruit or seedpods in retaliation, it was not long before they were swinging away though the trees, their mocking laughter fading away.

"Good shot!" Durrik said approvingly, sitting up and rubbing his aching leg.

"That filthy thieving wildkin stole my necklace!" Lisandre cried, touching her ear then looking with horror at the blood on her hand. "I command you to pursue him and retrieve my necklace!"

"I'm not retrieving aught," Pedrin said, stowing his slingshot back in his belt with a fond little pat. "You want your necklace, you go get it."

"I did warn you to take off your jewels, milady," Briony said, squatting next to Lisandre so she could examine her lacerated ear.

"My father gave me that necklace for my birthday," Lisandre said, her voice very wobbly. "You must recover it for me."

"I'm sorry, milady. I'm afraid your necklace is gone for good. Woods-sprites are impossible to catch, that's why you see them so close to the edge of the forest."

Lisandre looked appealingly at Durrik, who looked uncomfortable. "I'm sorry, milady, but Briony is right. Even if we were as good at tracking as your chief huntsman, I doubt we'd be able to find your necklace. The wood-sprites move so fast! Look, there's no sign of them now."

Lisandre sat for a moment in silence, her jaw thrust out. "I am tired," she said disdainfully. "I wish to rest. If you will not retrieve my necklace for me, you can gather some firewood and kindle a fire so that Briony can prepare me a repast of some kind. I am very hungry."

Briony looked troubled. "Milady, those soldiers were close behind us. I don't think we'd best stop yet. This is not a safe place, they could easily sneak up on us through all these trees. I'm sorry, but we must push on."

"I am tired," Lisandre said obstinately.

"I know it," Briony said gently. "But really, we mustn't stop yet, milady."

"Very well then," Lisandre said, holding her chin high. "I have no desire to lose all when we have come so far. Let us keep on walking until we find somewhere safer. You, goat-boy. Bring up the rear. Give us fair warning if the soldiers approach."

Gritting his teeth, Pedrin did as he was told. He was tired too, though. Try as he might he could not keep his mind from wandering into a miserable sort of daze. His thoughts went round and round, fretting about his mother and his sister, worrying about what Lord Zavion would do to him if he caught him, fuming about the starkin princess and her arrogance, and wondering with a truly acute anxiety what they were going to eat when their food ran out.

If it had not been for Thundercloud, Pedrin would have had no warning at all. He was jerked out of his abstraction by the sudden swift bound of his billy-goat back past him, bleating a loud challenge. Pedrin spun on one heel, nearly overbalancing, and realised with a nauseating drop of his heart that the forest behind him was full of soldiers. Even in the soft drifting clouds of mist and rain, their silver armour looked bright and hard. Pedrin cried a despairing warning, both to his friends ahead of him, and to Thundercloud, who was charging straight at a line of soldiers that had their fusilliers raised to their shoulders and fully cocked.

"Don't fire! Lord Zavion wants them alive!" the lieutenant cried.

The soldiers dropped their weapons, parting ranks swiftly so that Thundercloud charged straight through them. One used the butt of his fusillier to whack the billy-goat hard on the head. With a yelp, Thundercloud was knocked sideways. He got to his feet, shaking his horns dazedly, and tried to charge again.

"Nah, nah!" Pedrin cried desperately and gave a long, melodious whistle. Again and again he whistled, and Thundercloud wheeled away and came bounding back to his side, his black lip lifted in irritation.

The soldiers were all around Pedrin. His arms were seized and bent back cruelly, and he was cuffed on the side of his head so he fell to his knees, his arms almost pulled from their sockets. His head ringing, Pedrin looked up blearily, seeing his goats being seized by their collars and dragged back, Thundercloud struggling every step of the way. Blood was trickling down into Pedrin's eye, making it hard for him to see. He bent his head, wiping his temple on his sleeve. His vision clear once more, he looked anxiously up the path. He saw Durrik being hauled along by the collar of his shirt, the crippled boy clutching his crutch with both arms and making no attempt to defend himself. Lisandre was stalking along proudly, holding up her skirt with both hands, her body held away from the soldier who had her arm in a hard grip.

"How dare you lay hands upon me!" she cried in a ringing voice. "Unhand me, I say!"

"My lady," the lieutenant said with a low, sweeping bow. "My Lord Regent requires your presence back at the Castle of Estelliana. Your family has been most anxious about you. I have been given very strict instructions to escort you back to your home, at the very earliest convenience. We have our sisikas tethered in a clearing some distance from here. I must request that you accompany us without hindrance."

"I will not go," Lisandre said, her voice shaking. "What gives you the right to handle me with such discourtesy? Instruct your man to unhand me at once."

"I beg your pardon, my lady, we mean no discourtesy." There was a faint stress of sarcasm in his voice as he looked Lisandre up and down, noting her unevenly hacked hair, scratched face and muddied gown. "I must insist that you accompany us as the Lord Regent has commanded. Much as I would regret it, I have been given the authority to compel you, if necessary. If you would please come this way?" He made a sweeping gesture with his hand.

Lisandre was undecided. Although she clearly

141

wished to defy the lieutenant, it was clear she could not possibly escape. The soldiers stood in close ranks on all sides, their armour glinting in a brief ray of sunlight that struck down through the columns of trees. Pedrin and Durrik were on their knees in the mud, their arms twisted back so hard both were sobbing in pain. There was no sign of Briony.

Lisandre sighed, her shoulders slumping in defeat. She began to walk in the direction the lieutenant had directed, her face downcast.

There was a wild shaking of branches right above their heads, and the soldiers were showered with leaves and nuts. Pedrin could not look up, for the soldier behind him had his weapon jammed so hard against the back of his head that his face was only a few inches from the forest floor. His heart jolted, half with hope, half with trepidation. He heard a wild, melodious call and then there was another rattle of rain and leaves. Suddenly a great weight fell on him. His face was pushed deep into the mud. He tried to scream, thinking his arms were being dislocated. His mouth was full of leaves and dirt. Realising the pressure on his arms had been released, he tried to squirm away. He could not get away from the person lying so heavily on his back, though. Someone else trod on his hand. His face was squashed up against the hard chain-mail of someone's leg. All he could hear was a great confusion of shouts and cries, and a few loud bangs as fusilliers were fired. The stench of smoke filled his nostrils. He coughed, his eyes streaming. Then there was a hard jerk and he was hauled into the air. Rope grazed his cheek and arm. He realised they were all trapped in a net, struggling as helplessly as herrings.

Pedrin managed to wriggle through the mass of arms and legs so that he could see through the weave of the net, and then he wished that he had not. The net was being swung through the trees, bashing wildly against trunk and branch. Far below, the ground swung back and forth, back and forth. Occasionally the laden net swung right out through the branches and then there was only dizzying grey sky before once again the green-brown-grey lurch of the forest floor returned. Pedrin shut his eyes, the rope burning where it cut into his cheek, and tried not to vomit.

Some time later the net was dumped unceremoniously onto a wide wooden platform. As the net collapsed, everyone within flopped about, groaning, retching. Pedrin managed to get to his knees, hanging his head down and waiting for the whirling sensation to pass. One or two of the soldiers tried to get to their feet, only to stagger ludicrously and fall. As his vision cleared, Pedrin saw a small bare foot, very grubby, right in front of his nose. He seized it.

"Durrik," he hissed.

His friend only groaned.

Pedrin wriggled up so he was lying alongside Durrik, who smelt horribly of vomit. Durrik looked rather green and his shirt was stained with fresh blood where his half-healed welts had broken open. "Where are we?" he asked weakly. "What happened?"

"Wood-sprites," Pedrin whispered back. "I'd say

they be a-wanting the soldiers' armour and stuff. We've got naught much they'd want, though. If we lie low, we might be able to escape. Stick close by me."

Durrik nodded, and slowly followed Pedrin as he crept to the very edge of the platform, under an overhang of leaves. It was close on dusk. Beyond the spread of the tree's branches was the great green carpet of the forest, still burnished here and there with light, but under the canopy of the enormous leafy branches, a twilight gloom hung.

The wood-sprites were swiftly stripping the soldiers of their silver mail and breastplates. Some were leaping about with glee with silver helmets on their matted elflocks, others were squabbling over the long gleaming fusilliers with their glass barrels of thick, oily liquid. One broke, filling the air with a pungent stench that had the soldiers nearby trying desperately to crawl away and the wood-sprites wrinkling their pointed noses expressively. Then a loud bang filled the air, and there was an explosion of bright fire. Starkin and wildkin together screamed in agony as the spilt fuel ignited with a flash. As the seething crowd broke apart in confusion, Pedrin and Durrik carefully lowered themselves off the platform and into the shadows underneath.

Cold, hungry, shivering with shock, they clung to a branch, peering over the edge of the platform, trying to see through the writhing shadows of flame and smoke. Everywhere wood-sprites were leaping about in agitation, trying to extinguish the fire with cloaks of green leaves or wooden buckets of water they dragged up on long ropes.

144

Smoke billowed everywhere, but there was enough light left in the sky for the two boys to see that they were perched at the very top of a tremendously tall tree, hundreds of feet off the ground. All they could see when they looked down was the thick column of the trunk, with enormous branches radiating off in all directions, some of them as wide as a road.

Platforms had been built all through the tree's branches, and many vine-ropes hung down from one platform to another. There were ladders too, long flimsy structures of rope that could be rolled up and moved about as needed. Strangest of all were the hundreds of delicate ovoid nests that hung everywhere from the leafy tips of the branches. Taller than Pedrin, the nests had been woven from twigs, reeds and grass, and smoothed over with mud. Wood-sprites swung in and out of the nests, running along the broad grey branches with no hesitation or fear, or swinging nimbly down ropes, so quick and agile it was almost impossible to follow them with the eye.

Hanging everywhere were long wind-chimes made from hundreds of different kinds of silver objects – swords, teapots, ladles, sugar bowls, tankards, candlesticks, spoons. As they swayed in the wind, they chimed eerily, filling the air with their sound.

"Those wood-sprites are everywhere," Durrik said shakily, both his arms and legs wrapped tightly about their branch. "How are we meant to get down?"

Pedrin could only shake his head numbly. He risked another look down and heard the roar of vertigo in his ears, upsetting his sense of balance so that

145

he swayed. He grasped the branch tighter and put his forehead down on its smooth grey bark, his eyes clamped shut.

"There's Lady Lisandre," Durrik whispered risking the lift of one arm so he could point. Almost immediately he clutched the branch again.

Pedrin gingerly opened his eyes and raised his head over the edge of the platform, being very careful not to look down. He saw the distinctive billow of the starkin princess's red skirts. She was sitting bolt upright in the midst of all the confusion, her hands folded tightly in her lap, her most disdainful expression on her face. Pedrin felt a prick of admiration for her courage. She must have been sick with fear, all alone, her friends gone, the edge of the platform on which she was sitting all charred and smoking, flames still smouldering only a few yards from her foot. There was no sign of it on her face or in her demeanour, however. She watched calmly as wood-sprites worked frantically to lash the platform securely to another branch, for one of the ropes that tied it to the tree had disintegrated in the fire. Others were prodding the soldiers into tall cages with their own weapons, all their malicious glee vanished in the face of the disaster. Quite a few lay moaning, their smooth brown skin blistering horribly.

A tall wood-sprite dressed in a sweeping cloak of leaves, a crown of the same glossy green leaves on his head, was bending over the wounded, his face very grave. Although he had no beard, the smooth olive of his skin had hardened into lines about his eyes and mouth, and he moved with quiet deliberation. He straightened up and gave a series of swift orders to the wood-sprites clustering close about him, and they hurried to obey him. Some knelt by the wounded, trying to ease their pain and suffering with cool compresses and sips of water. Two more ran to the edge of the platform. They dragged on helmets made from giant nuts, then rolled out what looked like enormous, rough-hewn wheels. They knocked on the serrated side with a heavy hammer and the two sides of the wheel sprang apart. From within unfurled two fragile white wings, diaphanous as gossamer. The wood-sprites seized a little tuft at the centre of the seed-wings, ran towards the edge of the platform and launched themselves off into space. The seed twirled and danced, drifting down smoothly and swiftly, the two wood-sprites dangling beneath, steering the peculiar aircraft with lithe twists of their bodies.

"They don't seem to have noticed we're gone," Pedrin said, his eyes still on the starkin princess. A wood-sprite was now ordering her into another cage, gesturing menacingly with a long spear. Lisandre slowly stood up, shook out her skirts and, with great dignity, climbed into the cage. The door was slammed shut and fastened tightly, then her cage was swiftly lowered over the edge of the platform until it dangled in the breeze, nothing between her and the ground but four hundred feet of air. Each of the soldiers had been treated the same way, the wood-sprites obviously considering them dangerous indeed.

"Mebbe we can climb down when 'tis dark," Pedrin

said, laying his face back on the branch. He felt an irresistible desire to cry or laugh, he did not know which.

"What about milady? We can't leave her here, surely?"

"Well, what else can we do?"

"I don't know," Durrik said unhappily. "There must be something we can do."

"I don't know what."

"We can't be a-leaving her here," a soft little voice said from right behind them. Durrik was so surprised he shrieked out loud, while Pedrin felt a shock run through him as if he had been lashed with a whip. Luckily their hold on the tree instinctively tightened rather than loosened, else they may well have fallen to their deaths.

Briony was crouched on the branch behind them. In the deepening twilight, she was virtually invisible with her drab brown skirts and mass of tangled brown hair. Only her small, pointed face could be seen, a wedge of whiteness.

"Tessula's tears! How did you get here? What do you think you're doing, a-sneaking up on us like that!" A red wave of fury swept over Pedrin, so fierce that he was blinded and deafened by it.

"I'm sorry," she whispered. "I didn't mean to make you jump. I had to be quiet else the wood-sprites would've heard me."

"How in Liah's sweet eyes did you get here?"

"I caught a-hold of the net and got carried along too," Briony said quietly.

"What?" Pedrin said incredulously. "You must be tomfooling!"

She shook her head. "Nah, I'm not. I waited till they were almost at the platform and then I let go. I almost didn't catch a branch—"

"What a cabbage-head!" Pedrin said furiously. "You could've been killed."

She nodded, huddling her arms about her thin form. "Yeah, I know it. But if I hadn't I'd have been left far behind and not known where you all were. I had to come along too."

Pedrin was so angry and astonished he could not find words.

Durrik said wonderingly, "But why? The soldiers hadn't found you. You were safe. You could've stayed hidden."

"Yeah, I s'pose," Briony said awkwardly. "But 'twas me that brought milady here, to the Perilous Forest. I couldn't be just a-leaving her, when I'd promised and all."

Pedrin felt his stomach sink with shame and misery. He was so embarrassed he could not look at her, even though there was nothing of her to see but a crouched shadow among shadows. "But what can we do?" he said, almost pleadingly. "She's a-dangling over the edge in a cage, for Liah's sake!"

Briony gave a little shiver. "Mebbe we could throw her a rope, drag the cage in," she said hesitantly. "At first light, when all is quiet."

"Mebbe," Pedrin said doubtfully. "But then what?"

"Mebbe we could be a-stealing some of those seed-wings, and fly along out of here," Briony said, even more diffidently.

"Mebbe," Pedrin said, conviction growing in his voice. Then he remembered the drop and said in a hollow voice, "Mighty dangerous."

He saw her head jerk in agreement. He remembered that she had hung onto the bottom of the wood-sprites' net during all that long, wildly swinging journey and said in a loud voice, "Well, I'm game if you lot are!"

"Sh!" she whispered.

"Sorry," he whispered back. "So, are we going to give it a try?"

There was a short silence, then Durrik said rather hoarsely, "Well, I can't think of aught else to do."

"Me either," Pedrin said. Having a plan of action made him feel much better. He sat up, not so bothered by the free-fall below him when it was hidden by darkness, then said with a involuntary drop in his voice, "But we got no rope."

"That's all right," Briony said. "I'll spin us some."

11

She sat in the leaf-shifting darkness, her head bent. The boys could hear something whirring softly between her hands.

"What's that?" Pedrin whispered. "What're you doing?"

"'Tis me drop-spindle," she whispered back. "It means I can be a-spinning anywhere, without the need for a wheel."

"But 'tis dark."

"Yeah, I know it. But I've been a-spinning all my life, I can do it with me eyes closed, or in the dark if need be. Surely there's summat you can be a-doing in the dark too?"

"I could milk Snowflake," Pedrin said, feeling his cheeks curve in a grin for the first time in what seemed like ages. The smile faded very quickly. "I do hope me goats are safe," he whispered. "I wish I knew what had happened to them."

"The soldiers had them tethered to a tree," Briony said. "They weren't caught up in the net. I would've freed them if I could. I hate to think of them all tied up, unable to run if summat comes a-prowling round."

"No tether can keep Thundercloud tied up if he is not a-wanting to be," Pedrin said proudly. "Still," he said, his voice growing troubled again, "'Tis mighty dangerous in this here wood, and Snowflake is still all laden down with our stuff." His voice quavered despite himself.

Briony laid down her drop-spindle. "You're both a-weary indeed. Why don't you try and sleep. We can't be a-rescuing Lisandre until 'tis light enough to see."

"Rock-a-bye, baby, in the treetops..." Durrik sung. "Oh, yeah, I'm a-planning to sleep."

She moved, creeping forward on the branch. "How about if we had a hammock we could be a-tying up safely?"

"Why not a four-poster bed, on which to rest my weary head?" Durrik returned swiftly.

"I can't be a-managing a bed but a hammock I can do," she answered seriously. They sensed a few quick movements in the darkness and then heard something being shaken out.

"You're not tomfooling?" Pedrin said hopefully.

"I'm not one for much tomfoolery," she answered, a hint of a smile in her voice. "Are you two any good at knots?"

"I am," Pedrin replied, "but I wouldn't be a-trusting any knot Durrik tied."

"Then you can tie up the hammock and Durrik can keep an ear out, while I keep on a-spinning," Briony answered, passing Pedrin a length of knotted rope. He

152

felt along it in the darkness, still incredulous that she could be carrying a hammock about her when it was the very thing they needed. Then, relief springing up in him, he fumbled about in the darkness, tying the hammock securely to the same branches as the platform above. He and Durrik then crept thankfully into the swaying net of rope, which was surprisingly soft and comfortable. Since it had been raining that day, both boys were wearing their oiled capes and so they were able to draw them close about their weary bodies and fall instantly asleep.

Pedrin half-roused some time later, the hammock swaying under Briony's weight as the little girl crept in next to him, but he was asleep again the very next heartbeat, rocked gently by the breeze.

When he next woke, it was to the first sharp, clear sound of birdcalls. Briony was shaking him gently. Pedrin opened his eyes blearily, and realised it was light enough for him to see her silhouette. He tried to sit up and remembered with a jerk that he was in a hammock which rolled wildly at every movement. The turbulent swinging woke Durrik, who sat up, saying loudly, "Next shall be the king-breaker, the king-maker..."

"Shh!" Briony hissed.

"He always does that," Pedrin whispered resignedly. "I should've stuck me hand over his mouth."

"What?" Durrik said sleepily. "What did I say?"

"Gobbledygook, as always. Stop making so much noise."

"Sorry."

They managed to sit up, clinging to the net, and

look around them. It was in the hours before dawn, the sky overhead still dark enough for stars but beginning to brighten so that the stars were very faint, almost imperceptible. Apart from the shuffle of leaves and the crystal ting of birdsong, it was very quiet.

"I made us a lot of rope," Briony whispered and indicated a coil of thin rope hanging over a broken branch. "I thought we'd probably best tie ourselves all together, when we go a-flying away on the seed-wings, else we'll all get separated again."

Pedrin was not feeling so enthusiastic about their plan now that it was time to implement it, but he could not say so. He nodded his head jerkily. "How did you manage to make so much rope? Surely you can't have been a-carrying that much raw hemp around with you?" he asked, trying to focus his mind on practicalities so he did not have to think about how much air there was between his body and the ground.

"Nah, of course not," Briony said. "I borrowed bits from round us." She waved her hand vaguely. "Come on, if we're to rescue milady, we'd best be a-moving."

They struggled out of the hammock, amazed that they could have slept so comfortably now that the receding darkness showed them again the great height of the tree. Briony untied the hammock and deftly rolled it and shoved it in her little sack, which she slung on her back as usual.

"How do you fit aught else in there?" Pedrin asked. "That big hammock must take up every bit of available space!"

"'Tis only a bit of old rope, it rolls up small," Briony

said rather evasively. Pedrin would have questioned her further, but she was passing him the coil of rope, suggesting they tie themselves together in case one of them slipped and fell. Pedrin thought this was such a good idea he was quick to agree. Once they were all securely lashed together, Briony began to slowly edge her way along the branch and Pedrin's mind was soon fully engaged in not looking down. He followed close on her heels, keeping his eyes fixed on the very middle of the branch, glad it was so broad.

By the time they reached the edge of the platform, the wooden boards were pressing down upon their heads, making it hard to move. They could see the dim shapes of the cages dangling from their long ropes and swinging slightly in the breeze.

"Do you remember which one they stuck Lady Lisandre in?" Durrik said, leaning forward.

Pedrin pointed. "Can you see the bit of red a-hanging out one side? That's her."

Gingerly they manoeuvred themselves through the struts under the platform until they were as close to Lisandre's cage as they could get. All they could see of her was a pile of crumpled red silk. Pedrin hung on to one of the struts and very carefully reached out one hand as far as he could, wondering if he could grab the rope and swing her closer, but the rope was too far away.

"We'll have to throw her the end of our rope," Durrik said.

"She's a girl, remember? There's no way on earth she'll be a-catching it," Pedrin said. "I'll tie a pebble onto it and sling it to her." He put his hand into his bag of stones and realised with chagrin that he had not replenished his supply after peppering the wood-sprites the day before. He had only a few stones left.

"Your sister Mina's a pretty good catch," Durrik pointed out.

"Yeah, but I trained her," Pedrin answered. "I'll bet you me silver crown Lisandre can't catch!"

"No go," Durrik answered, grinning. "Those long nails of hers would get in the way."

While they'd been talking, Briony had quietly been rummaging in her sack. She drew out a handful of nuts that she had gathered the day before, chose one and dropped the rest back.

"Can I have your knife?" she asked.

"What for?"

"Too hard to be a-tying the rope to it. I thought I'd drill a hole through the nut and then we can be sure the rope is secure."

Pedrin gave her a quick glance of admiration. "Good idea." He took the nut from her and carefully used the sharp point of his knife to drill a hole through its centre. Briony then teased apart the end of the rope and strung the nut upon it, knotting it into place securely.

"We'd best be a-waking her," Pedrin said. He slung a nut at the cage and it flew swiftly through the air, rattling the bars before spinning away. Lisandre woke on the third nut. She sat up, gripping the bars anxiously and staring about. They waved at her, sure no one else could see them beneath the platform, and they saw her expression suddenly change. She struggled to her feet, waving and calling. Briony put one finger to her lips and Lisandre nodded, but stood pressed against the cage, her fingers gripping the bars. They tried to explain their plan to her by mime, but since none of them dared to let go of the branch they were clinging to, it was hard to express their meaning very clearly. She nodded her head, though, and stretched her hand to them through the bars.

Pedrin had been right. Lisandre was a very bad catch. On the thirteenth attempt Pedrin managed to get the nut to fly straight through the narrow crack between the bars, and Lisandre was able to wrap it round and round the bars until it was secure. The other three children then hauled on the rope until the cage was dragged right up to where they crouched, tipped at an oblique angle. It was then a matter of only a few seconds for Pedrin to cut the rope binding the door closed and for Lisandre to very shakily climb out.

There were white tear tracks through the grime on her face, and her eyes were puffy and red-rimmed. Her hair stuck up like quills, her dress was crushed and stained, and blood was encrusted on her ear. She was so pleased to see them, though, that she smiled brilliantly at them, saying in a tremulous voice, "Oh, I am glad indeed to see you all. I had thought myself forsaken."

Both Pedrin and Durrik felt themselves overtaken by awkwardness, their hands suddenly feeling too large and their necks too hot. Pedrin dropped his eyes and muttered something, but Durrik bowed his upper body, saying, "Our pleasure, milady." For the first time Pedrin envied his friend's quick facility with words. Durrik never seemed at a loss for the right thing to say, while Pedrin just blushed hotter and hotter, everything he felt dammed up in his throat so he could say nothing at all. He cast a quick look of resentment at Durrik and busied himself untying the rope so the cage swung back to its original position.

"The sun's a-rising," Briony whispered. "The wood-sprites will all be waking. Let's get a-going."

"How are we to descend?" Lisandre demanded. "Did you see how high we are?"

"See those enormous seed-pods hanging all over the tree?" Briony pointed to the very edge of the branch, where a cluster of the enormous wheel-shaped seeds hung, dark against the lucid sky. Lisandre nodded and Briony described to her how the seeds within had two wing-like projections that caused them to float upon the wind. "The wood-sprites hang below them and fly with them, milady. They must be able to travel a very long way."

"Are you mad?" Lisandre said, whiter than ever below the grime. "We shall all be killed."

"The wood-sprites—"

"I am not a wood-sprite!"

"Nah, I know it, milady. Still, it can't be too dangerous else they wouldn't do it. You just need to hold on long enough, and if a-letting go meant you'd be a-falling to your death, well then, you'd be a-holding on, wouldn't you? And we mean to tie ourselves to the seed-wings, and to each other. The wood-sprites steer themselves by shifting their weight one way or another. 'Tis a long way down. We'll have plenty of time to catch the knack of it."

At times like this, when Briony forgot her shyness and diffidence, her whole face glowed with colour, transforming her. Her green eyes were bright with resolve, her small face set in lines of such determination that all the others were convinced and even inspired. The very next instant she dropped her eyes and the glow faded, but an impression of it lingered with the other children so that they all followed her readily when she said, in her usual hesitant way, "I can't be sure, but I think the seed-pods a-hanging on the tree can't be ripe. We'll have to be a-stealing some of the ones on the platform. Mebbe we'd best be a-moving?"

With Pedrin's knife they cut the rope into lengths, constructing halters that passed over their shoulders and round their waists, with loose reins that were to be tied to the seed-wings, and another long line that tied all the children together. Lisandre stood like a doll, her arms held out stiffly, allowing the other children to prepare her but making no attempt to help in any way. Already she seemed to have forgotten her gratitude for being rescued, saying coldly, "I hope this madcap scheme of yours works, Briony, else we soon shall all be dead."

"I hope so too, milady," was all Briony said. "All we can do is try."

Pedrin busied himself checking the knots, trying to

ignore the incessant fluttering of his stomach. Eventually, though, he had to declare all was firm. He gritted his teeth together, determined no little serving-girl was going to outface him, and said, "Well, let's get a-going then."

Very quietly the four children climbed up onto the platform, keeping close under the overhang of leaves. A wood-sprite was sitting on the far edge of the platform, his arms wrapped around his knees, drinking in the sight of the dawn. To the east the sky was luminous, golden rays striking up into a welter of clouds, gilding them with light. He was so absorbed in the beauty of the sight that he did not notice the furtive movements of the children as they crept towards the seed-pods. His head swung round at the first blow of the hammer, however. When he saw the four children desperately banging open four seeds, he sprang towards the nearest wind-chime and shook it furiously. A cacophony rang out. He then seized his long spear and leapt towards them. It was too late, though. Lisandre, Briony, Durrik and Pedrin had all hurriedly tied themselves to the diaphanous white wings and launched themselves off into space.

All four screamed. They were not prepared for the speed of their descent. It felt as if their hearts had been kicked up into their throats and lodged there. Branches sprang towards them. Instinctively they arched backwards and the seed-wings swayed away in response. Pedrin caught his breath, swallowed a surge of hot bile, and dared to open his eyes again. Far below, the forest canopy was like a deep green carpet, glanced with light. He saw the sinuous gleam of the Evenlode a long way away, and beyond the river, high green hills that rose into grey mountains, sullen with cloud. He glanced behind him, but the movement caused the seed-wing to veer, making the line between him and Durrik go suddenly lax. He had only long enough to see wood-sprites hanging out of the branches, watching them. To his surprise, most of them were laughing and waving. Then he had to straighten his course again, before he crashed into Durrik.

Briony had been right. It did not take them long to begin to control the speed and direction of the seed-wings. Although the wind was the engine that drove their momentum, the children could slow the descent by slanting the seed-wings against the breeze, and change direction by tilting their bodies from side to side. Soon their terror was replaced with jubilance. To soar above the trees, as swift and free as birds, to see the whole world unfolding below them in all its vast-ness and beauty, to have escaped the soldiers and outwitted the wood-sprites – it was no wonder all of them shouted aloud for joy, even quiet little Briony.

The silvery-blue snake of the Evenlode rushed towards them. It was impossible to pick the spot where the soldiers had discovered them the previous evening. Pedrin cupped his hands about his mouth and gave a long, loud, melodious whistle. Again and again he whistled, hoping his goats were close enough to hear.

Then he had to stop, for their feet were beginning to

brush against the shaggy tops of the trees. Pedrin cleared his throat. "Any idea how to be a-landing these things?"

The wind was capricious down here, in the tree-tops. They were tossed about wildly, branches smashing against their legs, their sides. Briony's seed-wing tipped sideways and fell sharply, with a loud ripping sound as the gossamer tore. The rope that tied her to Lisandre dragged the starkin princess down too and she screamed in terror.

"Slow down, slow down!" Pedrin shouted. "Grab a branch or summat!"

"How, you imbecile?" Lisandre screamed back. "I'll break my arm!"

"Tilt your wing, make it slow down!"

But Lisandre's wing had flipped upside down and crashed down through the canopy, disappearing from sight. Desperately Pedrin tilted his seed-wing up against the wind. It flipped and crashed into the trees. Pedrin covered his face with his hands as twigs and branches tore into his skin. He was jerked around, and then down, and around again. When Pedrin at last dared open his eyes, blood roaring in his ears, he found himself dangling upside-down in a tree. He heard screams and the crashing of branches, then saw a flash of white as someone else was caught nearby.

"Everyone all right?" he cried.

"Yeah, sort of," came Durrik's voice.

"I think so," Briony answered, from quite a distance away.

Then Lisandre said, in an icy voice, "I am scratched

and bruised from head to foot, and I am dangling upside-down twenty feet above the ground. Of course I am not all right. Whose wonderful idea was this?"

12

◆ ◆ ◆

The Evenlode wound through the trees, brown where it was dappled with light, greeny-dark where the branches hung close. A path was worn along its ferny banks, leading down to a wide curve of pebbly sand. Here Lisandre sat, her scarlet silk skirts spread gracefully about her, her hands folded in her lap. The setting sun shone through her dandelion-seed hair so her beautiful, pale face looked as if it was haloed in light.

Cicadas sang in the bushes all about, and Thundercloud and Snowflake were knee-deep in a bed of thistles, contentedly grazing. They had come bounding up to the four children only an hour or so after they had finally managed to extricate themselves from the treetops, bowling Pedrin over in their excitement. The goatherd had been so relieved to see them tears had stung his eyes, and he had had to wipe them surreptitiously on his sleeve, afraid Lisandre would notice and jeer at him. Snowflake had been in great discomfort with bursting udders, and so he had sat down at once and milked her, pressing his face into her flank so he could smell her clover-sweet scent. The children had not eaten for almost a full day and so they all drank the milk gratefully, even Lisandre, and gorged themselves on stale bread and cheese from the nanny-goat's saddlebags.

The rest of the day had been spent walking, but the mood could not have been more different from the day before. The sun was shining, the starkin soldiers were hanging in cages four hundred feet off the ground and forty miles behind them, and they had managed to escape the wood-sprites with no more than a few nasty scratches and bruises. The ointment of Naoma of the Crafty had soon eased that discomfort, and they had found this peaceful clearing with fat silverbacks sunning themselves in the shallows, and the whine of cicadas to warn them of any disturbance to the peace.

Pedrin, Durrik and Briony were up to their knees in the river, casting their makeshift fishing lines into the swirl of water beyond the beach. Three fish already dangled from Pedrin's belt so the urgency had gone out of their task and they were happy to splash about a little and talk and joke.

"So why do seamstresses like wide-open spaces?" Durrik asked solemnly.

"I don't know," Briony answered uncertainly. "I certainly do but then I'm not like most seamstresses, I was born out in the open. Do most seamstresses like wide-open spaces?"

"Oh, they do," he answered. "'Tis because they

don't like feeling *hemmed in.*"

It took a moment for Briony to understand but then light dawned in her greeny-dark eyes. "Oh!" she cried.

"So where do seamstresses like to live?" he asked.

"Where then?" She was half-laughing, half-defensive.

"Why, on the *outskirts* of town, of course."

"Very funny," she grinned.

"Don't mind him," Pedrin said. "He's the master of the bad pun."

"My puns aren't bad," Durrik protested. "You're just jealous because you can't ever think of any yourself."

"I can too!"

"Well then?"

Pedrin coloured, swung his leg back and forth in the water, and said nothing.

"Told you."

"I'm a-thinking!" Pedrin protested. He took a deep breath, then, his ears turning red, asked: "So is it hard to sew, Briony?"

"Is this a pun?" she asked, bewildered. "How am I meant to answer?"

"You should say, 'Nah, 'tis *thimble'*," Pedrin answered, grinning widely. "Do you get it? Thimble. Simple. Hah, that's mighty good!"

"Mighty bad," Durrik said, once he stopped laughing. "You're good at catching fish, Pedrin, but gruesome at cracking jokes."

Pedrin splashed him with water. "You're just jealous 'cause you didn't think of it yourself," he cried.

A water fight ensued, the boys doing their best to drown each other. Laughing, Briony ran back to the shore. "Those boys are such tomfools," she said to Lisandre, wringing out the hem of her dress.

"With execrable manners also," Lisandre said coldly. "I am hungry. When do you intend to serve me my meal, Briony?"

Briony stopped laughing. "I'm sorry, milady," she said gently. "Indeed you must be hungry. 'Tis been a mighty long time since we last ate. I'll be a-kindling the fire now."

She busied herself gathering firewood while Lisandre watched, a little of the stiffness gone from her back. Pedrin and Durrik waded out of the pool to help her, their clothes and hair dripping wet.

"I see milady does not intend to lift a finger," Pedrin said with some acidity, taking the heavy load of branches from Briony's skinny arms.

"It wouldn't occur to her," she answered. "She's been waited on hand and foot all her life, you know."

"Yeah, but we're not at the castle now," he said rebelliously. "She treats you like dirt."

"She treats me as if I were her servant, which is what I am," Briony replied gently. "I don't mind, much. All this is hard for her. I'm happy to do what I can to make it easier."

"What's so hard for her? A-sitting around and a-watching us work?"

"But don't you see how weary Lisandre must be, and how a-feared? She's never left the castle before, except to be carried down the town in a litter. You sneered at her for her shoes but don't you realise she's got no others? I think she's amazingly brave, to leave the luxury of the castle and be a-setting out on such an adventure."

Colour had risen in her cheeks and she was gazing directly at him for the first time, so he saw how very bright her eyes really were. He looked back at her in surprise, and she blushed and dropped her eyes, bending to pick up an old dry branch. He had not thought of things from quite this angle before but he said stubbornly, "Or amazingly stupid."

"But she's not stupid at all. She knows there's summat wrong with her father's death and she's determined to find out what and set it right. She was the only one of the starkin to see behind Lord Zavion's charming smile."

She gathered up another handful of dry leaves and mosses, carrying them back to their campsite in her apron. Pedrin said nothing as he helped Briony lay the fire, but when he glanced at a white-faced Lisandre, sitting so still on the sand, the hostility in his eyes was a little tempered.

As was the usual practice among the hearthkin, Pedrin said a little prayer to Liah as he tried to strike a spark from his flint.

"O Liah, lady of the hearth,
Kindle our spark of light,
Bless our fire tonight,
Keep your flame bright,
All this long, dark night,

Watch over us while we sleep,
And keep us safe from harm,
O Liah, lady of the hearth."

"What is the goat-boy muttering about now?" Lisandre asked wearily.

"He asks for the blessing of Liah the Hearth-Keeper," Briony replied softly. "She's the goddess of the home fire, the bringer of warmth and light. It is Liah who grants the power to see clearly and understand what is seen."

"How quaint," Lisandre said.

Pedrin glared at her, all his hostility aroused once more, and laid the fish in his pan to fry.

"The best thing about fried fish is that 'tis so quick," Durrik said happily. "Imagine if we had to sit and smell that for an hour!"

"It does smell delicious," Lisandre admitted. "I am very hungry."

"It tastes even better," Pedrin said, licking his fingers a few minutes later. "Why does food always taste better outdoors?"

"Does it?" Lisandre said. "Until we left the castle, I had never eaten outside before and the food we have had since then has all been rather repugnant. Though I must admit this is the best fish I have ever tasted."

"Well, it was swimming about only half an hour ago," Pedrin said. "The fish you eat up at the castle must be a day old, at least."

She was too busy eating to answer. Apart from the fish, there was soft goat's cheese and freshly baked bread and delicious yellow yams that Briony had dug up in the forest and roasted in the fire. Soon all that was left was a scatter of bones and crumbs, which Briony carefully gathered up and buried out of sight. She then spread some of the bread with honey and poured out a bowl of Snowflake's warm frothy milk.

"What you doing?" Durrik asked as she carried the bowl and plate to the far side of the clearing, leaving them behind a big bush.

Briony looked at him in surprise. "A-leaving an offering for the wildkin, of course. It'd be very rude to fish in his pool and dig up his roots without a-leaving summat in return."

"Whose pool?" Pedrin asked, sitting up abruptly and reaching for his slingshot.

"The river-roan's, of course. Did you not see his hoofprints in the mud by the river?"

"A river-roan's hoofprints? No!"

"Did you think this pool unoccupied?" Briony was a little puzzled.

"But ... I didn't think, I suppose." Pedrin looked about uneasily. He lowered his voice. "Do you think he's a-watching us now?"

"For sure," Briony answered. "River-roans are very curious, you know." She saw the alarm on all their faces and said in her soft, gentle voice, "There's no need to be a-feared. He won't hurt us, as long as we don't make too much of a mess or try to harm him in any way."

"But I thought river-roans always be a-trying to trick people so they can drown them," Durrik said, staring around with wide eyes.

170

"Oh, they'll a-try to drown you if they think you're a threat, but river-roans are mostly pretty gentle. 'Tis the lake-lorelei you really need to be a-worrying about when it comes to drowning, and they never share a pool with a river-roan. It was when I saw his hoof-prints that I decided it was safe to camp here, didn't you realise?"

Pedrin's ears turned red. "Just so long as he stays away from us, I s'pose it'll be fine," he said gruffly, and got up to call the goats in from the forest.

They grew sleepy as the fire sank down into coals, and made themselves beds of bracken and grass. Lisandre sat and watched them in silence, her back very straight, then ordered Briony to come and brush her hair and wash her face and hands. Briony did as she was bid, trying without much success to smooth down the shock of unevenly hacked fair hair. When she was finished Briony passed Lisandre the silver mirror, and she examined her face and hair closely, frowning in displeasure at what she saw. "I look like some repulsive hearthkin brat," she said unhappily, and tried to smooth down her crumpled, muddied skirt. "Briony, you must wash my dress for me and set it to dry for the morning."

"Yeah, milady. Come, won't you lie down and rest? We have another long walk tomorrow."

"Very well," Lisandre said, and held up her hand imperiously. After a moment Pedrin realised she expected him to pull her to her feet. He blushed furiously and took her hand. It was very soft, but her long nails cut his palm cruelly. He hauled her up, and she came to her feet abruptly. He realised, with rather a shock, that she was not much taller than him after all. It was the preposterous high heels that all the starkin wore that made them seem so very tall. She stepped away from him haughtily, gathering up the great mass of her skirt with both hands so she did not trip over its trailing hem.

"You boys must turn your backs and cover your eyes while I undress," she commanded. "Do not dare try to cheat, for I shall know."

"Nah, of course not, milady," Durrik said in a scandalised voice, then flickered a wink at Pedrin. The goatherd could not help grinning in response. He knew his friend had every intention of peeking, just as he did himself. There was nothing to see, however, for Briony held up the long purple cloak as a screen and Lisandre undressed behind it, then wrapped herself up well before lying down on the bed of bracken Briony had prepared for her.

"Try to sleep, milady," Briony said.

"I'll try," Lisandre said rather pettishly, trying to get comfortable. "I must admit I am immensely weary."

It took a long time for Briony to wash the mass of red silk, and squeeze it out and hang it up to dry. Although both Pedrin and Durrik were so tired their bones ached, they were so indignant at Lisandre's behaviour that they made a point of sitting up to help Briony and keep her company. At first Durrik entertained her with jokes and funny stories then, when he grew so drowsy he could hardly keep his eyes open, Pedrin took out his wooden flute and began to play.

He had not had the opportunity since they had fled the Regent's crystal tower, and so he took pleasure in playing tune after tune, until at last Briony was able to join them in their rough bracken beds by the fire.

"You play well," Lisandre said sleepily. "When I have woken my brother, you must come up to the castle and play for him. I'm sure he will be able to find you a job as a court musician."

Pedrin had not yet forgiven her for her comment about hearthkin brats, so he replied rather curtly, "Thank you, but I like being a goatherd. *I* wouldn't like to spend all me days a-lying round, growing fat and lazy, unable to even wash me own face."

She did not answer, though they heard her turn away abruptly, the bracken crackling. Pedrin put his flute away and pulled his weatherproof cape up about his ears, having won first watch with the toss of his new silver coin. Silence fell.

It was sometime later that he woke with a start, hearing rustling sounds in the bushes. Pedrin held his breath, listening. He heard the sound of crunching and slurping. Suddenly the darkness was split by a broad ray of light. The massive trunks of the trees were illuminated brightly. He saw something move, something dark and quick, then all was still. Quickly he looked back towards the fire, startled and afraid, and saw Lisandre was sitting up, a blazing sphere in her hand. Then the light dwindled down to a muted glow that lit her face and Pedrin's, but no longer split the darkness.

"What was that?" Lisandre said shakily.

"I don't know. The river-roan, mebbe, though it did not look much like a horse." He got up and crossed the clearing, his hand on the billy-goat's tense shoulder. Thundercloud's head was lowered, his golden eyes narrowed evilly. There was just enough light left for Pedrin to see that the bowl of milk was empty and the bread and honey gone. He went back to the fire with a tight feeling in his throat, a coldness in the pit of his stomach. "Summat has eaten the offering anyway," he said, trying to sound light-hearted. "Let's hope it warn't a gibgoblin!"

Lisandre made a little sound, a sigh or a sob, it was hard to tell which. She raised high the sphere of light, turning it so that its bright beam swept through the trees. There was nothing to see.

"What is it?" Briony sat up, her ragdoll clutched in her arm, the blanket falling from her thin shoulders. "What's wrong?"

"Summat came and drank the milk," Pedrin said brusquely.

"Oh, that's good," she said.

"It didn't look much like a horse."

She gave a little nod. Durrik was awake now too, his blond hair sticking straight up, his face frightened. "What do you think it was? Will it come back?" he asked.

Pedrin did not want to admit he had fallen asleep, or that his heart was galloping along so fast it thundered in his ears. He gave a little shrug and looked at Briony but she said nothing, just yawned sleepily and snuggled back down in her blanket.

After a moment Lisandre brought the light back down to a muted glow that slowly sank away, leaving them in darkness. "Well, I cannot see anything out there," she said, her voice a little wobbly. "I think it must have gone."

"What's that light you keep a-conjuring up?" Pedrin asked curiously, throwing more wood on the fire so he could see. "'Tis so bright and you don't need no tinder or flint to light it."

"What, this? It's my night-light," Lisandre said carelessly, and held it out for the others to see. It was a jewelled orb, the shape and size of a sisika egg, enamelled a pale violet-blue and garlanded with flowers and ribbons of gold set with sapphires, blue opals and amethysts. At one end was a golden crown set with a brilliant diamond, at the other end a little oval knob that looked as if was designed to be set into a stand. A heavy gold chain was now threaded through so the jewelled egg could be worn hanging from Lisandre's waist. The two boys stared, open-mouthed. They had never seen anything like it.

Lisandre swung the jewelled egg idly. "It's pretty, is it not? It was my christening gift from the king. All children of the Ziv are given one, so we need not fear the dark. Look..."

She held the egg up and gave it a little twist with her hand. To the surprise and delight of the others, it opened like the bud of a flower, revealing within a golden bird sitting upon a blossoming branch of blue jewels. The bird spread its tiny wings, opened its golden beak and sang exquisitely. When the song was

175

finished, the bird folded its wings and closed its beak, and the four petals smoothly and silently shut once more, hiding the bird within.

"What about the light? Where does the light come from, the one a-shining like a lantern?" Pedrin asked, fascinated and envious.

"Here," Lisandre said, pointing one finger at the great spherical diamond set into the golden crown. At her gesture it began to glow with light, sending rainbow sparks flashing around the circle of intent faces. "I can make it as bright as I want," she said. "If I wanted to, I could light up this clearing as if it were day."

"How?" Pedrin asked.

"What do you mean, how? I've showed you how."

"I mean, how does it work? What makes the diamond shine with light?"

"I do not know," she answered irritably. "It just works."

"Is it some sort of magic then?"

"There is no such thing as magic," she said indulgently. "Believing in magic is just a symptom of a primitive philosophy, one that is based in superstition and fear."

The other three exchanged quick glances and Pedrin rolled his eyes.

"Can I hold it?" Durrik asked.

Lisandre frowned. "Absolutely not. Only one of the Ziv may touch it. Did I not say it was a gift from the king himself?"

"Yeah, you did," Pedrin said. She scowled at him.

"Isn't it pretty?" Briony said with a little sigh.

"How do you make it open?" Pedrin asked. She showed them how to twist the knob at the bottom and once again the egg split open, revealing the singing bird on its branch of opals and sapphires. When the song was finished, the petals closed shut once more, hiding the bird within.

Pedrin would have liked to examine the jewelled egg more closely and see if he could make the light shine himself, but Lisandre tucked it out of sight, saying, "Do you think it is safe to go back to sleep? For indeed I am weary still."

"I'll keep watch," Pedrin offered.

"Only try not to fall asleep this time," Durrik said.

Pedrin coloured hotly. "I was tired too," he said defensively. "We walked a mighty long way today."

"Yesterday," Lisandre said. "It must be tomorrow by now."

"Well, it must be my turn to keep watch now anyways," Durrik said. "You sleep and I'll wake you later."

Pedrin shook his head. "I'm fine," he said crossly. He stared out into the fire-lit darkness, sure he felt eyes watching them. Snowflake gave a little reassuring bleat and snuggled down next to him, and he stroked her head with his fingers. "Butt me if I fall asleep again," he whispered and she nodded her horned head and laid it against his knee.

"So what's the plan now?" Durrik asked the next morning, his mouth full of toast and honey. "How are we meant to find the place where the count and all his men died? This forest is mighty big!"

Lisandre frowned and tried to follow what he said, but he had slipped back into Adalheid, the complex phrasing of the starkin language just too difficult to keep up in everyday conversation. Seeing her puzzled frown, he obligingly translated for her.

"The sisika lords who led the search party said they found the bodies by the river, a few days' walk into the forest," Lisandre said, dabbing delicately at her mouth with her handkerchief while Briony tended her blistered feet. "That was why Lord Zavion said they must've been killed by the lake-lorelei, but Briony tells me the lake-lorelei always lure their prey into the water and then drown them, they do not kill on dry land."

"So I thought if we just a-followed the river we'd soon come to the right place," Briony said. "Me only worry is that Lord Zavion will surely reason the same way – the river is the only true constant in the forest. Surely he will get his sisika riders to fly up and down the river, a-looking for any trace of us? Then all they have to do is find a clearing big enough for the sisikas to be a-landing in, and they'll be hot on our trail again."

"We must just keep a close watch above and behind us as well as before us," Pedrin said, hoping no one remembered how he had failed to notice the soldiers behind them last time. No one said anything, though, and so he said, "I'll lead the way, shall I?" He bent and seized one of the saddlebags, saying, "Durrik, I think we should carry our own bags, in case we get separated again. At least that way we'll have some food and our blankets and stuff."

Durrik nodded, and picked up the other saddlebag, strapping it over his shoulder so it rested comfortably on his back. Pedrin took a deep breath then said, frowning, "All right then, let's get a-moving. Try not to leave a trail. Durrik, how about you bring up the rear?"

"Yessir!" Durrik said with a mocking salute. "Your wish is my command!"

Colour scorched up Pedrin's face, all the way to his ears.

.

13

♦ ♦ ♦

A week later the path began to climb steeply, through rocks all emerald-green with moss. The two goats bounded on ahead, leaping from one boulder to the next with amazing agility. The children did not have so much ease, panting along behind, using their hands to haul themselves higher. Once Durrik's makeshift crutch slid in the mud and he fell heavily, grazing his knees and palms. He did not complain, just hoisted himself up again and kept on going, blood discolouring the torn fabric of his trousers. Snowflake came leaping back, bleating softly, and ran by his side so Durrik was able to steady himself with a hand on her back.

They came to a dark, gloomy copse of trees, where the Evenlode slid down black and silent between the close-gathered branches. They made their way forward cautiously, finding it hard to see in the sudden dusk but unwilling to draw attention to themselves by illuminating Lisandre's night-light. Twice in the past few days they had seen or heard soldiers in the woods behind them and, although they had managed to hurry on ahead without being seen themselves, they were all too well aware that Lord Zavion had not given up his pursuit.

Pedrin felt something sticky across his face. He recoiled, putting up his hand to brush it away. "Spiderwebs," he said in disgust. He took another step forward and felt himself entangled in stickiness again. As he brushed the cobwebs away, he heard Lisandre shriek. Then the white radiance of her night-light shone out. They all screamed then.

All about them, as far as the eye could see, the intricate fretwork of spiderwebs stretched, the delicate lines gleaming in the light. Huge black spiders crouched in the webs, each as big as Pedrin's face and covered in bristling hair. There were hundreds of them, hanging motionless all about them.

"Jumping Jimjinny!" Pedrin seized a stick from the ground. To his surprise, Briony grasped the other end in both her small hands, preventing him from swinging it.

"What are you doing?" she cried. "There's no need to be a-killing them! They're not doing no harm. We're the ones doing the harm, stomping through here and destroying all their webs. Do you need to be a-murdering them as well?"

Pedrin could only gape at her.

"Whatever do you mean, Briony?" Lisandre cried, shrinking away. "Ooooh, look! It's coming!"

One of the spiders was rapidly descending towards them, swinging from a long shining filament. Lisandre

181

screamed and cringed back against Durrik, who lashed out at it with his crutch. He broke the filament. The spider dropped upon his arm. He screamed and flung it away from him. Lisandre screamed too and scrambled away, her hands over her face.

Briony fell to her knees, picking the spider up and cradling it in her hands. It was so large it filled both her palms, the hairy legs hanging over. She stroked its sides gently with her thumbs.

"She warn't a-coming for *you*, milady," Briony said. "She's a-coming to fix her web. See how you've torn it. Come, let us away from here before we do even more harm." She examined the spider anxiously, saying with a relieved sigh, "She's not hurt, only all shaken up, thank Imala."

Lisandre was staring at her with horrified eyes. "How can you stroke it like that? Urrghh!"

"She's soft, like velvet," Briony answered, lifting the spider towards the others. "Touch her, she'll not mind."

"Nah, thank you!" Pedrin said. Durrik shuddered and backed away, with Lisandre behind him, clinging to his arm, her face as white as whey.

"Let's get out of here," she whispered. "Look, another's coming!" She gave another high-pitched shriek and stumbled back.

"They'll not hurt you," Briony protested. "They're not poisonous." She lifted the spider up her neck, brushing her chin across its back. "Really, spiders are sweet creatures, very gentle and loving. You shouldn't be a-feared of them." She followed them towards the edge of the copse of trees.

"Get it away from me," Lisandre screamed. "Urrggghh, how can you bear it on your neck like that?"

She scrambled further away from the little seamstress, her mouth all contorted with revulsion. Suddenly she came to a halt, one hand flung out, the other raised to her lips in an urgent shushing motion.

"What?" Pedrin stopped beside her.

Lisandre pointed with a shaking hand. "Soldiers!"

He looked quickly. Climbing up the bank of the river was a band of soldiers, their white uniforms glimmering in the dusk. In their midst was a canopied litter, carried on the shoulders of four burly men. Reclining upon white satin cushions was a tall man in a sweeping white robe. The last of the sunshine seemed to linger in his long, smooth curls. He carried a sphere of white light which cast a bright ray before him, illuminating every nook and cranny.

"Lord Zavion," Lisandre whispered. "There's no one else with a night-light of his own. Only the Ziv may carry them. Oh, comets and stars, I cannot believe he has joined the soldiers himself! I have never seen Lord Zavion leave the court before, he has a great dislike of any exertion. He must be serious indeed about recapturing me..."

Pedrin's ribcage had tightened so abruptly he felt all the breath squeezed out of his lungs. He could not take another. He had begun to believe the starkin soldiers had given up and gone home, yet here was Lord Zavion himself less than a hundred feet away.

"Come," Briony whispered, drawing Lisandre back into the dark wood. "They mustn't see us. We have to be a-finding somewhere to hide."

"I cannot! The spiders…"

"They'll not hurt you," Briony repeated. "Come, get down low and crawl, so we pass right under their webs. The spiders don't seek to trap us, 'tis moths and flies they want. Don't be a-feared."

"I cannot!" Lisandre shuddered.

"Then Lord Zavion will have you. Look, they're almost upon us. He'll be a-seeing us any moment. Get down and crawl."

Lisandre shook her head mutely, though the bright ray of light was sweeping through the trees only a few scant paces from where they stood.

Briony dropped down to her hands and knees, and dragged at Lisandre's skirt. "Shut your eyes. Hold on to me ankles and crawl behind me. Pretend there's no spiders. Come on!"

After a moment, Lisandre obeyed. She fell to her knees and gripped Briony's ankles, crawling along behind her on her elbows and knees. The boys followed behind, though they were unable to help straining their necks to look up at the spiders, hanging black and motionless in the midst of their webs. The searchlight illuminated them starkly, so that the boys' flesh crept with revulsion.

"Whatever you do, don't scream!" Briony hissed. "They're close behind us now."

Thorns tore at their faces and hands, and stones and roots bruised their flesh. Every brush of leaf and twig

184

felt like spiders' claws. Lisandre moaned every now and again, and once uttered an involuntary shriek that she muffled by burying her face in the thick litter of decaying leaves. They could hear shouting behind them and the white ray of light glanced through the filigree of branch and twig and web, making the spiders' eyes glitter. They ducked their heads down low and crawled forward blindly.

"There's a little cave in the rock ahead," Briony whispered. "Come on, it may be big enough for us to hide in."

She wriggled out from under a bush and led them in a low staggering run to a narrow crack in the cliff-face. The light swept over the rock and back into the trees. In the darkness it left behind, they scrabbled inside the crack, one by one. Briony crept in last, barely able to fit her skinny little body inside.

"Durrik, get your elbow out of me face!" Pedrin panted.

"Ow! You're standing on my foot!"

"Can't you squeeze in a bit, Lisandre, that stupid skirt of yours is taking up a mighty lot of room."

"I cannot, this cave is far too small," Lisandre whispered in despair, trying in vain to press herself closer to the rock. The searchlight swept back, seeming to linger on the crack in the rock. They could see each other's faces clearly, all looking strained and frightened.

"They'll find us for sure," Durrik moaned. "This'll be the first place they look."

Briony lifted the spider from her shoulder. The others all muffled involuntary shrieks and scrabbled further back into the crack, not realising until then that she still carried the great arachnid, nestled into the dark riot of her hair. She lifted it level with her eyes, stared into its impassive face, and then gently deposited it on the rock.

The spider crouched for a moment and then swung nimbly across to the other face, causing all the children except Briony to once again shudder away, Lisandre uttering a little squeak of protest. It took them a few moments to realise the spider was spinning a web across the narrow cave mouth. Even then their reaction was one of horror and dismay. Lisandre was sure the huge black spider had trapped them in the cave so she could cocoon them in cobwebs and suck dry their life juices. Even Pedrin thought only of having to struggle out through the incredibly strong, sticky strands with the risk of brushing up against that repulsive hairy creature. Only Briony showed no perturbation, crouching within the shadow of the wall as the searchlight came closer and closer and closer.

The children were too afraid even to breathe. They could hear the crack of branches being broken, the crunch of leaves underfoot.

"Filthy spiders," a man said. "They're everywhere!"

"I do not think the young lady could have come this way, my lord," another man said. "Surely she would've been terrified of these spiders?"

"We heard a girl scream." Lord Zavion's voice was very, very cold. "And did we not find a scrap of red silk caught on a thorn? Lady Lisandre was here, and not so very long ago. We must find her and return her to her mother's loving embrace. My cousin the king has already expressed his astonishment at the count's death and this peculiar sleep of his son. I do not wish to arouse any stronger expression of displeasure so soon after I have been granted the Regency. Lady Lisandre's disappearance could not have come at a worse time. We must find her before the king hears of it!"

"She is only a child," the other man said. "We should have no trouble finding her, my lord."

"I certainly hope not!" Lord Zavion said. "I have never had to endure so much discomfort in my life. My only consolation is that the little brat must've been at least as uncomfortable!"

The cold, haughty voice was very close now, the probing searchlight very bright. Pedrin could feel Lisandre trembling against his back, though with fear or anger he could not tell. "There is the crack in the rock we saw, my lord," said the soldier. "It is very small. Do you think my lady could have squeezed in there?"

"She is only a child," Lord Zavion said contemptuously. "It is my experience that children can wriggle in just about anywhere."

The light shone full upon the cave mouth. The spider scuttled out of sight. All the children could see were the complicated strands of her web, shining a little in the light. They shrank back, expecting to be dragged out at any moment.

"Look, my lord, the crack is thick with cobwebs,"

the soldier said. "Nobody has passed through there, no matter how small. Lady Lisandre is hiding elsewhere, my lord."

There was a long pause, and then the light slid away. "She must be here somewhere," Lord Zavion said, in a high, fretful voice. "Find her! I cannot risk attracting the king's displeasure any more than I already have. I do not care if you must search all night – she cannot be far away!"

For a long time the children crouched, motionless, all their muscles screaming from standing so still for so long. All was dark. All was quiet. At last Durrik said, rather tremulously, "I think they've gone."

"Can we get out of here?" Lisandre asked, a thin thread of hysteria in her voice. "Is that horrible spider gone?"

"That horrible spider just saved our lives," Briony said. "Or at least our liberty."

"Come, let's find a place to camp the night," Durrik said, anxious to keep the peace. "Lord Zavion's gone now. We should be safe for a while, at least. In the morning we can be a-thinking about what to do. Let's just find somewhere to rest now."

"Not near these spiders," Lisandre said, her voice shrill. "How can you think of sleeping with all these spiders around?"

They all found it hard to look at Briony. Although the curly-haired girl had hidden them and kept them all safe, unconsciously the other three drew together, keeping their distance from her. Briony looked unhappy but she said nothing, leading them swiftly away from the spider wood. All was dark now, but Briony seemed to see as clearly at night as she did during the day. She led them without hesitation to a big willow tree, whose green hanging branches concealed a warm hollow where all four children could stretch out to sleep, hidden from prying eyes.

There was no joking tonight, no flute playing or silly stories. They ate the last of their bread, softened in milk, Briony putting a small share out for the wildkin as usual. Then all four lay quietly, listening to the night murmurs of the forest and thinking their own troubled thoughts. After a long silence Pedrin said, very gruffly, "Briony, how did you know about that little cave?"

"I don't know," she answered hesitantly.

"What do you mean, you don't know?"

"I mean I don't know," she answered miserably. "I know things sometimes. I don't know how."

After a long moment, Pedrin asked, "Like what sort of things? What do you know?"

"Not much," she answered, very quiet and low. "How people think, what they feel, what lies ahead. Not much."

This time the silence stretched on until it slid into sleep, a sleep haunted by spider claws and shadows.

14

"**W**hy did the fly fly?" Durrik asked. "Here we go," Pedrin said wearily. "I don't know, why?"

"Because the spider spied her," Durrik replied.

Pedrin and Lisandre both groaned. "That's gruesome," the goat-boy said. "Can't you do better than that?"

"I thought 'twas rather clever, actually," Durrik replied, leaning down to rub his withered leg. "Aught to distract me from how empty my tummy's a-feeling. Isn't there anything else t'eat at all, Pedrin?"

"Not a crumb," Pedrin answered forlornly. "We ate it all for dinner last night. Nah, I'm afraid 'tis air pudding for brekkie. Unless Briony knows of an inn just ahead that serves fried eggs and ham."

His rather lame attempt at a joke fell flat as a pancake. Lisandre and Durrik glanced at Briony, sitting silently, her ragdoll cuddled close to her thin chest, and then they glanced away, embarrassed. Briony said nothing.

"Well," said Pedrin, looking rather forlornly at the bowl that Briony had put out for the wildkin the night before and which had been licked well and truly clean, "I s'pose we might as well get on our way. We're a-going to have to get ahead of those soldiers, if we can."

"They will not be able to move very quickly if they need to carry Lord Zavion in a litter," Lisandre said. "Surely we can gain some ground if we hurry?"

The starkin princess had, in the last few days, grown quite fluent in Adalheid, for the other children tended to talk amongst themselves in their own language, which Lisandre had found very irritating. After much patient translation by Durrik, Lisandre had gradually picked up the most commonly used words, using Ziverian for any word or expression she did not know. Similarly, the other three peppered their speech with Ziverian words to help deepen her understanding, so that conversation between them now ran smoothly and comfortably.

Now the starkin princess was reluctantly easing her swollen feet back into Durrik's shoes, wincing at the pain of her blisters and uttering, quite unconsciously, one of the favourite curses of the hearthkin: "Tessula's tears, that hurts!"

"Are you sure you'll a-manage with your feet so sore?" Briony asked.

"I am sure I shall manage perfectly well, thank you," Lisandre said stiffly, unable to meet her eyes. "Do not concern yourself with me."

All day they felt awkward with Briony, unable to

forget how she had cuddled the huge black spider to her cheek. Even Pedrin, who prided himself on his stoicism, could not have borne the spider's touch with fortitude. None of them had ever known a girl that was not repulsed by spiders, at the very least.

Even more difficult to deal with was Briony's admission that she knew things that others did not. The other children could not help wondering uneasily if she was reading their thoughts. Such insight smacked too much of the Craft for anyone to be at all easy in their minds, particularly Lisandre, who had been taught to fear and revile the Crafty. Even Pedrin, whose mother regularly sought the advice of the hedge-witch Naoma, felt uneasy and even a little frightened. Briony had seemed such an ordinary sort of a girl but every day spent in her company revealed new and mysterious depths. Pedrin even began to doubt her motives, wondering why she was leading them ever deeper into the Perilous Forest. He had to remind himself quite sharply that she had put herself in grave danger to help rescue them from the wood-sprites, yet once again he wondered why she had done so, and to fear she had some other, hidden purpose.

It was a long, wearisome day. They walked for hours, following the river towards its source, each one of them tired and scared and troubled. All knew the starkin soldiers were there in the forest somewhere, searching for them, led by the sinister Lord Zavion. All knew the forest was filled with many perils, most of them unknown. All felt the strain of the past few weeks. Added to that was the discomfort of hunger, for they had not dared take the time for fishing. All they had to sustain them was the thin sweet milk that Snowflake never failed to provide, and a handful of mulberries Briony plucked from a tree.

At last they had to stop to rest, unable to walk another step on swollen, throbbing feet and aching legs. They chose a quiet pool, with a clear view down the river so that they would have early warning of anyone following them. The evening sun slanted down through the brown water, highlighting the softly waving weeds and lazy fish drifting along the bottom. Although Pedrin dangled a line in the water, none of the fish bothered to bite and so he lay back in the grass, the fishing line wrapped around his splayed toes, letting his weary body relax.

Thundercloud roamed all about the clearing, leaping onto the high roots of the trees, trying to reach the unripe nuts high in the branches. Snowflake lay beside Pedrin, her head resting on her dainty black hooves. Briony sat apart, her mouth drooping wistfully, playing cat's cradle with a loop of string. The sight made Pedrin rather sad. She seemed so very alone.

Along the banks were bushes whose long branches trailed in the water, coloured as vividly as the sunset sky. "Look at those gorgeous flowers," Lisandre exclaimed, dabbling her hot, tired feet in the water. "What a remarkable colour."

Briony smiled briefly, lowering the intricate net of string woven about her fingers. "I wouldn't try and pick a bunch."

"Why not?"

"They're not flowers," Briony answered. "Look." She pulled one hand free, reaching down and dragging one of the flowering branches towards her. With a little start of surprise, the others realised that what they had thought were blossoms were indeed tiny orange frogs, clinging to the twig with enormous green toes.

"Urgh!" Lisandre said, shrinking away.

"You thought they were pretty when you thought they were flowers," Briony said sadly, and let the branch dangle in the water once again.

"Well, so much for the perils of the Perilous Forest," Pedrin said, idly kicking his foot so his lure would bob up and down in the water. "From the stories I'd heard I thought we'd be a-fighting gibgoblins and hob-henkies every step of the way."

Like Durrik, he was trying to find a way to bridge the unease that had grown between them, but it was an attempt doomed to failure. Briony gave him an unusually direct look from eyes as clear and brown as the river. "We're only a few days into the forest," she said. "The wildkin hate and fear those of your kind. They don't live near the edge of the woodland but deep within the shelter of the trees. We shall be a-seeing more of the wildkin now we're a-venturing into the heart of the forest."

Pedrin frowned and chewed on a blade of grass. Something odd about Briony's statement was niggling at him but he could not put his finger on it. He glanced at her and she blushed and dropped her eyes to the geometric pattern of string laid out on her lap. He found himself wondering what colour her eyes really were.

Just then they heard a distant tinkle of music. Lisandre stiffened all over, her face draining of colour. "Ziggy's night-light!" she cried, jumping to her feet. "But who...?" Before the others could stop her, she ran down the path, her red skirt all bunched up in her hands. The others scrambled up, exchanging quick glances of dismay and anxiety.

"Go with her, Thundercloud!" Pedrin cried, struggling to untangle his fishing line from his toes.

The shaggy black billy-goat bounded after her, his horns low. Pedrin raced behind, fumbling for his slingshot. *Cabbage-head!* he thought to himself. *To go a-running off like that, just when we were a-talking about the dangers of the forest!*

Pedrin caught up with Lisandre just as she came panting into a small gully by a deep, shadowy pool of water. The air struck at them with a chill, causing their skin to shrink with gooseflesh. The gully was rimmed around by high cliffs, their mossy roots sunk in the green-dark water. The banks were overgrown with curling fronds of fern and bracken, while tall stately trees soared high into the sky, their branches intermingling so all was quiet and dim in the small clearing below. The only sound was the roaring of the waterfall where the river tumbled down the cliff in foaming white cataracts.

Where the waterfall hit the pool, the water churned and boiled but elsewhere the water's surface was dark and tranquil. No birds or frogs sang, no insect chirruped, no fish broke the mirror-still gleam. There was a great patch of burnt ground where a bonfire had once been lit, but otherwise there was no sign of life.

Then they saw him. An old man, sitting on a log, his bare legs dangling in the water. He was an odd-looking creature. He wore a long coat, woven from leafy willow twigs, over mud-coloured trousers rolled to the knee. On his head was a cap woven from rushes. His face was very long and thin and mournful, with a big, high-boned nose that jutted out from beneath the brim of the cap. Long straggles of gingery-white hair hung halfway down his back, all snarled with old leaves and burrs. His straggly white beard was so long the end dangled down into the water, while his mouth was completely hidden beneath a shaggy moustache.

Involuntarily Lisandre and Pedrin drew together, the goat-boy sinking his fingers into Thundercloud's shaggy black coat. Behind him he heard Durrik's halting step, Briony's light tread and the patter of Snowflake's hooves. He glanced back at them with a frown and a jerk of his head. There was something about this cold shadowy gully that made him feel uneasy, and he could see by their faces that the others felt it too. They all came together into a little bunch, the goats standing protectively in front.

The old man did not seem to have noticed them. He was looking down at something he held in his hands, something which glittered even in that uncertain light. Then the exquisite strain of music filled the air again.

Lisandre sprung towards him, all her wariness

forgotten. "That's Ziggy's!" she cried, half-sobbing. "What do you do with it? How dare you?"

He looked up at them, his eyes very dark and bright on either side of the preposterous nose, and swiftly tucked one hand beneath the skirt of his coat of willow twigs. He spread the other out in a deprecating gesture. "I'm just a-sitting enjoying the evening, little miss. What's in that to get you into such a botheration?"

"You have Ziggy's night-light! I heard its music and I saw it in your hand. Give it back! It's not yours."

"Now, now, not so hasty, little miss. Whatever you a-talking about? Do you mean the moon? That's the only light I ever have at night, unless I catch a glow-worm. And I certainly don't have the moon in me hand, nor a glow-worm neither."

"I'm not talking about a glow-worm," Lisandre cried. "I'm talking about my brother's christening egg. Do you not realise it was a gift from the king himself? How dare you lay your filthy thieving hands upon it!"

"Now, that's not polite," he said with great dignity. "I'll have you know me hands are very clean." He spread both of them out for her to see. They were very long and bony, and covered in gingery-white hair. "And to call someone a thief when you hardly know him is not at all nice, particularly when you're just a little girl and I am really quite elderly. I must say I wonder about the youth of today. They have no respect, no respect at all."

Lisandre blushed. "I'm sorry, sir, I did not mean to be discourteous," she said haltingly, the first time any

197

of the other children had heard her apologise. Durrik and Pedrin exchanged little grins as Lisandre hurried into speech again. "But you do have my brother's christening egg, I saw it in your hands and I heard it playing. Where did you get it? Give it back to me!"

"I thought 'twas a night-light you were a-talking about. Now 'tis an egg? I do wish you'd make up your mind. You young things are so muddled. Clear thinking, that's what you need, clear thinking and clear speaking."

Lisandre stamped her foot. "You had it, I saw it! Give it back now!"

"Now, now, little miss, manners!" he said reprovingly, so that Pedrin's grin grew wider.

Lisandre gave a little shriek of frustration and swooped upon him, searching him hastily. He held up both hands in protest. "So hasty! So rash!"

But Lisandre had given a little crow of triumph, finding a bulge within his twiggy coat. She tried to drag it free but could find no way to open the pocket. Frantically she tugged at it, and would have torn the twigs asunder if she could. He sighed and shook his head. "Is that any way to behave, young missy? Me father would have taken a willow-switch to me if I'd acted like that when I was your age. Stand back, I say, and bide your time."

Chastened, Lisandre fell back, though her face was hot and angry, her jaw thrust forward.

"Now, now," he said, sliding his fingers within his coat and pulling out a jewelled orb that flashed in the last rays of the sun. "I s'pose this is what you were after?" Lisandre gave a little sob. "Yes! That's my brother's night-light."

"Well, I don't know why you didn't say so from the very beginning," the old man said, waggling his beard from side to side. "All this talk of glow-worms and eggs, you had me fair befuddled."

Lisandre's chest rose and fell rapidly. "What are you doing with my brother's night-light?" she demanded, her voice trembling. "Where did you get it?"

She reached out both hands and tried to seize it, but he held it fast, saying reprovingly, "No snatching now, little missy. I must say, I wonder at your parents, they don't seem to have taught you no manners at all."

She let it go, biting her lip and bunching her skirt up tightly with both hands.

The old man's moustache twitched as if, underneath all that hair, he was smiling. He looked down at the glittering thing in his hands, and the moustache dropped mournfully once more, the shaggy brows drawing over the eyes, hiding them. Of midnight-blue enamel, the orb was crisscrossed with delicate bands of gold. At the point where each band crossed was a golden star set with a glittering jewel, while two narrow strips of diamonds circled the orb. Another big diamond was set at its apex, flashing with rainbow fire.

"I knew 'twas trouble the moment I first seen it," he said ruefully. "I felt it in me bones. I should've left it where I found it—"

"Where? Where did you find it?"

He gave Lisandre a reproving glance. "—But it a-glittered like the moon on water and when I picked it up, it opened up its secret heart to me. It seemed then it was meant for me, and so I thought, well, if you don't take it, Sedgely, the moon-cursers will. They took everything else."

He touched it with a long bony finger and the egg split into two, the top half rising up smoothly to reveal a little carousel of golden horses. Delicately wrought, each horse had a different coloured saddle and bridle, one set with rubies, another with emeralds, yet another with sapphires and the fourth set with yellow diamonds. As the music played, the horses rose up and down as they circled round and round. At last the music came to an end, and the two halves of the egg folded together again, hiding the carousel from view.

"Oh, 'tis lovely," Briony said with a sigh. She had drawn close to the old man and now gave him one of her rare, shy smiles.

"What do you mean, the moon-cursers? Who or what are they?" Lisandre demanded impatiently. "What do they have to do with my brother?"

Sedgely shot Lisandre a glance from under his bushy white brows and did not answer.

"He means the outlaws," Briony said quietly.

"Yeah. Outlaws. Big rough noisy men with sharp swords and quick tempers. You should keep out of their way, little missy. They'd cut off your pretty fingers for all those fine rings you're flashing about."

Lisandre looked down at her hands in dismay. She wore several rings set with amethysts, sapphires and diamonds. Selfconsciously she hid her hands under the folds of her skirt.

"Why do you call them moon-cursers?" Pedrin asked.

"Because they curse the moon, of course," the strange old man said. "They like the night to be dark so no one can see them as they lurk about. Though whether the moon shines or not, *I* still see them as they bring their boats up and down the river." He gave a dry chuckle. "I see them but they don't see me."

"Forget the outlaws, what about Ziggy's egg? Where did you find it? Take me there!" Lisandre was dancing about in her impatience.

"I wouldn't be forgetting about the moon-cursers if I were you, little missy," Sedgely said. "You don't want to fall into their clutches. They've a grudge against the starkin, the moon-cursers do, and I don't doubt they'd be pleased to lay their hands upon the dead count's pretty daughter."

Lisandre lost all her angry colour. "How do you know who I am?" she demanded. "Who are you anyway?"

The old man stood up, swept off his cap of rushes and made an elaborate bow. "I'm Sedgely, little missy. And you told me yourself who you were, for you said the boy who played with that starry egg was your brother and I'd seen for meself that he was the old count's son. Though I would've guessed for meself, I think, for you have a great look of the boy about you."

"You saw my father and my brother? You stole the

201

egg from Ziggy? What did you do to them? If it was you … if you were the one who hurt them, I'll … I'll…" Lisandre was incoherent with rage and grief.

Sedgely's shaggy brows drew together. "So now you accuse me of murder as well as thievery, little missy. What can have given you such an idea about me?"

"You have Ziggy's night-light," she stammered.

"And that makes me a murderer?"

Lisandre scrubbed at her eyes angrily. "You have his night-light. Do you not understand that it was a christening gift from the king himself, a mark of great favour and esteem? Ziggy would not lose it or give it away, particularly not to a ragged old man like yourself. What else am I meant to think?"

"You could mebbe ask me, politely, how I came to have your brother's starry egg?"

Once again Lisandre was confounded. Her face burnt with embarrassment. For a moment she had nothing to say, and then she asked stiffly, "Well then, how do you happen to have it?"

"Well, I've heard questions more prettily phrased in me time but I s'pose it shall have to do, the youth of today being what they are," Sedgely replied, tugging at his beard. "Well then, I guess you'll want the full tale, and me, I like t'take me time in the telling of tales. I don't s'pose you young ones are hungry, are you? For I've found a-eating and a-listening go rather well together, don't you agree? And certainly 'tis easier to keep things straight when the sides of your stomach aren't a-flapping."

"It certainly is," Pedrin agreed fervently. "And we're starving."

"'Tis me experience that young ones like you usually are," the old man said, his moustache twitching again.

"The count and his men were all in a merry mood," Sedgely said, a leg of roast pigeon in one hand, a wooden cup of goat's milk in the other.

"They came up the path along the river, a-talking and a-laughing, the dogs a-barking and a-rushing about with their noses to the ground. Such a noise they made! I could've told them 'tis asking for trouble, to be a-making such a noise in the heart of the Perilous Forest. But I doubt they'd have listened."

He sighed, shook his head sadly and took a bite of pigeon leg. Lisandre urged him on, saying, "So what happened? Was it the moon-cursers?"

He chewed ruminatively, then took another great mouthful. Lisandre gripped her hands together in frustration. "I'd eat up, little missy," he said. "I daresay it'll be a long while before you get a good meal like this again."

It was indeed a feast he had spread out before them. Five plump roasted pigeons, coal-baked yams, some crunchy green beans, and a bowl full of tiny fried fish, no longer than Briony's smallest finger but very tasty indeed. The others were all eating steadily, but Lisandre was too overwrought to eat. As if sensing her tension, Snowflake lay beside her, rubbing her horned head against Lisandre's leg.

Sedgely waited until Lisandre had picked at the laden plate before her, then said, "The starkin lords were all cheerful because they thought they were hot on the trail of the gibberhog boar, but roundabouts here the trail suddenly turned cold, Old Tusky being cleverer than they gave him credit for. So they set up camp, not a-wanting to try to climb the rocks in the dark, which shows some sense, at least, I suppose. It was a clear, moonlit night, though bitter-cold and with a nasty nip to the wind. I could've told them it would snow before morning, if I'd thought they'd listen..."

Lisandre gave a little sigh of impatience. Sedgely took a deep drink from his wooden cup, looked down into it and sighed also, though his was a sigh of the deepest regret. "Milk again," he said. "I must say, kind as 'twas of you to leave me a little present for all the fish and berries you've been a-taking, I would've liked a nice drop of apple-ale for a change. You should've thought to provide yourself with some, but there you have it. No foresight, the youth of today."

Pedrin let his pigeon leg drop as he stared at the old man, sitting all hunched by the fire with his long bony face surrounded by a wild halo of snarled and knotted hair. "So it was you who drank the milk," he said. "But I thought it was for..." He bit back the rest of his words but saw how both Briony and Sedgely looked at him. The tips of his ears turned red. He took refuge in his pigeon leg.

"The count and his men had a barrel of apple-ale but they did not think to leave out a cup for me," Sedgely said sadly. "No manners, those of starkin blood. I've often noted it."

Lisandre turned a deep crimson. "I'll have you know the court of the Ziv is renowned for its courtesy and chivalry."

"Is that so, little missy? Well, I've never been to the court of the Ziv so I can't comment, but I do know those starkin lords never gave a thought to any poor thirsty soul that might have appreciated a small drop of apple-ale. I don't know what you starkin consider good manners but I reckon if you traipse all through someone's home and help yourself to their larder, the least you could do is offer them a nightcap."

This time it was Lisandre who took refuge in her pigeon leg. Sedgely sighed and stroked his tangled beard. "They drank deeply, those starkin lords, of the apple-ale. They were very merry then. Most of them danced, all by themselves in the darkness, a-stamping down the snow, a-leaping over the fire, a-shouting and a-singing. The noise they made! I could've told them the Perilous Forest is not the place to be a-making such a ruckus..."

The children looked at each other, surprised. Hearthkin men always danced by themselves, with great vigour and pride, but the starkin thought such behaviour uncivilised. Starkin men danced only with starkin women, moving with slow and stately grace, no part of their bodies touching but their hands. It was most peculiar to hear of starkin lords dancing by themselves, in darkness, in snow, singing.

"Your brother didn't dance," Sedgely said. He shot Lisandre a glance from under his shaggy eyebrows. She was listening intently, her hands gripped together tightly. "He sat and listened and smiled, with the singing egg a-turning in his hands. They offered him a cup of the apple-ale too, with much a-laughing and a-teasing, but he drank only a spit's worth."

"Ziggy does not much like apple-ale," Lisandre said with a little gulp of breath. "The men were all teasing him about it as they were getting ready to fly out on the hunt. They said he'd be drinking it by the barrel-full by the time he came back, with the gibberhog's head on a spike. His first kill would make him a man, they said. Lady Donella told them to stop teasing him, for he was just a boy still. It would be a long while before he developed a taste for it, she said."

Sedgely shook his snarled white head. "Fancy not having a taste for apple-ale." He gazed sadly down into his own cup, raised it to his lips and drained the last drop with a little grimace. "Ah, milk just does not quench a man's thirst."

He sat staring miserably into his cup for such a long time that Lisandre rose to her knees and offered him the bucket. "Perhaps some more would help?" she asked.

Briony, Pedrin and Durrik all exchanged glances of incredulous delight. They had never seen Lisandre lift a finger to help herself, let alone anyone else. Whoever this strange old man was, he seemed to have a knack for humbling the proud starkin princess.

"Mebbe another cup will help," Sedgely agreed, though so gloomily it seemed clear he did not really expect so. Lisandre dipped his cup in the bucket and passed it back to him.

"So what happened next?" she prompted as he drank again.

He wiped his moustache with the back of his hand. "Naught," he replied sadly. "They fell asleep. But in the morning they didn't awake. Snow had fallen in the night and covered them up like a rug. Icicles sprouted in their eyebrows, and hung from the ends of their noses. Oh, it was a-cold! One of the dogs was a-howling and a-howling, loud enough to wake the dead, you'd have thought, though it didn't."

Lisandre was weeping. "But how? Why? Was it the cold?"

"And them all in their rich furs and velvets, and a fire high enough to burn an oak?" He swept out one hand, indicating the great burnt-out patch in the clearing behind them. "I wouldn't think so."

Lisandre hunched in on herself, looking sick. "It was here? This is where it happened?"

"Of course. Didn't you ask me where I'd found the singing egg? It was here." He pointed with one long bony finger. "It must've fallen from your brother's hand and been covered with the snow, for I didn't find it till the spring thaw. By that time the other starkin had come and shot the howling dog and gathered up the bodies and taken them away, and the moon-cursers had looted everything that was left. All I found was the singing egg and a gem-studded goblet, and that I don't like t'use."

Lisandre was too upset to wonder why, but Pedrin always had to know the why and the what and the wherefore, and so of course he asked instantly.

"I'll show you if you like," Sedgely replied. He got up stiffly, with a groan and a hand to his back, and dug around in the hollow end of the fallen log. He pulled out a golden goblet, all set with flashing diamonds and sapphires. Within was a black stain and corrosion, so that the goblet's lip was almost eaten away on one side.

"What could've caused that, I wonder?" the goatherd said softly, touching the corroded metal with one finger.

"Surely apple-ale wouldn't?" Durrik replied. The eyes of the two boys met.

"So was it poisoned? But what sort of poison would eat away gold like that? And who'd want to do such a thing?" Pedrin gave a little shudder.

"Lord Zavion would," Lisandre said miserably. "He's the closest male heir. Already the king has granted him the Regency and once Ziggy dies he'll be declared Count of Estelliana. And he's in love with my mother, I know he is. This way he gets both my father's crown and my father's wife, without having to get his lily-white hands dirty."

"Very quick you are to label a man a murderer," Sedgely said, lying back with his head pillowed on his hands. "Why, you called me one after you'd only

209

known me for five minutes. 'Tis a black label to fix to a man, on so little evidence." He yawned widely. "You shouldn't be so hasty, little missy. But that's the youth of today. Always in too much of a hurry. No time for reflection or repose."

He fell silent. After a moment of waiting politely for him to speak again, they realised he was snoring gently. His beard waggled with every snore.

Lisandre turned the corroded goblet in her hands. She gave a little heart-rending sob, and then covered her face with her hands, her shoulders shaking. Durrik and Pedrin tried to comfort her as best they could, but she was inconsolable.

"Not fair … my papa … no one… How can I … and Ziggy… I wish … oh, I wish … why? Why?"

Briony got up and went to kneel beside her, hugging her gently. Lisandre, forgetting her repugnance for someone who liked to cuddle spiders, pressed her head into Briony's shoulder and sobbed heartbrokenly.

After a long moment she sat up, hiding her face in her hands. Briony got her a cup of water and Lisandre drank obediently, her sobs finally subsiding. Briony handed her a handkerchief, and Lisandre wiped her eyes and blew her nose with great delicacy. Even with her eyes and nose all red and swollen, she looked so pretty that both Durrik and Pedrin were wrung with helpless pity.

After a while Pedrin said awkwardly, "I don't have a pa any more either, y'know. He died a few years back. Killed by a gibgoblin."

"And I haven't got a mother," Durrik offered, though he coloured hotly, looking down at the tip of his crutch as he dug it into the ground.

"I might as well not have," Lisandre sighed, dabbing at her eyes with her handkerchief, by now very crumpled and grimy. "Since my father died, she's been in another world. It's like not having a mother at all."

"What happened to your ma?" Pedrin asked Durrik, having never thought to ask before. "She died when you were a baby, didn't she?"

"She didn't die," Durrik replied curtly, not meeting anyone's eyes. "She left us. I don't know why. I never knew her."

"I never knew either of me parents." Briony's soft, shy voice fell into the silence. "I was abandoned – or lost – or stolen. I don't know what."

"That's dreadful," Lisandre said awkwardly. "I'm so sorry."

"At least you knew your father," Briony said. "And you had him for twelve years. You knew he loved you." This time the silence stretched a long time. "And there's still hope for your brother," Briony continued. "And for your mother too. Grief rarely kills." There was a sardonic edge to her voice, the first time they had ever heard her sound anything but timid and demure.

Lisandre stirred restlessly, crushing her handkerchief into a little ball. "But Lord Zavion's crystal tower only made things worse. And I've come all this way … and had all my hair cut off … and I hurt all over … and for what? I've discovered nothing. Nothing!"

"That's not true," Durrik said comfortingly. "We know your father and brother drank some kind of poison. That's something."

"But what am I supposed to do now!" wailed Lisandre.

"There's still the Erlrune," Briony said hesitantly. "She might have the answer, I s'pose. She's meant to be able to see many things in that pool of hers. They call it the Well of Fate, for if you look within you can see what was, what is and what shall be. Or so they say."

"Or so who says?" Pedrin asked, eyeing her curiously.

Briony went crimson and did not answer, dropping her eyes. After a moment, and with obvious difficulty, she said, "The Erlrune may help us in deciphering the prophecy too. For don't you think it interesting we now number five?" She nodded towards Sedgely, fast asleep on the far side of the fire.

Lisandre and Pedrin both looked baffled, but a grim shadow fell upon Durrik's face. He turned his head away, staring out into the night, and Snowflake crept closer to him, bleating gently. He rubbed her soft white ear between his fingers.

"Do you not remember? Durrik said summat about six separate threads, woven into one. Six different people, brought together. Milady and I set out on this adventure, just the two of us, and then we met you two boys, and now Sedgely…"

Lisandre was staring at her incredulously. "You

mean you take all that stuff and nonsense Durrik was spouting seriously? It was nothing but a bag of moonshine! His brains were fried by that bolt of lightning. It doesn't mean a thing."

Durrik stared at her angrily. "My brains weren't fried! I don't know where it all came from but 'tis not stuff and nonsense, that I do know!" His voice rose defiantly, yet his face was still set in lines of misery and uncertainty. Durrik had not once spoken of the cryptic prophecy he had made that day in the crystal tower and, troubled and uneasy about it himself, Pedrin had been careful not to bring it up.

Now he glared angrily at Lisandre as the starkin princess, always unheeding of other people's feelings, said contemptuously: "How do you know? Do you have any idea what it is all supposed to mean?"

"I can figure some of it out," Durrik said defensively. "The first few lines seem obvious, really." His eyes fixed dreamily on the flickering flames, he quoted softly:

"Under winter's cold shroud, the son of light lies
Though the summer sun burns high in the skies.
With the last petal of the starthorn tree
His wandering spirit shall at last slip free,
Nothing can save him from this bitter curse,
But the turning of time itself inverse.

"The son of light is your brother, obviously. Everyone knows that's what 'Ziv' really means. The children of light."

"Actually," Lisandre said coldly, "it means 'those that brightly shine'."

"Whatever," Durrik said rather huffily. "It obviously still means your brother. And when the last petal of the starthorn tree falls, that means the end of autumn and the beginning of winter. 'Cause the starthorn tree is all backwards. It blooms in autumn and is fruitful in winter, when all t'other trees are bare. So that means we've only got until the end of autumn to be a-finding the antidote, 'cause that's when the last petal shall fall."

"The antidote?" Lisandre sounded bewildered.

"Antidote," Durrik repeated loudly. "To counteract the poison."

"Poison?"

"Yeah, the poison." Durrik stared at her, surprised, and jerked his thumb at the goblet with its black corroded stain.

To his surprise, Lisandre's face crumpled again and she began to cry quietly. She really was the only girl he had ever seen who could look pretty while crying, even with her face all dirty and her fair hair sticking straight up like a duckling's down. He looked at her in consternation, and patted her arm ineffectually.

"So you ... really think ... we can find a cure for ... Ziggy?" she hiccuped.

"Well, don't you think that's what it means? That bit about the 'turning of time inverse'? 'Tis a bit obscure, I admit, but couldn't it just mean a-finding the antidote to the poison, and returning Count Zygmunt to the way he was before? 'Antidote' kind of means 'going back', doesn't it?"

"I suppose it could mean that," Pedrin said rather doubtfully. "Though it seems too easy."

"Well, 'tis not going to be easy to find the antidote to the poison, because we have no idea what the poison was," Durrik said.

"But maybe this witch could tell us," Lisandre said excitedly. "Witches know all about curses and poisons and things, don't they?"

Unconsciously all three turned and looked at Briony, who flushed miserably and looked away.

"Well, from everything I've ever heard about the Erlrune, 'tis not just a matter of knocking on her front door and saying, 'please, can you tell us how to break the curse on the count?' She doesn't exactly welcome visitors, does she?" Pedrin spoke quickly.

The others all looked back at him, Lisandre with consternation. "Why, what do you mean? I am of the Ziv. Surely she would welcome me gladly?"

"Yeah, with open arms," Pedrin said sarcastically. "Really, you are such a cabbage-head sometimes! 'Tis not just the moon-cursers who hate the starkin, you know. Why, the Crafty used to be well respected and even powerful before the starkin came. Now they are outlawed, and have to live in hiding and ply their trade in secret."

"They are nothing but frauds and charlatans," Lisandre replied hotly. "They dupe the credulous with their talk of being able to see the future or talk to ghosts. It is the starkin's responsibility to protect those less fortunate from their own folly—"

"And milady of the Ziv expects the Erlrune to welcome her gladly?" Pedrin said.

Lisandre thrust out her jaw stubbornly.

"If you think the Erlrune is a fraud and a charlatan, and her Well of Fate naught but trickery, why do you seek to consult it?" Briony asked gently.

Lisandre crimsoned. "I thought perhaps it was some kind of machine," she answered lamely.

The others all laughed at her, and her jaw thrust out further still. "I'm willing to try anything to save my brother," she said angrily. "Even if she cannot really see anything in that pool of hers, this witch may be able to tell us what sort of poison it was. She may even know the cure. It certainly makes more sense to go and consult her than it does to believe in a whole lot of gobbledygook. Durrik may think he understands the first half of his little rhyme but the rest of it makes no sense at all!"

"Nah," Briony said quietly. "I thought it made perfect sense, the last bit. Say it all again, Durrik."

The shadow on Durrik's face deepened. He hesitated, his face bent, then said gruffly:

"If those long apart can together be spun
Six separate threads woven into one,
Two seeking destiny in heaven's countless eyes,
Two of the old blood, children of the wise,
Two iron-bound, that tend the hearth's red heat,
Six brought together can the cruel bane defeat."

Lisandre shrugged contemptuously. "Very well then, Briony, tell me what it means."

"Well, 'Two seeking destiny in heaven's countless eyes', that has to be two people of starkin blood, doesn't it?" Briony said. "'Heaven's countless eyes' means the stars, don't you see? And 'Two of the old blood,

216

children of the wise', that means two of the wildkin. They are often called the Old Ones or the Wise Ones, didn't you know? And 'Two iron-bound, that tend the hearth's red heat—'"

"The hearthkin, of course," Pedrin said wonderingly. "But why 'iron-bound'?"

"Well, you are bound, aren't you?" Briony said. "Bound to the starkin's service, by plough-share, spade and hoe."

"Yeah, I see," Pedrin said and felt his ears begin to burn.

Lisandre said impatiently, "But that basically means it's an impossibility, doesn't it? Two starkin, two hearthkin and two wildkin, brought together as one? It's like saying the curse will only be lifted when hens grow teeth, or when pigs fly. It can never happen."

"Yet here we all are," Briony said softly.

Lisandre stared. "Whatever can you mean, Briony? There may be five of us here now but I am the only one of starkin blood, and I cannot see that changing, unless of course you expect Lord Zavion to join forces with us?"

Briony looked at Durrik. Unaccountably he went red and looked away.

"Shouldn't you tell them?" Briony said in her soft, gentle voice.

"Tell us what?" Pedrin felt a sullen rage take hold of him.

Briony said nothing, just kept looking at Durrik, who was digging at the earth with the tip of his crutch, unable to meet anyone's eyes.

"I s'pose she means I should tell you that my mother was one of the starkin," he said at last, raising his eyes to meet Pedrin's. "I don't see that 'tis of any real importance. I'm as much hearthkin as I am starkin, and I never knew her or any of her people. I was raised by my father. He was her music tutor, down in Zarissa, many years ago. They fell in love and eloped together, but my mother found it too hard to bear, all the whispers and sideways glances, and of course, a-giving up the life of the starkin to be with a mere hearthkin. They said it was her punishment, to bear a son who was crippled." There was real bitterness in his voice. "So she went back to her family and left me with my papa, which was just fine by me."

Pedrin stared at him as if he were a stranger. It explained many things, of course. The delicacy of Durrik's hands and face, the fairness of his hair, the fluency with which he spoke Ziverian, the many precious things in his house. Now he looked, Pedrin could see how similar Durrik was to Lisandre, especially now the starkin girl's fine blond hair was cut so short. He marvelled that he had never noticed it before. Briony had, of course. Her changeable eyes saw everything. He found he was as angry with her as he was with Durrik. He could not have explained why he was angry, he could not separate the hurt and jealousy and resentment and disappointment that knotted themselves together into a hard lump in his throat. He just knew it infuriated him that she should see so quickly and easily what he himself had never noticed.

Although Lisandre was not angry, she too was staring at Durrik with shocked and horrified eyes. "A half-breed!" she whispered. Unconsciously she drew a little away from the crippled boy, even as Pedrin had done.

Durrik gritted his teeth and looked down at his feet. His eyes glittered with angry tears.

Briony said miserably, "'Tis not Durrik's fault, Lisandre. He's still the same boy, regardless of who his mother was. It wouldn't matter a bit, except it shows there's some truth to the prophecy. There's two of starkin blood here, you and Durrik."

"Well, what about the wildkin then?" Lisandre said coldly, still holding herself aloof. "You cannot tell me you expect us to make friends with a gibgoblin now? There might be five of us here together at the moment but I don't see horns or scales or fangs on any of us!"

Briony bit back a smile. "Not all wildkin have scales or fangs, milady," she said gently. She nodded at Sedgely, sleeping peacefully on the far side of the fire. His nose stuck up out of the white tangle of his hair like a mountain peak out of a snowy forest, and his leafy coat rose and fell with every snore. "Didn't you realise?"

Lisandre looked shaken. "*He's* wildkin? Really? But I thought ... he looks just like an old beggar-man! Are you sure?"

"He told us so himself," Briony said. "You mustn't have been a-listening very closely."

Something in her tone stung Pedrin. He said, "And what about you, Briony? You always say 'you hearthkin', never 'we hearthkin'. So are you wildkin too?"

All the amusement died out of Briony's face. She hunched her shoulders, her arms wrapped close about her knees. Fire shadows danced over her face, making her eyes glint red. "I don't know what I am," she replied unhappily.

16

The wind was brisk the next morning, the leaves sharp-edged against the crystal-cold sky. The children were glad to huddle round the fire, exchanging rather stilted remarks on the weather as they held their numb hands to the blaze. All found it difficult to meet anyone else's eyes. Once again the confessions of the night had caused a chill, a constraint, to grow up between them.

"Jumping Jimjinny, I'm hungry!" Pedrin looked rather hopefully towards the pool, where Sedgely was wading, his ratty trousers rolled above the knee.

Pedrin was not yet sure how he felt about the revelation that Sedgely was a wildkin. His own father had died horribly at the hands of a gibgoblin, so horribly that the very thought of it made Pedrin's insides flinch and loosen. His fear and hatred of wildkin had been intense ever since, and the goatherd had only been able to sleep fitfully, waking several times to check that the old man still slept peacefully, his nose pointed to the stars. Not long before dawn, Pedrin's overwrought mind had decided it was all rubbish and he had slipped into a deep, dreamless sleep.

Now, in the bright light of morning, Pedrin found it even harder to believe. Apart from the preposterous size of his jutting nose and the wildness of his hair, Sedgely looked and talked just like any irascible old man who sat outside the village inn on a summer evening, complaining about the weather and the ache in his bones, and drinking a jug of apple-ale dry.

He certainly did not seem feral, like the wildkin were supposed to be. Pedrin had been taught that the wildkin were the creatures that had first swarmed out of the ocean of tears that Tessula had wept in his bitter loneliness. His tears had fallen upon the dry, lifeless womb of Imala, the earth-goddess, and his intense longing had given his tears power. Imala had given birth to a myriad of creatures, great and small, all of them wild, dangerous and unpredictable, carrying within them the desperate grief of a god.

This first creation of life had enthralled Tessula and Imala, however, and so they had come together to create six perfect children. Imala had taken the soil of her body and the salt-water of Tessula's tears and, in the resulting clay, formed the shape of three girls and three boys. She had laboured long in their creation so they would be as slim and supple and shapely as possible. Tessula had then breathed his god-force into them, and thus Lullalita, Liah, Taramis, Marithos, Tallis and Chtatchka were born. Made in love and joy, these six children were radiant with beauty and strength. Tessula was so pleased and overjoyed at their birth that he gave a great exhalation of breath and, without meaning to, animated the little, clumsy clay body that was Imala's first attempt at creating form. Neither boy nor girl, this child was named Jerimy and he was to be the eternal child, never growing beyond the innocent years of mischief and self-absorption.

The seven children of the gods played together happily, growing every day, and soon they too began to make shapes in the mud of the world and breathe life into them, and so all the birds and animals and reptiles of the world were made. But as the children of the gods grew older, they wanted new playmates and so they stopped experimenting with different shapes and forms and made a host of figures in their own shape. Each of the young gods and goddesses gave these figures a gift – Lullalita gave the capacity for grief, Liah the light of reason, Taramis the ability to dream and long for something beyond this world, Marithos the desire for order and the ability to create limits, and Chtatchka the power of anger. Jerimy the Eternal Child gave laughter and lies, and Tallis the moon god gave wisdom, the gift of the knowledge of death.

So the hearthkin were born, and soon spread and populated the world, giving the nine greater gods all the honour they deserved. Some mated with the gods and goddesses, giving rise to the ninety-nine lesser gods, and some, it was said, mated with those creatures called the Old Ones, for they were the first and oldest children of the gods, born without reason, imagination or the knowledge of death. Some said the

Crafty was the product of this mating between hearthkin and wildkin, carrying within them the wild magic and the seven gifts of the gods. Others said such a union was impossible, and the Crafty were merely hearthkin that rejected the ordered life of village and guild, and studied their own arcane mysteries without the need to submit to law and tradition.

Certainly that was the explanation most hearthkin accepted, because the idea of a coupling between hearthkin and wildkin seemed so abhorrent. Although the wildkin had always lived alongside the hearthkin, they were considered so very different, so very dangerous, that any other explanation threatened the harmonious order of the hearthkin's society. This was why Pedrin had such difficulty believing Sedgely really was a wildkin, as Briony had said. Deep in his heart he thought he was probably just a crazy old man who had wandered into the forest as a child, and had managed to adapt and survive.

At that very moment, Sedgely lunged forward and came up dripping wet, a fish flapping desperately in his hands. This evidence of skill impressed Pedrin greatly and he found the last vestiges of his fear dissolving away. Sedgely killed the fish with a dexterous slap on the stones and tossed it to a grinning Pedrin, before turning once again to scan the water. Soon three plump fish lay frying in the pan, the delicious smell working its magic on all of their spirits.

"Good old Sedgely," Pedrin said. "Fried fish for brekkie. I could get used to that. I'm a-wondering if he means to come with us? I hope so, if he can catch fish as easy as a-snapping his fingers!"

He asked the old man when he came to sit beside them by the fire.

"Well now," Sedgely said, rubbing the side of his big, bent nose. "I gather you're thinking of a-calling on the Erlrune?"

The children exchanged uneasy glances, wondering how he knew their plans, and if his blissful snores of the night before had been spurious after all. Lisandre in particular looked edgy, pausing with a piece of fish halfway to her mouth, her fair brows drawn close together.

"I can't say I'm on visiting terms with the Erlrune," the old man went on. "She's not the most cosy of acquaintances, if you catch me meaning. Still, I've eaten of your food and drunk of your drink, even though it was only goat's milk and not a nice drop of apple-ale, like I might have hoped. And there's no doubt you're as innocent as the day you were born, with no idea of the dangers you might face. Not that you'd be likely to listen to me anyway. That's the problem with the youth of today. Never a-taking the time to listen." He sighed and shook his wild white head. The children all sat silently, not liking to protest.

"So can you show us the way to the Erlrune?" Pedrin asked at last, when it seemed Sedgely had forgotten the question. "For we need to travel quickly, you know. Already the days are getting shorter."

"Yeah," the old man agreed miserably. "Me poor old bones ache as the weather turns cooler and they're aching today, that I can promise you. There'll be rain tonight, mark me words. If I were you, I'd be a-finding a nice cave to shelter in the next few days, instead of a-pushing on up the river, for the weather's turning nasty, I can feel it in me bones."

The children glanced up at the bright clear sky, then at each other with little grimaces. Lisandre said impatiently, "Yes, but we have not got the leisure to be sitting around in a cave, twiddling our thumbs! The Erlrune is to be found at the source of the river, isn't she? We need to find her, and with all haste."

"Yeah, the river flows down from the Evenlinn," Sedgely said. "Follow the river and you'll reach the Erlrune, sure as the sun will rise tomorrow. If you survive. 'Tis not the easiest of ways to go, following the river."

"Do you mean there are easier?" Pedrin asked quickly.

"Sharp you are, sharp as a bee's sting. Yeah, though 'tis true the Evenlode flows down from the Evenlinn, a-following her is not the best way to reach the lake. The Evenlode does not flow straight, she winds about like an adder. Follow her and you'll be a-winding about too, and it'll be midwinter before you reach the lake. If you cut through the forest, though, you can save a lot of time and bother."

Lisandre looked at Sedgely suspiciously. "But we could also get exceedingly lost," she pointed out. "The river is the only true landmark in this whole wide forest. If we leave the river, we shall have nothing to guide us, for all these trees look the same!"

"I daresay that is true for a little missy that has never before set foot outside her castle gates," Sedgely said. "Luckily for you, I've been a-roaming this forest since I was naught but an unbroken colt. All I need do is follow me nose."

He tapped it knowingly. Durrik gave a little choke of laughter that he swallowed hastily when Sedgely turned reproachful dark eyes upon him.

"Does that mean you'll come with us?" Briony asked anxiously.

"Mebbe," Sedgely answered briefly, pulling his cap of reeds down over his eyes so all they could see of him was a wild halo of snarled white hair and the great jutting nose.

"Please?" Briony asked.

Sedgely lifted his cap and peered at her from under his shaggy brows. "Well, at least one of you has some manners."

"Please, sir?" Pedrin and Durrik chorused.

Lisandre smiled at him winningly. "If you would agree to assist me in this venture, I would be most grateful, sirrah. I am sure my brother would reward you handsomely, once we have woken him from his accursed sleep."

"Indeed? What kind of reward?"

Lisandre tilted her head graciously. "Whatever you desired, if you guided and protected us well."

"Such promises are easily made and easily broken," Sedgely said. "What if I desired your hand in marriage? Would your brother grant me that?"

Lisandre was affronted. "Grant my hand in

marriage to a ragged old man like you? A wildkin? I think not!"

"And what if I asked for your first-born child? Would he agree to that?"

All the colour drained from Lisandre's cheeks. She tried to speak but her throat muscles had tightened so convulsively she could not find her voice.

"I thought not," the old man said. "Luckily I don't want your first-born child, nor to marry you, for that matter, as pert and unmannerly as you are. I like a peaceful life, I do."

After a long silence, Briony said wistfully, "Does that mean you won't come with us and show us the way?"

For the first time Pedrin realised that she found the responsibility of guiding them a heavy burden and felt a stirring of sympathy for her.

Sedgely said reprovingly, "Now, did I say that? You shouldn't be so hasty. Though I s'pose that's the way of the world. You young things, with all your life a-stretching in front of you, are always in a hurry, while we old ones, who have so little time left us, are content to sit and watch, a-pondering." He sighed heavily, and unconsciously all the children did too, their spirits quite depressed.

No one said anything for a while, though Lisandre stirred restlessly then held herself in check. At last, though, her impatience broke free and she said, "Well, then, sirrah? What is it you want? You say you will lead us to the Erlrune for a price. Name your price then."

228

Sedgely drew his shaggy brows together and stared at her. She flushed and said in a much more conciliatory tone, "If you please, sir."

"I need very little," the old man replied rather sadly. "A patch of sun to warm me poor old bones, a nice mess of fried fish every now and again, that's all I need." He sighed and pulled his beard once or twice. "Though I must say I like that little singing egg. I've always liked a bit of music, to help while away the time."

Lisandre said angrily, "But the king himself gave that to Ziggy!"

"Well, I daresay your brother would rather be alive and without his little trinket than dead and in the ground with it," Sedgely said. "Besides, finders keepers, losers weepers is what we always used to say as colts, and I daresay not much has changed. I could've just kept the little egg and never let you see I had it, you know. I always had a soft spot for young things, though, and it troubled me sorely to see you a-wandering about with no more sense than a newly born foal. Come now, you must admit you'd never have found the place where your father died if I'd not led you here, would you?"

Lisandre had nothing to say. Sedgely tugged at his long snarled beard, the suspicion of a twinkle in his deep-set eyes. "Well, then, why are we all a-sitting here, miserable as crows at a wedding? If we don't want to draw any more attention to ourselves, we should be on our way. The Perilous Forest is not the place to be a-sitting around in the sun, a-waiting for trouble."

Briony had been playing cat's cradle with her loop of string as she listened, her green-dark eyes often lifting to scan the forest all about them. Now her nimble fingers paused, and she said apprehensively, "Are we likely to meet with trouble?"

Portentously the old man said, "Well, they don't call this the Perilous Forest for naught, little missy. This is bandit country, this is. This stretch of river is the last port of call for the moon-cursers, for they hide their contraband in the caves in these cliffs. I wouldn't be surprised if they're a-spying on us now, a-wondering what we do here and eyeing those pretty jewels young missy keeps a-flashing."

Lisandre glanced down at the rings on her fingers, then looked nervously at the forest towering high all around them. As she dragged the rings off her fingers and thrust them into the pocket of her cloak, Sedgely went on ruminatively, "And of course Old Tusky and his sow have their hide somewhere hereabouts. Their piglets will be just getting old enough to be mean, yet not so old that Old Tusky won't still be feeling protective. You don't want to arouse a gibberhog's protective instincts, that I promise you!" He tapped his beaky nose with one finger.

Briony looked down at the spiderweb of string strung between her hands, her face unfathomable. Then she tucked it into her pinafore pocket and got to her feet with a sigh. "Well, we'd best get a-moving then, hadn't we?"

17

▲ ▲ ▲

hey gathered up their belongings rather hastily, all of them looking around with sudden quick fear. Thundercloud was leaping over the roots and boulders in his usual manic fashion when he unexpectedly paused, calling a challenge. Briony looked up, her ragdoll clutched to her chest, and Snowflake bleated unhappily. They heard a peculiar gibbering noise from the bushes behind them, then the crack-crack of twigs snapping and the crash-crash of branches smashing.

"Jumping Jimjinny, what's that?"

"I don't know," Briony admitted. "But I don't like the sound of it."

"Old Tusky," Sedgely said succinctly and began to run. He moved with surprising speed and agility for such an old man. After a moment, the others ran too, but they were not fast enough. An enormous black boar charged out of the bushes, straight for them. Yellow tusks curved up from either side of a slobbery snout, their tips stained a horrible brown. His mean little piggy eyes glared red. He was as large and fast as a pony and much, much heavier, with enormous slabs of shoulders all covered in black bristles. He gibbered as he charged, dirty-looking foam spraying from his snout.

Lisandre tripped on her voluminous skirts and fell, screaming in terror. Pedrin hesitated, then with a dreadful sinking sensation in his stomach, spun on his heel, his slingshot flying up. In a single fluid motion, he spun a pebble about his head and flung it straight for the gibberhog. *Ping!* It hit him right between the eyes.

The boar did not even falter. The pebble spun harm-lessly into the grass. Lisandre scrambled away, frantic with fear. Thundercloud bounded before her, his horns lowered, but the boar sent him head-over-heels into the bushes with a single swipe of his tusks. The billy-goat lay still, whimpering. Lisandre managed to regain her feet, only to trip again in her fear, hitting the ground hard. She cowered down with her hands over her head as Pedrin desperately pelted the boar with pebbles that he seemed to notice no more than the bite of a flea.

Suddenly someone hung upside-down from the tree branch directly above Lisandre's head, seizing her wrists and swinging her up and out of the boar's way. The gibberhog charged right through her hanging red skirts, ripping them to shreds. For a moment he was blinded by the silken rags, and slowed, shaking his brutish head in confusion. Pedrin took advantage of his bewilderment to run and leap up into the tree him-self, yelling at Durrik to follow.

Durrik scrambled up onto the tree-roots just as the gibberhog shook away the last rags and spun on his little black hooves – incongruously dainty for such a colossal creature – looking angrily for his prey and gibbering with frustration. The boar saw Durrik and immediately charged once more, while the crippled boy struggled to climb the tree that Pedrin had scaled so quickly and easily. Pedrin reached down his hand and caught Durrik's, trying to haul him up. Just as he thought the weight of his friend would drag him out of the tree, someone else reached down and added their strength to his. Durrik was dragged up into the branches, just as the boar slammed into the trunk of the tree.

Panting, Durrik clung to the branch, the force of the impact almost knocking him down again. Below, the boar had been knocked off his feet. He lay for a moment, disorientated, shaking his tusked head and gibbering softly in pain and bewilderment. More foul foam splattered the grass. Then he was on his feet again, his little red eyes peering up at them, his snout snuffling as he sought their scent. He gibbered in triumphant joy at the sight or smell of them, they did not know which, and rose up on his hind legs, placing his forefeet on the tree-trunk. He shook the tree. Lisandre screamed as she almost fell, and wrapped both arms and legs tightly about her branch.

"Jumping Jimjinny!" Pedrin cried. "He means to shake us down as if we were hazelnuts! We're trapped up here."

"We can swing away through the trees," said an

unfamiliar voice. Pedrin cast a glance that way as the boar determinedly shook the tree once more. All he got was an impression of a very dirty, very freckled face under a shock of tangled hair before his attention was again firmly returned to the need to hang on tight. Leaves and twigs were raining down all about the boar as he shook and shook and shook the tree. Lisandre lost one handhold and almost fell but the ragamuffin stranger swung down one dirty hand and caught her under the shoulder, allowing her to grab the branch once more.

The gibberhog gave up shaking the tree and prowled around its bole, sniffing and snuffling. He caught a new scent and began to gibber happily as he once again charged ahead, tusks low.

"Oh, no, Briony!" Lisandre cried, terror in her voice.

Sedgely was crouched at the edge of the clearing, beckoning Briony urgently, but the little seamstress had stopped to bend over Thundercloud, who was shaking his horned head dazedly and struggling to rise. Bearing down upon her was the enormous boar, in full gibbering cry.

All those in the tree shouted a warning and Briony looked up. Her face blanched. The children in the tree all hunched down, sick with horror, covering their eyes, expecting to hear Briony scream. Instead, they heard the gibbering strangled into high-pitched squeals. Silence. Cautiously they looked again.

Briony stood unmoving, one hand still flung up, Snowflake pressed close to her side. The huge black boar lay only a few paces in front of her, struggling and grunting under a large, intricately woven net. Despite all his squirming and struggling, he could not break free of the netting, which held him captive as surely as if it was woven of steel and not of string.

"By the moon and the stars, how?" Lisandre breathed.

"Is that Briony's hammock?" asked Durrik. "But..."

Filled with dread for his billy-goat, Pedrin jumped down from the tree. Lisandre followed in a rush, bringing a shower of leaves and bark with her. She landed clumsily on all fours. The ragamuffin girl laughed at her, saying, "Leeblimey, what a lubber!" She swung from the branch by her knees, somersaulted down and landed lightly on her feet, giving Lisandre, still on all fours, a mocking bow.

She was not very old, probably no more than twelve, and very grubby indeed. Her tousled brown hair was full of knots and leaves, and her clothes were so torn and grimy it was impossible to tell what colour and shape they had been originally. Her legs and feet were bare and badly grazed about the knees, and she wore a little leather scabbard thrust through the cord she wore knotted about her waist.

Lisandre flushed crimson and held up her hand imperiously for Pedrin, who once again found himself responding automatically to help her to her feet. Lisandre shook out the red rags of her skirt, looking the little ragamuffin up and down disdainfully. "Heavens, what a tatterdemalion."

Immediately the little girl scowled, her hands clenching up into fists. "Tatter-doozit yourself, frog-face!"

Lisandre stepped away with her nose in the air. "Pooh! What a reek! One would think soap had not yet been invented, so few in this forest seem to employ it."

"You're not so sweet-smelling yourself, frog-face!" The girl darted forward and plucked a mouldy black leaf out of Lisandre's hair. "You're just as dirty and tatty as me, so what gives you the right to look down your nose at me?"

No one could live in the forest for weeks and climb up trees, and grapple with a gibberhog, and not show the marks of it on their clothes and person. Lisandre was indeed a far different picture from the starkin princess they had first known. Her silken skirts were badly torn and stained, her dirty hair stuck up like a porcupine's quills and her face was scratched, bruised and smeared with mud. She drew herself up like a princess, however, saying coldly, "How dare you speak thus to me, you ill-mannered guttersnipe! Do you not know I am one of the Ziv?"

The little girl stuck out her tongue rudely. "And what if you are? Starkin scum! You lot should go back where you came from. Snooty stuck-up tyrants, you think you rule the whole leeblimey world!"

"What's all this?" Briony said quietly, coming up beside them. "Where did she spring from?"

"Out of the trees," Pedrin said, rather bemused. "I don't know what she is, some sort of wildkin, I suppose? She swings about in the trees as nimbly as any wood-sprite."

"Wood-sprite!" The ragamuffin stared at him furi-

236

ously, then swung a punch that Pedrin only managed to avoid by scrambling backwards quickly. "I'll sprite you, hayhead! I'm no wildkin, I'm a girl."

Pedrin was disappointed. "Oh, what a shame! I thought we might've found our second wildkin. For the prophecy, you know."

"Well, I'm no wildkin and I'll thank you to remember it," the little girl said belligerently.

Briony smiled at her. "What's your name then?"

"Maglen," she answered, her fists relaxing a little. "Though they call me Mags."

"A good name," Lisandre said disdainfully. "Mags-in-Rags, we'll call you."

"And we'll call you 'frog-face', frog-face," Mags flashed back, her hands doubling up into fists again.

Pedrin remembered his billy-goat. "Thundercloud?" he cried in alarm, scrambling across the tree-roots.

"He's got a nasty gash and is a bit shaken up," Briony said. "He should be all right, though, thank Imala. He's a tough old goat."

Durrik flashed her a smile, appreciating the pun, but then his face suddenly changed as he perceived the gibberhog, still thrashing and jabbering under the net. "Liah's eyes!" he breathed. "Look at the size of that thing! Briony, where on earth did that net come from? 'Tis not your hammock – the weave is much tighter."

"'Tis me cat's cradle," she answered.

"But it was naught but a loop of string that you tangled about your fingers," Lisandre said in amazement. "How on earth?"

237

"'Tis a little trick I know," Briony said. "It can be rather useful. Like the rope I made for you to climb down out of the castle, milady. I would've needed a room full of hemp to make a rope long enough to reach the ground from your room, but all I had was a little bobbin of thread. I had t'spin it very long and strong to support our weight, and I must admit I was worried it wouldn't last until we had both set foot on the ground."

Lisandre looked at her indignantly. "You mean I climbed down from the castle on a rope spun out of just a bobbin of thread and you only tell me now?"

"Well, you did insist I spin a rope for you," Briony said.

"What about the hammock?" Pedrin demanded. "Was that your cat's cradle too?"

She nodded, colouring and dropping her eyes.

"You mean we slept all night in a hammock made from naught but an old bit of string?" Pedrin was just as incensed as Lisandre had been.

"I made it as strong as I could," she answered rather pleadingly. "And I wound the end tight around me finger. Me magic always lasts longer if I'm still touching it."

The word "magic" dropped into the silence like a stone into a still pool. All the children stared at her in amazement and fear, though Sedgely was as placid as ever, taking out a long clay pipe and puffing away at something that smelt truly horrible. Lisandre took an involuntary step away, but the alarm on her face was not, this time, touched with revulsion. Pedrin felt a

238

difference in his emotions too. His apprehension was not a little tempered by respect. As uncomfortable as he was with Briony's strange powers, he had to admit they were very useful.

Briony gave a troubled little sigh and bent to pick up her ragdoll, which she had dropped in the grass. "Come, let's get a-moving while we can," she said. "That gibberhog doesn't look happy, and I don't know how long 'twill be until me net turns back into just an old loop of string."

They stared down at the big black boar, rolling a red eye full of inarticulate rage.

"I bet his piglets don't pay much attention to him," Durrik said rather shakily.

"Why? What do you mean?" Mags said, poking the gibberhog with one grubby foot. He snorted, spraying yellow foam, and thrashed about furiously.

"'Cause he's a real boar," Durrik answered, grinning weakly.

Mags stared at him and then went off into peals of delighted laughter. Her amusement was infectious and the others all laughed too, partly in heady relief at the danger being past. The gibberhog grunted angrily and heaved with all his strength against the confines of the net.

"You're such a ham, Durrik," Pedrin said with a grin. "I don't think that pig much appreciates your sense of humour. Let's get a-moving before he manages to get free."

"Yeah, I can't see him giving up the chase easily. He looks real pig-headed, don't he?"

Again Mags laughed delightedly. Surprised, Durrik smiled back at her. He was not used to such warm-hearted appreciation of his puns. He picked up his little bundle and said to her, "So where did you spring from, anyway, Mags? What are you a-doing here in the heart of the Perilous Forest?"

"I live here," she said. "What are you a-doing here?"

"We're a-heading up the cliffs right now," he answered gravely. "Hopefully old pig-face is as bad at climbing cliffs as he is at climbing trees. I'd be getting as far away from here as you can right now, before that net turns back into string."

"I might just climb up the cliffs too," she said. "I've always wanted to see what's up there. I might as well go the whole hog…" – she flashed him a wide, gap-toothed grin – "…and go on up. Me pa won't think to follow me up there!"

"Ah, I see," Lisandre said, rolling her eyes. "A run-away. Do you not think you should go home, little girl? I'm sure your family must be concerned for you." The cool ironic tone of her voice expressed, ever so subtly, her actual disbelief in her words.

Mags fired up immediately. With clenched fists, she said, "Go home yourself, frog-face. I do what I want, I do, and no stuck-up starkin scum is a-going to tell me different."

"Well," said Lisandre, gathering up the torn rags of her skirt in one hand, "if you must tag along behind us, do, please, try and stay downwind?"

18

◆ ◆ ◆

If it had not been for the goats, the children might never have been able to clamber up the cliffs. Thundercloud led the way, leaping from boulder to boulder with incredible ease and assurance. He always managed to find a path, even when Pedrin himself was clinging to the cliff with all his fingers and toes, unable to see which way to move.

The little nanny-goat, meanwhile, ran close by Durrik so that he could grip her collar when the way grew too hard and let her drag him higher. He found the climb very difficult, and had to stop often, clinging to the rocks, his breath wheezing in his throat, his face white under the grime.

Of them all, Sedgely seemed to find the climb the easiest, though he leant heavily on his walking stick and complained often that he was far too old for such foolhardy exercise. When they finally reached the top of the cliff, though, it was the children who threw themselves on the ground, panting and groaning, and the old man who stood calmly, leaning on his stick and waiting for them.

It was a different landscape above the cliffs. All about reared high hills, clothed in the dark green of tall trees and hanging vines, and wreathed with thin wisps of mist. The Evenlode pelted forward in white rushes of foam and spume, its progress hampered by ugly great boulders that thrust out of its midst, sending gushes of spray high into the air. Their ears were filled with the clamour of the river as it leapt out over the cliff and poured down to the valley below.

Once they had recovered their breath, the children all rushed into excited speech, reviewing the climb and arguing about the best course of action now they were safe on the bluff.

"Looks like rain," Sedgely said despondently. "If I were you, I'd be a-looking for somewhere dry to shelter. Unless, of course, you don't mind a-getting wet."

This time the children believed him. Looking up at the sky in consternation, they saw dark clouds pouring down over the shoulders of the grim grey mountains. There was a low rumble of thunder.

"But it was so bright and sunny this morning," Lisandre cried. "Who would've believed a storm could roll in so quickly?"

Sedgely shook his head. "I did warn you," he said sadly.

"We'd better try to find a cave or summat," Pedrin said uncertainly, looking around.

"No caves hereabouts," Sedgely said. "Plenty of caves in the cliff we could've sheltered in, but you wouldn't listen to me."

242

"Oh well, at least we've left the gibberhog far behind us," Briony said. "If we'd taken shelter in a cave, it would've been bound to be his home and we would've had the sow and all the piglets to worry about as well. Let's get a-moving and see if we can't find somewhere to shelter. Those clouds look nasty."

The children set off up the side of the river, Thundercloud and Snowflake bounding before them. The trees rose high all around them, tall and grey and silent, their roots like a tangle of ossified snakes. Mist reached down from the mountains to brush their cheeks with soft, indifferent fingers. Pedrin and Durrik were glad of their capes, and Lisandre wrapped her heavy cloak close about her. Briony pulled her shawl up about her hair, while Pedrin gave little Mags-in-Rags his blanket to wrap about her head and shoulders.

"Now, if I remember a-rightly, there's a place not far from here that might do the trick," Sedgely said ruminatively. "Though 'tis probably home to a bear now. If not summat worse."

It began to rain, light and stinging at first, and then in great blowing sheets that soaked them to the skin.

"Bear or not, lead us to this place," Lisandre commanded. "It is near nightfall and we are all tired. I cannot and will not flounder on in all this mud."

"If there is a bear there, I warrant you'd rather we were a-floundering," Sedgely sighed. "Bears don't much like uninvited visitors."

"Briony will weave a net to entrap the bear, if there is one there," Lisandre snapped. "Just get us out of this rain!"

On they went, tired, wet, cold and very uncomfortable. Branches slapped them in the face. Their feet sank deep into mud. The tree-trunks were wreathed in mist, so that they could hardly see their way. From time to time, Sedgely stopped and stared about him, tugging at his long white beard dispiritedly. "Things do change a lot in twenty years," he said once, and another time, "I do hope there's no bear living there now."

At last he stopped, nodding his head in satisfaction. "Here we are then. I thought I hadn't forgotten the way. Just follow your nose, Sedgely me lad, I always say. Just follow your nose." He tapped it knowingly. Durrik and Mags shared a grin of pure, mischievous delight.

They were standing at the foot of yet another giant of the forest, a tree that soared so high its upper branches were lost in clouds. The tree-roots enclosed the children like thick, groping arms, creating a dusk even darker than the one now closing in over the forest. It was so dark it was hard to see more of each other's faces than vague white blotches floating in the grey. The children all huddled together, shivering.

"Well?" Lisandre demanded. "Where is this cave?"

"What cave?" Sedgely asked.

"The cave you were leading us to, the cave in which you said we could shelter," she said impatiently.

"Oh. There's no cave. 'Tis the tree I was a-talking about. 'Tis hollow. Some little weevil must've eaten out its heart. It'll be a little cramped with all you big lumbering children, but at least it'll be dry. That is, if there's no bear."

The old man clambered up onto one great writhing root and jumped down on the far side. "Well, no smell of bear," he said in quite a cheerful tone. "Though that's not to say a snake mightn't a-slithered in to get out of the rain. Couldn't smell a snake over all this water."

"A snake?" Lisandre recoiled.

"A snake would be better than a scorpion." Sedgely's voice was muffled as he groped around in his coat pocket. "At least we'll know straightaway if there's a snake, while a scorpion tends to sneak up on you while you're asleep." Light suddenly illuminated the dusk all about them, turning the rain into long strokes of quicksilver. There was a moment of silence, the children standing shivering in the rain, then Sedgely's head popped up again. "No snake," he said succinctly. "Come in out of the rain before you all catch your death of cold."

One by one they clambered in over the high root. In the pale radiance of the light shining from the old man's hand, they could see a wide gaping crack in the trunk. They examined it rather fearfully. All, that is, except for Mags. Her eyes were fixed greedily on the jewelled orb in Sedgely's hand. There was a fierce longing there, a covetousness that Pedrin recognised well, having felt much the same desire himself. Something about her expression bothered him, though. It was the depth of the longing, as much as the absence of some emotion he thought should have been there. Wonder, perhaps, or surprise that such a ragged old man should possess something of such

245

opulent beauty. There was no such amazement in her face, only greed.

Just as he recognised the look in her eyes, it vanished, and Mags was wondering aloud with the others at this doorway into the heart of the tree. "Leeblimey!" she cried. "Is there really a little room in there? Are you sure 'tis empty?"

"If anyone lives here, they're not home now," Sedgely replied. "Go on. No point a-standing about in the rain. We'll find out soon enough if we're not welcome."

One by one they crawled in through the crack, Sedgely setting his night-light in the centre so it illuminated the small chamber within brightly. The walls narrowed overhead so that they banged their skulls if they stood, but once seated there was plenty of room as long as they kept their knees bent close to their bodies. At least, there was, until Thundercloud came butting his way in, shaking his shaggy coat so they were drenched anew.

"Oh, no!" Lisandre cried. "Get your goat out of here, Pedrin. It's bad enough that we have to smell that Mags-in-Rags girl without having the stench of wet goat as well."

As Pedrin hastily chased a belligerent Thundercloud back out into the night, Mags thrust her fist into Lisandre's face, saying furiously, "Smell this, frog-face!"

Briony dragged her back. "There aren't enough room for punch-ups in here, Mags. Please don't start a scuffle! We're all tired and wet and cold. Let's just try and get warm and dry, and get some sleep while we can."

"What gives her the right to sneer at me!" Mags cried. "She's just as tatty as me, for all her airs and graces."

Lisandre looked down at the ruin of her red silk dress. In the steady glow of Sedgely's night-light, they could see she was close to tears. "What is this appalling child doing here anyway?" she asked icily.

"What indeed?" Briony said. "For now we are six."

As the import of her words sunk in, there was silence for a long moment. "But she says she's not wildkin," Pedrin objected. "If she's not wildkin, that must mean you are." He said it challengingly, not really meaning it, but Briony nodded her head slowly.

"At least I know now."

Pedrin was instantly sorry he had spoken. He could see the shock on Lisandre's face, the instant recoil. He felt the same recoil in himself. All his life he had regarded the wildkin as dangerous, unpredictable, and even evil. The last few weeks travelling through the Perilous Forest had caused a gradual stretching of this belief. The wood-sprites had been heedless and lawless, for sure, but they had been merry-hearted too, and had cared for their wounded with true compassion. He liked Sedgely and enjoyed his sly humour, and had tried to tell himself that such a kindly old man could not really be a wildkin. It now seemed certain that he was, and Briony too, and Pedrin had to come to grips with the idea that wildkin could look just like normal people, walking about and living amongst them without anyone ever knowing the difference.

He stared at Briony and saw again how pale and pointed was her face. Her ears, usually hidden by her dark curls or by a kerchief, were now revealed by the wetness of her hair as being as long and pointed as the ears of a wood-sprite. He remembered how her eyes were always changing colour, reflecting her mood or the colour of the world around her. He thought about how she could turn a knotted loop of string into a hammock or a net, and a length of cotton into a rope. He remembered how loyal and brave she was, and how hard she worked to keep the peace between them. She had saved them again and again, and all with no trace of conceit or demand for gratitude, that hardest of all debts to bear.

Now Briony was looking tense and unhappy, waiting for them all to shrink from her as they had after the spider wood. Pedrin saw with a sudden flash of insight that she had lived all her life in fear of that instinctive recoil, yet a lifetime of enduring it had not hardened her to it. Although he was still troubled and a little repelled by the realisation that Briony was indeed wildkin and thus unknowable, he tried to smile at her in reassurance, though his cheeks felt stiff as if carved from stone.

The smile on Durrik's face was far more genuine and sympathetic. Pedrin realised with the same sudden shock of clarity that Durrik was feeling an eager kinship with Briony. Durrik had also lived his life with the fear of being reviled and rejected, an outcast hiding his secret nature under the mask of normality. This insight shook and disturbed Pedrin, revealing subterranean depths to his friend that Pedrin had never before recognised.

Sedgely too was looking at Briony kindly, nodding at her and smiling a little. There was no such sympathy on Lisandre's face. She was genuinely shocked and horrified. They could all see how she drew herself away so no part of her touched the wildkin girl, and how the mask of pride and disdain closed down over her face.

Mags was looking from one face to another. "What are you all a-talking about?" she asked rather shrilly. "What's all this blather about wildkin? What does it matter that there's now six of us?"

They hesitated a moment, looking at each other, then Lisandre said coldly, "I do not see how that is any of your business, Rags."

"If 'tis not me business, why do you keep a-talking about me as if I warn't here?" she snapped back.

"I'm sorry," Briony said miserably. "'Tis just…" She looked appealingly at Lisandre. The hope and longing on her face cut Pedrin like a knife. He felt a sudden hot shame and, though he could not smile, the stone of his face dissolved so she could see his very real and deep desire to understand and accept. It gave her strength. Her shoulders lifted a little and she said, with new ardency in her voice, "Can't we tell her about the prophecy, milady, and what we're a-doing here in the Perilous Forest? For it does seem too much like coincidence that we should just meet up with her like that, don't you think?"

Lisandre thrust out her jaw stubbornly. Briony added pleadingly, "And Mags did save you from the gibberhog, remember?"

"Not that I've had any thanks," Mags said piously.

Lisandre saw that Sedgely was about to add something and said coldly, "Very well, I thank you!"

"I think Briony's right," Durrik said. "I think you should tell Mags all about the prophecy, Lisandre—"

"I am of the Ziv," Lisandre said icily. "Who gave you the right to call me by name, sirrah?"

19

◆ ◆ ◆

Durrik was taken aback. For a moment he stared at her, then his face burnt with colour. He could find nothing to say.

"Briony, I am cold and wet still. Why have you not lit a fire to dry my clothes?"

"I'm sorry, milady. I haven't had a chance," Briony faltered. She looked about her, and made an effort to rise, though her face was white and pinched with tiredness and misery. "I don't know … could we be a-lighting a fire in here, Pedrin? Surely it'd smoke us out?"

"Indeed it would," Pedrin said shortly, looking angrily at the starkin girl, sitting very stiff and proud on the other side of the hollow tree. "I'd say we'd all better just be glad we're out of the rain and make do as best we can. Though I must say I'm hungry," he finished in a plaintive rush, undermining the stiff righteousness of his previous words.

"So am I. Fair gutfoundered," Mags agreed.

"Now let me see," Sedgely murmured, thrusting his

hand into first one pocket then another. He pulled out five small birds' eggs, blue and speckled, a handful of mushrooms, a little bunch of spring onions, dirt still clinging to their bulbs, and finally, with an air of triumph, a long yellow marrow. "I picked up a few things along the way, a-knowing you young things are always hungry," he explained. "Now, a fire. I agree a fire would be nice. Though how we're to manage it, I can't say. We can't be a-lighting one in here, for even if we could stand the smoke in our eyes, we'd be a-toasting our toes a little too warmly for me liking. Nah, nah, we'd best be a-thinking of summat else." He tugged his beard and then, finding it dripping wet, absentmindedly wrung it out all over Pedrin's bare feet. Luckily Pedrin's feet were already so wet and cold he hardly noticed.

Sedgely put his head out of the crack in the tree-trunk. Outside the rain was still blowing in heavy sheets. They could hear him scuffling about outside. Then he pulled his head back inside. "Can I have your oilskins, young fellers?"

A few minutes later he requested a handful of dry twigs and leaves from underfoot, and then Pedrin's tinder and flint. Soon, incredulously, they smelt wood smoke and heard the merry crackle of a fire. The old man had draped the boys' oilskins over some long sticks, making a little tent between the high tree-roots, before lighting a fire under its shelter.

"The wood's all damp, it'll smoke," he said dubiously. "Still, we'll at least be able to make a nice hot omelette and hang some of our clothes up to dry. It'll help keep us warm too, though I daresay we'll choke on the smoke if the wind turns."

Sedgely's stream of ordinary, everyday conversation had calmed the overcharged atmosphere in the little room. Gratefully the children began to struggle out of their damp clothes, passing them out for Sedgely to hang on a little line he had rigged up. Under the red rags of her dress, Lisandre wore a white camisole and pantaloons, all trimmed with satin ribbons and lace, while both Briony and Mags wore nothing but drab cotton shifts, rather damp about the neck and hem. Durrik had stuffed his rolled-up blanket into his bag at the first hint of rain and he took it out now, and offered it to Briony. She tucked it around Lisandre's shoulders but the starkin princess flinched away from the touch of her hand. Briony sat down as far away from everyone else as she could get, arms wrapped about her knees, her eyes as black and full of storms as the sky outside.

"What about me?" Mags said belligerently. "I'm cold too, but I can't see anyone offering me a blanket."

"I'm sorry," Durrik said, his words rather muffled as he pulled his shirt over his head. "I only have the one." He handed the wet, tattered, stained rag of a shirt to Sedgely and turned back to find the three girls all staring at him in horror. They had all just seen his bare back for the first time, the white skin marred with great red welts, some still oozing pus.

"Leeblimey!" Mags said in great distress. "What happened to you? A gibgoblin?"

Colour had scorched up Durrik's face. He squatted

253

down, his back hidden against the wall, and said with a bitter twist of his mouth, "A gibgoblin in human form. A delightful starkin guard, that had the charge of me and Pedrin at the glass factory."

"But why? Why would he flay you like that?" Mags cried, her hands clenched into fists.

"I stumbled," Durrik said and gave a deprecating little wave of his hand down at his thin, crooked left leg, the foot curled now in a cramp that he bent down and tried to massage away.

"Starkin scum," Mags hissed, and cast a look of virulent hatred at Lisandre, who had gone first white, and then red, and now shut up her mouth tightly and raised her chin in a way they all knew well.

"Does it hurt, Durrik?" Briony asked anxiously. "I have some ointment that might help…"

"I was a-rubbing it with some stuff me ma got from one of the Crafty," Pedrin said, "but we ran out a while back and all the running and climbing we do seems to keep opening up the sores."

"Let me rub some of me stuff in," Briony said. "I don't know if 'tis as good as the stuff you had, 'cause I made this meself, but it'll be better than naught."

"All right then," Durrik said reluctantly, and shifted round a little so Briony could reach his back, yet not enough that Lisandre and Mags could see much of the ugly scars. Briony seemed to understand, for she knelt between them, shielding Durrik from everyone else's sight.

Pedrin hunched at the dripping end of the tent to milk a very wet and miserable Snowflake, passing the foaming bucket back to Sedgely so the old man could briskly whisk the milk together with the eggs. The mushrooms and marrow sizzled together in the pan, then Sedgely poured in the egg mixture, tilting the pan so it swirled about, turning a warm golden-brown. All the children leant in expectantly.

The omelette was delicious. As Pedrin finished the last warm, luscious mouthful, he gazed at Sedgely in open admiration. "I'm mighty glad you decided to come along with us, Sedgely!"

"Me too!" Durrik and Briony echoed.

"I'm full as a body louse," Mags said with pleasure.

"I know what you young things are like," Sedgely answered tolerantly. "Always hungry, yet never wor-rit about where the next meal's a-coming from." He lay back against the curved wall, pulling the brim of his reed cap over his eyes. "Lucky for you I felt a whim to come along," he said to no one in particular.

"I am grateful," Lisandre said stiffly, the first words she had spoken in some time. "Thank you." She then turned to Briony, drawing the blanket up to her chin. "Where is my mirror?"

Briony drew the hand-mirror and the silver-backed comb and brush out of her sack. As Lisandre exam-ined her face anxiously, Briony struggled to comb the knots out of her matted fair hair. Lisandre sat very stiffly indeed.

"Heat me up some water so I may wash," Lisandre ordered. "*I* do not wish to go to sleep all muddy and smelling of the mire. In the morning, if it is fine, you shall help me bathe properly, but for now just wash

255

my hands and face and feet. And you must do something about my dress. I cannot wear a dress all torn to rags."

Briony nodded and obeyed, her face unhappy.

"What's she meant to do?" Durrik burst out. "How is Briony meant to mend your dress, Lisandre? We're a-sitting inside a tree in the pouring rain, in the heart of the Perilous Forest, a million miles from anywhere."

"I cannot call upon the Erlrune in rags," Lisandre said obstinately.

She darted a look at Briony that was oddly anxious, and the little seamstress said reassuringly, "Of course not, milady." She sighed. "I shall need to be a-spinning some new silk, having only a few bobbins of thread with me. It shall take some time, I'm a-feared, milady."

"Very well," Lisandre replied, obviously mollified. She gave her face one last dissatisfied scrutiny then gave the mirror back to Briony, allowing her to wash away the mud smears with a warm, damp flannel.

The others washed too, all but Mags, who had obviously decided to wear her grime like a badge of honour. Even Pedrin found himself wishing she would consent to a good scrubbing. In the close confines of the tree, she did smell a little too much like wet dog.

Warm and pleasantly full at last, the children began to feel sleepy. They wriggled down into the pine needles and leaves, watching the mesmerising dance of the flames through the crack in the tree-trunk. Rain pattered on the leaves. Sedgely began to snore and soon both Durrik and Lisandre were asleep too, worn out by the exertions of the day.

Only Briony did not snuggle down. She took down the red dress and spread it across her knees, examining the many rents in its silky fabric. Then she drew out a spool of red silk from her sack and threaded a long silver needle. It flashed in the low glimmer of the night-light as she began to sew, swiftly and deftly.

"You should try to get some sleep," Pedrin said drowsily. "Need you do that now? Surely me precious milady doesn't expect you to sit up all night a-fixing her stupid dress?"

"We need to be on our way again tomorrow," Briony replied softly, not lifting her gaze from her task. "Time's a-running out."

"But 'twill take you all night to sew up those holes," he protested, rousing himself from the heavy exhaustion dragging him down.

"Probably."

"It doesn't seem fair," he said rather inadequately.

"Of course 'tis not fair," Mags said passionately. "When are the starkin fair? They grow fatter and richer on the toils of our bodies, and what do they give us back in return? Naught!"

Briony glanced at her. Her eyes looked very black. "I doubt they'd agree with you," she answered mildly. "Besides, not all starkin are like that. Lisandre's father, the old count, he was always very just, I've heard."

"No doubt she's the one that told you so," Mags said sarcastically. "Did you ever see aught like the

257

way she drooled over herself in that mirror? Talk about vain!"

"Well, mebbe she is," Briony said. "But she's starkin, you see. I'm so glad I'm not starkin! All I have is the skill of me hands, but I am free to go where I will and do what I want. Lisandre's not. She's a prisoner of her own beauty. It'll fade one day and then she'll have naught. Look at Lady Donella, the chief lady-in-waiting. She married well, because she was beautiful, but now her husband's dead and she has naught left. 'Tis very sad. And Lisandre is a-feared for her own mother, now her father is dead, can't you see that? If Count Zygmunt dies, Lisandre and her mother will be destitute, unless Lord Zavion cares for them. Her only hope to be free of him is to marry well herself, and then she'll have to submit to her husband instead of to Lord Zavion. Do you wonder she's so a-feared?"

Briony was leaning forward, her hands clenched to her breast, all her face aglow in her passionate desire to make them understand. As usual, Pedrin felt his emotions swayed by her so that he was filled with pity and dread for Lisandre. He glanced at the starkin girl and saw her face relaxed in sleep, all the stubborn pride and determination smoothed away, her mouth drooping softly so that she looked sad and vulnerable. He did not want to feel compassion or sympathy for Lisandre. He hated the starkin, and his hatred was just. He looked away, hardening his heart, his teeth clenched together.

"She don't seem a-feared to me," Mags said, though without her usual conviction.

"Don't she? She does to me. Very a-feared and very lonesome."

There was a long, thoughtful silence. Pedrin found himself wondering how Briony saw him. With a rueful grin he decided that he did not really want to know. She saw things too clearly with those strange, changeable eyes of hers. A little self-delusion never hurt anyone, he told himself.

Mags had rolled away from them, huddling her arms around her shock of matted brown hair. He heard her mutter something to herself, though the only words he caught were "spoilt rotten ... like all the starkin." She almost sounded as if she was trying to convince herself.

Though Pedrin was very tired, he only drifted in and out of the verge of sleep, the dim glow of the night-light pressing against his eyelids like heavy golden coins, the constant rustle of the silk abrading his nerves. He heard Briony rise some time later and throw some more wood on the fire. The familiar crackle of the flames soothed him, and he slid deeper into sleep.

When Pedrin next opened his bleary eyes, the little wildkin girl had laid down her needle and was bending her head over the ragdoll cradled in her arms. Feeling a sudden pang of contrition, Pedrin raised himself on one elbow. He was about to speak but bit back the words when he saw she was not merely seeking comfort from the raggedy old doll, as he had thought. She was slowly, carefully, extracting something from a hole in the side seam of the doll. He saw with a sudden squeamishness that it was the cocoon of some insect.

She looked up suddenly and saw he was awake. For a moment she hesitated, biting her lip, then she said, very softly, "I couldn't leave me silkworms at the castle, they're the secret to me silk weaving. No one else knows how to breed them or what to feed them, or how t'spin the silk. 'Tis why I have a place at the castle at all. Lady Donella would not take a little foundling child in out of the goodness of her heart, you know." There was a faint shade of bitterness in her voice. "So I had to smuggle some out. I would've taken more if I could – all the ones I left will die because no one there knows what to feed them."

She laid down the ragdoll and hung the small yellow cocoon upon Pedrin's toasting fork, holding it in the smoke of the fire. "I'm a-killing the larvae within," Briony said matter-of-factly. "Its cocoon is made of one long filament of silk. I shall spin the filaments of three cocoons together to make a strand, and then spin together three strands to make a thread. Then I shall have enough to finish mending the dress. I shall need to find a bush of kindleberries too, to dye the fabric red again. I saw a bush not far from here. I shall go in the dawn to gather the berries."

Pedrin nodded. "I hope it stops raining," he mumbled.

"It stopped some time ago," she answered, pulling out the little drop-spindle from her sack and giving it a spin with one finger. "Go back to sleep, Pedrin. Don't mind me."

He tried to think of something to say, but as always the right words eluded him, even in the familiar language of the hearthkin which they now spoke together. "I don't," he said, and felt his whole body grow hot with inadequacy.

She smiled a little, though she did not look up. "I know," she answered.

20

In the dark stuffiness of the hollow tree, the children all slept late. They woke to find long rays of sunlight striking down through the soaring trunks of the trees, the sky a shifting canopy of green and gold.

Lisandre's dress was hung up to dry from a branch, a waterfall of shimmering red silk. Scrambling out of the hollow tree, their eyes dry and scratchy, their mouths tasting like a bear's den, all were stricken into an awed silence. There was no sign that the dress had ever been torn by thorns, ripped by rocks, slashed by gibberhog tusks, bedraggled by mud and rain, slept in or scrambled in. It looked like it had never been worn.

"Leeblimey!" Mags said. Once again there was a fierce yearning in her face. She stepped forward almost blindly, and lifted one finger to stroke the sensuous crimson shimmer.

"Do not dare lay your filthy fingers upon my dress," Lisandre said fiercely. She stepped forward, tears on her face, and embraced a startled and wan-faced Briony. "Thank you!"

"It was me pleasure," Briony answered, very gently. She yawned and added, without any acerbity whatsoever, "Though it may have been better if I'd mended it for you the night before we visit the Erlrune, for I have used up all me silks now and we still have some way to go."

"I shall not wear it," Lisandre said, her mouth still soft and quivering with surprise and pleasure. "Can we fold it so it will not crush? How did you do it? I did not mean … I'm sorry, Briony," she said in a rush. "It was horrible of me to make you sit up all night like that. I did not really mean you to. I was just … I was upset…"

Briony nodded. "'Tis still damp, I'm a-feared. Do you really want me to carry it for you? I admit, I'd be sorry to see it being torn again."

"I'll carry it," Lisandre said in a sudden rush. "You've carried all my things as well as your own all this way. I'll take a turn today."

"That would be nice," Briony said. "Though the sack's not heavy, except when I have to carry your cloak as well. That does get a bit awkward."

"I'm sorry," Lisandre said. "I did not think…"

"What will you wear if we're to carry your dress?" Briony said. "We have no spare clothes."

Lisandre look down at herself, startled, and realised she was standing in nothing but her lacy underwear. She coloured with embarrassment, instinctively wrapping herself in her arms.

"You may wear me pinafore," Briony said. "'Tis just as long as a dress, really."

263

Lisandre nodded. "If you don't mind."

"Of course I don't mind," Briony answered with a smile. Her eyes were a brilliant sunshiny green, her rather peaky face flushed now with pleasure.

Lisandre was rather an odd sight in the long, drab-coloured pinafore, with the long, lace-trimmed pantaloons poking out beneath, and Durrik's heavy brogues on her feet. Mags crowed with laughter at the sight of her but although Lisandre blushed, she just shouldered the bulky sack and rolled-up cloak with grim determination and set off down the path with the others. Mags went with them, saying with an air of insouciance, "May as well stick around for a while longer, I s'pose. Got naught else to do."

In the sombre hush of the evening, the dark-clad trees wearing petticoats of mist, the six weary companions came to another high waterfall. Shaped in an uneven horseshoe, the river poured down, down, down in a white roar. The cliffs loomed wet and black above them. It seemed the only possible way forward was over a long, thin, mossy tree which had fallen many years before, bridging the river from one steep, rocky side to another. The waterfall thundered past it and under it and sometimes over it, a turbulent mass of foam and lather.

The children stood and stared in incredulous horror.

"If we're a-wanting to cut across the loop of the Evenlode, this is the place to do it," Sedgely said. "We either cross here and angle through the forest to the mountains, a-finding ourselves a pass through to the

Evenlinn, or we climb up these here cliffs and follow the river. 'Tis a long, slow way, though, a-following the river. Weeks of walking."

"I can't be a-crossing that," Durrik said, staring at the thin stride of the fallen pine, his eyes dark with fear.

"We'll just run a rope across for you young ones to cling to," Sedgely said encouragingly. "If an old, old man like me can do it, a young one like you should run across as sprightly as a wood-pheasant's chick."

Durrik shook his head emphatically. "I can't!"

"I don't much like the look of it either but if it saves us days and even weeks, I think we should do it, don't you?" Lisandre said cajolingly.

All day Lisandre had been making a visible effort to be conciliatory towards the others, especially to Briony and Durrik. She had asked the crippled boy, with red staining her throat and cheeks, if his back felt any better, and had offered him her hand over several rough spots, until she finally realised he hated to have anyone notice his disability. After that she left him alone, though it was clear to everyone that she had been shocked and shamed by the scars on his back and was trying, awkwardly, to make some sort of amends. Mags did not like Lisandre any better for all her new-found sensitivity, scowling at her now and muttering, "Humbug."

"'Tis a-getting dark, mebbe we should set up camp and cross in the morning," Pedrin suggested. To his surprise, Briony frowned and gave a little shake of her head.

The wildkin girl was usually the first to note signs of trouble in others and search for solutions, and so Pedrin looked at her in alarm. "Why? What's wrong?" he asked, his hand moving to his slingshot for the first time that day.

"I don't know," she answered. "I feel uneasy. I feel like we're being watched."

"Watched by what?"

"I don't know. Summat ... curious ... yet implacable. It makes me ... twitchy... Me fingertips are tingling."

Durrik gave a nod of surprised agreement.

"Everything's too quiet," Briony said and gave a convulsive shudder.

"Yeah, too true, too true," Sedgely agreed. "Too quiet all week, if you ask me. Not that you ever do." He sighed in resignation.

"We're asking you now!" Pedrin said impatiently. "Is summat out there? What do we do?"

"Cross the river," Sedgely said placidly. "I already said that, but mebbe you warn't a-listening? Never listen, the young of today, I often notice it."

"But the light is almost gone. We can't be a-crossing that slippery old log in the dark," Durrik said, panic in his voice.

Briony shrugged her shoulders uneasily. "I think I'd sleep better if we were on t'other side of the river."

Just then Sedgely leant forward, pointing with his stick. "Me poor old eyes aren't as good as they used to be. What's a-moving down there?"

In sudden trepidation, Pedrin stared down the river. At first he could see nothing, but then a brief, shifting gleam caught his eye. Sunlight glancing on metal. He shaded his eyes against the glare of the setting sun and stared some more. Now he knew where to look he could see the furtive movements of forty or more soldiers creeping up on them from behind. His pulse accelerated so fast he had to grasp a tree-trunk to steady himself.

"Soldiers," Briony whispered. "Though that's not..." She came to a halt, staring around uneasily. "This place is a trap," she said very quietly. "We'd best be a-getting out of here!"

Pedrin rested his head on his hands for a moment. How could he have been so stupid to have thought the starkin soldiers had given up? They would never give up. He would be hounded all the rest of his life. He swallowed hard, saying gruffly, "No doubt about it, we cross that log and we cross it now!"

"Why will they not leave me alone?" Lisandre whispered. "Why is Lord Zavion so intent on recapturing me? He never liked me anyway."

"Mebbe he don't want all the starkin a-wondering if he's a-killing off the whole ziv Estaria family," Pedrin said grimly. "Anyways, he's not a-giving up so we'd best be a-moving on – fast!"

Hurriedly they gathered together all their various scraps of rope and knotted them together, then Sedgely took one end in his big bony hand and cautiously began to edge out along the slippery, precarious bridge. Durrik watched, clinging tightly to the same tree as Pedrin, looking like he was about to vomit.

"You come up last, little missy," Sedgely said to Briony, "and bring along the bit of rope. We don't want the starkin a-getting hold of it."

"But Briony will need it too," Pedrin protested.

Sedgely twinkled at him from beneath his bushy white brows. "Yeah, mebbe so. Though with the blood that runs in her veins, she'll be a-needing it less than you, young feller!" He snorted with laughter then, with that last rather cryptic comment, turned and shuffled forward, arms held wide.

Pedrin was too busy watching the soldiers to puzzle over what the old man meant. The soldiers had still not seen them, and so were proceeding quite slowly, searching carefully for tracks and prodding under bushes with the butts of their fusilliers. The children had all crouched down behind the upflung roots of the fallen tree and so were hidden from view, while Sedgely was almost invisible in the dusk, his shaggy hair and beard as white as the weltering foam, his willow-leaf coat as green as the moss.

At last the old man reached the far side of the fallen log, having to climb through a maze of old dead branches to reach the shore. In a few seconds the rope Pedrin held tightly in his hand was drawn taut as Sedgely tied it on the far side. Pedrin tied his own end firmly to a thick root and then nodded urgently at the starkin princess. Lisandre took a deep breath and then stepped out onto the log, holding tightly to the rope with both hands. Very slowly she edged her way forward, Pedrin sick with impatience and trepidation. When she was almost halfway across, he turned and said to Durrik, "Mebbe you'd best go next. Will you be all right?"

Durrik hesitated then shrugged. He straightened up, tucked his crutch under his arm and seized the rope with one hand. For a second he looked as if he meant to say something, then he gave them all a strange smile and a wave of his hand. Without any more hesitation he began to sidle his way across the log, moving quickly, almost recklessly. Briony stared after him, frowning.

Just then the sun slid down below the bank of heavy cloud into a thin line of pure, shining radiance at the horizon. The whole scene was lit up warmly, the long rays of the setting sun lingering on the fair heads of the two children making their halting way across the log. There was a distant shout, and Pedrin and Briony exchanged horrified glances. The soldiers had seen Lisandre and Durrik.

"Hurry!" Pedrin said to Mags. "Be careful!"

She nodded and clambered up onto the log, giving them her gap-toothed grin before quickly and easily following Durrik, hand over hand.

"You sure you want to come last?" Pedrin said to Briony. "The soldiers will be here mighty quick!"

She nodded and flapped her hand. "Go! Go!"

"The goats'll be here to protect you," Pedrin said awkwardly, then he too climbed up onto the fallen log, careful not to pull too hard on the rope in case he caused the others to overbalance. He had both the saddlebags slung over his shoulders, which made movement a little awkward, but he had wanted to relieve Durrik of his burden, recognising how difficult the crossing would be for the crippled boy.

Pedrin glanced along the log. Lisandre was still moving very slowly, shuffling her feet along, one arm hooked over the rope as she used her other hand to haul herself along. Even hampered with his crutch and weak, crooked leg, Durrik was quickly gaining ground on her, while nimble-footed Mags was close behind. Pedrin silently urged Lisandre to hurry up, while casting another anxious look back the other way.

The soldiers were running up the hill, though they were finding the narrow, rocky path hard going in their high-heeled boots and heavy armour. Pedrin gave a grim little smile as he saw more than one stumble and trip. Then he concentrated on his own feet, for the mossy log was very slippery and angled down slightly with the occasional broken branch to negotiate.

A terrified scream rang out. The rope jerked wildly. Pedrin clung on desperately, looking quickly along the log. His heart moved sharply in his breast. Lisandre had slipped and fallen. She was clinging tightly to a dead branch, her lower body immersed in the foaming river. He could see her white terrified face, and Sedgely kneeling to try and reach her, and Durrik frozen where he stood, staring down at her. She was right below him and as Pedrin watched, she let go one arm so she could reach up to him.

"Your crutch!" Pedrin screamed. "Durrik, reach out with your crutch!"

Durrik did not move. Shouting at him, begging him, Pedrin hauled himself down the slippery log. Mags was hurrying along as frantically. She reached Durrik's side and seized the crutch from him, leaning over as far as she could, the crutch stretched out in her hand. They were all shouting desperately at Lisandre, but it was too late. She had lost her hold. Pedrin watched in sick horror as she plunged down into the river, her screaming face disappearing beneath the water.

Pedrin felt a cry force its way up from the very depths of his being. He threw off the saddlebags, tossing them to Mags, and then he dived forward off the log. The river swallowed him. He was shocked by its power. At once all the breath was pummelled out of him, his body was churned round and round, over and over, tumbling head over heels till he was unable to tell which way was up, which way was down. It felt as if the river had thrown him into a dark sack and was beating him with a stick. He was blind, deaf, panicked, water forcing its way down into his lungs.

The next second he was flung upwards. His head broke the surface and he managed to take a few ragged breaths before he was again sucked down. Something hard banged into him. He groped out and managed to grab something made of cloth. It ripped in his hand, but he had managed to seize Lisandre's arm, and then her waist. He held on grimly. Again his head broke through and he struggled to drag Lisandre up as well. She was limp in his arm and incredibly heavy. He looked about desperately, realising they were caught in the maelstrom below the waterfall. He got a whirling glimpse of Mags and Durrik stretching out their hands to him, but they were six or more feet above him. Then he saw Sedgely on his knees on the cliff-edge, throwing down what looked like another dead tree.

The splash it made swamped him. Pedrin went down again, swallowing water. All he could do was cling on to Lisandre. His vision was filled with swirling, hissing foam. His skull felt like it was about to explode. With an enormous effort, Pedrin kicked his legs, straining upwards. Though his arms ached and the muscles of his legs screamed, he managed to bring both their heads above water. He flung out one hand, caught the thorny end of the dead tree and heaved himself into its branches. There he and Lisandre hung, the starkin princess lying white and limp in his arms, her eyes closed. Pedrin's breath rasped in his throat.

Sedgely began to drag them up. Pedrin vomited up a gush of vile-tasting water, then closed his eyes for a moment, coughing weakly. He managed to catch his breath and at once bent over Lisandre, queasy with dread. Her cheeks were icy cold, completely colourless. Her head lolled on her neck. He could not tell whether she was breathing. With one arm hooked through the branches and the other supporting her weight, he could do nothing but press his face against the tree and pray to Lullalita, the goddess of water and grief and lost causes, to spare her.

21

◢ ◢ ◢

Sedgely, Durrik and Mags were all there on the shore, working together to drag them higher. Pedrin was so exhausted he could do nothing but cling to the branch. As the dead tree was hauled over the edge of the cliff, he let go and fell back to the ground in a sort of faint. He felt Durrik lean over him, calling his name and he managed to sit up, hanging his head forward between his arms.

"Is she dead?" he asked.

"What?"

"Is she dead?"

"I don't know. I don't think so. Sedgely's pumping water out of her."

Pedrin sat up more strongly, looking around. He saw Lisandre lying on her stomach on the ground, while Sedgely knelt beside her, his hands gently pumping together in the middle of her back. Lisandre suddenly vomited up a big rush of water. Sedgely sat back and let her lift herself to her hands and knees, so she could vomit again. When at last she was finished

273

she laid her head back down on her hands, crying softly. Pedrin was all choked up with tears himself. He watched Sedgely pat her gently, murmuring something in his deep, low voice, and then put his head back down on his knees.

"No thanks to you," he muttered.

Durrik leant closer. "What?"

"I said, 'no thanks to you'. Lisandre could've drowned and it would've been all your fault. Why didn't you stretch down your crutch to her?"

Durrik sat back and looked away, biting his lip. He was clutching his crutch close to his chest. He made a motion as if about to speak, just as Pedrin too opened his mouth again. Their words clashed, drowning each other, and both boys stopped, frustrated.

Suddenly Pedrin remembered the soldiers. Adrenaline surged through his body. He scrambled to his feet, looking about him wildly.

Briony was running lightly and easily across the fallen log, her sack slung over her one shoulder, the coil of rope over the other. The goats were close at her heels, not at all troubled by the slipperiness of the moss or the narrowness of the trunk. The soldiers were all at the other end of the log, milling around uncertainly. They certainly did not wish to follow in their boots and armour, with the last light fading quickly and no rope to guide them. One of the soldiers gave a quick gesture, and six of the soldiers went down on one knee and raised their fusilliers.

"Briony! Snowflake!" Pedrin screamed. "Run!"

He covered his eyes.

A spine-chilling cry rose high above the roar of the waterfall. All the hairs on Pedrin's arms stood straight up. He had never heard such a sound. Trembling in every limb, his shoulders hunching in an instinctive motion of protection, he looked up through his hands.

An immense, bat-winged creature was plummeting down from the cliffs. In the dusk it was just a shadow among other shadows, except for its face, which was illuminated from below by the red flames leaping from its mouth. It was a thin, cruel face, black-skinned, with slitted eyes and red, flaring nostrils. Two small, sharp horns rose from its forehead, and its ears were very long and pointed, rising from a magnificent golden mane that flowed down onto its powerful shoulders.

Pedrin did not need to see the rest of its body to know what it looked like, although he had never before seen one and knew no one who had. It was a grogoyle, a creature out of legend. With the face and wings of a bat, the body of a lion, and the tail of a giant scorpion, the grogoyle was the most dangerous of any of the wildkin. Even without the cruel, poisonous sting of its tail and its fiery breath, the grogoyle would be deadly, for it moved with incredible speed and agility and its sheathed claws were tipped with poison.

The soldiers had seen it coming too, and had raised their fusilliers against it. Again and again the starkin weapons spat blue lightning, but the grogoyle easily evaded their fire, tilting its wings up and twisting its graceful body. Before the soldiers had time to refuel, the grogoyle had struck. Some soldiers fell shrieking, enveloped in flames. Others were crushed below the immense body as the grogoyle landed with a thump that jarred the tree-bridge and caused it to slowly slide over the edge and into the foaming river. Others were stung by the darting tail, falling like stones, paralysed and in agony. Others were tumbled about by the heavy paws, the poison-tipped claws unsheathed and ripping apart armour like paper. The children crouched on the far shore could only watch, horrified and mesmerised, as the grogoyle destroyed the entire squad of soldiers in just a few seconds.

Briony and the goats had barely managed to leap to the shore in time and Snowflake, in the rear, would have fallen into the river if Briony had not caught her collar and hauled her to safety. Now Briony sat shivering on the very edge of the cliff, her face buried in Snowflake's shaggy white coat, listening to the screams of the soldiers slowly fade away.

Pedrin staggered to his feet. "Come on!" he cried, his voice so hoarse the words barely came out. "We got to get out of here!"

He caught up the saddlebags, half-dragged Lisandre to her feet, and began to run into the forest, whistling to the goats, who bounded past him with golden eyes wide in terror. Sick with fear and horror, exhausted and trembling in every limb, they all stumbled into the forest, expecting to hear the flap of leathery wings falling upon them, and that spine-chilling shriek of triumphant glee echoing in their ears. They heard nothing but the crash of their own headlong race through the forest, however, and saw nothing but the black entanglement of branch and vine and thorn that slashed their faces, tripped their feet and stabbed their flesh.

Soon Pedrin had to stop, panting. He was still holding on to Lisandre's hand and she was clinging to him tightly, trembling violently and trying to stifle her tears.

"This is stupid," Pedrin said angrily. "We'll all be lost in the forest. We'll have to call out, find the others."

"But ... that thing! That thing ... will ... hear us."

"If the grogoyle wanted us, it would've found us by now," Pedrin said, only half-believing his own words. He peered through the darkness, but could see no one. He tried to disengage his hand from Lisandre so he could cup his mouth to call, but she would not let go. He realised she was dripping wet and shivering so much her teeth were chattering. Gently he made her sit down and took his blanket out of his saddlebag and wrapped it about her shoulders. She gripped his hand in both of her small, cold, wet ones. "You saved my life," she said with great difficulty. "I thank you."

Overcome with embarrassment and pleasure, he muttered something in return and stepped away, calling out, "Durrik, Briony! Sedgely! Where are you?" At first he dared not call too loudly but then anxiety sharpened the edge in his voice. Then he heard Durrik's voice, shouting in response, his voice high in alarm. He called back, heady with relief, and Durrik and Mags came blundering to the spot where he and Lisandre were huddled. Then the goats and Briony came running in, Snowflake bleating in joy. The friends all embraced, their faces wet with tears of relief, pounding each other's backs.

"Sedgely?" Pedrin asked. "Anyone seen Sedgely?"

But there was no sign of the old man. The five children huddled together, too frightened to make a fire. They had no food left but Pedrin managed to bend his stiff, cold fingers enough to milk Snowflake, so they were able to comfort themselves with her warm, sweet milk and fall asleep at last, too worn out by the exertions of the day to even think about posting a watch.

It was a cold, misty morning when Pedrin woke. His wet clothes had stiffened in the night so he felt that he was clad in steel-cold armour and all his joints ached. He sat up, groaning, then suddenly realised that he smelt wood smoke. The very whiff of it was comforting and when he looked around and saw Sedgely was feeding a fire with kindling, and that his pail was hanging over the fire with something bubbling inside, Pedrin could have wept with relief and happiness.

"Oh, Sedgely, I'm mighty glad to see you," he said and shuffled forward to give the old man a little punch in the shoulder and to see what was in the pail.

"I couldn't find much," Sedgely said. "'Tis just milk and honey and some herbs, but at least it'll warm your innards. Shouldn't have slept in your wet clothes, you'll catch your death, you will."

Pedrin grinned and took the cup of hot milk the old man poured him, sipping it gratefully. He looked round and saw the others all sleeping together like a litter of puppies, huddled under the two blankets. The goats were lying contentedly back to back, though both had their heads raised to watch and listen.

"How did you find us?"

The old man's shaggy white moustache twitched. "Followed your trail," he said laconically. "Good thing no other wildkin seem to live hereabouts because it was a good mile wide. Found you all sleeping sweet and foolish as babes."

Pedrin coloured hotly. He spread his hands to the warmth of the fire and said nothing.

"Too much to hope I'm the only creature to see your trail," Sedgely said. "Though if a grogoyle has taken it into its head to roost hereabouts, mebbe all t'other wildkin have fled. Wise, really. We should too, is me advice. Not that I expect you to…"

"No, no," Pedrin said earnestly, laughing despite himself. "'Tis very good advice. We'll listen and obey, I promise."

Briony was stirring sleepily. She sat up suddenly and looked about her, and smiled widely at the sight of Sedgely. The smile completely transformed her face, making her almost pretty. He smiled back at her and slipped again into his grumble, all the while pouring her a cup of hot milk and exhorting her to drink it up. By the time she had finished the others were all awake too. As they quickly packed up the blankets and doused the fire, they all talked excitedly about the day before.

"What was that thing? I've never seen aught like it!"

"'Twas a grogoyle, and deadly dangerous 'tis too."

"Did you see how it stung with its tail? Horrible!"

"Why didn't it come after us? Had it enough to eat with all those soldiers?"

"It didn't seem to want to *eat* them, just kill them all." Mags gave a shiver of delicious horror.

"Do you think it was the grogoyle that you sensed watching us, Briony?" Durrik said, still very wan-faced and weary-looking.

She shrugged and nodded. "I think so. Though if it was a-watching us the whole time, why didn't it attack us?"

"Mebbe it just doesn't like starkin," Sedgely said.

Colour rose in Lisandre's cheeks and she said defensively, "Well, if it doesn't like starkin, why didn't it attack me?" And then she shot a look at the crippled boy and said, with rather a cruel edge to her voice, "And Durrik, for that matter?"

Durrik coloured and turned away. Presented with the sight of his back, the shirt all stained with ugly brown lines, the disdainful anger on Lisandre's face faded and she looked troubled and even remorseful. Everyone else felt awkward too, unable to forget how Durrik had crouched motionless on the log, Lisandre stretching her hand up to him desperately. Mags shot Lisandre an angry, resentful look and followed after Durrik, though she did not speak.

Sedgely continued comfortably, "Mebbe 'tis just soldiers it don't like. Don't ask me, little missy, *I* don't know how a grogoyle's mind works. Come, stop your a-blathering and let's be on our way. I mislike the quietness of this forest. Seems to me 'tis too quiet!"

All day they walked in single file through the damp,

gloomy forest. Without the river to guide them, the children all felt rather vulnerable. Pedrin in particular did his best to fix various landmarks in his memory in case they became lost or were separated again. Within the green gloom of the trees, however, it was impossible. Everything looked the same under the tangled canopy of vines and leaves, and the paths were uncertain, meandering through the ferns and saplings, round bulging rocks and twisted tree-roots, and petering out near the dens of various small animals.

In the grey dusk of the evening they wearily made camp near a small stream. Sedgely and Pedrin cast their fishing lines to try and catch some fish while the others searched through the forest for birds' eggs, fruit, nuts, roots, wild grains, vegetables and anything else they could find. The need to forage was a constant drag on their progress, and so they hoped to find enough to keep them going for several days.

By the time they rolled themselves in their blankets to sleep, pleasantly full and very tired indeed, a string of fish hung above the fire to smoke and two round loaves of bread, made from laboriously ground wild grains, were stowed away in Pedrin's saddlebags. Although it had been hard work, everyone felt a warm sense of satisfaction and camaraderie.

"Another week or so and we'll be at the Evenlinn," Sedgely said as he crossed his hands over his stomach, his nose pointing to the stars. "That is, if we don't run into any boo-bogeys."

22

◆ ◆ ◆

Pedrin opened his eyes and stretched, wondering what had woken him. It was almost dawn, the trees black against a pewter-coloured sky. Mist was rising from the pool but through the drifting tendrils he could see Thundercloud standing guard over someone cowering on the ground. The billy-goat's horns were lowered menacingly and he was rumbling deep in his throat.

"What happened? Who is it?" Pedrin asked rather stupidly, rubbing the sleep from his eyes. Thundercloud looked back at him, lifting his black lip, then butted the cowering figure with his long, sharp horns. She whimpered and huddled closer to the ground.

"Mags?" Pedrin asked, getting up. "What's going on?"

He stepped closer and realised, with a sudden upsurge of anger, that the little girl was hiding Briony's sack and his saddlebags beneath her. The others were all sitting up, rubbing their eyes, a little murmur of surprise and concern running between them.

"Naught," Mags said shortly. "That bad-tempered goat of yours just rammed me over. Ow! His horns are sharp. I'm covered in bruises."

"What you a-doing with me saddlebags?" Pedrin asked sharply.

She looked surprised. "Me? Naught. I must've tripped and fallen on them."

"But they were over there before, beside me. What are they doing all the way over here?"

"How would I know? That billy-goat gruff of yours probably dragged them off, a-trying to get at the food inside. You know what goats are like, they'll eat shoes if they can't get aught else. He was probably having a chew on the leather."

Pedrin reached down and seized the sack and the saddlebags.

"I said not to let that dirty ragamuffin accompany us," Lisandre said piously. "Of course she was only waiting for an opportunity to rob us."

Mags glowered at her from under the tangle of brown hair. "Warn't," she said rather weakly.

"Look, Lisandre, your dress!" Pedrin cried, pulling out handfuls of shimmering red silk. "And she's got your night-light and all your rings too."

Lisandre clapped a hand on the empty pocket of her cloak, colour flaming in her cheeks. "Why, you little sneak-thief!"

"Look, Lisandre, your bag of money too." Suddenly he gave a cry of outrage and pulled out a handful of loose coins. "The coins you gave me!" Pedrin clasped his silver crown close to his chest. "They were in me pocket. How did she get them out without me feeling her?"

"Sticky fingers," Mags said with a grin, wiggling her fingers.

"Look!" Durrik cried, rifling through one of the saddlebags. "All our food, our fish and the bread we baked and all the nuts and berries. And my bell! I can't believe she took Papa's bell."

"Mirabel!" Briony snatched up her little ragdoll and cradled her tightly, gazing at Mags with huge accusing eyes.

"That's me good knife. The rotten little thief."

They were all standing around the culprit now, exclaiming as they pulled out their most precious belongings. Mags lay back on her elbows resignedly.

"I told you we should not have trusted her," Lisandre said.

"Mags, why would you do such a thing?" There was deep reproach in Briony's voice.

Mags shrugged.

"Is that why you followed us around, because you wanted to rob us?" Durrik sounded hurt.

"Sure," she said. "Why else?"

"I told you—" Lisandre began.

"Oh, shut up," Pedrin said. He tossed her back her jewelled egg and dropped his own coins back into his pocket. Scowling, he said, "So what are we meant to do with her? There's not a reeve for miles, nor any stocks!"

"She should have her hand cut off for stealing from one of the Ziv," Lisandre said coldly.

"Oh, nah," Briony said involuntarily.

Mags went rather white but said defiantly, "I suppose you'll cut it off yourself? Starkin scum!"

"We'll just have to tell her to get lost," Pedrin said in disgust.

"But what would prevent her from following us and stealing from us again?" Lisandre demanded.

"We could tie her up to a tree," Durrik suggested.

"But these forests are so dangerous," Briony protested, at the same time as Mags said, "Leeblimey, I'll be monster bait!"

"What if we get Briony t'spin us a rope from a bit of thread? That way it'll only last long enough for us to get away."

"Long enough for a gibgoblin to flay the skin from me bones," Mags said.

"We'll hide our trail so she can't follow us," Pedrin said.

Mags laughed mockingly. "Leeblimey, I've been following you lot for days and you never knew it, what makes you think you'd be able t'stop me now?"

Pedrin shot an accusatory glance at Briony. "I thought you were able to sense that sort of thing?"

Briony flushed and dropped her eyes. "Many creatures live in this forest and they all watch us pass by. I can't always tell what 'tis that watches, you know."

"I must thank you for all the food you left out," Mags said with an impudent grin. "Saved me from having to hunt many a hungry night."

"I thought it was Sedgely eating the milk and honey," Pedrin objected.

"Not if I could get there first," Mags grinned.

Only then did Pedrin realise the old man was nowhere to be seen. Suspicion flared instantly. "A-talking about Sedgely, where is he?"

He saw his dismay and chagrin mirrored in Lisandre's and Durrik's faces, but Briony just gave a little shrug, saying, "I imagine he's a-swimming. He does most mornings, hadn't you noticed?"

"Nah, I hadn't," Pedrin snapped. "Not being a wildkin, I try to mind me own business."

He saw hurt in Briony's face and felt immediate remorse, but the curly-haired girl had moved away, her face downcast, and was bending to pick up their belongings spilt all over the ground.

Water splashed behind them. Pedrin whirled, his hand automatically flying to his slingshot. Sedgely was rising out of the mist-wreathed water, shaking drops from his matted beard and hair like a dog after a bath. He was covered in gingery-white hair, all plastered against his pale, freckled skin.

"Moon-cursers coming," the old man said without preamble. "We'd best get a-moving, they're hot on our trail."

Mags slammed her hand into the ground. "Chtatchka shake it!"

The others looked at each other in shock and dismay. To call on the god of earthquakes and thunder was to call on trouble, and never done lightly. Mags looked like a little black thundercloud herself, glowering with rage. "Blast that billy-goat! If it hadn't been for him, I would've been clear away, me pockets filled with coins and jewels and a swishy red dress too. That would've shown him I was as good a bandit as any of those bully-boys!"

She leapt to her feet. "Shake a leg, you lot! I'm not having me father a-getting hold of *me* loot."

"Your father?" Pedrin asked rather stupidly.

"Yeah, it'll be him, Chtatchka blast him! And just when I was a-getting ready to go home of me own accord, with me pockets bulging with booty. Come on, what're you all a-waiting for, he'll be here in half-a-crack!"

She began to throw their possessions at them, dancing up and down on the spot, and urging them to hurry. They did not hesitate, cramming their things into their bags and setting off up the path, Sedgely struggling to drag his clothes on over his wet limbs.

"You mean your father is an outlaw?" Pedrin asked, having to jog to keep up with the quick pace the little girl set.

She laughed mirthlessly. "He's *the* outlaw, hayhead! Diamond Joe himself."

"Diamond Joe?"

"Yeah, are you deaf?"

"Jumping Jimjinny!"

Unconsciously they all quickened their pace, looking about them for an escape route. The soaring trees crowded in close to the path, however, the spaces between their trunks crammed with ferns and brambles. The shrubbery sometimes leant so close they had to hold back branches for each other or duck under briars. Thundercloud raced ahead, his golden eyes glowering with pride and satisfaction, and Snowflake leapt behind him. Pedrin glanced back over his shoulder, and saw Sedgely close behind him, moving surprisingly quickly for such an old, bent man. Then, through the trees, some way back, Pedrin saw a group of big, hairy, dirty men, all bristling with weapons. A shout went up as they spotted him, and they broke into a run.

"Come on!" Pedrin shouted and took to his heels. Briony and Lisandre scrambled ahead, the little seamstress again carrying the heavy sack, with Mags disappearing into the green distance. Durrik swung his makeshift crutch furiously, racing after them. Suddenly his crutch slipped in the mud. He fell heavily, crying aloud. Pedrin dragged him up but Durrik could only hobble, his face twisting as he tried to keep back tears of pain. Pedrin swore and tried to help him along, but then they were surrounded by the bandits, all laughing and joking.

"Where's Maglen?" one of the men cried. "Where's me daughter?"

Diamond Joe was not at all what Pedrin had expected. He was a slim, lithe figure, not much taller than Pedrin, with long dark hair tied back with a silver clasp and a long green coat with silver buttons. He wore black boots to above the knee, and carried a sword at his hip. A diamond glittered in his ear and on his thumb. As Pedrin stared and stammered, the sword flashed out, the point pressing against Pedrin's throat.

288

"Where's me daughter?" Diamond Joe said in icy tones. Wordlessly Pedrin pointed up the path.

Diamond Joe jerked his head and half the men went hurrying on up the path, while Pedrin and Durrik stood close together, trying not to show their fear.

Diamond Joe leant on his sword, looking the boys over with a rather puzzled frown on his face. "Now what do we have here?" he mused.

Assuming he did not expect an answer, the boys stayed silent.

The goats had paused at the top of the path, looking back for their master. Seeing Pedrin held at sword point, Thundercloud and Snowflake came bounding back down the path, horns held low. One of the men shouted a warning and Diamond Joe wheeled, his sword flashing up. Pedrin cried out in horror and darted forward, but the goats avoided the sword gracefully, ramming two of the men and knocking them over.

Diamond Joe dropped his sword in disgust, saying curtly, "You fools! Get up and catch those goats. To be floored by a nanny-goat!"

Rubbing their posteriors ruefully, the two men got up and tried to catch the goats, who leapt about the rocks nimbly. Thundercloud knocked down one of the men again, but was caught by the deft throw of a lasso and dragged back to the bandits, tossing his horned head angrily and trying to twist away. Snowflake was caught as quickly, and they were lashed tightly to a low bough of a tree, the billy-goat still struggling and bleating with rage.

Then they heard Lisandre scream. Her furious voice came closer and closer, saying, "Unhand me, you great lumbering oaf, you asinine fool. How dare you touch me! I shall have the skin flayed from your back. Unhand me, I say!"

Pedrin could only hope the bandits did not speak Ziverian.

A struggling Lisandre was unceremoniously dumped at Diamond Joe's feet and he surveyed her with interest, one hand caressing his pointed black beard. Briony had been dropped as roughly. She crouched where she had landed, clutching her ragdoll close to her chest, her gaze fixed upon the ground.

Then they heard Mags as she too was carried kicking and screaming down the path. "Put me down, you cabbage-head! Fish-breath! Frog-face! Put me down! Leeblimey, I'll make you sorry." The man carrying her was stoically enduring her kicks and blows, but once he had deposited her at her father's feet, he rubbed his bruises ruefully, saying, "'Tis a hellcat you've got yourself there, sir!"

"So it seems," Diamond Joe replied coolly.

He regarded Mags sternly as she leapt to her feet, crying, "How dare you set your bully-boys upon me, Pa! I'll not—"

"That's enough out of you, Maglen," he snapped. To the surprise of the others, Mags fell silent, twisting her bare toe in the mud and regarding it unhappily. "How dare you disappear like that, a-wasting me time and the time of me men! You get back to camp before I give you a beating you'll never forget."

Mags looked up, sulky and defiant. "I won't!"

"You will, young lady, believe me! I haven't the time for this rubbish. There's a starkin lord camped out only a few miles from here and he's a-dripping with jewels. You should see the size of the diamond he's a-wearing on his finger. I want that diamond and me men want his men's weapons and no spoilt little girl is a-going to stop us a-getting them!"

Lisandre exchanged quick glances of dismay with the other children from Levanna-On-The-Lake. Lord Zavion!

Mags, not knowing or caring that the Regent of Estelliana was nearby, said sullenly, "Well, go and do your stupid robbery then. I'm a-doing just fine, thank you very much."

"Indeed? Is that so? You look like you've been dragged through a hedge backwards. And who are these raggle-taggle gypsies? What kind of company have you taken up with?"

Lisandre had scrambled to her feet and was dusting off her mud-smeared pinafore but at this comment she turned crimson and said in a clear, ringing voice, "How dare you, sirrah! Do you not know I am one of the Ziv?"

Pedrin rolled his eyes. "That's torn it," he whispered to Durrik.

Diamond Joe stared at her incredulously. She stared back at him, her chin raised proudly. Suddenly the bandit chief began to laugh. After a moment all the other bandits joined in, slapping their legs, holding their sides, wiping their eyes.

"How dare you mock me!" Lisandre cried. Diamond Joe only laughed louder. "You imbecilic oaf, how dare you laugh! When my brother has woken, he and his legions will march into this forest with spears and torches and he will drag you back to the castle in chains. You will beg him for mercy but his retribution will be swift and terrible. Your head will be impaled upon the battlements as a warning to all others that those of the Ziv will not be mocked and reviled!"

Diamond Joe managed to catch his breath. "I think she means it, boyos!" he cried. "A starkin princess walks among us!" He spat into the bushes and said contemptuously, "Starkin scum!"

She bit her lip, and stared at him haughtily. He walked around her, looking her up and down insolently. "Well, milady, you must forgive me surprise. One doesn't expect to meet a lady of the Ziv here, in the depths of the Perilous Forest." He made a sweeping gesture with his hand, then waved it up and down her person. "Nor is this what one expects a lady of the Ziv to wear." He smiled and all his men sniggered. Lisandre's face scorched with colour. She clenched her hands in the mud-streaked cloth of the shabby old pinafore but did not drop her eyes.

"Well, well, very interesting. I can almost forgive you for a-running away, Maglen, when you find yourself such charming and – dare I say it? – potentially profitable company."

"I found her, she's mine," Mags said flatly. "If you hadn't come a-barging in where you warn't wanted, I would've made off with all her jewels and money and her red swishy dress too."

"Jewels? Money? All very nice but your vision is a-lacking, I'm a-feared, Magsie me darling. Come, let us head back to camp and think about how we can best turn this to our advantage. No doubt the new Regent of Estelliana will be anxious indeed to clasp your charming young friend to his bosom once more. Anxious enough to pay a pretty penny for her!"

"I would not want to allow you to raise your hopes unnecessarily," Lisandre said sweetly. "Lord Zavion would not care if I never returned home!"

"Well, that too can be arranged if the price is right," Diamond Joe replied, striding down the path, the children and goats pushed and prodded along behind him. Lisandre faltered to a stop, her cheeks whitening, but the bandits only hustled her along, growling at her to shake a leg.

Mags skipped at her father's side. "I found her, Pa, the jewelled egg is mine. And the red dress."

"Of course, me dear," he replied urbanely. "If all goes according to plan, you can have as many dresses as you want."

"And her rings."

"Rings, brooches, bracelets, you can have a tiara if you wish, Magsie."

"Bully beef!" Mags said in delight.

23

♦ ♦ ♦

The children sat disconsolately within a cage woven from saplings and willow twigs, picking at a mess of boiled potatoes, and watching the bandits celebrate. Roaring with laughter, singing drunkenly, the bandits toasted each other with great tankards of apple-ale and stuffed themselves with roast pork. Mags was mincing around the camp in Lisandre's high-heeled ruby shoes, the red silk swishing about her. She wore all of the starkin girl's rings and the jewelled christening egg hung from her girdle.

"She had better not tear my dress," Lisandre said savagely. "Just wait until I get my hands on her! I'd wring her neck ... if only she'd wash it first!"

Despite himself, Pedrin laughed. Lisandre looked at him, surprised, then reluctantly smiled.

"All we can do is hope that Sedgely will come and rescue us," Pedrin said. "He wouldn't just disappear and do naught to help, would he? I can't believe he managed to slip away like that. One minute he was there, the next he was just gone."

"I'm sure Sedgely will come," Briony said. "Once all the bandits have gone to sleep, he'll find a way to get us out."

"I can't believe that little brat took me silver crown again," Pedrin said bitterly. "The first silver crown I've ever had and a cheeky good-for-naught bandit girl has to go a-stealing it."

"When I have woken my brother I will give you fifty silver crowns," Lisandre said grandly. "And a bag of gold too."

"Forgive me if I don't hold me breath," Pedrin answered sourly.

Lisandre thrust out her jaw and looked away. Pedrin, with an expression of intense dislike, picked up a long droopy curl of potato peel and threw it out through the bars of the cage. "I hate boiled potatoes."

"Who doesn't?" Lisandre snapped.

"What potatoes look alike?" said Durrik.

"All potatoes," Lisandre answered crossly, pushing her plate away.

"Nah, imitators," Durrik replied solemnly. "Get it? Imi-taters."

"Yes, I get it," she answered wearily.

"And what potatoes stir up trouble?"

"I don't know."

"Agitators. Get it?"

"Yes, I get it," she replied, smiling despite herself. "Very funny."

"And what potatoes never make up their minds?"

"Why don't you tell me?"

"Hesitaters, of course," Durrik said with a grin.

"And what potatoes get on your nerves?" Pedrin said peevishly, having heard all these jokes many times before.

"You can't mean me, surely? Milady, you don't find me irritating, do you?"

"Yes, I do," she answered. "Very irritating. I have never heard such feeble witticisms in all my life. You boys are truly tomfools, just like Briony said."

"Well, aught is better than just a-sitting round and a-waiting for Mags's father to hand us over to Lord Zavion," Durrik said. "Do you think he'll still be angry about his lens being broken, Lisandre?"

She just looked at him. Durrik sighed. "I suppose he will be. Tessula's tears, I wish I'd never set foot in his stupid crystal tower."

"Me too," Pedrin scowled.

Some time later, Diamond Joe and his two favourite henchmen came over to their cage, the bandit chief smiling widely. "I hope you find your quarters comfortable, milady?"

"This is an outrage," Lisandre said stiffly. "How dare you treat one of the Ziv in this manner! Do you not understand I am the second cousin, once removed, of the king himself?"

His smile widened. "Indeed I do, and I'm glad of it, I assure you, milady."

"If you think keeping me in a *cage* and feeding me *pig-food* is the way to improve your fortunes, you are very much mistaken," Lisandre said in her iciest voice. "If you approach Lord Zavion with your ridiculous demand for ransom, he will simply send in his soldiers and kill you all. The so-called Regent is not known for his clemency. He thinks my father was far too lenient in not curbing the depredations of your criminal associates a long time ago. He will raze this camp to the ground, and anyone left living will be hung. I can promise you this with all assurance."

Diamond Joe still smiled, but his henchmen looked rather nervous.

"However, if you allow me to go on my way unmolested, I assure you my brother Count Zygmunt of Estelliana will grant a pardon to you and to all your men and family, despite the grievous insult offered to me." Lisandre cast a venomous glance at Mags, who was lolling nearby, listening. Mags tossed her head and impertinently swung the jewelled christening egg to and fro.

"But everyone says your brother is so close to death, he barely breathes," Diamond Joe protested. "I think I'll try me luck with the starkin scum who actually rules."

"My brother will die if you do not let me go," Lisandre said, her voice shaking despite all her attempts to preserve her icy calm. She took a deep breath and said urgently, "I give you my word Ziggy will grant you all a pardon. You will no longer be an outlaw, forced to beg and steal for a living. You will be able to return to Estelliana, a free man, nay, a hero even. My brother will give you land, a house, gold, whatever it is you want. You'll be able to walk the streets of Levanna-On-The-Lake with your head held high, instead of creeping about in the dark of the moon, a price on your head and every man a potential traitor."

Mags had crept closer and was listening with a look of longing on her face. Her father laughed, though, and said, "You think I'm such a cabbage-head that I'd trust the word of a starkin?"

"My word is my bond," Lisandre said desperately, but he only laughed and stepped away.

"Lord Zavion will not pay you a ransom for my release!" Lisandre called after him. "He will descend on you like a gibgoblin upon a baby goat. You will all die a traitor's death and I'm glad!"

There was no one left to listen, though, and Lisandre flung herself upon the muddy ground and sobbed heartbrokenly. Briony comforted her as best she could, but all the starkin girl could say was, "Ziggy's going to die, he's going to die."

"Sedgely will come, he'll rescue us," Briony said. "We just need to wait."

But Sedgely did not come. Eventually the bandits began to snore loudly, most of them lying where they had fallen. Once all was quiet, Pedrin and Durrik began desperately to test the bars of the cage, but the saplings had been hammered deep into the iron-hard ground and the boys were not strong enough to shift them. The door was tightly chained and fastened with an enormous padlock they had no hope of breaking. They tried, though, spending all their strength on the effort, until at last they had to stop, trembling with fatigue and grinding their jaws in frustration.

Exhausted with emotion, Lisandre fell asleep with

her head on Briony's lap, but the others were all too cold and uncomfortable and anxious. They knew Diamond Joe had sent one of his men to seek out the soldiers still searching for Lisandre in the forest. They knew from the bandits' conversation that the soldiers were not very far away. There was little doubt they would be in Lord Zavion's hands by morning time.

There was a faint rustle. Briony's head jerked up and she leant forward. A small, quick shadow darted through the mist beginning to rise from the ground.

"Is it Sedgely?" Durrik whispered hopefully.

Briony shook her head.

"'Tis me," Mags whispered. She had taken off the red dress and looked like the girl they knew again, though very much cleaner.

"Come to crow?" Pedrin said bitterly.

"Nah. Wouldn't waste me breath," Mags replied. "I've come to help – mebbe."

"Why would you want to help us?" Pedrin demanded. "You got what you wanted."

She hesitated, then jerked her head at the sleeping Lisandre. "You been with that starkin scum for a while. Her word any good?"

"If you mean does she a-keep her promises, well, I think she'd try," Briony answered quietly.

Mags was silent for a while, then she asked abruptly, "What about this Lord Zavion? Is it true what she says about him or is it all bluster?"

"I think 'tis true," Briony said. "He's a vain, ruthless man, and doesn't care about the hearthkin or anyone else for that matter. It would irk him bad to be beholden to a bandit. He's likely to pretend to be a-willing to talk terms and then set a trap for your father. All he needs to do is fly in more troops on his sisika birds, under the cover of darkness, and a-land in the nearest clearing."

Mags made a little murmur in her throat. She was silent for a while, then said gruffly, "Wake her up. I want to make a bargain with the starkin scum."

"Don't call her that," Durrik burst out. "She's not scum. I know she gives herself airs and graces, but she's really a nice person underneath."

"She has you bedazzled," Mags said scornfully. "I suppose you think so because she's pretty. Boys are all the same."

"Am not," Pedrin snapped. "*I'm* not bedazzled."

"Could've fooled me!"

"I'm not!"

She shrugged her shoulders impatiently. "Stop all your a-blathering, I haven't time for it. Wake her up."

Gently Briony shook Lisandre awake. She yawned and rubbed her eyes and sat up, murmuring, "Huh?"

"Mags wants to talk to you."

Lisandre was awake instantly. "Well, I do not wish to converse with her. Tell her to go away."

"She says she'll help us."

"I think she has helped quite enough already."

"I think she wants to make a bargain."

"Indeed?"

"Did you mean what you said, about your brother giving me pa a pardon?" Mags burst out. "And a fine townhouse? With glass in the windows and pink silk curtains? And a real fireplace with a chimbley?"

Lisandre nodded slowly, surprised out of her hostility. "If you helped us, I'm sure Ziggy would be grateful," she said. "And he truly is very fair. If he knew I'd promised you something, he would honour that promise, I'm sure of that."

Mags pulled out a small leather wallet and opened it to show a collection of slim steel tools. "Me pa's a-going to be so angry," she said, half-fearfully, half-joyfully, as she slid two of the tools into the lock and carefully manipulated them. "I'm a-going to have to run away again."

"What are those things?" Pedrin asked curiously.

"Me pa's lock-picking tools," she answered with a grin. "I nicked them from his coat pocket. Oh, he's a-going to be spitting blood!"

"Would he really beat you?" Briony said sympathetically.

"Pa? Leeblimey, nah! Of course not. But he'll yell at me, and forbid me from a-leaving camp. He always does."

"What about your ma?" Pedrin asked, thinking with a pang of his own mother and wondering if she and Mina were still locked up, and how they were faring.

"Don't have nah ma," Mags said matter-of-factly. "She were killed by the starkin. When Pa couldn't pay the taxes, they a-burnt down our home. Me baby brother was asleep inside and me ma ran in to try to save him. They both got killed. That's why me pa turned outlaw. He swore revenge on the starkin and

301

he's been a-bothering them ever since, a-stealing their gold and jewels, and a-trying to persuade the hearthkin to turn rebel. They all be too scared, though, the cabbage-heads."

Lisandre was staring at her with horrified eyes. "Oh, that is so awful," she whispered. "Surely the soldiers could not have known your brother was in the house still?"

"Didn't stop t'ask," Mags said simply. "Me whole family could've been in there for all they cared. They just rode up, beat me pa into a black-and-blue swoon, and then a-fired the cottage. Didn't give us time to get aught out, not a scrap of clothing or a bite of food. There'd been a drought that summer, which was why the crops had failed. House didn't take long to burn. I was out a-tending the pigs when I saw the smoke. By the time I ran back across the yard there was naught much left but cinders."

Lisandre's hands were clenched tightly. "Lord Zavion has a lot to answer for!"

"Oh, it warn't the Regent who ordered it," Mags said, "'Twas your precious pa."

"My pa?" Lisandre whispered. "You don't mean it was my father who…"

"Yeah, sure. And me pa's not the only one. Justabouts every man here has a similar tale to tell."

Lisandre was stricken into silence. Her fingers worked at the coarse cloth of her pinafore, but her eyes stared blindly out into the night.

Just then the lock clicked open. Mags gave a mocking bow. "Your freedom, milady."

As she stowed the tools away in her pocket, the children crawled out thankfully, stretching their cramped limbs.

"We'll need all our stuff," Pedrin commanded. "And where are Thundercloud and Snowflake? I hope someone milked her, she'll be in pain otherwise."

"They're in with t'other goats, I can't be a-getting them," Mags said. "You'll have to leave them."

Pedrin was outraged. "I can't leave me goats! Nah, we have to get them."

"And I want my christening egg back," Lisandre said. "And my dress."

"Nah, they're mine now! Losers, weepers."

"They're not yours, they're mine."

"Not any more."

Lisandre sat down. "Then the bargain is void. I cannot and will not give away my christening egg. It was a gift from the king himself. Besides, you are not permitted to carry it. If you were ever seen with it, you would lose your hand, if not your life. Only the Ziv may own such a thing."

"You let Sedgely have your brother's egg."

"I did not let him have it, he took it and I have not been able to get it back. Besides, Sedgely is a wildkin, he lives in the Perilous Forest a million miles from anywhere. You want to live at Levanna-On-The-Lake where other people will see you. That's different."

"Will you girls stop a-bickering!" Pedrin hissed. "You'll wake the bloody bandits!"

"I will not go without my egg," Lisandre said obstinately. "I'll give you all my other jewels and the dress too, if you want it, but not my egg."

Mags suddenly gave in. "All right then, let's just get the stuff and get out of here before somebody hears us. The goats are penned up over there, Pedrin, if you want to risk a-waking everyone up with the bleating. I'll sneak in and get everything else. That'll show Pa I'm as good a thief as any of his bully-boys!"

Mist swirled and scudded along the ground, though overhead the sky was thick with stars. Pedrin crept along to the pen where the livestock were all tethered, having to step over the occasional snoring bandit. They all stank of apple-ale and he thought with some scorn how stupid they all were, to drink until they could not move in the very heart of the Perilous Forest. Even the man who had been given the watch lay sleeping, a ceramic pot hanging from his hand.

Thundercloud heard him coming and leapt to his feet, bleating his outrage at being locked up in a pen crammed with dirty swine and common, woolly-brained sheep. In vain Pedrin tried to shush him, but Thundercloud only tossed his long horns and broadcast his displeasure. Pedrin scrambled over the paling fence, landed on his hands and knees in squishy, stinking mud and seized the goat's nose in his hand, pinching the nostrils shut. Thundercloud could not bleat if he could not breathe, and so eventually he had to quieten, though he put up a good fight first.

When Pedrin had finally subdued him, he knelt in the vile-smelling muck and listened intently, terrified one of the bandits would have woken at the ruckus. All was quiet. There was only the soft shuffling noises of the forest at night. He relaxed his hand on the high-boned bridge of Thundercloud's nose and the billy-goat shook his head irritably and tried to swipe Pedrin with his horns, but did not trumpet again.

All the animals in the pen were uneasy, though, milling around and muttering. Pedrin had to fight his way through to the gate, dragging Thundercloud by his collar. His hand was on the latch when he heard something that made his heart jolt and a cold sweat break out on his body. It was the flapping of wings.

He leant on the gate, listening so hard his ears felt as unnaturally large and sensitive as a bat's. The sound came again and he looked fearfully up at the sky. High in the sky, the moonlight shining on their outstretched white wings, were rank upon serried rank of sisika birds. They were descending quickly, the only sound of their approach the ominous beat of their wings.

For a moment Pedrin was paralysed with indecision. He could not let the bandits lie there snoring, though, with starkin soldiers descending upon them in deadly silence. They would all be slaughtered, Mags's father among them, and then the soldiers would simply fan out through the forest until they caught the children too. So Pedrin swung open the gate and, as a triumphant Thundercloud went bounding away through the camp, Snowflake leaping beside him, Pedrin scrambled atop a barrel, beating a feed tray with a metal ladle. The sound was horrendous.

"Starkin a-coming," he shouted. "Wake up! Starkin a-coming!"

All round the clearing, bandits woke with grunts and confused mutters. They rolled over, groping for weapons, shouting the alarm. Pedrin whistled to his goats and they came leaping to his side, one slim and white, the other shaggy and black, both bleating with joy to be united with him again. The three of them went hurtling through the camp, bounding over sleepy, bewildered bandits, until they reached the others, who crouched half-terrified, half-indignant on the far side of the camp.

"What are you doing?" Lisandre demanded. "I thought the idea was to creep out of here as quietly as we can. The whole camp is awake now!"

"Starkin," Pedrin panted and pointed up at the sky. The stars were all swamped now by waves of white wings, for the sisika birds were coming down to land.

Mags leapt to her feet, dropping the bags and bundles she had been carrying in her arms. "Me pa!" she cried. "I have to warn him!"

Pedrin held her back. "There he is, he's awake, he knows," he said all in a tumble. "Come on, we have to get out of here while all is confusion. I've done what I can to warn the bandits, 'tis up to them now."

Battle had begun in the clearing. They saw the flash of steel as the bandits attacked with swords and knives and axes, and the thrust of spears as the starkin retaliated, and then the first stab of blue lightning as one of the starkin fired his fusillier.

Mags was sobbing. "They'll all be killed."

"I did warn them," Lisandre said.

The bandit-girl turned on her, hands clenched.

"Shut up, shut up! I hate you! This is all your fault! You starkin scum are all the same, smug arrogant bastards…"

To everyone's surprise, Lisandre burst out crying too, saying incoherently, "We're not, we're not. I swear it's not my fault. I did try to warn them. Oh, I'm sorry, I'm sorry."

"Hush, hush," Briony said. "Come, Pedrin is right, we can't stay here, we'll be killed or captured. Come away, come away." She drew both girls away into the concealing mist, Durrik limping along behind. Mags dragged against her hand, staring back at the bandit camp. The scene was suddenly lit with an eerie blue glare as more fusilliers were fired. Mags gave an ear-piercing wail. "Nah, nah, me pa!"

They all turned back, in time to see Diamond Joe zapped by a bolt of blue lightning. For a moment he was silhouetted mid-thrust, black outlined in crackling blue, then he simply dissolved away into nothing.

Mags screamed but in one quick stride Pedrin had his arm about her shoulders, his other hand clamped over her mouth. She fought him, trying to get back, but he dragged her away, hissing at the others to follow. In a dazed, stumbling run they obeyed, the goats leading the way through the dark forest tangle.

24

♦ ♦ ♦

For a time they could only stumble forward, sometimes running, sometimes walking, clinging to
each other and to their baggage, desperate to get away
from the bandit camp. Mags moved like a sleepwalker,
quiet now except for an occasional shuddering sigh. It
was very dark and gloomy under the trees, mist
swirling up about their faces. If it had not been for the
white bob of Snowflake's tail they would have wandered off the path and been lost, but the little
nanny-goat led them true, bleating occasionally in
reassurance.

After a long while, Pedrin called a halt and they all
sat down and rested, limp with shock and weariness.
No one had a word to say. It had grown light enough
for them to see each other's strained, white faces but
everyone looked away into the dripping, fog-
shrouded undergrowth. Mags had her face buried in
her knees. It was cold and the children were glad to
huddle into their cloaks and blankets.

"Does anyone have any idea where we are?" Pedrin

whispered at last.

Briony shook her head. "I'm sorry," she said. "I tried to watch where the bandits were a-taking us but they seemed to lead us in circles. I couldn't keep me sense of direction straight."

Mags laughed bitterly, lifting her face. "They did. Lead you in circles, I mean. Me pa was good at that."

Briony gave her a little rub on the arm in sympathy but Mags shook her off irritably. "So that's that," she said. "Pa's gone too. I'm an orphan." She spoke in the same matter-of-fact tone as when she had spoken of her mother's death.

"I'm so very sorry," Lisandre said with awkward but heartfelt compassion.

Mags shrugged, not returning her gaze. "'Twas me own fault. I was greedy. I wanted your little singing egg and your swishy red dress and so I got meself involved with a starkin. Should've known it'd lead to trouble."

"Not that kind of trouble, though," Lisandre said. "I never meant – I never wanted…"

"Yeah, I know. Didn't know I existed, did you, me and me pa? Had to happen one day. Can't go a-pulling the Regent's nose and a-trying to blackmail him and not get yourself into a pot of trouble. I knew it. That's why I thought if I helped you … mebbe, just mebbe…"

She buried her face again and her shoulders heaved. The others all exchanged glances of misery and compassion over her head. Snowflake thrust her nose into the crook of her arm, and Mags flung her arms about Snowflake's neck, burying her head in the soft white coat.

After a while she lifted her head and wiped her nose defiantly on her sleeve. "Mebbe you'd all better tell me what's bin going on," she said. "Seems like I'm with you now, willy-nilly, and I feel I've a right to know what you're all doing here, a-traipsing through the forest with a starkin princess and a-talking all the time about magic and wildkin and prophecies."

Pedrin was surprised. He had forgotten that Mags did not know their true purpose in journeying into the dark heart of the Perilous Forest. By the look on the others' faces, they too had forgotten.

So they told her how the count and his men had been poisoned; and how Lisandre's brother had drunk only a mouthful and so had not died like the others but was sunk in this strange, unnatural sleep; and how they planned to seek out the Erlrune of Evenlinn and see if she knew the antidote; and how Durrik had foretold that only a party made up of six of the land's ancient and irredeemable enemies could break the curse.

By the time the whole story had been told it was fully light, though still very dank and gloomy with mist. Mags cast Durrik a look of frank admiration out of her bright hazel eyes. "So you be the one a-prophesising and a-telling the future? I knew you were summat special, the first time I saw you, I knew it."

Colour scorched up Durrik's face. He shook his head. "I aren't special," he said very gruffly. "I don't know when 'tis a-coming or what I'm going to hear. It just comes and there's naught I can do but listen and speak. It's awful."

"What do you hear?" Mags asked, wide-eyed.

Durrik looked at her rather shyly. "'Tis just voices, sometimes very faint and far off, like voices a-crying in the wind, sometimes clear as a bell, right in my ear. That's how it was in the crystal tower, I could hear it so loud it was almost talking *through* me. But I'd been a-hearing those words for a while then, mainly in my dreams. Or if I was really tired and sort of slipped off into a daze, then I'd hear the words, fragments really, a-floating past my ear." He paused, discomfited, but then, encouraged by her amazed interest, said shyly, "I thought I was a-going mad. I didn't want anyone to know."

Briony was as intent and interested as Mags. "Nah, not mad. 'Tis the gods, a-talking through you. It must be." She spoke with awe in her voice.

"But why? Why me?" he demanded rather wildly. "I don't want it! I want to be like other folks, just happy and quiet and without voices in my dreams all the time."

"Mebbe 'tis because you listen," Briony said gently.

"But I don't," Durrik said. "I cram my fists in my ears and refuse to listen. I hum and whistle and make up jokes so I don't have to listen."

"You mustn't," Briony said. "If the gods speak to you, you must hear what they have to say."

"Have you always heard the gods?" Mags whispered, so awestruck she could hardly speak.

Durrik was unfolding under the warmth of her interest like bread dough rising by the fire. "Just scraps before that time in the crystal tower." He shot a

311

look at Pedrin, who was staring at him as if he never knew him. "The first time was that time our raft capsized and I almost a-drowned in the river. I heard a deep, calm voice say to me, 'He who was born under water shall under water die.' So I knew I was a-going to drown and was just resigning myself to it when Pedrin dived down and dragged me back up to the surface. I remember it every time I go near deep water and I heard it again, milady, on the log when you were a-hanging on and a-reaching up to me, I heard it clear as a bell in my ear. 'He who was born under water shall under water die.'"

"That's why you didn't try and help me," Lisandre exclaimed. "I thought it was because you hated the starkin, because they'd rejected you. I thought it was because you hated me and wished I was dead."

"I could never hate you, milady," Durrik said softly and blushed.

Lisandre coloured too and looked away. For a moment there was an awkward silence and then Briony said, puzzled, "But how did you a-know the prophecy meant you'd die by drowning, Durrik? Were you born under water? 'Cause I never heard of anyone but a lake-lorelei being born under water before."

Durrik grew so hot and red and uncomfortable it was painful to watch. He dug at the ground with the rough end of his makeshift crutch and would not meet anyone's eyes.

At last he said, with a gulp of breath, "I *was* born under water, you see. My mother ... when her family found out she and my father ... they threw her out,

312

she had to flee. Papa says she was very distraught. He could not comfort her, she wept and wept. They were a-travelling on a ship up the coast, and she was sick something terrible, he says. Anyway, one night it seemed she couldn't stand it any longer and she … she threw herself off the ship. My father … he had awoken and known something was wrong, and he jumped in after her and managed to keep her afloat till they dropped a lifeboat in … but the shock of it all made me come early, and so I was born there in the sea, in the darkness, my father a-holding my mother up so she didn't drown. He says they all thought I was dead, I was that blue and would not breathe, but there was a woman on the boat, he thinks she might have been one of the Crafty, she rubbed me and breathed her own breath into me and worked on me for a long time until I breathed for myself. So you see, that's how I know I'm a-going to die by drowning, for I *was* born under water, just like the voice said."

There was a very long silence as they all absorbed the many ramifications of this story. Pedrin in particular was stricken. He had always thought rather vaguely that Durrik had made up his declaration in the crystal tower like he made up puns and riddles and silly rhymes. If Pedrin had ever really wondered if the prophecy was a true foretelling, he had pushed the thought away, uncomfortable with anything that smacked of the Crafty. He had been conscious of a widening gulf between him and his friend ever since the catastrophic events in the crystal tower, but had blamed it on their weariness, their preoccupation, their anxiety over the fate of their families. Every now and then he had been conscious of a pang of jealousy, because Durrik was so much better-looking than him, and always knew what to say, and could speak with Lisandre in flawless Ziverian while Pedrin mangled every word and made her laugh with his rough accent. He had stamped down these feelings too, not wanting to admit even to himself that he cared if Lisandre smiled at Durrik's jokes or if she admired his fair delicate looks, so like the starkin men of her acquaintance.

The revelation that Durrik was half-starkin had only widened the gulf between the two boys, for Pedrin had been hurt that his friend had never confided in him, and angry that Briony could see what he could not, and vaguely disgusted that Durrik was a half-breed and one of a race that Pedrin had learnt to hate with every fibre of his being. Paradoxically, Pedrin had been both angered and repelled by Durrik's failure to help Lisandre during the crossing of the log bridge, not knowing whether to think him a cowardly weakling, too afraid to stretch out his crutch, or a ruthless knave that would rather watch a beautiful young girl drown than hold out a helping hand to one of the starkin.

Pedrin's emotions about Durrik and Lisandre had all been in such a tangle that he had not been able to sort them out, and so he had busied himself with practicalities like food and finding the path and keeping his pouch full of well-shaped stones and minding the goats. Now, all at once, he knew the pitiful story of

Durrik's birth and how deep the injury ran, and understood his terror of water and why he had failed to help Lisandre, and saw, with a little sinking feeling of shame, how he himself had helped to make Durrik fear and dread this uncanny ability of his to hear the future.

These revelations should have made Pedrin feel even more tangled up and confused but instead they acted like a knife, cutting through the snarl of his feelings like his own knife had once slashed through Lisandre's hair, emancipating him in one quick, ruthless cut. He saw that the gulf between him and Durrik was of his own making, and that it had caused his friend grief; and he saw that being born of a starkin mother and having the power to hear the gods were what made Durrik what he was. His eyes smarted and his throat closed up and he tried to smile, but could not, so leant over and gave his friend a hard punch on the shoulder.

"You're such a cabbage-head, Durrik," he said.

Durrik looked at him in surprise and grinned, and the chasm between them closed without a single grind or shudder and everything was as it had always been.

The other three children had been making their own adjustments. Briony's eyes were soft and grey with sympathy and understanding, Mags was gazing at Durrik with a look of fierce protectiveness mingled with wonder, and Lisandre was once again grappling with a world that was very different from what she had imagined.

"What about me?" she asked then, with her voice

full of stifled longing. "What do you hear about me?"

Durrik gave her a troubled look, and drew a little pattern in the mud with the tip of his crutch. "Next shall be the king-breaker, the king-maker, though broken himself he shall be…" he whispered.

"What does that mean?" she asked blankly.

Durrik shook his head. "I don't know. How could I know? 'Tis what I hear when I think of you. Sometimes I hear more, but 'tis only fragments … mebbe I will hear more later, but now … naught is clear."

"What about me?" Mags demanded.

He smiled at her dreamily. "A crutch for the crippled, a shield for the meek…"

"Naught about a nice house with glass in its windows and a chimbley and rose-coloured curtains?" Mags said with bitter disappointment in her voice. "Mebbe you're a-hearing wrong?"

"A voice for the speechless, a sword for the weak…"

"Surely you don't be a-hearing all of that?"

Durrik nodded, looking sad. "I do."

Mags scowled and clenched her fists together. "Well, I must say, there's need for someone to be a-doing some loud talking and fighting in Estelliana," she said. "'Tis uncommon cruel that a little girl like me can be left all lonesome in the world, with not one bit of family left anywheres and no home of me own. 'Tis mighty mean, that's all I can say."

Everyone had to agree, even Lisandre, who nodded her head in sympathy.

"Well, I don't know about the rest of you but I'm

mighty hungry," Pedrin said. "Does anyone have a bit of food about them, for me sides are fair flapping together?"

Forlornly they all shook their heads.

"Thank Liah we've got Snowflake," Pedrin said. "Though I'm beginning to feel a mite of sympathy with Sedgely and think milk just does not quench a man's thirst."

He called the little nanny-goat to him and sat before her, leaning his head against her warm flank and milking her swiftly and expertly, as always soothed by the sound of the squirting milk and by her sweet, clover smell. She turned her head and nudged him with her nose, and he kissed her on the little whorl of hair between her horns.

"You coddle that nanny-goat," Durrik said, surreptitiously rubbing his leg. "What's the only thing you'll get from a pampered goat?"

"What then?" Pedrin asked, glad for once that Durrik was asking riddles.

"Spoilt milk," Durrik answered with a grin, stretching his toes to try and relieve the cramp in his calf.

"Very funny," Pedrin replied. "I s'pose that means you don't want none."

"Yeah, please," Durrik said. "I'm starving too."

They were taking turns to dip the cup into the bucket when suddenly there was a rustle in the bushes right behind them, then a tall, bent shape loomed up out of the mist. Lisandre screamed.

"Whist, no need to be a-screaming," Sedgely whispered. "'Tis only me."

Lisandre had her hand to her chest. "Do not creep up on people like that," she said sternly. "I almost expired of heart failure."

"No need to bite me nose off," he said reproachfully. "I thought you'd be glad to see me, little missy."

"Oh, Sedgely, I am – we all are – so glad to see you!" Briony said and embraced the old man affectionately. "What ever a-happened to you?"

Sedgely blushed and rubbed his nose in pleased embarrassment. "Oh, I didn't much feel like being poked and prodded by a bunch of bandits, little missy. They have very sharp swords, you know. Besides, I thought it might be useful to have one of us still at liberty, so to speak. So I just sat down in the undergrowth and then when you all went a-blundering off down the path, I just followed along behind, quiet like."

"But why didn't you come and rescue us when the bandits were all asleep?" Pedrin demanded. "We were stuck in that cage thing for hours."

"They warn't all asleep," Sedgely said simply. He nodded his snarled white head at Mags. "This one here was still wide awake and a-creeping about, and forgive me if I mistook the matter, but she didn't seem to be that kindly disposed towards you all. So I just nosed about the forest for a while, breathed up a little mist to provide some cover, and a-waited me chance. You could have knocked me over with a feather when I saw Missy Mags let you all out."

"What do you mean, you breathed up some mist?" Pedrin asked curiously.

"Oh, that's just a little trick I know," Sedgely said. He breathed in deeply, held it for a long moment, then breathed out through his nose. Two long streamers of mist flowed out and roiled into the air.

"Jumping Jimjinny!" Pedrin cried. "That's a useful trick to have. How do you do it? Could I learn?"

Sedgely tugged his beard. "I don't rightly know," he said cautiously. "Mebbe."

"Sedgely, did you see what happened at the bandits' camp?" Briony said very seriously.

"I heard," Sedgely replied. "Didn't want to get close enough to be *seeing*."

"Do you know … how did things fare for the bandits?" Mags said anxiously.

Sedgely blew out through his nostrils noisily. "Not good," he admitted. "They put up a good fight, though, for men half-addled with the apple-ale. It'll be a while before the soldiers' heads stop a-ringing, I'd say."

Tears ran down Mags's face. She sniffed defiantly, scrubbing her eyes with her sleeve.

"Sedgely, do you know where we are?" Lisandre asked. "I'm afraid we are lost."

"Yeah, I think I might know whereabouts we be," the old man answered, without any real conviction in his voice. "We've come a long way out of our way."

"Do you know how to get to the Evenlinn from here? Every day brings Ziggy closer to death. We must get to that witch just as soon as we can."

"Well, yeah, I do know the way from here, though 'tis not a way I'd ever choose to go meself. The hills

319

are steep this way, too steep to climb, even for your goats. There is one pass through the hills, only a few days' march from here. That would bring us right to the shore of the Evenlinn, but indeed, I do not think you want to be a-going that way."

"Why not?" Lisandre demanded. "If it brings us right to the shores of the Evenlinn, I think we should go that way."

Sedgely tugged his beard. "'Tis not a way I'd be a-choosing, little missy."

"Why not?" she said again. "What's wrong with it?"

"Boo-bogeys," he said succinctly.

"Boo-bogeys? Boo-bogeys are nothing but stories made up to frighten small children."

"Is that so, little missy? Well, no doubt you would know best, having spent all your life within the safety of your castle walls while I'm naught but a poor wild-kin who has lived nowhere but the Perilous Forest."

Lisandre had the grace to blush.

"What kind of boo-bogeys, Sedgely?" Briony asked anxiously, knowing it was a term used to describe a wide array of different spirits and ghosts, both mischievous and malevolent.

Sedgely looked unhappy. "They call it the Gorge of Ghouls."

In the warmth of the midday sun, the six companions stood at the mouth of the ravine in real trepidation. The Gorge of Ghouls was a deep, narrow chasm that cut its way through the rock. Although the sun was high overhead, the ravine was black with shadow so that they could only see ahead a few feet.

"So do we still want to go through there?" Pedrin said, scowling ferociously to hide his fear.

"We have to," Lisandre said rather uncertainly. "It would take us a month to backtrack and find another pass through the mountains, you know that. We've come too far to turn back now."

Pedrin nodded. It had taken them over a week to reach the pass, for the way was steep and all were tired from the exertions of their long journey. They had also had to take the time to forage for food, and to find a way to make torches that would burn for some length of time.

"Well, let's get it over with," the goatherd commanded. "You all heard what Sedgely said. Ghouls only eat corpses, and prefer rotting meat, so they will only try and kill us if they're really hungry. They're afraid of fire, so as long as we keep close together and keep our torches lit, we should be fine."

"Just bully," Mags said in a hollow voice.

Pedrin ignored her. "Durrik's got his father's bell, and we all know boo-bogeys will flee at the sound of a bell, which is why we have bell-criers at all. So he will go first, ringing the bell every step of the way. The girls can go in the middle, and Sedgely and I behind with the goats."

He paused, half-expecting Mags to protest, but she said nothing. Pedrin knelt with his tinder and flint in his hand, chanting the prayer to Liah the Hearth-Keeper with more than usual fervour.

A spark kindled, leapt, dwindled, caught hold. Pedrin thrust the torches they had made into the heart of the fire until they began to flicker with a sullen flame.

"They aren't burning very well," Briony said nervously.

Pedrin blew on them, and the flame flared yellow for a mere instant, then sank again. "Lisandre, mebbe you'd better keep that night-light of yours close to hand, just in case," he said, his scowl growing deeper. "Briony, have you got a cat's cradle woven?"

She nodded, patting her pocket.

With the flickering torches in their hands, they stood for a moment longer, then Pedrin gave Durrik a little shove with his hand. "Go on, cabbage-head. Ring your bell."

Durrik took a deep breath, unswaddled his bell and swung it in his hand. A deep melodious tone rang out. He swung it with greater confidence, and slowly moved forward into the gorge. The girls followed close behind, holding their torches out like spears. Thundercloud shoved his way to the front, horns lowered, yellow eyes baleful, while Snowflake trotted close by Pedrin's side, bleating rather piteously.

Sedgely shook his matted head. "You're too old for this, you fool." He gripped his torch in his gnarled hand and followed the others into the shadowy gorge. Cold struck at them like a knife. There was a most unpleasant smell, which made Lisandre gag and almost drop her torch. She clamped one hand over her mouth and stumbled on, the smoke from her torch wavering wildly.

The ringing of the bell echoed all around, so that it sounded like a legion of bell-criers marched with them. Their step grew more confident, though it was hard to walk with the ground so rough and uneven, littered with rocks and dry sticks that snapped beneath their feet. Pedrin glanced down, wondering rather vaguely how there came to be so many sticks in the gorge when there were no trees. Vomit suddenly rose in his gullet. They were not sticks that broke beneath his bare feet, but bones, thousands of them, dry white bones piled high all about. He stopped abruptly, and Mags turned and hissed, "What's the matter?"

"Naught," Pedrin said, swallowing his gorge, and gingerly walking on. He could hardly bear the crunch of bones beneath his feet but to stop would be worse, and so on he floundered, the bare soles of his feet, as hard as the hooves of his goats, flinching at every step as if he trod on glass.

Their eyes had adjusted to the gloom, and they could see deep caves and ravines lining the steep cliffs. All were black as night and, as the six companions apprehensively passed by, a cold, fetid breath of air gusted out, making the flame of their torches flicker and almost snuff out.

It seemed to Pedrin that something moved in the corner of his eye. He turned his head abruptly, his pulse hammering, but saw nothing except a wavering shadow that could have come from their torches. Again and again his head jerked around, and he saw the others were glancing about as wildly. Lisandre gave a little panting sob.

"I told them, I did, but no one a-listens to Sedgely," the old man muttered behind them. "You'd think they'd have the sense to listen to the counsel of their elders, but nah, headstrong as always, that's the youth of today."

"Shut up!" Mags hissed. "Just shut up."

"May as well. You wouldn't listen to me anyway."

"Shut up, shut up, shut up!"

Sedgely shut up.

The gorge narrowed until the sky overhead was a mere thin line of blue. It felt as if the walls were closing in on them. Lisandre had her arm up over her mouth, trying not to gag as the smell of rotting meat grew more pervasive. The children clustered as close together as they could get, Durrik ringing the heavy bell gamely, though his arm was beginning to ache. Suddenly he tripped and fell. The bell flew from his hand and clanged to the ground, rolling away, jangling dolefully. Durrik looked up, straight into the gaping eyes and toothy grin of an enormous skull. He screamed and flinched away, only to scream louder as he saw hundreds of pale, skinny shapes swarming out from the caves.

"Ghouls!" he screamed. Desperately he scrabbled for his bell, clambering over piles of bones to reach it. Lisandre screamed too, and waved her torch wildly as the ghouls flowed down towards them. They were tall, emaciated creatures, all bone and withered skin, with huge black staring eyes and mouths filled with row upon row of needle-sharp teeth. They moved with unnatural speed and agility, swinging along on all fours like an animal one moment, standing up on their hind feet and gesturing with their bony hands the next.

"Don't let them touch you!" Sedgely cried. "They freeze your blood with their touch. Keep them off with the torches. They hate fire!"

"Durrik, get that bell!" Pedrin shouted.

Durrik reached the bell, seized it with both hands and rang it with all his might. The ghouls shrieked, their hands to their ears, many fleeing back into the caves. Those nearby cowered down, howling. Pedrin waved his smouldering torch so it burst into flame once more. "Come on!" he cried.

They scurried forward, having to climb over piles of

broken skeletons. There were skulls of all sizes and shapes, some huge and horned, others small and delicate, like a baby's. The goats bounded forward with their usual nimbleness, but Pedrin found he had to use his spare hand to keep his balance on the constantly shifting mass of bones and skulls. He heaved himself to the top of the pile, putting down his hand to help Lisandre, who had fallen behind. She stretched to grasp it, but stumbled and fell with a shriek, sliding down in a great avalanche of bones. Her torch spun out of her hand and was extinguished. Lisandre landed in a heap at the bottom, screaming as a ghoul rose up right in front of her, grinning evilly, its white, skeletal fingers reaching out for her.

Pedrin dropped his torch, grabbed his slingshot and seized a tiny round skull from the ground. Quick as thought, he spun the slingshot over his head and flung the skull straight at the ghoul. It slammed into its forehead and knocked it down, and Lisandre was able to scramble back up the incline, sobbing with fear.

Their torches were scorched right down to their handles, the flames mere flickers of colour within the ashes. "How much further?" Pedrin panted.

Sedgely shrugged. "How would I know? I've never been foolish enough to travel this way before. It could be miles."

"Miles?" Mags groaned. "Me torch is almost out!"

"My arm is aching," Durrik panted. "Not sure I can—"

"Give it to me," Pedrin demanded. He snatched the bell and rang with renewed vigour, so that the ghouls drew back again, shrieking. "We'd … better … run!" Pedrin panted. The others needed no persuading. They all ran down the gorge as fast as they could, smoke trailing from their dead torches. Mags glanced at hers, then flung it at a ghoul that was braving the bell to try and reach her with its bitter-cold fingers. It ducked and she was able to run on. Sedgely and Briony also cast their burnt-out torches away, scrambling over the bones and stones as fast as they could.

Then Pedrin tripped and fell, hitting the ground so hard he could not breathe for a moment, red stars bursting in his vision. Although he clung to the bell still, he did not have the strength to lift it. Immediately the ghouls swept down upon them again. A strange sort of wailing filled the air. Mags screamed and cowered down, and Briony desperately threw a cat's cradle net at the ghouls closest to them. About six fell down in a tangle but there were hundreds more, and Briony had no time to weave another net.

Lisandre seized her night-light in both hands and thrust it towards a ghoul, silver light blossoming within the diamond's heart. It lanced into the ghoul's eyes like a sword and it howled and cowered back. She spun on her foot, the ray of light sweeping the shadowy gully. All the ghouls recoiled, hiding their sensitive eyes with their long, bony hands. Pedrin managed to sit up, tolling the bell once again. Pressed shoulder to shoulder, the clanging bell on one side and the blazing sphere of light on the other, the six managed to run down the last length of the gully and out into sunshine at the other end.

They did not stop running till the slope of the hill led them all the way down to the lake's edge and they could run no further. They bent over, hands on their knees, trying desperately to get breath into their starving lungs. At last they were able to straighten, and look about them, though their breath was still harsh in their throats.

The Evenlinn was a great lake which stretched along the floor of a valley, surrounded on all four sides by tall peaks, some so high they were dusted with snow. The lake was surrounded by forest, many of the great trees beginning to flame with autumn colour. In the centre of the lake was an island which rose into a steep pinnacle. In the red light of the sunset, they could see a tower poking out of the trees that clustered close about the base of the pinnacle.

As the sun sank behind the mountains, the light quickly faded. Above the far horizon they saw the round curve of the moon, just a few days past its prime. Even though all were exhausted, it was decided, with no argument at all, that they should cross the lake at once and spend the night within the shelter of the island's trees. No one wanted to spend the night with the gaping maw of the Gorge of Ghouls behind them. In the morning, when they were well-rested and recovered from their ordeal, they could seek the counsel of the mysterious Erlrune.

"What we need is a raft," Pedrin said. "Though we have naught to lash the logs together. If only I'd thought to bring me hammer and some nails!"

"Well, we've got plenty of nails," Durrik said with

his familiar, puckish grin. "Not that they're much use t'us."

Pedrin looked at him suspiciously. "What do you mean?"

Durrik waggled his fingers and toes. "Twenty nails each, we've got, but not much good for nailing wood together."

It took Pedrin a while to work out the pun, he was so focused on solving the problem at hand. When he did, however, he flushed with mortification. "Would you stop your tomfoolery!" he snapped. "If you haven't got aught constructive to add, don't open your mouth!"

Durrik grinned and exchanged a quick twinkle with Mags, who had also picked up Pedrin's unintentional pun. The goatherd was oblivious, however, wondering aloud whether it was possible for Briony to spin them some rope to tie some logs together into a raft.

"I have very little thread left," Briony said unhappily. Pedrin knew she was reluctant to kill any more of her precious silkworms but thought their immediate need was urgent enough to warrant the sacrifice. He was just opening his mouth to say so when Sedgely said, rather diffidently, "No need for a raft, young feller. I can swim the lake."

Incredulously Pedrin looked at the wide expanse of water, all lilac and silver now with the coming of evening, then back at the old, stooped man. "Well, mebbe you can, but I don't know that the girls could."

"If you can swim it, I can too," Mags fired up.

Pedrin looked back at the glimmering stretch of

water and slowly his ears turned red. "I don't think I could swim that far either," he admitted.

"No need for you young ones to swim that far," Sedgely said. "You can all ride on me back."

This time all the children turned to stare at him, eyebrows raised. All except Briony.

"Didn't you a-realise Sedgely's a river-roan?" she asked in true surprise.

"Sedgely? A river-roan?" a chorus of voices cried.

"But river-roans are like horses," Pedrin said stupidly.

"Sometimes," Sedgely said. "Other times not."

Lisandre looked at him suspiciously. "Do river-roans not seek to trick one into mounting upon their back so they can gallop into the water and drown one?"

"Sometimes," Sedgely replied placidly. "Other times not."

She frowned and thrust out her jaw, scraping the sand with one foot.

"If you wish to be a-crossing the lake, you must be a-trusting me," the old man said gently. "'Tis your choice, of course. Mebbe you could make a raft in the morning, and get across all right and tight. If the lake-lorelei do not drown you, or the ghouls freeze your blood in the night."

"'Tis a-getting late," Mags said belligerently. "I say we trust him."

"Of course we must trust him," Briony cried. "Hasn't he brought us this far? If he wanted to drown us, he could've tried the first night we camped by his pool."

"Why would I want to drown you?" Sedgely said, taking off his coat of willow twigs and dropping it on the ground. "I like young things about me. Oh, I know you're rash and hasty and a-lacking in respect, but an old horse like me needs a bit of livening up. And there's no doubt you're all as innocent as the day you were born, and a-needing someone with a steady head about you."

"Of course we do," Briony said, giving his scrawny arm a little pat. "So, please, can we ride on your back?"

"Surely we couldn't all fit?" Durrik said. "There's five of us."

"Five skinny little things like you? Of course you'll fit," Sedgely said. "Me back is broad."

"What about Thundercloud and Snowflake?" Pedrin said unhappily. "Goats hate water, and aren't very good swimmers. They'd stand with all four hooves on a pebble rather than step in a puddle. There's no way they could swim that far, even if I could coax them into the water."

"We will have to leave them," Lisandre said.

"I can't leave them! They'd be eaten by a hobhenky or summat. 'Tis much too dangerous."

"We have to," Lisandre said. "What other choice do we have?"

Pedrin looked obstinate. "We have to build a raft or summat. I can't be a-leaving them here. Snowflake will pine for me."

"They'll be fine," Briony said reassuringly. "Thundercloud will look after Snowflake – and it'll only be for a day or so."

"But you don't understand," Pedrin said desperately. "I can't be a-leaving them. Snowflake needs to be milked, it hurts her if she's not milked. And they've never been away from me before, except for the month I had to work in the glass factory, and then Snowflake almost lost her milk, a-fretting for me. I can't be a-leaving her."

Pedrin knew everyone could hear the catch of tears in his voice but he did not care. He had to make them understand. He had raised Snowflake from a newborn kid with long, trembling legs who had bounded everywhere behind him, and had slept in his arms at night. She had been born in the weeks after his father's death. The birth had been long and difficult, the doe greatly distressed by Mortemer's absence, and Pedrin not knowing what to do to help her, being only six.

When Snowflake was finally born, she was not breathing and the doe, panting heavily and covered in blood, had died soon after. Pedrin, bewildered by so much death, had keened over the dead kid, rocking her back and forth, rubbing her reddened body with frantic hands, soaking her coat with his tears, until at last she struggled weakly and bleated. It had been a miracle. Pedrin had suckled her with warmed goat's milk strengthened with herbs, waking six or seven times every night to feed her, and had kept her warm with his own blanket, and carried her when she was too weary to walk. He could not be leaving her alone in the Perilous Forest, with grogoyles roosting and gibgoblins stalking.

"We don't have the time to be a-building a raft for a couple of goats!" Mags said. "Look how dark 'tis already."

The sun had slid down behind the mountains and stars were beginning to twinkle in the great expanse of purplish-dark sky. The wind rattled the pine trees, smelling of snow. Briony gave a little shiver and dragged the blanket close about her shoulders. An eerie singing sound rose through the dusk, so sweet and ethereal that all turned to listen, staring through the gloaming.

"That's the lake-lorelei you can hear," Sedgely said, straightening abruptly. "I'd be a-stuffing your ears if I were you – and fast!"

"'Tis so beautiful," Durrik said softly. "It reminds me..." He fell silent, though a look of longing was on his face. He took a few eager steps forward, staring out at the moon-glimmered lake, his face transfigured by a yearning sadness.

"I'd be a-stuffing your ears," Sedgely urged, taking hold of Mags's arm to prevent her following. "Candle wax is best."

"It sounds so far away," Mags said dreamily. "Yet somehow..." She took another step towards the water, dragging against Sedgely's hand.

Pedrin was gazing out at the lake, his face screwed up in concentration. "Surely it can't be..." he whispered. Suddenly his face was transformed by joy.

"Pa!" he cried.

He ran forward eagerly. Snowflake bounded in front of him, bleating urgently, but he pushed her away, not even seeing her. Again she leapt in front of him, butting him with her hard little head so that he stumbled and fell to his hands and knees.

"What's wrong with you!" Pedrin cried. "Not now, Snowflake! Me pa's a-needing me!"

Once more the little white goat butted him. Pedrin struck her hard across the face so that Snowflake yelped and leapt away. Pedrin hardly noticed. He was running forward, straining to pierce the gloaming with desperate eyes. "Pa!" he cried. "Where are you?"

26

◆ ◆ ◆

"Pedrin!" his father called. "Help me. I can't get away, they have me, they're a-holding me back. Pedrin, only you can save me! Help me!"

Pedrin had always hoped and wondered, deep down in the most secret chamber of his heart, if his father still lived. He had never been able to believe that the flesh-red carcass they had found on the mountain, peeled of his skin like an apple so that the convoluted mess of capillary and vein and artery could clearly be seen – Pedrin had never been able to believe that soft red pulp was all that remained of his strong-armed, quick-tempered, big-bearded, belly-laughing father.

So now, hearing his father's voice calling him through the *lap-lap-lap* of the waves, he struggled to see him, to find him. Was that his father, that beckoning arm, at the very edge of his vision? Was that his father, holding out two imploring hands, there where the glimmering shine of the water struck at his eyes, bedazzling him with tears? Where, oh where was he?

Mortemer's voice was growing more frantic yet ever more distant, as if he were struggling against hands that sought to drag him away.

Hands were holding Pedrin back. He struggled against them wildly and then, when he could not break free, swung around with his clenched hand as hard as he could.

His fist connected with a thin, bony shoulder. Sedgely cried out in pain and indignation. "Hey, young feller! No need to lam me! Come back, come back. 'Tis the lake-lorelei you're a-hearing. You must come back else they'll have you. I need your help, I can't be a-saving them all!"

Pedrin glared at him with hatred. He had never trusted Sedgely. What was the old man doing, a-coming along with them anyways? He must have some trickery up his sleeve, to face so much danger when he had naught to gain himself. He should've known better than to turn his back on a wildkin. Scowling ferociously, Pedrin punched the old man again, hard, right on his huge, hooked nose.

Sedgely howled in pain and let go, grasping his nose with both hands. Pedrin turned and lunged away from him, a little surprised to find he was up to his armpits in water. He kicked out strongly, striking out across the water, but Sedgely caught hold of his foot, dragged him back and slapped him sharply across the face. The blow knocked Pedrin right under the water.

He came up fighting but Sedgely seized his ear in a painful grip and bawled in it, "Whatever you're a-hearing, young feller, 'tis not true! 'Tis a lie! 'Tis the lake-lorelei and they're a-seeking to drown you. Stuff your fingers in your ears and look! Look! All your friends're a-drowning…"

At first Pedrin tried to hammer the old man with his fists but Sedgely kept that vice-like grip on his ear and kept on yelling in it, drowning out his father's voice and the poignant, ethereal singing that filled his mind and his heart, echoing like nothing he had ever heard before. As the meaning of Sedgely's words penetrated his brain, Pedrin stopped trying to punch him and then, feeling dazed and confused, did as he was told. With his fingers jammed hard in his ears, he looked about him.

Mags was crouched on the shore, rocking back and forth, her hands clamped over her ears, muttering over and over to herself, "Shut up, shut up, shut up!" As Pedrin stared, she lifted her face, ravaged with tears, and howled, "Shut up! You're all dead, you're all dead, you're all dead! Shut up, I say!"

Lisandre was up to her armpits in the water, forging forward, her face incandescent with joy. "Father! Where? Where are you?" She stumbled and went under the water, but struggled up the very next instant, holding out her arms pleadingly. "Father!"

Briony was even deeper, her curly hair floating out behind her like seaweed, splashing wildly as she struggled to swim out further into the moonlit lake. Durrik was so far out his head was just a dark shape against the glimmer of the water, his threshing arms only just managing to keep him afloat. As Pedrin watched in horror, he went under, only to struggle above the surface again a few seconds later. He was above water for only long enough to gasp a breath before going under again.

Just beyond him, Pedrin could vaguely see slender, shapely forms with dark flowing hair and shining eyes, swimming lithely through the water. They held out their white arms to Durrik, beckoning, calling, trilling with musical laughter. Pedrin had dropped his hands in dismay and he once again heard the silvery song, weaving its enchantment under the moon. At once it began to work upon him, bemusing his senses, muddling his memories, filling him with a joy so intense and poignant it was like a stab of pain. But Pedrin was too filled with fear about his friends to listen. "Durrik!" he screamed. "Briony!"

They did not hear.

"Young Durrik will be in their arms any instant," Sedgely said urgently in his ear. "You must help the little misses, I'll get the young feller. Quick now! Once the lake-lorelei have you in their toils, 'tis too late to save you."

Pedrin nodded and struck out for Lisandre, having to whistle loudly to stop the echo of the lake-lorelei's song from winding about his heart. It was hard, though. Every intake of breath was enough for the song to begin working its evil enticement and it took all Pedrin's strength not to listen.

Meanwhile, the old man gave a little hurrumph and shook himself all over. Somehow, he shook himself out of his skin and into the shape of a big old horse.

338

He was a dappled roan colour, with a shaggy white mane and fetlocks and a flowing white tail, all knotted and snarled. He surged out into the water, moving with immense speed and creating such a strong wake that Pedrin was swept up into the air, coming down again with a slap that knocked all his breath out of him. He had no breath for whistling and so heard his father crying to him, "Pedrin, Pedrin! You must believe me! I'm here, I'm alive, Pedrin, I need you..."

Though it cost him dearly, Pedrin refused to listen, muttering, as Mags had done, "Shut up, shut up, shut up!" He reached Lisandre in a few swift strokes and seized her in his arms, treading water strongly. She hammered him with blows, screaming, "No, no, let me go, my father is here, he needs me..."

Pedrin tried to reason with her but she was hysterical, slapping him, punching him, screaming at him to let her go. He shook her, yelling, but Lisandre brought her knee up sharply into his groin and, enveloped in a white flare of agony, Pedrin let go abruptly.

She lunged past him, going under the water in her desperation. It was clear Lisandre could not swim, for despite a great deal of splashing and gulping, she kept on going under. Pedrin tried to straighten but his whole body was paralysed with pain. He dashed tears away from his eyes, reached out and caught Lisandre by her hair, dragging her to the surface. Then he grimly towed her towards the shore, though the starkin princess fought him every step of the way and he was still bent over like a very old man. When it was shallow enough for him to stand, he seized Lisandre and dragged her up, still struggling and crying, and pressed his hands over her ears as hard as he could. She tried to wrench her head away but he would not let go, wresting her around so that together they looked out into the lake.

Briony was struggling feebly to keep her head above water as six pale, lissom shapes plunged and dived about her, rocking her with the waves of their motion, submerging her again and again. When Briony managed to raise her head above water, it was to gaze desperately about, calling a name the two watching children could not hear. Closer and closer the lake-lorelei swam, singing and mocking, then one reached out her hand and put it on Briony's head, pushing her under the water. Briony went down in a great sucking splash, her arms and legs flailing, her mouth wide open in a scream. She bobbed up again a second later but she was clearly losing strength quickly, while the lake-lorelei smiled and sang and circled her ever more closely.

Where Durrik had been was now only thrashing water and foam. In the darkness it was hard to see more than the occasional upflung white arm, abnormally long and supple, sinuous as a snake, tensile as a tentacle. Towards this maelstrom swam the river-roan, head held high, a long wake arrowing behind him.

The lake-lorelei's song had deepened, built to a gleeful crescendo. Lisandre no longer struggled against Pedrin's grasp, but stood stiff, her hands to her mouth in horror. He turned her back to him, and risked releasing her ears, though he cupped her face with his hands still.

"Lake-lorelei … seek to drown us," he managed to say. "I must … Briony … Lisandre, cover your ears … go back to shore … in me bag … candle wax…"

She nodded, her hands still covering her mouth. He took them, pressed them together between his own, and nodded urgently at the shore. She nodded again and began to wade towards the shore, her fingers jammed in her ears. Pedrin turned and dived into the water.

He had never swum with so much desperate speed in his life. The water was silky-cool and the moonlight gleamed all about him, so that every arc of his arm sent a spray of quicksilver through the air. In the great arch of the sky above, stars glittered and the round-bellied moon rode, haloed with a dim radiance. On the shore, invisible trees rustled and murmured in a black assembly, gathered at the foot of the lofty mountains, so tall and sombre with their silvered heads and implacable bulk. The air was filled with the most bewitching of music, airy and silver as the wind on the water.

It was all so beautiful, this moonlit swim should have been the most wondrous experience of his life. Instead it was nightmarish. His body could not answer his need. Every stroke of his arms and kick of his legs was too slow, too weak. He could see the lake-lorelei's sinuous white arms closing about Briony's dark head. The wildkin girl was able to keep her face above water for only a few scant seconds before she sank again, and the circle of plunging bodies was now so tight she was buffeted by rocking waves and cruel hands from all sides.

Pedrin kicked mightily, and reached the circle. He seized one of the lake-lorelei's arms. To his disgust it was slimy. He dragged her away from Briony but immediately the lake-lorelei coiled herself about him, pressing her slim, white, naked body so close against him he could feel her with every inch of his skin, so cold she was like fire, so close it was as if their bodies were fused. He could see her face laughing up at him, only a breath away, a face of wild, cruel beauty. Her eyes were filled with cold fire. Her hair was a living thing, black snakes that coiled about his arms and legs, dragging him ever closer to her. She raised her mouth to his and kissed him as if seeking to devour him. His body was already quivering and aroused with the feel of her cold, wet, writhing body. The shock of the kiss went through him like a bolt of lightning. He could not move. He could not breathe. His ears were filled with a roaring blackness. He jerked as she bit him, tasting the sweet gush of blood, and felt her whole body move with him. Pedrin tried to wrench his mouth away but could not. His limbs were bound tightly by her hair, her arms and legs twining about him like tentacles, their mouths, hearts, groins, legs, all pressed together, swaying, quivering, igniting.

His fingers found the hilt of his knife, still strapped to his belt. Awkwardly he eased the knife out of its sheath and into her. It did not need much movement, she was so close. At once she jerked away. He could feel long, slimy limbs flailing madly about him, then she turned and shot away at speed, hunched around her wound.

Suddenly he could breathe. Instead of air, Pedrin swallowed water. Black, swampy, foul, tasting of mud and weeds. He choked, kicking out with his feet, feeling below him the slimy ooze of the lake bottom. She had dragged him deep, that lake-lorelei with her cold eyes and passionate mouth, she had dragged him right to the very depths of the lake.

Pedrin pushed off, thrusting towards the surface. His legs were leaden, his head was bursting, he felt a dangerous trembling inside, but doggedly he kicked his legs. At last his head broke through the water's surface. He took deep, gulping breaths, his heart hammering horribly, and vomited up the slime of the lake's deep waters till his body was as scoured clean and empty as a clamshell.

27

◆ ◆ ◆

Briony was lying limply within the tight circle of the lake-lorelei's arms. They were crooning soothingly like a mother rocking her child to sleep, the black eels of their hair winding about her and slowly strangling the breath from her body.

Pedrin felt like a whole lifetime had passed, but it could only have been a few minutes. He still had his knife in his hand. He dogpaddled forward, as weakly as a young child. One of the lake-lorelei smiled enticingly and held out her arms to him. He swam into her embrace, and brought the knife up, ramming it into her breast with all his strength. She screamed, showing a mouth full of fangs, and fought against him, but Pedrin hung on to the knife wearily, all his weight pressed against her so that her own struggles forced the knife deeper and deeper into her breast. At last she hung as limply as he. They began to sink, but Pedrin put forth a great effort and dragged his knife free. She sank. He managed to keep his legs moving.

They all came at him them, four black-haired

women of bewitching beauty, their fangs white in their smiling mouths. The knife and his hand were all sticky with something black, and Pedrin was so tired he could hardly keep himself afloat. He saw Briony sink away under the water, her eyes closed, and made another stupendous effort, lifting the knife and lunging forward. They laughed and moved easily out of his reach, holding out their hands to him and singing. They did not sing to him with his father's voice this time, but with their own dark, mysterious, alluring voices that spoke of a pleasure so exquisite, so profound, it was worth drowning to experience. Pedrin felt himself stir in response, a wave of heat scorching through him, all his nerves coming thrillingly alive. He could not forget the feel of the lake-lorelei's body against him, the shock of her hungry mouth. He shook his head dazedly and gripped the knife tighter.

Suddenly a large, dark, warm body came surging up through the circle of lake-lorelei, scattering them with a neigh like thunder. They laughed and dived away, and Pedrin flung out a trembling hand and gripped hold of the river-roan's mane. His fingers met another hand, clenched as tight as his on the coarse white mane. He opened his eyes and dimly saw Briony, her face buried in the river-roan's shoulder, her great mass of dark wet hair streaming down her shoulders. She managed to look at him before burying her face again. Sedgely neighed reassuringly and swam strongly for shore.

Pedrin allowed himself to be towed along, his eyes closed, his hands still clenched on his knife. It seemed he felt the knife's odd halt of resistance, the sudden quick slide inside, the writhing of the wounded lake-lorelei again and again. It made him feel nauseous, yet he could not stop his mind from replaying the scene, or from remembering the ecstasy of the lake-lorelei's kiss. Pedrin had not known it was possible to feel such things. One part of his mind wanted to dwell on it, to relive the sensations again and again. The rest of him flinched away, sick with revulsion. He tried hard not to think at all. He wished he could just drift away into sleep, floating dreamless upon the cool, dark water.

There was to be no rest, however. Mags and Lisandre were crouched on the sand in the windy darkness, leaning over Durrik and weeping.

"He's dead, he's dead," Mags screamed. "Oh, Pedrin, he's dead!"

The world seemed to stop moving. Pedrin let go of Sedgely's mane and fell to his knees in the shallows, retching. Briony was beside him, floundering weakly out of the water on her hands and knees. Sedgely shook himself out of his horse-shape, seemingly mid-stride, and back into the shape of an old man. Naked, his skinny limbs gleaming in the moonlight, he knelt beside Durrik, feeling for his heart, listening for his breath. He rolled him over and leant his weight on Durrik's back, pumping the water out of his lungs as he had pumped the water out of Lisandre after she had fallen into the river. Though water gushed out of Durrik's mouth, there was no other response. He lay slack, loose-limbed, his head lolling.

"You must breathe your own breath into him,"

Sedgely ordered. "Cover his mouth with yours so that all your air goes into him."

The children stared at him uncomprehendingly. Sedgely hurrumphed impatiently. "Breathe your air into him now else we have no chance of saving him. I can't be a-doing it, a river-roan's breath is cold. Your breath is warm."

"He who was born under water, shall under water die," Briony said fatalistically, sounding as if she was talking in her sleep. She stood stiff and still, her hands hanging by her sides. Pedrin felt the same numbness, as if he was watching from a very long distance. Mags gave a little whimper and threw herself on the sand beside Durrik's unmoving body. "Show me what to do!" she cried.

Following Sedgely's instructions, the little bandit girl knelt and pressed her mouth against Durrik's, breathing her own breath into his lungs, lifting her head, pressing her mouth to Durrik's again. Watching her, Pedrin felt an unbearable coiling of lust and grief deep in his groin. He retched again, coughing up bile that tasted of slime. He spat it as far from him as he could, wiping his mouth again and again, then he hid his face in his hands. He could hear the uneven pant of Mags's breathing, though, and it had the same erotic effect on him, so that he had to press himself into the sand, trying without success to control his agitation.

Sedgely began to speak, very softly, alternating Mags's breaths with the firm pumping of his clenched hands on Durrik's chest. "'Tis a cruel enchantment, the beguiling of the lake-lorelei. They sing of your deepest longings, they get you all a-twisted up inside, so that whatever you most want to be true, you start a-thinking *is* true. They can fill you with such a yearning that you almost wish to be dead, once you realise 'tis all a lie. Oh, we river-roans, we hate the lake-lorelei, for we have longings and desires just like you young things do, and we know 'tis uncommon cruel to sing a man his deepest longings and then show 'tis all a mockery and a sham. And the worse thing about a lake-lorelei's song? 'Tis so beautiful you wish all your life you could be a-hearing it again, even though you know 'tis enticing you to death."

Listening to Sedgely's deep, melancholy voice helped Pedrin overcome the craving in his belly, but at his last words, he felt a surge of tears that swept over him with such intensity that he could only lie on the sand and weep. He felt a soft hand stroking his hair and realised Lisandre was kneeling beside him, stifling her own tears so that she could comfort him. He buried his face deeper into his arms and let the shuddering sobs subside.

"He's a-breathing!" Mags cried. "Sedgely, he's a-breathing on his own!"

"Let him rest awhile and keep him warm," Sedgely said wearily, letting his hands drop. "We can't tarry long, I feel ghouls a-breathing down me neck and the lake-lorelei will come back, a-singing and a-drowning if they can. We shall have to cross the lake tonight."

Pedrin sat up and rubbed his eyes roughly, and pushed his wet hair out of his face, aware now of a cramping cold that crept right into his very bones so that he could not stop shivering. He crawled forward so he could see Durrik, who had opened his eyes and was staring around blankly. "I'm alive," he whispered hoarsely. "I'm not a-drowned?"

"Sedgely saved you," Pedrin whispered, "and Mags."

Durrik shook his head in disbelief. "But I was a-drowning…"

"Sedgely saved you, and me, and Briony, in fact he saved us all," Pedrin said gruffly. "And I punched him in the nose."

"I slapped and kicked you," Lisandre said remorsefully. "I am sorry."

Pedrin coloured hotly and muttered something incoherent. She knelt and put his blanket about his shoulders. "What happened?" she asked. "Mags and I could see hardly a thing from the shore and we could hear nothing, for I'd put candle wax in our ears, like you said. All we could see was a lot of splashing, and then Sedgely swam up with Durrik draped over his back and dropped him on the sand and went galloping off into the lake again."

"I killed her," Pedrin said blankly. "She kissed me … and then I stuck me knife into her. It was horrible."

"She kissed you? A lake-lorelei kissed you?" Lisandre said indignantly.

Pedrin nodded.

"What was it like?" she asked after a moment's pause, half-curious, half-cold.

349

"Slimy," Pedrin answered without looking at her.

"Urrgh!" Lisandre said.

"Exactly," Pedrin said and crossed his arms on his knees, his head pillowed upon them, the blanket pulled close.

Sedgely woke him from an uneasy half-doze a few minutes later. "We must cross the lake now. Will you manage?"

Pedrin looked at him sideways, wondering how much he knew. He nodded and got to his feet, shivering as the cold air struck through his wet clothes. He rolled up the damp blanket and stowed it in his saddlebag, rubbing his arms and stamping his bare feet.

"Better be a-stuffing your ears," Sedgely said gloomily. "The lake-lorelei hate to lose their prey. They'll be a-coming again, mark me words." Pedrin nodded numbly. "I'd tie the young feller to me, if I were you, and probably the little missy too. Once you've succumbed to the lake-lorelei's song, often you're eager to meet with them again, no matter how clearly you see their evil."

Heat washed up Pedrin's face. "I'll be a-tying us all on," he said gruffly.

Sedgely nodded. "Wise decision. Glad you're a-listening for a change, young feller. Let's get a-going then, 'tis late and me poor old bones are weary indeed."

Pedrin nodded and gathered together the coil of rope. In the bright moonlight, he could see the goats lying together on the grass at the edge of the shore, Snowflake curled within the shelter of the billy-goat's

350

body. He remembered how he had struck her and was filled with shame and remorse. Slowly he went over towards them and was stricken when Thundercloud leapt to his feet and stood belligerently, horns lowered.

Pedrin held out his hand and whistled gently. "I'm sorry," he whispered. "I didn't mean to hurt you, Snowflake. I was ... enchanted, I s'pose. Please forgive me."

She stood up and took a few tentative steps towards him, her nose outstretched. He sat down, his hand still held out pleadingly. She came and smelt his hand, and then nudged her soft nose into it. He wrapped his arms about her neck, burying his face in her white coat that smelt of sunshine and clover and milk, all good, wholesome things.

"I have to leave you," he said in a muffled voice. "I'm sorry but I have to go. It doesn't mean I'm not a-loving you. Please, please, stay safe and I will be back just as soon as I can."

She bleated unhappily and nudged him again, and he dried his tears on her coat as he had done so many times before. Then he stood up and made his way back to his friends on the lakeshore, feeling as if a great hole had been torn out of him.

"They'll be all right," Lisandre said sympathetically, and gave his arm a little rub. The others all made little murmurs too, though all were so shocked and weary and overwhelmed by the day's events that it was as much as they could do to keep standing. They shouldered their bags and sacks and stood waiting by an old log for Sedgely to once again take on the form of a river-roan.

Sedgely gave a little hurrumph, and shook himself all over. In a heartbeat, he transformed into the shape of a magnificent old horse, with powerful haunches, huge black hooves covered with a long fringe of white hair, a tail like a waterfall and a thick white mane, as knotted and snarled as his hair had been. His coat was dappled red, he had a long white beard like a billy-goat and his splayed hooves were split in three, almost like a duck's webbed feet.

The transformation was so quick and so absolute it was hard to take it in, though Pedrin was watching avidly, curious indeed about this magical ability of the old man's. Although there were so many startling similarities between the two forms – the out-curving line of the great nose, the dark liquid eyes, the shaggy white hair and beard, the mingling of red and white hairs on his body – it did not seem as if one shape stretched to make room for the other. Sedgely just shook it off as if he was shaking away water.

Astonishing as this was, the children hardly reacted at all, so numb were they with shock and exhaustion that they moved like sleepwalkers. One by one they climbed onto the log and then onto Sedgely's back. Though they all had to cling close together, all five fitted easily upon his back.

The river-roan turned and trotted down into the water. The last of the day had gone, the dark arch of sky overhead strewn with stars. The lake seemed to catch the starlight, glimmering with a silvery-blue light against the blackness of the shore. Into the water they rode. It flowed like silk along the river-roan's sides, shocking them with its coldness. They were all wet to the waist, clinging tightly to Sedgely with their legs, their arms about each other's waists. Beside them swam the lake-lorelei, laughing, seeking to drag them from the horse's back. In the darkness, all that could be seen of them was their slim white arms and their pointed faces, though their eyes glittered with starlight.

Pedrin kicked out angrily and the wildkin dived away with little flurries of foam, only to surface a few feet away, their arms held out imploringly. They were so beautiful and so strange that, despite his terror and revulsion, Pedrin found himself leaning towards them, wanting to see more, wanting to hear their song. Durrik would have fallen into their arms if it was not for Mags's tight hold about his waist, so transfixed was he by the lake-lorelei's beauty.

Steadily the horse swam onwards. The dark pinnacle of the island slowly grew closer. Soon the lake-lorelei ceased swimming alongside, and the children no longer felt the sudden tug of malicious hands about their ankles or, worse, the sensuous stroke of their fingers up their legs.

Sedgely's webbed hooves found purchase. He rose out of the lake, water streaming from his hide, then they were upon the island, sand crunching under his hooves.

Trees crowded close about the beach. Sedgely made his way forward slowly, the children crouching down

353

low on his back as branches whipped their faces. Lisandre gave a little cry as her arms and legs were scratched but Sedgely pushed on until the glimmer of the lake was far behind them. At last he came into a small clearing, the stars bright in the ragged hole of the trees' branches. Exhausted, the children slid from his back and curled on the ground where they fell, too weary to do more than huddle together under their blankets and shawls and cloaks. In an instant, all were asleep.

28

♦ ♦ ♦

Pedrin was rudely awoken by a cruel sting across his cheek. He recoiled with a cry, sitting up with his hand to his face. The sun fell through the branches in long, slanting rays, the dew upon the leaves sparkling. Pedrin looked around crossly, then froze into stillness, his throat closed with terror.

A gibgoblin stood nonchalantly in the middle of the clearing, expertly coiling a long black whip into one claw. He was very tall and thin, and elegantly dressed in black leather. His skin was of very smooth, shiny green scales and he had narrow black eyes, set at a distinct angle in his tapered face. A long green tail snaked out from under his leather coat and his oily black hair was slicked off his face and combed into a little curl at the back of his head. In his other claw he held a slim cigar. He lifted it to his green, scaly lips and took a luxurious drag. Smoke curled lazily from its glowing end.

"Ah, ssso you're awake at lassst," the gibgoblin said in a low, menacing hiss.

His neck was so stiff, Pedrin could only look up at the gibgoblin with difficulty. Of all the possible dangers they might have had to face in the Perilous Forest, it was gibgoblins that Pedrin had dreaded the most. He had seen what a gibgoblin could do to a man. The sight haunted his dreams.

Many times he had wondered what it must have felt like for his father, having his skin slowly, languorously, peeled away with flick after lick of the gibgoblin's long whip. Many times he had wondered how long it had taken his father to die once his skin, the largest living organ, had been so dexterously removed.

Now Pedrin was so paralysed with terror that the only thing that moved was his heart, threatening to hammer its way right out of his ribcage. He could not even swallow, though his mouth felt like a bucket of sand. He became aware of a creeping wetness down his leg and began to burn with shame and misery. His bitter humiliation was the spur that enabled him to move. Pedrin knew only that he did not intend to die like his father had. Very slowly he slid his hand into his pocket, seeking his slingshot.

The others were all sitting or lying with the same rigidity, staring at the gibgoblin with the fascination of mice looking at a snake. Even Sedgely seemed mesmerised. The gibgoblin smoked his cigar affably, his other hand toying with the end of his whip.

"I'm ssso glad. I had ssstarted to think you would sssleep all day which isss mossst monotonousss. I much prefer my victimsss to be consciousss when I ssscourge the ssskin from their flesh. Ssso much more amusssing."

Pedrin tried to swallow. A boulder seemed to have lodged itself in his throat. His fingers had touched the familiar shape of his slingshot, delicately hooking about it. Slowly he began to draw it out, his other hand groping through the grass for a stone.

"However, I mussst not amussse myssself yet. I mussst ask you firssst what your busssinessssss here isss. The Erlrune mossst dissslikesss unsssolicited visssitorsss."

Suddenly the gibgoblin turned and, quick and graceful as a striking snake, lashed out with his whip. Pedrin screamed and sucked his hand, and deftly the gibgoblin caught his slingshot in his claw.

"Ssso, the boy thinksss to ssstrike me with ssstonesss. How amusssing. I am sssorry to disssappoint you, my child, but being ssstoned would not sssuit me at all."

Pedrin looked down at his hand in chagrin. A thin red welt was oozing blood. He sucked it again and tried not to show how very frightened he was. He was shivering, though, and the brightness of the day seemed to have dimmed.

"Ssso once again I mussst asssk you to ssstate what your busssinessssss upon the island of the Erlrune isssssssss..." The gibgoblin's malevolent hiss drawled away. He yawned, lifting one claw politely. It was very cold now. The dew had all turned to frost. Mist crept along the ground and writhed up the gibgoblin's leather-clad legs. Pedrin shivered and rubbed his

357

arms. He saw Lisandre was huddling into her purple velvet cloak, and Briony had dragged the rough old blanket up about her shoulders. Suddenly he realised the mist was flowing out of Sedgely's enormous, high-boned nose. Two long, steady plumes of fog that gusted and whirled and eddied, as cold as the iciest winter blast. The gibgoblin yawned again.

"Ssstrange, I feel sssleepy ... 'tisss grown ssso chilly ... time for a sssiesssta, perhapsss..." Slowly and gracefully, the gibgoblin sank down into the mist and disappeared. Then they heard thin, hissing snores.

The children sat, too terrified to move. Sedgely had no such hesitation, however. He bounded up, showing no sign of age or infirmity, and hustled them all to their feet. "I can't be sure how long the fog'll last, never having waited around to see," he said. "Let's get out of here!"

Pedrin risked one quick look at the gibgoblin, who slept all coiled up like a snake, his green eyelids fluttering slightly. Pedrin's slingshot was half underneath him but Pedrin did not even consider trying to ease it out. He hurried away from the clearing just as fast as he could, feeling rather light-headed.

"Oh, that's an old river-roan trick, that one," Sedgely was saying. "Gibgoblins hibernate in winter, you know. They hate the cold. He'll be spitting poison when he wakes. We'll have to find running water so we can drown our scent. Gibgoblins have an excellent sense of smell. Why don't you all ride, so we can get along a little faster?"

The children were only too glad to comply, being

tired still and rather shaken by their encounter with the gibgoblin. They were glad to cling to Sedgely's back as he galloped through the forest, all the leaves above them stained with brilliant autumn colour. They came to a clear, sparkling brook and he plunged in, swimming strongly upstream. Pedrin was glad to let the water wash up over his legs, hoping no one had noticed the telltale stain on his breeches. He bent and grasped the water with his cupped hand, drinking thirstily and splashing away the nightmares of the night.

He had not slept well, despite his bone-dense weariness. The song of the lake-lorelei wove its way all through his dreams, keeping him in a fever of horror and shameful desire. Again and again Pedrin had seen the black coils of hair and starshine eyes laughing at him, had bent his head to kiss that fanged mouth, had drowned again in her embrace. Again and again he relived the easy way his knife had slid into her, with no more than a little catch, like a gasp of breath. Pedrin had killed fish before, and birds, rabbits, chickens, kids. He had even helped an old doe to death, when her pain had grown so intense he could bear it no longer. Killing the lake-lorelei did not feel like killing a chicken for his supper. It felt like murder.

He had not been the only one to suffer nightmares. Half-rousing through the night, he had heard Briony sob in her sleep and turn convulsively, hunching herself into a ball, and he had heard Durrik muttering and calling out. Much later, he half-roused as he felt Mags grow agitated in her sleep. She had sat up, crying aloud for her father, her hands stretched out imploringly. They had all felt her jerk as she woke and realised where she was, then heard her little despairing sob as she flung herself down again, burrowing under the blanket. Dumbly they all pressed close about her, offering what little warmth and comfort they could. She was very subdued this morning, her mouth set in an expression of misery and anger.

Briony's pointed face was also tense and strained, and she flinched at every rattle of twig or susurration of wind in the dry leaves.

Durrik was sunk so deep in a miserable abstraction that he noticed nothing, not even the crack of a branch breaking that had all of them startling violently. His cheeks were like chalk, and his eyes glittered with a feverish light. He did not answer when Pedrin asked him how he was, and had said not a single word all morning. Pedrin tried hard to think of something to say that would rouse him from his preoccupation, but his skull felt like it was stuffed with wool. He could think of nothing.

So Pedrin could have kissed Mags when she turned around and said, with a determined attempt at her usual cheeky grin, "Hey, what kind of wildkin thinks life's a laugh?"

"What?" he asked.

"Guess."

"I can't. Tell us!" Briony begged.

"Can you guess, Durrik?" Pedrin said.

Durrik smiled rather faintly and shook his head. "It has to be something to do with a gibgoblin."

"Go on, guess. What kind of wildkin thinks life's a laugh?"

"Tell us, Rags," Lisandre demanded.

"A giggling gibgoblin," Mags answered, grinning.

They all laughed, and then began to try to make up other jokes. "What kind of wildkin is always hungry? A gobbling gibgoblin!" Pedrin said.

"What kind of wildkin talks too much? A babbling gibgoblin," Lisandre offered.

"A gibbering gibgoblin would be a better answer," Mags objected.

"Gibbering does not mean to talk too much," Lisandre said haughtily.

"Yeah, it does!"

"No, it doesn't."

"Yeah, it does!"

"Well, you ought to know," Lisandre said crushingly.

"Babbling gibgoblin's not funny at all, gibbering gibgoblin is much better."

"Well, what kind of wildkin always wants to argue?" Durrik suddenly said.

"What?" Pedrin said encouragingly.

"A squabbling gibgoblin!"

All five of them laughed, and once they started, could not stop. Clinging to each other, they laughed hysterically. Whenever one began to stop, someone would call out "squabbling gibgoblin" or "gibbering gibgoblin", setting them all off again. They were all so weak with laughter they would have fallen off Sedgely's back if it had not been for the tight hold they had on each other.

The river-roan hurrumphed disapprovingly and shook his mane, splashing them with water, which only made them laugh harder. Suddenly they saw a glimpse of something through the golden-red foliage which made all their laughter die in their throat. An incredibly huge, incredibly ugly creature stood beside the stream, an enormous war-axe held in its great fist. It was about eight feet tall, almost as wide as it was tall, with a horned helmet crammed onto its head. Below the helmet were a pair of deep-sunk eyes, set close to a squashed-looking nose and a crack of a mouth. It wore a battered and tarnished breast-plate, and beneath its skirt of rusted chain-mail were two of the thickest, hairiest legs anyone had ever seen. It roared at them and shook its war-axe.

"Oh no, a hobhenky!" Pedrin and Briony cried together.

Sedgely reared back, threshing the water with his great hooves, then turned and galloped out of the water and into the forest. Through the thin white trees he raced, the children hanging on grimly. They could hear crashing behind them as the hobhenky lumbered in pursuit, but the river-roan was fleet and soon the din faded away. Sedgely did not slow, foam flecking his dappled sides. The children all stared back anxiously, but there was no sign of the hobhenky.

Suddenly there was a roar from right in front of them. Sedgely neighed and reared in fright. Taken by surprise, Pedrin, Durrik and Lisandre all slid off, landing with a bone-jarring thump on the ground. The hobhenky roared again and swiped his mace at Sedgely, who leapt away over the children's heads.

"Jumping Jimjinny, how did he get here so fast!" Pedrin breathed, even as he ducked down into the bracken. Automatically his hand sought for his sling-shot, only to remember with a sinking heart that he had left it under the sleeping gibgoblin. His mind raced as he tried to think of some way to defend him-self against the hobhenky now barging towards them through the bracken.

Although Pedrin had only seen a hobhenky once before, he knew quite a lot about them. Of all the wild-kin, hobhenkies were those most prone to attacking flocks of goats, or invading outlying villages. Though extremely strong, hobhenkies were also extremely stu-pid. They were easily tricked and tended to be rather cowardly, despite their huge size.

Remembering how easily he had been able to drive away the big, simple-witted creature on his previous encounter with a hobhenky, Pedrin whispered hur-riedly, "I'll distract him, while you two get back on Sedgely! I'll meet you back here later."

"But he'll kill you!" Lisandre was white to the lips, and she clutched Pedrin's arm fearfully.

"Don't be a-worrying about me," Pedrin said gruffly, conscious of the admiration in the starkin girl's eyes.

"But—" Durrik protested.

"Don't argue, just run!" Pedrin ordered. "Look after milady."

Durrik raised an expressive eyebrow, but he nodded and jerked his head to Lisandre to follow him. Quickly they swarmed away through the bracken, as Pedrin leapt up right under the hobhenky's huge, flat feet. The wildkin swiped at him with his mace, and Pedrin scrambled out of its way. He then ran swiftly back the way they had come, knowing the hobhenky would follow. Hampered by his heavy armour, the hobhenky was slow and rather cumbersome, and Pedrin was confident he could easily outrun and outwit him. He could hear crashing behind him as the hobhenky trampled down bushes and small trees, and Pedrin increased his pace, looking for somewhere to hide.

Then, to his utter bemusement, he saw the hobhenky charging towards him, waving his war-axe. Pedrin skidded to a halt, panting, then glanced back over his shoulder. There was the hobhenky again, roaring with rage, the ground shuddering at every step, a cruel studded mace dwarfed by his enormous fist. For a second, Pedrin thought he was back in the Hall of Mirrors, seeing a double reality. Then, with a sickening drop of his stomach, he realised he was caught between twin hobhenkies, the only difference between them the weapons they wielded.

Despairingly Pedrin looked one way, then the other. The hobhenkies were now only a few strides away from him. With a desperate effort, Pedrin leapt up in the air, caught the branch above him and swung his legs up. Below him the hobhenkies crashed into each other. Each fell down, roaring with pain. Sitting with their hairy legs splayed out, they held their heads in their beefy hands. Then, to Pedrin's surprise, each opened their mouths and began to wail, showing broken teeth of a most unsavoury brown colour.

"Boo hoo!" one wept. "Smash crashed."

"Boo hoo!" the other wept. "Crash smashed. Boo hoo!"

The crying went on for some time, but eventually gave way to mere sniffles, the hobhenkies wiping their noses on their sleeves.

"Crash smashed me," one said reproachfully. "Hurt head."

"Smash crashed *me*," the other said defensively. "Hurt *me* head."

Crash and Smash argued on for a few more minutes, then realised their prey was gone. For a while they searched for Pedrin, lifting up fronds of bracken and looking behind rocks, then stood around scratching their heads, perplexed. Meanwhile, Pedrin sat quietly at the very top of the tree, wishing there was another tree nearby that he could swing to, and that his branch was a little bit sturdier.

If luck had been with him, the hobhenkies would have forgotten what they were looking for and wandered off into the forest. Luck was not with him, however. The branch Pedrin was crouched upon began to crack under his weight. The sound, although slight, was enough to cause Crash to look up and immediately he began to roar with excitement.

As the hobhenkies jumped up and down, trying to reach him, Pedrin groped in his saddlebag for something to use as a weapon. He found the frying pan just as the hobhenkies began to lam into the tree-trunk with their axe and mace. The tree had only a slim trunk and even with such ham-fisted woodcutters, it did not take long to fell. Pedrin leapt desperately out of its falling branches and onto Smash's massive shoulders. As the hobhenky swung around, shouting in fury, Pedrin repeatedly beat the wildkin over the head with the frying pan. To his dismay, the hobhenky only shook his head as if shaking away a fly, and whammed him with one immense fist. Pedrin was flung across the clearing, landing so hard all his breath was knocked out of him.

Pedrin felt as if all his ribs were broken. He held his side, wheezing, watching the hobhenkies lumber towards him with grim fatalism. There was nothing he could do.

The goatherd had dropped his saddlebag when he had fallen and it lay half-open, spilling his belongings upon the ground. Pedrin managed to reach across and drag the saddlebag towards him, groping inside for something, anything, that might distract the hobhenkies. His fingers closed upon the cool, slender length of his flute.

Amidst the welter of jostling, panicked thoughts, a memory suddenly crystallised in the very forefront of his brain. Pedrin remembered that he had been playing his flute the last time he had battled a hobhenky. He had been absorbed in his music when he had suddenly noticed the huge, hulking creature in the corner of his eye. The hobhenky had been crouched only a few feet away, listening intently, a beatific smile on his ugly face. Pedrin had screamed and dropped his flute, and the hobhenky had immediately lurched to his feet, scowling and roaring with rage. It was then Pedrin had pelted him with the first rock.

He was having trouble catching his breath but, unable to think of anything else to do, Pedrin lifted his flute to his lips and began to play.

Delicate music faltered into the air. It took a while for the sound to penetrate the hobhenkies' skulls but when it did, the effect was astounding. Both the hobhenkies stopped mid-step, their mouths open. Their weapons dropped from their hands and one of them gave a high, gusting sigh. Encouraged, Pedrin played on, his song growing in strength and confidence. The other hobhenky sighed too, and then they sat down with an earth-shuddering thump, their hairy knees only a few inches from Pedrin's head. Cradling their weapons in their laps, they swayed gently from side to side, humming tunelessly.

Pedrin did not dare stop. One lilting tune followed another. The hobhenkies sighed and sniffled, occasionally wiping away a tear from the corner of their eyes. The more melancholy the tune, the more they seemed affected, and so Pedrin played every lament, dirge and elegy he knew. When he reached the end of his repertoire, he began again. The hobhenkies did not seem to notice. They certainly did not seem to mind, if a rising crescendo of sobs and whimpers was any indication of their appreciation.

When the hobhenkies were leaning on each other's shoulders, weeping openly, Pedrin slowly and very gingerly rose to his feet. He did not dare stop playing to reach down and pick up his saddlebag, so he left it lying in the grass. Slowly he backed away.

The hobhenky Crash wiped his nose on his sleeve, scrubbed his eyes with the backs of both hands, and lumbered to his feet. Smash did the same. Pedrin stopped moving, and both the hobhenkies stopped too. Pedrin took a few more steps back, and Crash and Smash ambled after him. Watching them intently, Pedrin kept walking backwards and the two hobhenkies followed after him like enormous, clumsy puppies.

When it seemed clear the hobhenkies were going to follow him as long as he kept playing, Pedrin risked turning around so he could see where he was going. The hobhenkies did not seem to mind. They trudged along behind him, weapons over their shoulders, only stopping to wipe their eyes. Growing tired of being splashed by huge hobhenky tears, Pedrin changed his tune to a rather martial march but that meant he had to run to avoid being crushed by huge hobhenky feet, so he settled on gentle lullabies and love songs.

The sound of his music preceded him and so, when Pedrin came into the clearing where the others were waiting anxiously, they came running towards him with their arms outstretched, exclaiming with joy and relief. The expressions on their faces when they saw the two hobhenkies were ludicrous. Pedrin dared not lift the flute away from his lips to explain, but the others were quick to understand. They had a hurried conference among themselves while Pedrin began yet another tune, his arms aching, his lips numb, his lungs labouring. The hobhenkies were swaying from side to side, drumming their thick fingers on their weapon hilts and humming contentedly.

"Pedrin," Durrik said rather carefully, "we think mebbe we'd best just head to the Erlrune's house as fast as we can. We can see the top of the tower through the trees. 'Tis not far. Can you keep a-playing that long?"

Pedrin managed to jerk his head up and down and began walking again, following the direction of Durrik's pointed finger. Smash and Crash followed along happily, and all the others fell into place behind, torn between grinning in amusement and shaking their heads in wonder.

29
...

uilt of silvery-grey stone, the Erlrune's house
stood tranquilly in a garden of apple trees, roses,
foxgloves and herbs. It was an old, low house with
peaked gables and one round tower, only just high
enough to peek out above the forest canopy. It was
topped with a lichen-green pointed roof and three
rows of tall, arched windows. There was no glass in
the windows, of course, but shutters could be drawn
against the winter storms and they could see white
curtains billowing in the breeze. Behind the house
towered the bare stone pinnacle, cutting dramatically
into the sky.

Outside the narrow lychgate into the garden, the six
companions stopped and made some effort to tidy
themselves. All were nervous and rather apprehensive
about the forthcoming meeting with the Erlrune. They
had come so far and suffered so much, but now they
were filled with foreboding, remembering all the tales
they had heard about the Erlrune's mysterious powers. So they washed their hands and faces and necks

370

and combed their hair with Lisandre's silver comb, struggling to get it through the knots. Briony washed Pedrin's face for him as best she could with the flute still lifted to his mouth.

Their clothes were all filthy and torn, so they brushed them off with Lisandre's silver-backed brush and Briony went down on her knees and effected a few rapid repairs with her needle and thread. Sedgely was once again dressed in his willow coat and cap of reeds, as fresh and green as if they had just been picked, and he had tucked a yellow daisy in his buttonhole.

Mags took out the red silk dress and shook it out, admiring the way the skirt shone in the sun. Lisandre looked at it longingly, biting her lip as she glanced down at her shabby old pinafore and heavy black brogues. She said nothing, however, smoothing the pinafore down and then taking out her purple velvet cloak to hang about her shoulders.

Mags held the dress against her, twirling about a little, then abruptly held it out to Lisandre. "Here. You take it."

Lisandre reached for it eagerly, then dropped her hands. "Are you certain? It's yours. I gave it to you."

"Briony fixed it for you, so you could be a-wearing it when we saw the Erlrune. You said you couldn't be a-calling upon her in rags. Well, I'm used to rags." She gave a little grin, saying with mock-pride, "Mags-in-Rags, that's who I am."

Lisandre flushed. "Are you sure?"

"Yeah, I'm sure. You can give it back to me later.

Here, take the shoes too. I'll be happy to be a-wearing a flashy diamond ring, that'll do me."

So, the two girls quickly swapped clothes behind a bush. When they finally came out, Lisandre was once again wearing her red silk dress and ruby-heeled shoes, with her jewelled christening egg hanging from her girdle. Her high heels sank so deep into the ground that she could hardly walk and she said irritably, "Stupid shoes! I've always hated them."

Pedrin could not grin because he was still blowing fervently into his flute, but he saw the rueful glance she cast him and gave her a little nod and twinkle of acknowledgement.

Briony was looking about, a troubled frown on her face. She held her ragdoll clutched close to her chest.

"What's wrong?" Durrik asked apprehensively. "Can you sense danger?"

"Are we being watched?" Mags cried shrilly. "It's not the gibgoblin, is it?"

Briony shook her head, her frown deepening. "Nah," she said hesitantly. "I don't think so. Everything seems still and quiet. I can sense … naught at all."

"Then what's the problem?" Mags asked.

"Naught," Briony answered, more hesitantly still. "Except…"

"What?"

"Surely it's too quiet? There's no guards, no sentry, nobody around at all."

Sedgely gave a hurrumph of heartfelt agreement, his shaggy brows knitting together as he stared around suspiciously. "Yeah, you're right, little missy. Too quiet, far too quiet."

Lisandre said, "Obviously the gibgoblin and hob-henkies were the guards, Briony, but we've managed to out-wit them, haven't we? Why look for trouble when we don't need to?"

"I can't help a-wondering, though..." Briony faltered.

"What, Briony?" Lisandre said impatiently.

"Naught," she said. "I'm sorry. It's just that I know the Erlrune is meant to be a mighty enchantress and I feel we should be on our guard."

"We shall be," Lisandre said. "But surely, if you can't sense anyone watching us now, all must be safe. We'll just make sure we keep a close ear and eye out. All right?"

Briony nodded unhappily.

Bunched close together, they approached the gate, Pedrin still valiantly playing his flute. Made wary by Briony's unease, they stared at the gate rather apprehensively then Sedgely stepped forward and pushed it open with his walking stick. At once he leapt back as if stung by a bee.

"What? What's wrong?" the children cried in fright.

"Naught, naught," Sedgely replied sheepishly. "Can't be too careful, you know."

They all looked through the narrow gate into the garden. All that could be seen were peaceful stretches of grass scattered with flowers, and the gnarled trunks of ancient fruit trees. A few tiny white butterflies fluttered above the clover, and a bird sang cheerfully.

"It looks peaceful enough," Lisandre said hopefully.

"Too peaceful," Sedgely muttered.

"We've come this far, no point a-hanging about, jumping at shadows," Mags said and walked swiftly through the gate and into the garden. She turned back to them smiling. "See? Naught to it!"

One by one the others followed, all rather hesitantly. Pedrin came last, the hobhenkies having to bend almost double to avoid banging their heads on the lintel. Once inside the green serenity of the garden, they all relaxed, smiling and murmuring with pleasure. It was cool and quiet under the trees, and the breeze was soft and sweet-scented, caressing their faces. The apple trees were all heavy with fruit, and apples lay scattered through the long grass. Bumblebees buzzed contentedly in the herbs, and blundered about the heavy heads of the roses. Even though winter was only just around the corner, flowers still bloomed in the sheltered corners of the garden and many shrubs were bright with berries or fruit. The only sound was the faltering song of Pedrin's flute.

Looking about them with delight, the children's steps quickened as they made their way through the green hush under the trees. The hobhenkies blundered along behind Pedrin, smiling rather foolishly, knocking the trees with their heads and shoulders so apples rained in their wake.

They came along an avenue of flowering shrubs, breathing in their heady perfume with great enjoyment. There was a pool filled with water-lilies and the children all leant on its rim, dabbling their hands in the warm water and laughing as enormous golden fish came swimming up lazily to try to nibble their fingers.

An archway in the tall green hedge led them to a wide expanse of lawn before the house. They could see a number of inviting-looking paths running away through other archways, and the children would have liked to have explored further, but Sedgely shook his head and said mournfully, "Best get it over with quickly, is what I always say."

So they came through clouds of daisies to a square courtyard before the house, and there they stopped, their voices dying in their throats.

A grogoyle lay sleeping in the sun, his grotesque head pillowed on his paws. His leathery wings were folded against his fur and the barbed tail was coiled neatly about his hindquarters. Little tendrils of smoke rose from his nostrils, which flared red as he breathed.

No one dared move or speak. Even Pedrin stopped playing his flute, giving no thought at all to the hob-henkies who merely squatted down and began to play marbles on the worn cobbles of the courtyard. The only sound was the clink of their marbles and their low, growling conversation.

"No, Smash, mine!"

"Mine! Not Crash's, Smash's!"

After a long, tense moment spent watching every twitch of the grogoyle's hide and every flicker of his leathery eyelids, Sedgely and the children at last moved a little, murmuring to each other.

"What do we do now?"

"He's asleep. Do we dare try and get to the house without a-waking him?"

"We cannot stand here all day. Pedrin, go bang that front door knocker!"

"If you think I'm a-going to walk right under the nose of a grogoyle, well, you're very much mistaken. Do it yourself!"

"Very well, I will," Lisandre said rather surprisingly. She took a deep breath and straightened her red silk dress with both hands. Then, with her head held high, she glided across the courtyard towards the great, arched door.

The grogoyle opened one eye. Lisandre stopped. Everyone stood very, very still. The flaming red eye regarded the starkin girl for a long moment, then the grogoyle rolled back the other leathery eyelid so both eyes were open, burning as red and hungry as the furnaces at the glass factory. The grogoyle yawned, sending out a little blast of fire and smoke, then stretched out one paw and then the other, extending and retracting his cruel, curved claws. Lisandre took a trembling step back. The grogoyle yawned again, turned round and round on the spot, then settled down to sleep once more, his back now turned towards the children.

Lisandre walked rather unsteadily up the three curving steps to the door and laid her hand upon the knocker. It had been forged to resemble the cruel face of the grogoyle, with slitted eyes and two pointed horns protruding from the vigorous waving mane. The ring of the door knocker was held in its fanged mouth.

As Lisandre laid her hand upon the knocker, the eyes suddenly opened, glaring red. The door knocker said malevolently, "What is your business with the Erlrune?"

Lisandre screamed and stumbled back, dropping the knocker. The eyes did not shut, however, the voice repeating sharply, "What is your business with the Erlrune?"

"I ... I ... I wish to ... consult..." Lisandre stammered.

"Visiting hours are from nine o'clock in the morning to one o'clock in the afternoon," the door knocker said. "Please return tomorrow." Its eyes shut.

Lisandre glanced up at the sun which was directly overhead. "But ... but it's only midday," she protested. There was no response. She seized the door knocker with both hands and pounded it vigorously. The eyes snapped open.

"What is your business with the Erlrune?"

"I wish to consult the Erlrune's acclaimed wisdom and insight," Lisandre said courteously.

"Visiting hours are from nine o'clock in the morning to one o'clock in the afternoon," the door knocker said. "Please return tomorrow."

"But it is only midday," Lisandre said. "See, the sun is still high overhead."

"Visiting hours are from nine o'clock in the morning to noon," the door knocker said. "Please return tomorrow."

"But that's not fair!" Lisandre cried. The door knocker's eyes had shut, however. Once more she

pounded upon the door. Behind her, the living grogoyle twitched and hissed, sending out a plume of
smoke and ashes. Although Lisandre flinched, she did
not let go of the knocker, banging it until the door
knocker's red eyes snapped open once more.

"What is your business with the Erlrune?"

"Please, I must see the Erlrune! My brother Ziggy is
ill, dying, poisoned…" Her voice broke. She steadied
herself with an effort and rushed on, "We do not have
much time! Only until the first snow falls. Please…"

"Visiting hours are from nine o'clock in the morning to noon," the door knocker said. "Please return
tomorrow."

"Oh, but, please…" Lisandre pleaded as the glowing eyes once again shut.

"'Tis no use a-trying to argue with it," a sweet,
rather faded voice said. "I'm afraid it's very old now
and rather cranky."

Everyone spun around in surprise. An old woman
stood at the edge of the courtyard. She was dressed in
a faded gingham dress, very saggy about the knees
and stained with soil, a disreputable straw hat and
gardening gloves. On one arm she carried a basket full
of carrots and cabbages, and in the other hand was a
very dirty spade.

"Perhaps you could tell me what it is you want?"

"Oh, please, we must see the Erlrune," Lisandre
said in a rush. "We have come so far and we have so
little time left. My brother Zygmunt, the Count of
Estelliana, has been poisoned or cursed, we do not
rightly know. He will die if I do not find the cure.

Please, can you not ask the Erlrune to help us?"

"But I am the Erlrune, my dear," the old woman said. "And I really have no idea what you think I could be doing for you."

"*You* are the Erlrune?" Lisandre stared at her incredulously.

"Yes, my dear." Then, as Lisandre's face crumpled and she began to cry, the old woman came forward, stripping off her muddy gloves so she could pat the starkin girl's arm. "Come, come, can it be so bad? Why don't you all come in and we'll have a spot of lunch and you can tell me the whole story."

Pedrin's face brightened considerably at the mention of lunch, and he came forward in a rush, shoving his flute into his pocket. The grogoyle leapt to his feet with a warning gust of flame and smoke. Pedrin recoiled as if he had been stung by the creature's cruel, barbed tail.

The old woman patted the thick, golden fur. "No need to fret, Gnash my dear, go back to sleep, there's a good grogoyle." Grumbling in his throat, the grogoyle turned round and round on the spot and settled back down again, though he still glared at the intruders with his flaming slits of eyes.

"Please excuse Gnash. He's very protective of me, as you can see. All my friends are, and I cannot but be grateful, irksome as it is at times. Come in, come in. Please don't mind the mess."

Rather warily, the six companions made their way past the crouching grogoyle and in through the great oaken door. Within was a rather dark hallway, panelled in wood, with a staircase at the far end. Rubbing the banister with beeswax was a wizened old wildkin, not much higher than Pedrin's waist, with a pair of velvety grey wings like a moth's. At the sight of the strangers, she gave a frightened little murmur and flew behind the banister, where she crouched, peering at them through the bars.

"Look, Flutter, guests! We have not had anyone come to stay for such a long time. Will you go and turn down the beds for me, dear? Make sure you give the sheets a good airing, there is naught worse than damp sheets."

As she spoke, the Erlrune laid down her gloves and spade on a hall-stand set against the side wall. She hung her shabby straw hat upon a hook, next to some other old, battered hats, an unravelling shawl and a very faded blue cloak with a fur-lined hood. A bucket crammed full of walking sticks and magic wands stood next to the hall-stand, along with a collection of muddy boots, some tiny, others so huge they could only belong to the hobhenkies.

The Erlrune led them down the hall and through a door into the kitchen. This was a big, warm, welcoming room, rather thick with smoke from the fire, with onions and garlic hanging in ropes from the mantelpiece, along with many bunches of dried herbs and flowers. Copper pots, pans and ladles dangled from hooks in the beams and there was a hand pump in one corner, above a wooden bucket standing in a puddle of water. Dirty pans and plates were piled on the bench, and there was a basket of kittens under the kitchen table.

"Do, please, excuse the mess, I warn't expecting visitors," the Erlrune said, dumping her basket of cabbages and carrots on the floor.

"I thought the Erlrune was meant to be a powerful enchantress, able to see the future," Lisandre hissed at Briony.

The old woman turned and twinkled at her. "Only if I look, my dear."

Both the hobhenkies had followed Pedrin and were now crowding into the kitchen, banging their heads against the copper pans hanging from the beams. "Ow! Smash crashed head! Ow! Crash smashed head!" they howled.

"Smash, Crash, what are you doing in here? Outside! Outside!"

"Boy pretty tune play," they said, rubbing their heads and pointing at Pedrin.

"Oh, and you do so love music, don't you? Well, mebbe he will play for you again this afternoon. He's hungry now, though, and wants his lunch."

"Smash, Crash, hungry too," the hobhenkies said.

"Of course you are. When are hobhenkies ever not hungry? You boys go outside and I'll put a bucket of stew out for you in just a moment. Good boys! Out you go!" She ushered the hobhenkies out the back door and shut it smartly behind them. "Such dear boys, but they can't help smashing and crashing everything and I'm running rather short on china. Please, sit down, sit down."

Rather bemused, the children cleared the kitchen

chairs of buckets of apples, jars of pickled onions, marmalade and chutney, sacks of flour and spices, and piles and piles of books with names like *The Genealogy of Grogoyles*, and *Divination and Demonolatry*. The old woman bustled about, stirring pots and pans, all the while talking genially about the weather. Lisandre looked despondent, leaning her head on her hand and occasionally giving a heavy sigh. The others were all very animated, however, looking about them with interest and telling the Erlrune some of their adventures. She exclaimed with admiration, setting the table with a motley collection of china, all rather chipped and cracked.

"Well, well, I daresay you could all do with a good meal then," she said. "Come, let us eat!"

"**J**umping Jimjinny!" Pedrin exclaimed, his eyes widening as he took in what could only be described as a truly magnificent feast. The long kitchen table was absolutely laden with delicacies of all kinds, all steaming and smelling delicious.

"Roast pork with crackling and apple chutney," Durrik exclaimed in satisfaction. "My favourite!"

"Mmmm, fried fish and baked potatoes," Sedgely said, tucking a napkin into his beard and beginning to eat with relish.

"And a nice drop of apple-ale," the Erlrune said with a twinkle, pouring him a cup. The river-roan heaved a huge sigh of happiness and drained his cup. The Erlrune filled it up again and he drained his cup again. "A very nice drop, ma'am," he said at last, his words rather slurred.

"Thank you, I made it myself," she replied. "Here, Pedrin, try this."

"Chicken-and-bacon pie," Pedrin said in amazement. "Just like me ma's."

"What's the best thing to put into a pie?" Durrik said with a puckish grin.

"Your teeth!" Pedrin cried and demonstrated enthusiastically.

"Lobster bouillon!" Lisandre's miserable expression disappeared like magic. "And can that be roast peacock? And asparagus with hollandaise sauce?"

"Indeed it is. Eat up, eat up! Enjoy."

"Oh, bully beef! A nice steak with mushrooms. I've been longing for a nice bit of steak."

Briony looked down at her bowl, which was filled to brimming with potato-and-tarragon soup. "How could you know?" she said slowly. "How could you possibly know?"

"But I am the Erlrune, my dear. Of course I know."

Everyone else stopped eating and looked at Briony, and then down at each other's plates, marvelling as they realised they each had been given their very favourite dish.

A little murmur of surprise and contentment rose, then everyone hurried on with their eating, only pausing to ask someone to pass the salt or to refill their cup. Lisandre was drinking a goblet of foaming sherbet, Pedrin had a tankard of sweet apple cider, Mags a mug of hot chocolate with whipped cream and marshmallows, and Durrik was enjoying a frothy concoction of fruit and ice. The expression on Briony's face as she sipped a little glass of some clear golden liquid was that of mingled bliss and sorrow, so that Pedrin nudged her and asked, in an undertone, "What's that you're a-drinking?"

"A cordial made from elderflowers," she said rather shortly. "The old witch who raised me used to make it. It was a secret family recipe of hers. I've always loved it and wished I knew the recipe."

Pedrin shook his head admiringly. "That Erlrune!"

As soon as all the plates were wiped clean, the Erlrune gave a little wave of her hand and the table cleared itself, a whole host of new dishes waltzing in to settle down. Once again everyone exclaimed with delight.

"Blackberry tart," cried Pedrin. "Me favourite!"

"Passionfruit soufflé!"

"Jam tarts. Yum yum."

"Oh goody, apricot turnovers," said Durrik.

"So why did the jam roll?" Pedrin asked, before Durrik could.

"Because it saw the apricot turnover," his friend responded, laughing. "You a-stealing my jokes now, Pedrin?"

Somehow they all managed to find room for the puddings, all except Sedgely, who was busying himself emptying the Erlrune's barrel of apple-ale. At last Pedrin pushed his chair away from the table with a groan, holding his stomach with both hands. "That was the best meal I've eaten in me whole life," he pronounced.

"Thank you, my dear," the Erlrune said with a quizzical smile. She turned from the fire, where she was stirring a big black pot.

"I don't think I can move," Mags said.

"Good," the Erlrune said.

Briony looked up sharply and then tried to rise. She was unable to do so, her arms and legs refusing to respond. With sudden frightened cries, the others tried to move too, but all were held fast in their chairs by some invisible force.

"We've been enchanted," Briony said, her voice cold with dread. "How? Why didn't I sense it?"

The Erlrune smiled. There was nothing left of the amiable old woman they had thought her. She was all hard bone and implacable power.

"Do you really think my power so unsubtle that a little girl with no education at all could be a-sensing it? My dear Briony."

The wildkin girl went crimson. They had never seen her so discomposed. She dropped her eyes and stared at her dirty plate, biting her lip.

"But why?" Pedrin said indignantly, struggling to move but unable to lift even a finger. "Why enchant us? We mean you no harm."

She frowned and instinctively he shrank back. "My island is strongly protected indeed and yet you were able to come a-walking right up to my very door, unhindered. That does not happen often. It speaks of great determination, at the very least. Few have the wit and courage and, yes, the power, to come a-knocking on my door as if I were merely some old country dame with a few simples to sell. This house, this garden, the Evenlinn itself, are very old. Many an Erlrune has lived and worked here and their magic has soaked in deep. From the moment you set foot inside my gate, the house and garden have been a-working to protect me, to lull and stupefy you."

The six friends were silent for a moment, each castigating themselves for being so unwary and foolish.

Then the Erlrune glared at them with a look of such fierce intensity that they all pressed their spines against the back of their chairs. "Nonetheless, do you really think you would be here, in my house, if I had not allowed you to come? Do you think the perils of the Perilous Forest so easily overcome?"

"The wood-sprites," Pedrin said, remembering how they had laughed and waved mockingly as the children had escaped on their seed-wings.

"The grogoyle!" Briony cried. "It was your grogoyle that saved me on the log bridge."

"Gnash is not mine," the Erlrune replied austerely. "One does not make a pet of a grogoyle."

"But it was Gnash, warn't it, who killed the soldiers before they could a-shoot me?"

"I have no liking for starkin soldiers," the Erlrune said coldly.

As they absorbed the implications of what the Erlrune had said, she called, in sweet, lilting tones, "Grim, Grisly, wake up, my dears."

Managing to roll his eyes upwards, Pedrin saw with a horrible little jerk of his heart that two omen-imps were perched on the rafters right above their heads. With wings like bats, hideous little faces with fangs and pointed ears, orange fur all over their bodies and black scales on their arms and legs, they were ugly enough to turn milk sour.

The omen-imps stretched and yawned, then flew

down, screeching, to land with a thump on the table. Nimbly they jumped over the dirty plates and cups, and searched through all their bags and pockets with quick and agile fingers. Once again, Pedrin's precious silver crown was stolen and he could do nothing to prevent the theft. He swore crossly, and the omen-imp only giggled and tweaked his nose derisively. They pinched Mags's arm, pulled Briony's long brown plait, tugged Sedgely's knotted white beard, and quarrelled over Lisandre's glittering christening egg. Suddenly the egg opened up, revealing the tiny jewelled bird within and causing the two omen-imps to tumble back head-over-heels. They lay amidst the piles of dirty bowls, their mouths open in surprise, then shrieked with laughter, drowning out the sweet song of the bird. When the egg had once again folded its petals and hidden its secret heart, they dragged it to join the big pile of belongings in the middle of the kitchen table.

"Good boys," the Erlrune said and scratched one omen-imp between his pointy black ears. He wriggled and squirmed with pleasure, then flew to perch on the back of one of the chairs, grinning with malicious glee.

The Erlrune turned over all their belongings, frowning a little, then picked up the two jewelled christening eggs in her hands. "Starkin artefacts," she mused. "Only limited powers, but interesting. Yeah, interesting." She laid them down on the table and turned to look them all over. "So you have come to ask for my help. Why?"

"I didn't know where else to go," Lisandre said

simply. "Please, you must help me."

"Why?"

"My brother…" she began, and found herself choking with tears. "My brother is dying … I … please, we have come so far…" Her voice suspended with tears, Lisandre could only look at the Erlrune pleadingly.

The old woman steepled her gnarled fingers. "Now, let me see if I understand the situation. You are the sister of the Count of Estelliana, who has been sunk in an unnatural sleep since midwinter. You've come here a-wanting my help in awakening him from this sleep. You hope that I will allow you to gaze into the Well of Fate, thus seeing the cause and the cure of the enchantment."

"Yes, please," Lisandre said with a little shake in her voice.

"But why should I help save a starkin prince? I have no love for the starkin. They have done naught but harm since they came here."

"But he will die," Lisandre pleaded.

"And I am meant to mourn his passing?"

"Ziggy's only fifteen," Lisandre said. "And really, he's a very nice boy. Not like most brothers. He's always let me play with him and he showed me how to heft a spear, and said he would take me out hunting with him one day. Starkin women aren't allowed to hunt, you know. He used to make up stories for me, every night before we went to bed, so I wouldn't be afraid of the dark. If I was sent to bed without any supper, he'd always smuggle something up to me. Oh, please, you have to help me! If Ziggy dies, Lord

Zavion will inherit and he's a cold, hard man, he'll be much crueller to the hearthkin and the wildkin than Ziggy would ever be. And we'll be destitute, my mother and I. We'll be at his mercy."

"Why should you not suffer poverty and hardship and thralldom like so many others have suffered?"

Lisandre did not know how to answer. At last she said helplessly, "I do not know. Please, I never understood before…"

"Now you do understand, what do you plan to do about it?"

"I don't know. I'll do something, I promise. I'll tell Ziggy when he wakes. Together we will change things, make things better."

"How?"

"I don't know," Lisandre faltered again. "But I'll find a way, I promise. The others will help me, they all want to make things better too."

"Is that true?" The Erlrune glanced around the table sternly.

Unable to nod, everyone said, "Yeah, of course, ma'am," with as much sincerity and enthusiasm as they could muster.

"How do I know you will keep your word?"

Lisandre looked steadily at the Erlrune, colour rising in her cheeks. "I don't know," she said for the fourth time. "I can only give you my word as one of the Ziv."

"Not a pledge that inspires trust in me," the Erlrune said dryly. She gave one of the christening eggs a spin with her finger and watched it twirl, the jewels all glittering.

"Very well, I shall help you, not because you command me to or because I have any desire to save the life of a starkin princeling. No, I shall help you because I see clearly that this quest of yours could be the catalyst for great events, events that could reshape our world. Never before in the history of Adalheit have starkin, hearthkin and wildkin come together and helped each other, and saved each other, and forged bonds of love and friendship. That alone has to mean something. So, yes, if you pass the test as all those who wish to gaze into the Well of Fate must do, I shall allow you to gaze into my pool. I have only one condition."

Emotions flitted across Lisandre's face like glimpses of sunshine amidst clouds. Triumph, relief, bewilderment, pleasure, and finally, suspicion.

"What test?" she asked first and then, "and what condition?"

"The river-roan once asked, in jest, for your first-born child as the reward for his help. I now make the same demand, though not in jest."

Lisandre stared at her, the colour draining from her face. She tried to speak but her throat muscles would not work. "My first-born child?" she faltered at last. "But how do you know about that?"

The old woman gazed at her levelly. "Do you really think I do not hear when my name is spoken, or do not see when strangers trespass on my province? Of course I have heard and seen all that has passed between you. Did you expect aught else?"

Lisandre's lips were white. "But Sedgely only spoke in jest. He did not mean … you cannot really want my first-born child!"

"But I do. You must send him to me when he is the same age as you are now. In the eighteen years between now and then, you must work to heal the rift in the land."

"But…" Lisandre faltered.

"That is the cost for my help," the Erlrune said implacably. "Your first-born child."

Lisandre stared at the Erlrune anxiously, her face white as chalk.

"I do not mean to eat him, you silly child," the Erlrune said with a sudden smile. "I mean only to teach him and guide him. You will get him back one day."

Slowly Lisandre nodded her head. "Very well then," she said through stiff, white lips. "I promise you my first-born child."

31
♦ ♦ ♦

From the outside, the Erlrune's house had looked rather small but the six companions soon learnt that, rather like the Erlrune herself, appearances could be deceiving. Accompanied by six grey-winged wild-kin, they were led through long halls, up sweeping staircases, along endless corridors, galleries and antechambers to a hallway with six bedrooms, three on either side.

The rooms were once again uncannily suited to each of the six companions. Lisandre's goose-down bed was hung with billowing white curtains and her ceiling was painted with silver stars and moons. There was a great hip-bath before a roaring fire, and a table crowded with different creams, perfumes, bath salts and a bottle of chamomile shampoo.

The walls and ceiling of Sedgely's room were painted with tall trees so it looked as if he slept in a forest. His mattress was, rather oddly, filled with water instead of straw so that the whole bed rocked when the children jumped on it, like a boat upon a river. His eiderdown was the deep green of a shadowy pond and a big ceramic jug of apple-ale and a tankard stood waiting on the table by the fireplace.

Mags's room was a frothy concoction of pale pink and lace, with delicate china figurines on the mantelpiece. A beautiful big doll with golden curls and lots of lacy petticoats sat on the pink satin eiderdown, and the wallpaper was sprigged with dainty flowers. On the table by her bath was a scrubbing brush, a wide-toothed comb and a huge lump of oatmeal soap, which made Lisandre laugh and say mockingly, "How well the Erlrune meets our needs!" Mags ignored her, her gaze fixed upon the doll. She sat down, cradling the doll in her arms, and soon was so absorbed the others left her playing, going on to explore their own rooms.

A wing-shaped spinet took up most of one wall in Pedrin's room, its case beautifully decorated with curling fronds, flowers and dancing wildkin. There was also a lute leaning against the wide-seated chair by the fire, and a collection of different pipes and flutes laid out on the table nearby. On his mantelpiece were two lovely dancing goats, one black, one white, and a tapestry of a goatherd playing a flute to a flock of grazing goats hung on the wall. There was also a box stuffed full of sweetmeats and cakes by his bed, which Pedrin immediately delved into before picking out a delicate tune on the lute.

The tapestry in Durrik's room showed a jester entertaining a royal court. Durrik grinned when he saw it, appreciating the joke, then he looked about his

394

room with pleasure. There was a new crutch leaning against his soft white bed, and a hip-bath filled with steaming water that smelt of wintergreen, rosemary, thyme and lavender, a combination of herbs designed to ease his aching leg. A music box on the table sang sweetly when opened, with two solemn figures gracefully turning and bowing within. The table by his fire bore a pile of books and a cup of steaming chamomile tea, which the weary boy gratefully sipped as he began to turn the pages of one of the books.

With the others all busy and preoccupied in their own rooms, Briony was alone when she opened the last of the six doors. She stepped inside with a glad sigh and shut the door behind her.

The walls of Briony's room were a soft pale green, with a simple design of forget-me-nots, roses and lilies-of-the-valley painted above the architrave. The same pattern was embroidered upon her green eiderdown and pillows, and green silken curtains were held back with an embroidered ribbon. A great bunch of wild-flowers on her bedside table sweetened the air. A hip-bath steamed gently nearby, its water green with mineral salts and herbs. A gilt mirror glimmered on the wall, with a pretty white gown hanging beside it.

A spinning-wheel stood in one corner and there was an embroidery stand by the fire, with many spools of coloured silk hung below it and a pincushion in the shape of a pink rose. On the table was a wooden box with a wreath of roses, forget-me-nots and lilies-of-the-valley carved upon it. When Briony opened the lid, she saw it was filled with mulberry leaves and silkworms, many already spinning themselves a little yellow cocoon.

Next to the box was a crystal glass and a decanter of elderflower wine, and a plate of little sweet biscuits, each with a sugar-frosted flower on top. There was also a very thick, ancient-looking book.

Pouring herself a glass of the sweet-scented, golden wine, Briony slowly undressed in the warmth of the crackling fire and climbed into the hip-bath. The water was hot and smelt delicious. She lay back, wondering at the powers of the Erlrune. She had such insight into all their hearts and minds. Briony shivered a little, knowing how dangerous such insight could be.

She soaked in the bath for a long time, enjoying her solitude, but at last the water grew cold and she got out and dried herself and dressed in the soft white gown. She combed out her long mass of dark curls and suddenly realised that her own clothes had disappeared, the curtains were drawn and candlelight illuminated the room with soft, golden light. She wondered how or when this had happened, for she had noticed nothing. It disturbed her a little, but she felt so clean and reinvigorated that it was easy to smile and shrug, and let her sense of unease dissipate.

She poured herself another glass of elderflower wine and sat sleepily by the fire. Her gaze strayed to the thick brown book. She wondered what it was doing there, for Briony had never been taught to read. She opened the cover and the indecipherable squiggles within turned and twisted and resolved themselves into a drawing of a face. It was the face of a woman with a mass of dark curly hair, a pointed chin and ears, and slanted eyes. The face looked up at her and said in a sweet, melodious voice, "Magic is the art of bringing change as a consummation of one's own will…"

With a little gasp, Briony shut the book. She held it closed, took a gulp of her wine, and then rather fearfully opened it again. The face looked up at her, smiled a little ruefully, and began again.

"Magic is the art of bringing change as a consummation of one's own will. All the world moves upon a wheel of constant change. Season follows season, life follows birth, death follows life. A seed falls, a sapling sprouts and grows slowly into a tree, bearing within its trunk the circles of its time. The tree blossoms, the blossoms harden into seeds and the seeds fall, to begin another tree. In due course, the tree shall fall and rot away, to feed the earth so another seed may grow. Onwards and upwards, the spiral continues. From the helix of life to the celestial dance of the stars, all life spins, a-growing and a-changing…"

Absorbed, Briony sat in the chair, sipping her wine and listening.

She came back to herself many hours later. The decanter of wine was empty, the biscuits all gone. Briony felt dreamy and light-headed. She closed the book and laid it carefully back on the table, then looked about her with an expression of serene joy. She could not remember ever feeling so safe and content.

There was a discreet tap on the door. Briony smiled and called, "Come in."

The little grey-winged wildkin looked in shyly and beckoned her. Briony nodded and got up, following her out into the corridor. All the others were just coming out too, all pink and sweet-smelling from their bath and with the same glow of contentment that Briony radiated. Sedgely in particular looked very well pleased with himself, grinning foolishly at the sight of the others and mumbling, "A very nice drop of apple-ale, me word! A lovely woman, the Erlrune, lovely! Knows just what a poor old river-roan's a-needing to be comfortable."

All were dressed in simple white clothes, without any adornment of any kind. Sedgely and the boys wore long shirts over loose trousers, and Mags and Lisandre were dressed in the same soft dress as Briony. All were barefoot. They smiled to see each other and a little hum of conversation rose as they each began to describe the treasures of their room.

"I had such a lovely nap," Durrik murmured. "And my leg does not ache at all! I dreamt ... oh, I dreamt so many things and now they're dissolving away. I wish I could remember..."

"Did you see the lute?" Pedrin's eyes glowed. "It has such a gorgeous sound. I wish I had one like it at home."

"Well, look at you," Lisandre said to Mags. "Who would've thought there was such a pretty girl under all that dirt?"

"Yeah, I scrub up mighty well, really, don't I?" Mags said proudly, giving a little twirl so her skirt billowed out. "Did you see me doll? Warn't she bully?

398

Do you think the Erlrune will let me keep her?"

The grey-winged wildkin led them down through the maze of galleries and staircases to a great hall where a pair of ornate wooden doors stood firmly closed. The panels of the door were carved with the faces of wildkin, some achingly beautiful, others hideously ugly, some grinning with spite, others frowning sadly. No one was surprised to see their eyes glowing with life. All those watching eyes made them feel rather uncomfortable, and they bunched close together.

The doors swung open. The gibgoblin stood inside, smiling malevolently.

"Sssalutationsss, my dearsss," he hissed. "Pleassse, passssss through."

They did not move a step, staring at him in chagrin. He waved his cigar nonchalantly, smoke trailing. "Pleassse, no need for disssmay. I ssshall not ssscourge you thisss evening. You are the Erlrune'sss honoured guessstsss ... for now. Later, perhapsss?"

Still they did not move. He made an impatient gesture, hissing, "Passssss through, my dearsss, passssss through."

Huddled together, they walked through the doors, trying to keep as far away as possible from the gibgoblin. He laughed and lashed his whip mockingly, so that they all flinched.

Beyond was a long dark hall, lined on both sides with great glass doors that stood open to the evening. White gauzy curtains billowed in the breeze. Outside, the sky was velvety-dark and glittering with the icy pinpoints of stars. The round orb of the moon irradiated the garden with silvery brilliance. It was cold and they shivered in their thin clothes.

At the far end of the room was a dais with a tall, elaborately carved wooden throne upon it. On either side of the throne was a candelabra, blazing with twelve white candles in three concentric rings. Sitting upright upon the throne was the Erlrune. The light fell full upon her face and figure, making her gown of silver-blue silk shimmer like the lake at moonrise and illuminating her ancient, high-boned face. They all wondered how they could ever have thought her a frumpy old serving-woman. Her lined face was full of power and mystery and pride.

Between them and the Erlrune was a round pool of water. The candlelight gleamed upon its still surface. The pool was surrounded by a mosaic of small blue tiles, bordered in black, set in whirling lines like a hurricane. The pool in the centre was the quiet eye of the storm. Around the edges of the room the tiles were set in coloured patterns of fronds and flowers and faces. The ceiling above them was painted with innumerable stars that glowed eerily, while a forest of trees grew upon the walls, framing the glass doors with their trunks and branches. As they tentatively moved forward a few steps, Briony saw forms and faces in the dark foliage of the trees. It seemed they moved, tiptoeing through the shadowy trunks, watching from behind the leaves.

All was silent. Sedgely and the children moved forward a few more steps. All their bonhomie had fallen from them, replaced with a little frisson of nervousness.

"Look," Briony whispered. "The tiles are set in a path. I think we should follow it."

"Whatever do you mean?" Lisandre whispered back.

"Follow the shape of the tiles, a-whirling about. See? They form a pattern. 'Tis a path that leads round and roundabouts to the pool. I think it would be wrong not to follow the path. Just come along with me. You'll see what I mean."

So, in single file, the six companions slowly wound their way into the pool, following the swirling shape laid down in mosaic upon the floor. The path led them inexorably to the pool in the centre of the room and then, rather to their surprise, out again and to the foot of the throne at the far end. The Erlrune regarded them with inscrutable eyes.

"I hope you found your rooms comfortable."

"Just bully!" Mags said as Pedrin and Durrik both said, "Yeah, rather."

"Yeah, ma'am," Sedgely said, rather abashed.

"Indeed I did. I thank you," Lisandre said regally.

"So are you ready to look into the Well of Fate?"

They all murmured a rather apprehensive affirmative.

"Very well," the Erlrune replied. "First of all you must understand that the Well of Fate may only ever be consulted once in a lifetime. All of you have secret longings and desires that the pool could answer. It could tell you, Briony, who you are. In its depths you could see your past and know who your parents were and why you were lost or abandoned. It could show you your mother, Durrik, and tell you whether she ever wishes she could hold you in her arms."

Both Briony and Durrik stared at her with stricken faces, their eyes very dark in the flickering candlelight. The Erlrune held their gaze for a long moment, and both dropped their eyes, shamed to have their hidden longing so clearly perceived.

The Erlrune looked then at the goatherd, saying, "Pedrin, in the Well of Fate you could know your future, whether you are destined to be a great musician or merely a lowly goatherd, as you fear. You too could see your future, Maglen. Will you be forever an outcast, cursing the moon's brightness, or will you ever have the home you've always wanted?"

Pedrin felt his ears turn red. He glanced at Mags and saw the wistful longing on her face. "I'm happy the way I am," Pedrin said loudly. "I don't need to look in the pool to know what me future will be. Me father was a goatherd and so was his father, and so shall I be. You should not try a-tricking us." Yet even as he spoke, he thought of the joy he had felt all that long afternoon, creating sweet music alone in his room, and his whole body felt hot and uncomfortable.

"I do not try to trick you," the Erlrune said sternly. "I just tell you that you must gaze into the Well of Fate with a clear and pure focus, else your visions will be sullied. You must all be sure of what it is you want to see."

They were silent and fidgety, unable to meet

Lisandre's anxious eyes. Sedgely said mournfully, "Oh well, no need to worrit on me behalf, little missy. An old man like me knows the only thing that lies ahead for him is the long, quiet sleep. No need to be a-feared *I'll* be distracted by a wish to know the future."

The Erlrune smiled in real amusement. "Life is full of surprises, Sedgely. I would not be too sure it holds naught new for you."

The river-roan hurrumphed in polite disbelief.

Lisandre said urgently, "Oh, please, can I not look in the pool by myself? The others can all look later and see whatever it is they want to see. Ziggy is my brother, it is me that needs to know what has happened to him."

The Erlrune shook her head. "'Six brought together can the cruel bane defeat,'" she quoted. "No, the six of you came together to seek my help. Often the visions in the Well are clearer if more than one mind and heart are bent upon it, and six is a good number for seeking such visions. 'Tis the number of perfection, being divisible by both two and three. It represents harmony, beauty and trust, which seems fateful indeed. Besides, the Well of Fate may be used only once a month, when the moon is full. If you do not look now, you cannot look for another month."

Surprised, Briony glanced out the window. Only when she saw the round brightness of the moon in the sky did she realise the moon was now radiantly full. It had been only a few days past its prime when they had crossed the Evenlinn. Surely that had only been yesterday? How long had she spent reading the book?

403

She gazed at the Erlrune, her hands clasped close to her breast. "How is it that the moon is now full when yesterday it was old? How long have we been here, in your house?"

"You were all a-weary," the Erlrune said. "You needed to rest. One needs strength and courage to gaze into the Well of Fate."

The others cried out in consternation. Lisandre said furiously, "Do you mean we have been here a month? A whole month? But we do not have the time! We only have till the beginning of winter. The prophecy says—"

"You couldn't have looked into the Well of Fate until tonight anyway," the Erlrune said indifferently. "You could have spent the month a-fretting and a-worrying and a-getting in my way, or you could have spent it a-resting and regaining your strength. You must admit you all feel better for your rest."

It was true, they all felt greatly invigorated. They looked at each other in chagrin, murmuring, "A whole month? But how can it be? It seemed only a few hours…"

"Do you mean I haven't eaten in a month?" Pedrin cried. "But I'm not hungry at all!"

"You all had sustenance," the Erlrune said, a smile flickering on her withered mouth. "And I fed you well before you went to your rooms."

"The food was all enchanted?" Briony asked in amazement.

"Of course," the Erlrune replied. "I would have thought you, of all people, would have been wary of eating such a feast, Briony. But come. We waste time.

'Tis the night of the full moon and midnight is almost upon us. Lisandre, you wish to gaze into the Well of Fate?"

"I do," Lisandre answered nervously.

"All those who come to the Well of Fate must first answer three riddles. Thus it is and thus it has always been."

"Very well," Lisandre said with a quick nod of her head and a glance at Durrik.

"The first riddle is a simple one. I shall ask you a question, and if you answer correctly, you may step to the pool and gaze into its waters. If you answer incorrectly, you shall die."

That made them all shuffle and sigh and look at each other in consternation.

"What, all of us?" Mags cried.

"All of you," the Erlrune said implacably.

"How?" Pedrin asked in very real dread, remembering the gibgoblin's smug smile.

She ignored him. "Are you ready for the first riddle?"

"Wait!" Lisandre cried. They huddled together, conferring rapidly. Though all were angry and troubled by the cost of the test, everyone but Sedgely was sure Durrik would be able to answer any riddle the Erlrune could throw at them. The river-roan just sighed and said, "Well, I've had a long life and most of it pleasurable. If I must be a-dying, it might as well be now as later."

Lisandre rolled her eyes at him, and turned back to the Erlrune, saying anxiously, "Very well then. Ask us the riddle."

The old woman said, very gently, "You understand 'tis you who must answer this riddle, Lisandre, since 'tis you who wish to question the pool?"

The colour slowly drained out of Lisandre's face. "But ... that's not fair..."

"You are not the first to come to the Well of Fate and face this quandary," the Erlrune said. "Time hurries on, though. 'Tis almost midnight. Do you wish to gaze into the Well of Fate or not?"

"Yes, yes, I do," Lisandre faltered. "But..." She looked at the others and though they had gone as pale as she had, they gave little shrugs and nods of encouragement.

"All this time in Durrik's company, you must a-learnt summat about riddles," Mags said in a high, strained voice.

"Let us hope so," Sedgely said mournfully.

Lisandre looked sick. She steadied herself with a hand on Pedrin's arm and said shakily, "What's the riddle then?"

"What is it that trembles with each breath of air, and yet can the heaviest loads bear?" the Erlrune asked.

Lisandre was baffled. She repeated the question once, twice, looked at the others pleadingly, looked back at the Erlrune.

"Lisandre!" Durrik said. The Erlrune looked at him sharply but did not speak, as he continued, "Here's a riddle for you! Why is a riddle like a sword?" He paused for a moment and then said with clear and heavy emphasis, "They're no good unless they have a point."

Lisandre looked thoughtful. Pedrin gripped his hands into fists, willing her to understand. As the silence grew longer, he felt his tension grow until he was sweating and trembling. The same strain showed on everyone's faces, except for that of Sedgely, who simply had too much facial hair to ever show much expression. The old man was clutching his pipe tightly, though, putting it in his mouth and taking it out again, showing how dearly he wished he dared smoke. Durrik was staring at Lisandre as intently as if he was trying to send her the answer telepathically, and Mags was biting her lip, her hazel eyes hard and bright, her hands clenched into fists. Briony was playing with her cat's cradle, her eyes lowered.

Lisandre looked up quickly, glanced at the others apologetically, and said, "I think I know. I hope … I hope I'm right."

"So do we all," Sedgely said gruffly.

"Very well. Answer me this then. What is it that trembles with each breath of air, and yet can the heaviest loads bear?

"Is the answer … water?"

"Is that your answer?"

Lisandre hesitated, then nodded her head. "Yes. It is."

"Water is the right answer." There was a great exhalation of breath all around the circle of tense white faces. Lisandre rocked on her feet as if her legs threatened to give way beneath her. The others all crowded around her, the girls hugging her ecstatically, Pedrin giving her a congratulatory thump on the arm.

Lisandre was quite limp and shaky, saying, "I can't believe I got it right! It was a guess, really – to think of all our lives, depending on a mere guess!"

"An inspired guess," Durrik said and she smiled at him brilliantly.

Their relieved babble died away as the Erlrune rose stiffly. At once tense and wary again, they all turned to face her. The old woman came slowly down the steps. She suddenly seemed very tall, her white hair shining in the candlelight. The glimmering silk flowed about her like water. Briony longed to stroke it and feel the texture of its weave. She did not dare, however, and so only gazed at it wonderingly, knowing it was the finest craftsmanship she had ever seen.

The Erlrune stood before them, regarding them with dark, hooded eyes. She said in a commanding voice, "You may gaze into the Well of Fate now, but if you do not decipher the second riddle, you will see naught but your own faces staring back at you."

"What's the second riddle?" Pedrin asked apprehensively.

"To make whole what was torn,
Kith must be as kin.
For kith to be as kin,
What is whole must be torn."

32

◆ ◆ ◆

They stared at her in puzzlement. "But … that's a paradox," Durrik protested. "'Tis impossible."

She did not answer, just stared at them with those impenetrable dark eyes.

"To make whole what was torn,

Kith must be as kin.

For kith to be as kin,

What is whole must be torn," Durrik repeated slowly. "It must make sense somehow. 'Kith' means friends. 'Kin' means family. So it means that friends must be as family."

"So, 'To make whole what was torn' – does that mean healing Ziggy?" Lisandre asked blankly.

"And the land," Briony added quickly.

"And everyone in it," Mags said passionately.

"So if we want to heal Ziggy…"

"And the land…"

"And everyone in it," Mags cried, laughing.

"…friends need to be as family. Does that mean us? The friends, I mean."

"Of course it does," Briony said. "Have you ever had better?"

Lisandre shook her head, her face crumpling.

"So the six of us … we have to be like a family," Mags said, her laughter dying and replaced by something scared and solemn. "But we are, sort of. After all we've been through…"

There was a long pause, broken only by mutters: "To make whole … kith must be as kin… For kith to be as kin … What is whole must be torn."

"Durrik?" Pedrin asked hopefully.

Durrik clutched his head and muttered some more. Then he looked up, his eyes shining, and said in a ringing voice, "What is it that binds family together?"

"Oh, please, not more riddles!" Lisandre said in disgust.

"Blood!" Durrik cried. "Blood binds family together."

"Yes," Lisandre said uncomprehendingly. "Ties of blood."

"Blood is thicker than water," Mags contributed with a return of her impudent grin. "Me own flesh and blood. It runs in the blood. Blood brothers…"

Durrik returned her grin with a sparkling one of his own. "Exactly. So to make us family, to make us blood brothers and blood sisters, we need to mingle our blood. We have to cut – or tear – our flesh, our whole, unmarred flesh, to make the blood flow so that we can bind ourselves together as family! Is that right?" He turned to the Erlrune triumphantly. "It has to be right!"

The Erlrune smiled at him enigmatically and pulled a long, wickedly sharp dagger from a sheath at her waist. "'Tis midnight. Time to gaze in the pool. Mingle your blood, with full knowledge of the sacredness of the ritual, and see if you have guessed a-right."

The Erlrune gave them all a candle and then they followed her round and round the circling path of blue mosaic, back to the Well of Fate in the eye of the storm. She instructed them to place their candles in a circle around it. They obeyed.

"Now, mingle your blood and let it fall into the water," the Erlrune said. "Then you must sit, a-holding hands and a-gazing into the pool. You must all focus your thoughts upon what it is you wish to see. Be very clear in what you wish for. Do not allow your thoughts to wander, for the visions will follow your thoughts. You shall receive three visions, of the past, the present and the future. Understand this. The visions you see in the pool are the third riddle. You must decipher what you see to understand the meaning hidden behind. The visions are not always clear, particularly the visions of the future, for they show what may be, not what shall be. Do you understand?"

They nodded and murmured in response, feeling a sudden quickening of their blood. The Erlrune bowed her head and walked swiftly away, following the spiral shape of the path. Her form was soon swallowed by shadows.

"We want to know the truth of this sickness that has befallen my brother Zygmunt, the Count of Estelliana," Lisandre said rather tremulously, "and to

411

discover the cure, so that we may save his life."

She held out her hand and swiftly slashed the palm with the dagger. Blood welled up, thick and dark. Cupping her hand so the blood did not drip, she jerked her head furiously at the others. One by one they reluctantly held out their hands. The pain of the knife was sharp but quick. Standing in a circle about the pool, all six of the companions held up their bleeding palms and clasped each other's hands above the water. Blood ran down their wrists and dripped into the pool, sending out ever widening ripples of red-gold flame and shadow.

They let go, sitting down and joining hands, bloody palm to intact palm, all round the circle. The palm that had been cut was sticky and wet, and stung. They hung on grimly, though, staring down into the pool, trying to think only of the sleeping Count of Estelliana.

Slowly the water in the pool began to rotate, swirling round and round in an anti-clockwise direction. Faster and faster the water swirled, and then suddenly it cleared and steadied, becoming as still and bright as a mirror. They did not see their faces, however, in the still surface of the pool. Instead they saw a moving scene, a scene with colour but without sound.

It was winter at the Castle of Estelliana. Snow lay heaped about the courtyard and icicles hung from the pointed roofs of the towers. The pool in the centre of the courtyard was frozen over. Above the pool, the starthorn tree lifted green, leafy branches to the steely

412

dawn sky. Peeping out from the shiny green leaves were large, golden apples. A few apples lay scattered through the snow.

A cloaked and hooded figure came furtively out of the castle, carrying a large covered basket. The figure came to the foot of the starthorn tree and searched through the snow, picking up the fallen apples with a gloved hand and stowing them in the basket. There were evidently not enough, for after a while the search grew more frenzied. Then the figure stood looking up at the tree. It grasped the trunk with both hands and shook the trunk vigorously. The starthorn tree was a tall and ancient tree, however, and not easily shaken. Only a few apples fell down and were hastily collected. The figure shook the tree again, but no more fruit fell. The figure went back into the castle, clearly displeased.

The picture blurred, then resolved itself once more into clarity. Lady Donella, the chief lady-in-waiting, was beckoning a small hearthkin boy to her side. Pedrin and Durrik both widened their eyes in surprise. They knew the boy. Named Garvin, he had been a pot-boy up at the castle. He had fallen ill with a mysterious ailment the previous winter and died.

Lady Donella spoke to the boy with a sweet smile, and he nodded. She pressed a copper coin into his palm and he scampered away, looking pleased. Once again the scene blurred. When the vision cleared, it was to show Garvin shivering and stamping his bare feet in the snow piled high under the starthorn tree. It was dawn. He rubbed his numb fingers together, looked about him furtively, and then began to climb the tree. He reached the fruit-laden branches and began to pick the star-apples, dropping them down into the snow below. Suddenly he seemed to cry out and wince. He looked down at his arm. The sleeve was torn and there was a long, bloody cut in the flesh beneath. He had scratched himself on one of the cruel-looking thorns. Garvin sucked the cut tenderly, plucked a few more star-apples, then slid down the tree.

A wave of dizziness seemed to overcome him, for he stood holding on to the trunk, his head bowed. When he raised his face, it looked pinched and white. Unsteadily he bent and picked up all the star-apples, stowing them away in a basket. He made his way through the heavy drifts of snow, leaving a few scarlet drops of blood behind him like rubies scattered on white velvet.

Lady Donella waited at the side door for him, a hood drawn up over her silvery-fair hair. Now the boy was sweating and trembling. He gave the basket to Lady Donella and showed her the long cut, bleeding profusely. She smiled and made some gesture of reassurance, giving him another small coin. He took it and turned away, making his unsteady way back towards the kitchens.

The vision accelerated, blurring in whirls of smoke, blood and shadow. When it steadied, they saw Garvin lying on a pile of blankets in a huge, dark, smoky kitchen, moaning a little, moving his head restlessly as if it pained him. His face was slick with sweat, and the bandage on his arm was dripping with blood. Through his half-closed eyelids they saw the white of his eyes, twitching horribly. An enormously fat woman knelt beside him, blotting the sweat from his face with a damp cloth and dribbling water into his mouth. He did not swallow, his throat muscles standing up rigidly, quivering with strain. Gradually the twitching of his eyeballs, the spasms in his arms and legs, the working of his throat, all slowed until he was still and lax. The fat woman sighed and shook her head, perplexed, drawing up the ragged blanket to cover the white slits of his eyes.

Pedrin could feel Lisandre's hand trembling in his but she said nothing, leaning forward, watching intently. The six companions were now looking into a comfortable room, a fire roaring in the hearth. Lady Donella sat at a table, wielding a slim silver knife. On one side was a pile of golden apples, on the other side a bowl full of chopped fruit. As Lady Donella delicately cut another apple in half, the watching companions could clearly see the shape of a six-pointed star inside. When all the apples were chopped, Lady Donella crushed them and extracted the juice, then mixed the juice with sugar and spices and poured the frothy liquid into a barrel, which she placed near the heat of the fire.

Once again, the vision returned to the snowy courtyard. This time it was filled with men upon horses, stamping and blowing frosty breath. The men were all grandly dressed in velvets and furs, and all were laughing and talking. Count Zoltan was there, his huge mastiff sitting panting beside him, the falconer handing up a hooded bird of prey. At the sight of her father, Lisandre gave an anguished cry but she did not break the circle. The castle doors opened and out came the countess, dressed all in white velvet and fur. Beside her walked her son Zygmunt, talking animatedly. Behind them was Lady Donella, smiling sweetly. She beckoned forward a servant, who carried the barrel of fermented star-apple juice. Though they could not hear what was said, there was clearly a lot of joking and laughing, as Lady Donella handed the barrel to one of the count's servants.

The next vision showed the clearing by the pool where they had first met Sedgely. They saw the starkin lords drink deeply of the apple-ale made from the starthorn fruit. They were possessed by a fervent excitement, talking and gesticulating wildly, singing and dancing about the fire. Only the young heir to the throne did not quaff his cup. He tasted only a few mouthfuls, then surreptitiously poured most of his apple-ale away. Again and again the men refilled their cups, and the dancing and talking grew ever wilder. At last men began to slump sideways where they sat, or fell mid-step, lying still and motionless as snowflakes drifted down, covering them with a cold, white counterpane.

The pictures in the pool dwindled away. Pedrin had to clear his throat, and he could hear Lisandre trying to stifle her sobs.

"I'm glad I warn't made an offering of *that* apple-ale," Sedgely said gruffly. "What kind of fruit was that?"

416

"No wonder they all died," Lisandre said miserably. "Apples from the starthorn tree! Why would Lady Donella do such a thing? Why, why?"

"She loves Lord Zavion," Briony said simply. "And power too, I think. I have always seen it in her."

"She loves Lord Zavion?" Lisandre said. "But why murder my father…?" Her voice trailed away.

"We all know star-apples can make a man dance until he dies, why did we not guess what had happened when Sedgely told us he saw the starkin lords dancing?" Durrik said. "We should've guessed."

"Do you know the cure for starthorn poisoning, milady?" Pedrin asked eagerly.

Lisandre shook her head miserably. "I do not think there is one. If there is, I have never heard of it."

"Poor Garvin," Durrik said. "The thorns must be poisonous too. It looked like a mighty awful way to die."

Lisandre said shakily, "The thorns are poisonous. My … my father always warned Ziggy not to try to climb the tree, that the risk was not worth the dare. He did not warn me, of course. What starkin lady would ever desire to climb a tree?" Her voice was full of bitterness.

The water had begun to swirl again, this time spinning in a clockwise direction. Faster and faster it whirled, a dark funnel at its heart sucking them down, making them lean closer and closer, their heads spinning.

"Look," Mags said hoarsely. "There's more."

When the whirling water stilled, they found themselves looking at the starthorn tree once more. Its black thorns were covered in drifts of delicate white blossom, with little buds of leaves just beginning to burst open along the stems. A gust of wind blew, tossing brown leaves about in the courtyard and dragging away a shower of white petals. The men digging over the bare earth in the kitchen garden shivered and huddled their chins into their scarves.

The vision moved to a room in the castle. The young count lay on his bed, covered with a white eiderdown. His eyes were closed, his hands folded. The slight flutter of a pulse in his throat was the only sign that he was still breathing. Lady Donella glided silently out of the shadows and stood, looking down at him, her lips gripped into a thin line. She watched him for a long moment then turned, quietly lifting a pillow from a chair behind him. As she bent over him, a little old hearthkin man rose from his seat by the fire. He was dressed in the white and gold livery of the Estaria family, the swan and starthorn blossom device upon his breast. They saw his lips moving, and Lady Donella paused with a sudden jerk. Then she was smiling sweetly, lifting Count Zygmunt's head so she could slide the pillow underneath. She smoothed his long, fair curls, nodded to the old man, then glided swiftly out of the room.

A few moments later, they saw her enter the Hall of Mirrors. Lord Zavion reclined upon a throne of cut crystal, sipping wine and ignoring the merchants on their knees before him, pleading. Lady Donella came and stood behind the Regent, smiling adoringly at him and laying her hand on his shoulder as she bent to whisper in his ear. He nodded, yawned behind his delicate white hand, then waved the hand nonchalantly. Soldiers dragged the merchants away and Lord Zavion ate another sweetmeat.

Lady Donella then made her way back upstairs, giving crisp orders to various servants as she went. In the solar, Lisandre's mother sat staring with vacant eyes out the window. She was as thin as a scarecrow, with great hollows beneath her cheekbones. Lady Donella looked at her with a small, secret smile, then bent over her, persuading her to drink a glass of some deep red cordial. After the dowager countess had obediently drunk it, she closed her eyes and seemed to sink into sleep. The smile on Lady Donella's lips grew.

The scene in the pool shifted to show Durrik's father, lying on a straw pallet in some kind of prison, looking dirty, thin, haggard and very unhappy. Many others were locked up with him. With a jerk of his heart, Pedrin recognised his mother and sister among them, as well as many friends and neighbours. Pedrin's little sister was crying quietly, and Pedrin's mother was rocking her gently in her arms, a look of despair on her face.

The vision widened to show the harvest rotting in the fields, as a few painfully thin people strove to bring it in alone. They saw a young mother struggling to hoe the fields, a wailing baby tied to her back. In the next field, a ragged bunch of children did their best to pick shrivelled, worm-eaten apples from the trees. The streets of Levanna-On-The-Lake were filled with people begging. Soldiers prodded them with spears, driving them out to starve in the countryside.

The vision faded. The six companions had to hang on to each other's hands tightly to avoid breaking the circle. All were horrified by what they had seen. Briony and Lisandre were both weeping, and Durrik was white as whey. Pedrin felt his anxiety about his family as heavy as a stone in the pit of his stomach, but he knew there was nothing any of them could do now. Sharply he called them all to order.

"Look, the water is turning again! Watch! Watch!"

Faster and faster the water spun, then slowly stilled. Once again they saw the starthorn tree. New leaves were bursting open all along the thorny branches, green buds of apples forming where the starthorn flowers had once hung. Only one spray of blossom remained, hanging from the very highest branch. A blast of cold wind came with a flurry of snowflakes. The petals were torn from the branch. Winter closed upon the Castle of Estelliana with grim, grey shadows. They saw the white flags being dragged down to half-mast and then they saw a sombre funeral procession, clad all in blood-red robes, carrying the dead count down to the burial ground. Lisandre sobbed out loud.

The water swirled back. Snowflakes spun back into white blossom again. They saw the flowering branch bending and swaying in the wind. A girl's hand carefully broke off the flowering twig. A few petals twirled away into the wind, and were joined by a flurry of snow. They saw the arm suddenly jerk and wince, as one of the cruel thorns tore open the skin from wrist to elbow. Blood fell in a scatter of bright red. The vision spun, the colours all blurring. Then they saw Lisandre bending over her sleeping brother. She held the cluster of snowy-white blossoms beneath his nose. His nostrils flared as he breathed in the scent. Colour tinted his cheeks. His eyelids fluttered and then slowly the young count opened his eyes. He smiled. Her eyes wet with tears, Lisandre threw herself upon him, kissing him joyfully. His thin arms tightened about her back, then, when she did not move, held her away. Blood from the wound in her arm stained the white satin in a great, widening pool. Lisandre was limp, her eyes closed. Zygmunt bent over her, shaking her, but she did not move. He shook her more urgently and, when she did not wake, bent his head over hers, weeping.

A flurry of visions followed, so fast and fragmented they had trouble understanding what they saw. Lisandre and Count Zygmunt embracing joyously, smiling faces all around. Lady Donella holding Lisandre tightly, her silver knife glinting. Lady Donella holding a pillow over Count Zygmunt's face. White feathers bursting, a flurry of white that could have been feathers or blossom or snow, concealing a whirl of faces, sometimes weeping, sometimes smiling. Then the silver knife stabbed down once more, and all they saw was blood.

The red, swirling water slowly, slowly calmed, became a pool of water reflecting the dancing flames of candles and their own faces, cavernous with shadows.

There was a long silence, fraught with tension. Lisandre clung tightly to Pedrin and Durrik's hands, bending over at the waist as if trying not to be sick.

"What … what did it all mean?" Mags asked tentatively, letting go of Durrik and Sedgely's hands and sucking at the cut on her palm. "Surely it didn't mean…"

"You can't be a-going back, Lise!" Pedrin said urgently. "You saw … we all saw … it means you'll be a-dying if you go back!"

Lisandre shivered.

"Mebbe not," Briony pointed out. "Only if she cuts her arm on the thorns. She mightn't."

"But we all saw—" Pedrin protested.

"Remember what the Erlrune said? It shows what may be, not what shall be."

"Even so," Pedrin said. He grasped Lisandre's hand tightly, turning her towards him. "You can't take the risk, Lise! 'Tis a mighty high price to be a-paying. You don't need to go back. You can stay here in the forest, we'll all stay! We'll be like wood-sprites, a-living in the trees and a-catching fish for our supper, same as we done all summer."

Lisandre's lip was trembling. Her breath caught. "Oh, if only I could! If you only knew…"

"But you can! Why can't you? We've managed this long, we can manage for longer." Pedrin's voice was rough and urgent. He looked at the others for support.

Sedgely was nodding and smiling at him, though his dark liquid eyes were sad. Mags was frowning and biting her knuckle, and Briony was shaking her head, though her moon-silver eyes were soft with sympathy. Durrik, although obviously troubled, nodded, saying, "Yeah, milady, of course there's no need for you to be a-going back if you warn't a-wanting to. We've lived this long in the forest, I'm sure we could find somewhere safe to keep on a-living." He hesitated, then said, "Only ... well, there's my papa still in the dungeon, and all t'other folk too. I ... well, I..."

Bitter shame and remorse filled Pedrin. He dropped Lisandre's hand and turned his face away, not wanting anyone to see how sick he felt. How could he be forgetting his mother and his sister, and Johan Bell-Crier, and all the other folk he had known all his life? Yet, for a moment or two, he had forgotten, the vision of Lisandre's death blotting out everything else, just for those few minutes. After a long moment of frozen blankness, his mind began to grind again. He began to say *We others can rescue our kinsfolk, while Lisandre stops safe in the forest*, but he could not say it, the obstacles were so enormous and the implications so difficult, more than his heart or mind could grapple with. He cast a quick look at Lisandre.

She had her face bent into her hands, shaking her head back and forth. "I cannot, I cannot," she said. "I came this far to save Ziggy, how can I turn back now? Besides, I gave my word of honour to the Erlrune. I know you all think me starkin scum and my word of honour as worthless as sisika dung, but ... it's not to me, it's not to me!" She was crying loudly now, as lost in her grief and bewilderment and indignation as a small child.

423

Briony took her in her arms and rocked her against her shoulder. "Ssshhh, sweetie-pie, ssshhh," she crooned, as if Lisandre were still only a little girl and did not have the blood of the Ziv running in her veins.

At last Lisandre sat back, wiping her face defiantly with the heels of her hands and looking pleadingly at the others. "Besides, do you not see? I know the antidote now. The blossom of the starthorn tree is the antidote." She gave a strange, merry laugh. "Is it not amusing? We came all this way to discover the cure is growing in my very own courtyard!"

She laughed again, peal after peal of high, gasping laughter that had the others looking at each other in concern. Briony was just moving to grasp her shoulders and shake her out of it when Lisandre managed to get herself back under control. She wiped her eyes again, saying with a distinct tremble in her voice, "If I didn't at least try to give Ziggy the antidote and he died, it'd be murder, don't you see that? And my mother ... I'd be murdering her too."

They all gave a little murmur of discomfort and reassurance, though the force of what she said struck them all powerfully. Durrik leant forward and grasped both her hands, saying, "Are you sure, milady? Are you sure? For I swear none of us would blame you if you were a-wanting to stay."

"No, I have to go," Lisandre answered. She bent forward, resting her forehead against Durrik's for a moment. "It was all there, in your prophecy, you know. Think about it! That bit you said, about his spirit slipping free 'with the last petal of the starthorn tree'.

Meaning that his last hope of a cure would be gone too. And that bit about time turning inverse. We should have known that was all about the starthorn tree! Because the starthorn tree is all backwards, isn't it? Blossoming in autumn, covered in fruit in winter, bare as bones in summer. It makes perfect sense that the starthorn blossom should reverse the star-apple poison. If only I had listened to you properly. If only I had thought..."

"None of us understood what it meant," Durrik said, gripping her fingers tightly. "If anyone should have known what it all meant, it was me. I'm meant to be the riddle-master!"

She nodded and sighed, drawing her hands away so she could wipe her nose and eyes again. Durrik sat back, looking as troubled and miserable as they had ever seen him look.

"So then. All we have to do now is get back to the castle before the last petal of the starthorn tree is blown away," Pedrin said very matter-of-factly. His hands were clenched into fists and he did not look at Lisandre.

A long silence fell.

"And climb the tree without getting scratched," Lisandre said, her voice shaking.

"And manage to get the blossom to your brother without any starkin scum a-stopping us," Mags said. "She looked mighty nasty, that starkin lady, and those soldiers have been a-chasing us and a-hounding us all along, they have."

"And 'tis not enough to just awaken your brother,

milady, we'll have to prove it was Lady Donella who poisoned him and your father," Briony reminded her. "And Lord Zavion won't be a-wanting to give up his Regency without a fight."

Everyone looked depressed. It seemed an impossible task, so impossible no one knew how to even begin.

"Oh, well," Sedgely said, getting to his feet. "Best be on our way, I s'pose. By the ache in me bones, winter's a-coming."

33

The Erlrune sat on her throne, her eyes shut. She opened them as they approached and regarded them silently.

"You saw?" Briony said.

The Erlrune nodded.

"Please, you need to help us," Lisandre said in a rush. "We have to get home as fast as we can. Winter is almost here."

"Yes," the Erlrune said rather dreamily. "And early this year. The cold mist of a river-roan's breath always brings winter early."

Lisandre cast an accusing look at Sedgely, who shifted his shoulders uncomfortably and muttered something about gibgoblins under his breath.

"It took us so long to get here," Lisandre said despairingly, hands clenched before her. "Oh, how can we get home on time!"

The Erlrune sighed and got to her feet. In her hand she held a long, supple wand, made of some silvery wood. "I can think of only one way," she said rather apologetically. "And you tempted me, Sedgely, a-saying you had naught before you but your own death. Will you change shape for me?"

He cast a suspicious look at her but did as she asked. With a hurrumph and a shudder, he turned himself into the big old roan-coloured horse again. Lightly she touched him, first on one shoulder and then on the other. "Sprout," she said, very softly.

His hide gave a little twitch, then a bud of feathers suddenly swelled at the points where the Erlrune's magic wand had touched. Swiftly they grew into two magnificent spreading wings, red and white feathers intermingled near the roan hide, and snow-white at the tips. Sedgely gave a little whicker of surprise then began to buck and prance like a colt, testing his wings. With a great whoosh, he soared up towards the ceiling, then swooped about their heads, neighing in excitement.

The children were overcome with amazement. With those two gentle strokes of her magic wand, the Erlrune had overcome the first and worst of their obstacles. Flying upon the river-roan's back, the children would be able to reach Levanna-On-The-Lake in days rather than weeks, and they would soar high over the most dangerous regions of the Perilous Forest.

Lisandre seized the Erlrune's hand and kissed her lined and sunken cheek. "Thank you, oh, thank you," she whispered. "Oh, I will try to do as I promised, truly, I will."

The Erlrune's face had softened at Lisandre's

impulsive action and now she gave her shoulder a brisk pat. "You have the chance now to bring about a true change for the better, my dear. I hope you do not disappoint me."

"I'll try not to," Lisandre whispered, swallowing hard. She hesitated, then said diffidently, "Erlrune ... I mean, my lady ... please, can you tell me—"

"No, I cannot," the Erlrune answered sternly. "The Well of Fate has given you the answers. 'Tis not my place to interpret or elaborate on the visions you received. Remember, the Well of Fate is the third riddle that you must solve."

Lisandre nodded, unable to hide her disappointment.

Sedgely had landed again and was craning his head around, trying to see as much of his wings as he could. The children all reached up their hands to stroke his feathers, marvelling at their softness and strength.

"I have packed some supplies for you," the Erlrune said with a wave of her hand. Pedrin saw two enormous panniers leaning against the dais, with thick straps designed to buckle around the river-roan's back. "There are warm blankets for you all as well, and a few other little gifts. Oh, and of course I sent Lash to retrieve all your belongings for you."

The gibgoblin bowed sardonically from the corner. "My pleasssure, my treasssuresss."

Pedrin and Durrik were rummaging through the pile of belongings piled neatly beside the panniers of food. "Look, Lisandre, your brush and mirror! You won't be a-wanting to lose those," Pedrin said mockingly as he tucked his slingshot and bag of pebbles into his pocket. For some reason, Pedrin was angry. He would have liked to punch someone or, at the very least, to have spent an hour skimming stones into a pool and seeing how far they could skip. When Lisandre cast him a hurt, surprised look, he clenched his jaw and occupied himself with counting his newly regained coins.

"Oh, Briony, look, here's your little ragdoll. And your sewing basket," Durrik called.

Briony took Mirabel eagerly and cradled her in her arm as she looked over her sewing kit, noting the many spools of coloured thread, the new pincushion in the shape of a rose, and the paper filled with bright new needles. With a little thrill, she saw also a bottle of elderflower wine, the wooden box of silkworms and the book of magic. Quietly she packed them away in her sack and slung it over her shoulder.

"You know you may return whenever you wish," the Erlrune said to her quietly.

Briony nodded. "I know," she answered. "Thank you."

There was a corked jar of apple-ale for Sedgely, the golden-haired doll for Mags, a bottle of sweet-smelling ointment for Durrik, a lute for Pedrin and, rather surprisingly, the long silver dagger they had used to cut their hands for Lisandre. She took it warily, with a wide-eyed glance at the Erlrune's impassive face, then bent her head, examining the magical runes engraved along its blade.

"I thank you," she said in a rather hushed voice, her

430

blue eyes very sombre, sliding the dagger back into its sheath and strapping it at her waist.

Lisandre's gift had made them all fall silent again, exchanging looks of foreboding. Even a flying river-roan was not going to make their task easy. Pedrin clenched his hands into fists and shoved them deep into his pockets. He felt an all too familiar curling and uncurling deep in his stomach, a combination of dread and longing.

"I have warm coats for you too," the Erlrune said, indicating a pile of white wool and fur. "It will be very cold flying up in the air."

As the others thanked her and tried on the long, white coats, Pedrin went suddenly very still, sitting back on his heels with his bucket clasped on his lap. "What about Thundercloud and Snowflake?" he said in a strained voice. "How are they meant to get home? They can't fly. Oh, I hope they're all right! A whole month..." He got up, his mouth set grimly. "I can't go with you," he said to Lisandre. "I have to go and see if me goats are all right. Aught could a-happened! Oh, me poor Snowflake! She must've been in such pain, with no one a-milking her. She'll have all dried up..."

"Oh no, Pedrin," Lisandre cried, clasping his arm with both her hands. "You have to come with us! We need you. Please..."

"I can't. I can't be a-leaving me goats." He held himself aloof, expecting her to offer to buy him a whole flock of goats when they had saved her brother, or to command him to accompany her.

Instead she nodded rather miserably, saying, "No,

of course not, I see that. Oh, I hope nothing has happened to them."

He gave her a wan smile. "Thundercloud would have kept them safe. Not even a gibgoblin could catch Thundercloud!"

"I detessst having to disssenchant you but I fear I mussst," Lash said with a sneering smile, playing with the end of his whip. "I had enormousss eassse ssseizzzing your goatsss."

Pedrin went very white, staring at the gibgoblin in horror. He swayed and had to put out a hand blindly for something to support him. His hand found Mags's shoulder and gripped so hard she winced but stood her ground, giving him the support he needed.

"Don't tease the boy," the Erlrune said rather sternly. "No need to be a-feared, Pedrin, your goats are safe and well. Lash brought them here for me and they're a-getting fat and lazy out in my stables."

Pedrin sat down rather limply. "Thank Liah!"

"Thank Lassshhh," the gibgoblin sneered.

"Come, you can see them if you like," the Erlrune said. "I will have them brought into the garden."

They all followed her out one of the great glass doors, Pedrin throwing the panniers across Sedgely's back and then surreptitiously leaning on the river-roan to hide the fact that his legs were still shaking. The soft feathers of Sedgely's wings warmed and comforted him, and he was soon able to recover his composure.

Outside, the horizon was striped with pale citrus colours. It was cold and they were glad to snuggle into the heavy coats and pull on their new fur-lined boots. It surprised no one that the boots and coats fitted them all perfectly.

A wizened old man with long shaggy hair and beard came through the garden, leading the goats. They both looked very healthy, their coats thick and shiny, their hooves and horns trimmed and polished. They bleated joyfully at the sight of Pedrin and bounded around him, almost knocking him over. He knelt down, embracing them fervently.

"Please," he said to the Erlrune, "can't they have wings too? Then they could a-fly home with us. Please?"

She regarded him silently, playing with the wand in her hand. "Do you not feel I have done enough to help you?" she said at last, rather irritably. "I have quite enjoyed fresh milk every day. It would be a fitting parting gift, to leave them for me, don't you think?"

"Please?" Pedrin begged. "I'll do aught. I don't want to leave them and I don't want to stay behind. I must get home and save me ma and me little sister. Please?"

"You'll do aught, will you?" the Erlrune said slowly.

Pedrin lost his colour, having spoken without thought, but he gritted his teeth and said obstinately, "Yeah, I will. Even me first-born child, if that's what you want!"

The Erlrune smiled as if at some secret joke. "Your first-born child ... well, why not? Tell him to bring me one of Snowflake's great-great-grandkids too. I do enjoy a nice drop of fresh milk in the morning."

Before Pedrin could change his mind, she touched the goats with her wand. A pair of black wings sprouted from Thundercloud's shaggy shoulders, and a pair of snowy-white ones from Snowflake's. The goats had been cavorting about in their excitement and suddenly, to their surprise, found themselves soaring through the air. They bleated in amazement, but were soon darting about as swiftly and nimbly as any swallow.

"I wish you well," the Erlrune said. "I shall a-watch and a-wait with great interest."

They nodded and tried to smile, but now it was time to leave all were filled with a deep apprehension that tied their stomachs in knots.

"I look forward to meeting your first-born child," the Erlrune said to Lisandre, with a nod and an odd sort of smile to Pedrin. "Don't forget about the kid."

"I won't!" Pedrin called, climbing up on a low wall so he could mount Sedgely.

"Thanks for the doll," Mags cried. "She's real bully!"

"Thank you ... for everything," Briony said. She suddenly seized the old woman's hands and gave her cheek a quick, shy kiss.

"I am not sure you will all thank me in the end," the Erlrune said with a compression of her mouth that made all their hearts sink. "Few do."

When all five were safely mounted and Sedgely was tossing his mane and pawing the ground, eager to test his wings against the wind, the Erlrune suddenly

stepped forward and chanted in a low, deep voice that
sent a thrill of holy fear down their spines:
"Deep peace, I breathe into you,
Deep peace, an end of strife for you
Deep peace, a soft white dove to you,
Deep peace, a quiet rain to you,
Deep peace, an ebbing wave to you,
Deep peace, the pure red flame to you,
Deep peace, the pure white moon to you,
Deep peace, the pure green trees to you,
Deep peace, the pure brown earth to you,
Deep peace, the pure grey dew to you,
Deep peace, the pure blue sky to you,
Deep peace of the running wave to you,
Deep peace of the flowing air to you,
Deep peace of the sleeping stones to you,
Deep peace, the cold fire of the stars to you,
Deep peace, the balm of a loving heart to you,
Deep peace, deep peace, deep peace!"
When the toll of her blessing had died away, the
silence seemed more absolute than ever. The children,
clutching each other with their arms and Sedgely with
their legs, called out a rather shaky farewell. Then the
big river-roan wheeled, galloped down the garden
and launched off into the air, the goats flying close
behind. The children waved until the Erlrune and her
small grey house had dwindled away into darkness.
Then they turned, clinging tightly to each other, looking down at the undulating landscape with mingled
delight and terror.

The sun was a molten curve above the horizon. Far

435

below them the dark forest rolled away on either side of the glimmering Evenlinn. The wind stung their eyes, and they had to blink away tears, drawing up their fur-trimmed hoods against the biting cold. Only a few stars still glowed in the sky and, as the sun slowly rose, they faded and flickered out. The sky blazed with vivid colour, red and gold and violet, and Sedgely's wings glowed like the shade of a lantern. Ahead of them were great mountains of soft billowing cloud that mounted up to the very heavens. They too glowed, rose-pink, lavender-blue, molten-gold.

Lisandre's arms tightened about Pedrin's waist. "I've never seen anything so beautiful in all my life!"

He turned. "What?"

"Never seen ... anything ... so beautiful." Her voice and her eyes were full of tears.

Suddenly choking with tears himself, Pedrin smiled, nodded, and turned back, his hands gripping Sedgely's flowing white mane tightly.

On they flew, the day brightening about them. Ahead were the mountains that ringed the Evenlinn. Sedgely had to beat his great wings hard to rise high enough to clear the peaks. The air was so thin it burnt their lungs. They saw plumes of snow blown from the highest spires. Pedrin looked back anxiously, and saw the goats cavorting about the pinnacle playfully. He called them sternly and they spread their wings and darted in pursuit.

Down the far side they glided, plunging into fog. Buffeted by strong winds, their faces lashed by sleet, Sedgely spiralled down. Lightning flashed by, reeking of sulphur. Lisandre shrieked and clung even tighter to Pedrin's waist. Then they slipped below the cloud, finding themselves flying only a few feet above the forest canopy. Treetops brushed their feet. Sedgely swerved to avoid a tall fir tree, and Mags yelped and clutched at Durrik's waist.

Up Sedgely soared again, filling their mouths with clouds. All they could see was greyness; all they could feel was the damp clutch of foggy fingers on their faces. Then they burst out above the cloud, flying in the brilliant sunshine above. Below lay billowing fields of cloud, occasionally broken by the dark spear of a fir tree.

At last Sedgely's strength began to falter. He descended slowly, landing lightly in a misty clearing. The children slid off, stiff and sore, and stretched thankfully. They all felt tired and rather numb, as if their hearts and minds simply could not deal with anything more. So it was a relief to make lame jokes about saddle-sores and Sedgely's bony spine, and to remark on the difference in the weather down on the ground, and to wonder what there was to eat, poking fun at Pedrin's hollow legs.

With great interest they delved into the panniers and found all sorts of delicacies to eat – cold chicken legs, pork pies, gingerbread men with candied cherry eyes, an egg-and-bacon flan, jam tarts, a bag of apples and another of carrots. Sedgely snorted mournfully, cropping at the grass with a most melancholy air as the children thankfully tucked in. He did not dare change shape in case he lost his magical wings. Briony took pity on him and poured some apple-ale into the bucket. At once the river-roan's ears pricked forward and he drank thirstily, then delicately took a carrot from Mags's outstretched hand, crunching it up with relish.

Once they had eaten and rested awhile, they quickly ran out of banter, for all of them felt the shadow that pressed on their spirits. Lisandre was particularly edgy and fidgety and, when she asked rather gruffly if they could fly on, no one argued or protested. Everyone got up at once and packed up the remains of their lunch and pulled on their coats, all with hardly a word spoken.

Sedgely flew on until the sun was merely a red smear on the horizon. They found a safe place to camp and, after eating another hotchpotch meal, hunched about the warmth and comfort of their fire, all very subdued and preoccupied with their own thoughts.

Durrik broke the silence. "Milady," he said timidly, "I don't know if this will make any difference but … I thought mebbe you should know … I've been a-hearing stuff about you."

"Hearing *stuff*!" Lisandre cried with a return of her old hauteur. "What kind of stuff?"

Durrik flushed uncomfortably. "In my dreams sometimes … and when I look at you or think of you…" His face grew so hot and red he could not meet her indignant, questioning gaze. He busied himself poking the fire with a stick. "I heard it the clearest at the Erlrune's house," he mumbled to the fire. "When we all slept a month, I had many dreams, full of rhymes and riddles and strange paradoxes I couldn't decipher ... most of it I've forgotten but the words about you I remembered."

"Why?" she cried. "What did you hear about me?"

He sent a gust of sparks whirling into the sky. "What I'm a-trying to say is, would I be a-hearing anything if you were about to die?"

Lisandre gripped her hands together. "I don't know. Would you? I suppose it depends on what sort of thing you hear."

"If you were a-going to die, surely I'd be a-hearing about your death, but I'm not, I'm a-hearing about your life ... or not your life, but what comes after you, your son..."

"What do you hear?" Lisandre screamed.

There was a long pause. Durrik stirred the glowing coals and gave a strange, sad, secretive smile. He said, very softly:

"Three times a babe shall be born,
Between star-crowned and iron-bound.
First, the sower of seeds, the soothsayer,
Though lame, he must travel afar.
Next shall be the king-breaker, the king-maker,
Though broken himself he shall be.
Last, the smallest and the greatest –
In him, the blood of wise and wild,
Farseeing ones and starseeing ones.
Though he must be lost before he can find,
Though, before he sees, he must be blind,
If he can find and if he can see,
The true king of all he shall be."

There was a long, daunted silence.

"I really have had enough of riddles," Lisandre said faintly. "What has this to do with me, Durrik? I don't understand."

"I hear this when I think of you ... when I think of what's a-going to happen to you," Durrik said stumblingly, the glow fading from his face. "You're one of the star-crowned, one of the ones who will have a child one day, a son ... who's going to be important somehow ... the king-breaker, the king-maker. I've a-heard it dim and I've a-heard it loud and I know it to be true." He cast a quick, shy glance at Lisandre and returned his eyes to the fire. "I thought at first ... I knew it was connected to words I'd heard about myself and I thought ... I hoped ... but now I've a-heard the whole riddle, I know I'm the first of the babes, the soothsayer, the one who must travel afar. It'll be someone else who's 'ironbound', some other hearthkin boy..."

Although Durrik looked at no one and his voice was flat, without expression or implication, Pedrin heard a roaring in his ears as if his skull was suddenly filled with churning water. A scorching-hot wave swept up his body, all the way to the very tips of his ears. He could only be thankful it was night-time and all was dark. Through the churning in his ears he heard Lisandre say in a bewildered voice, "I still don't understand what you mean, Durrik."

"If you're to one day bear a child who's going to be some kind of king-maker, like the gods have been a-telling me, well, then you can't be a-going to die, can you?" Durrik said fiercely.

"Except that what you hear, your riddles of the future, they're just like the visions in the Well of Fate, aren't they?" Briony said, apology in her voice. "I mean, they tell what *might* happen, not what *will* happen."

Lisandre's shoulders fell. "So I could still cut myself on the thorns and die," she said miserably.

"You aren't a-going to die," Pedrin said, his voice coming out much too high. He blushed, coughed and said, now much too low, "We'll figure summat out, Lise … milady, I mean. We'll be mighty careful and make sure you a-keep yourself safe."

"Sure, of course we will," Lisandre said with forced cheerfulness, and rolled over so that no one could see her face. The other four children all exchanged miserable glances and then lay down to sleep as best they could on the cold, stony earth, with their hearts and minds all filled with scrabbling thoughts like a box full of scorpions.

34
◆ ◆ ◆

For the next three days, Sedgely followed the sinuous gleam of the Evenlode as it wound through the forest. They flew over the tall, white waterfall where they had first met Sedgely, all growing tense and quiet when they saw the black ashes of the starkin lords' fire below. That night snow began to spit at their heels. Lisandre was so anxious and restless, they packed up camp at the first dull gleam of light and flew on, the goats labouring to keep up.

Their final night in the forest, hunched in their coats against the bitterly cold wind, the five children made and discarded plan after plan. All were tense and edgy, so that the discussion deteriorated many times into quarrelling.

"Don't be such a cabbage-head!" Pedrin snapped. "Your brother's been asleep for months. Even if we manage to wake him and convince him we're not mad as merry mummers, the castle garrison aren't going to listen to him. He's naught but a boy himself! They'll do what Lord Zavion tells them to do."

"But he's the Count of Estelliana!" Lisandre hissed. "They will not dare disobey him."

"With Lord Zavion there, a-telling them your brother's still sick, still weak, still confused?" Durrik asked.

"But Ziggy is the rightful count..." Lisandre faltered.

"Tell that to Lord Zavion," Pedrin snorted, bending his head over his knife which he was sharpening with the whetting stone.

"We need to know whose side the castle guards are on," Mags said. "Do they like Lord Zavion or would they rather do your brother's bidding?"

"Of course they're loyal to my brother!" Lisandre cried. "Lord Zavion is cruel and ruthless and manipulative. How could anyone like him?"

"But they do," Briony said quietly. "They all do. You were the only one to mistrust him, remember? Everyone else admired him and were a-swayed by his charm. Even the men." As she spoke, the wildkin girl was swiftly weaving a cat's cradle net from a piece of thread, knotting it and tying it without the need to look down at her hands. "Don't you remember? They all began to wear their hair like him, and to talk like him, in that weary way like they were bored to tears. It'd be easy for the Regent to say that Count Zygmunt was still ailing, and not in his rightful mind. No, no, Pedrin's right, we have to free the prisoners first and make sure they have weapons and stuff so that we have some kind of support."

"But Ziggy could die in the meantime," Lisandre

cried in frustration. "And what if we fail in releasing the hearthkin? We'll be captured ourselves and all will be lost. I say we must save Ziggy first and worry about the prisoners later."

Once again they began to argue vociferously. Briony tried to calm them but she could not make her soft little voice heard over the babble. Sedgely snorted and pawed the ground irritably, and Thundercloud gave a low growling noise in his throat but no one listened. Briony had to beat on the frying pan with a spoon before they all quietened down and turned to her, cheeks hot, eyes blazing.

"We mustn't fight like this," Briony said in a rush. "Are we not kin now, blood brothers and sisters? How about this? We split. Three of us go to waken the count, t'other three go and rouse the hearthkin. One of them will have to be Mags, for she's the only one that can pick the locks. T'other had best be Pedrin, I s'pose, for there'll be guards and he's the only one that's any good a-fighting..."

Pedrin hesitated, glancing quickly at Lisandre and then down at the ground. The starkin princess frowned and looked as if she wanted to protest, and then bit her lip and coloured, saying nothing.

"No, if Pedrin's the best fighter he'd best go with you and milady, to wake the count," Durrik said unexpectedly. "We're a-going to need stealth, not strength, to rescue my pa and t'others, anyhow, so it won't matter so much that I'm no good a-fighting or a-running."

They all looked at him in surprise.

"All right," Pedrin said gruffly. "Mebbe you'd bet-

444

ter have me knife. I'll have me slingshot and I can't be using both at once. Lisandre has the knife the Erlrune gave her if we need one."

Durrik nodded and gingerly took the fishing knife with its sharp, notched blade, sheathing it carefully in its leather scabbard.

Lisandre gave a little shudder. Mags leant forward and touched her arm lightly. "Are you sure you want to be a-cutting the branch yourself? You know I'm good a-climbing trees, I've been a-doing it all me life. Mebbe you lot can distract the soldiers while I'll climb the starthorn tree and—"

Lisandre was almost in tears. "Thank you," she breathed. "But how can I let you? No, I have to do it. Ziggy's my brother and besides, why else did the Erlrune give me the knife? I have to do it. I shall just have to be very, very careful."

Everyone was silent. There was nothing more to say. They knew what they planned to do was virtually impossible. How could five children and an old river-roan hope to storm the Castle of Estelliana by themselves, with only a few knives and a slingshot between the lot of them? All they could do is hope the starkin soldiers felt the same reluctance to shoot their fusilliers at Lisandre as they had shown all along, and that the element of surprise would be enough to sweep them through.

"Well, we'd best chuck out anything we don't really need," Pedrin said in his most matter-of-fact voice. "Sedgely's a-carrying enough weight already and we're a-going to want him to be nimble and fleet.

We'll take only our clothes and our weapons, we can stash everything else here somewhere and come back for it when we've won the day."

Everyone nodded and began to rummage through their belongings. Mags sat for a while with the red silk dress billowing over her lap, stroking its sensuous fabric, her face very reflective. Then she sighed, folded it up briskly, and shoved it into the pile of things to be left. "Where would I wear it, anyways?" she asked of no one in particular.

Briony was having as much difficulty leaving her ragdoll and an old, battered-looking book. She sat with them clutched to her chest for a long time before brusquely putting them on the pile.

Rather to his surprise, Pedrin felt the same reluctance. The dented frying pan, the toasting fork, the whetting stone, the stubs of candles, they were all he had left of his home. Discarding them somehow made the little cottage by the river seem a very long way away, when he was in fact closer to it than he had been in months. He did not allow his reluctance to show, though, tossing them all into the pile with a show of insouciance and suggesting they find a hollow tree in which to stuff them.

"I'll take the frying pan," Mags said, picking it up and hefting it in her hand. "I can see that a-coming in useful!"

"I'll keep me sewing kit and the little jar of stuff I made," Briony said, very softly. "Though I do hope I won't be a-needing them."

"I need my mirror and comb," Lisandre said plead-

446

ingly, one hand tugging at the irregular ends of her hair, which had grown to just past her ears. "I cannot let Ziggy see me like this."

Mags rolled her eyes but said nothing, fingering one of the diamond rings which she had slid into her pocket without anyone noticing. They all had their own vanities.

No one slept well that night. Pedrin's mind went round and round like a mill-wheel, churning the same doubts and fears over and over again. Despite the cold, his palms and feet were sweaty, his head was hot, he felt like he could not breathe. His heart was hammering so loud he worried the others would hear it and know how desperately afraid he really was. Snowflake was lying close beside him, as she always did. She bleated quietly in reassurance and love, and nudged his face with her soft nose. He rolled over, flinging an arm across her back and burying his hot face in her snowy white coat. He must have slept then, for it was grim, grey light when next he opened his eyes. Briony was busy spinning a rope with her drop-spindle, though the others were still all asleep.

"I thought I'd best make as much rope as I can," she whispered, her eyes as grey and miserable as the sky. "We're a-going to need it."

He nodded and got up to stoke the fire and rummage through the panniers.

"We might as well have one last feast and eat most everything that's left," he said. "No point a-leaving *all* the food for the wildkin."

Briony nodded. "Though I don't feel much like eating," she said. "I feel a bit sick."

"Me too," Pedrin said. "Have to, I s'pose, if we're not complete cabbage-heads."

She smiled wanly and coiled up the rope and put away her drop-spindle. "Let's wake t'others. 'Tis a-snowing again. I think we should be on our way just as fast as we can."

In a few hours they had reached the edge of the Perilous Forest. The sight of the rolling brown fields beyond gave them all new heart. The wide surface of the Evenlode scudded with clouds, glinting with stray beams of sunshine. As Sedgely flew above it, Pedrin saw the blurred reflection of wings and his heart gave a sudden, unexpected lurch of excitement. He had never dreamt of such a grand adventure. Until Durrik had made his pronouncement in the Regent's crystal tower, Pedrin had expected to be nothing more than a simple goatherd all his life. The world seemed much bigger now, filled with more menace and grandeur than he had ever imagined.

Hearthkin in the fields saw the flying horse and dropped their tools, pointing in amazement. The children waved to them and they waved back wildly. A strange sort of exhilaration filled them all, a sense that it was too late now to turn back.

"Not far now," Lisandre cried, her short blonde hair flying in the bitter wind. "Are we all ready?"

"Yeah!" the others cried, gripping their weapons.

They soared over the curve of a hill and saw before them the great sweep of the lake, all grey and moody under the ominous sky. The crystal tower stood tall upon its island, its walls reflecting the sky with even greater clarity than the water. Lightning suddenly flickered down towards its pinnacle like a white-hot lizard's tongue, and they saw the quick zigzag reversed in the gleaming length of the walls.

The castle towers rose high above the roofs of Levanna-On-The-Lake, trailing tattered banners of cloud. Snow lashed Pedrin's face and he turned to look anxiously at Lisandre. Her cheeks were pale, her teeth gripping her lip. The scene was so like the one in the Well of Fate, where they had seen the young count's body being carried down to the burial ground, that their triumphant courage ebbed away.

"Oh, let us be on time," Lisandre muttered, and dropped one hand down to the dagger at her waist, clutching the hilt with tense fingers.

Aaaark! Aaaark!

The air was filled with the harsh screech of sisikas. They all cried aloud in alarm and Sedgely neighed defiantly. A drove of the great white birds plummeted down from above, great black talons outstretched. On their backs rode starkin lords, all gripping long spears, their fusilliers still strapped to their backs. Four of them flung their spears simultaneously. Sedgely folded his wings and plunged towards the ground, the spears whizzing over the children's heads. All five were hunched down as low as they could get on his broad back, their eyes closing involuntarily.

Sedgely's hooves hit the ground, and he galloped away as fast as he could, his mane and tail flying. The sisika birds followed, screeching loudly. As one plummeted down with talons spread, the river-roan swerved and launched back into the sky. The sisika slammed into the ground, screeching with pain and tossing its rider over its head.

Sedgely soared up past the other birds, who had to wheel about to pursue him. Briony leant forward and cast out a little tangle of string that spread out into an enormous net that captured three of the birds, sending them crashing down to the ground.

Using his black wings nimbly, Thundercloud butted a starkin lord from the back of another bird. He fell screaming, landing with a thud that made all the children wince and turn their faces away.

"Gruesome," Durrik muttered.

Sedgely beat his wings strongly, endeavouring to shake the remaining birds off, but they were strong, swift flyers and harried the flying river-roan all over the sky. Three times Sedgely was not quick enough to avoid a cruel swipe of beak or talon, so that he was bleeding from deep gashes on flank and shoulder. Pedrin's shoulder was lacerated too, and again Mags almost fell off Sedgely's back as he swerved unexpectedly.

The two goats were darting nimbly about the sky, enraging the sisika birds with their antics. Snowflake had lured one away from the phalanx and was darting about its head, butting it with her curving black horns. The soldier on the bird's back had already lost his spear and so he had unstrapped his fusillier and was now trying to aim at the nimble little goat, who was almost invisible against the snow drifting down from the sky.

Trying to swipe Snowflake with its talons, the sisika did not notice the ground hurtling up towards it. The white bird crashed to the ground, crushing its rider beneath it. The bird screeched in pain and rage, trying to lift a broken wing. Its rider managed to crawl free of its weight and, although obviously badly wounded himself, raised himself to examine the injury. The sisika turned its head and slashed at him cruelly with its beak.

Three more sisikas were circling Sedgely, tearing at his wings with their talons. The river-roan soared high into the air, and quickly Briony cast out another net, entangling all three of their pursuers. They fell heavily, crushing and injuring their riders. Cries of pain and loud screeches of rage filled the air. Although Sedgely's flanks were heaving and his coat was damp with mingled perspiration and blood, he valiantly beat his wings and flew on.

"Well done, Briony!" Durrik cried. "I knew those nets of yours would come in handy."

"Yeah, but I've only got one left," Briony said. "I didn't think I'd be a-throwing two before we even got to the castle."

"Oh, well, you have plenty of thread left," Lisandre said comfortingly. "You can always weave another if we should need it, you're so quick and clever about it."

The castle walls loomed up before them. Sedgely and the goats flew up and over the soaring towers, descending inside the castle walls. Guards on the outer wall ran, pointing and shouting in amazement.

One or two threw spears, though there was no chance of impaling the river-roan at that distance.

Below them was the central courtyard. Soldiers ran out of the guardhouse, pulling on their armour. Lisandre drew her knife. "Carefully, Sedgely, old thing," she said, patting his shoulder. She was unnaturally calm, her face set with determination, her fingers clenched white on the hilt.

Below them the starthorn tree lifted its black, thorny branches to the leaden sky. New apples were burgeoning within the clusters of fresh, green leaves. There was only one spray of blossom left, the petals drooping. A gust of icy air swirled past, flurrying with snow. It caught the blossoming branch, shaking it, tearing away a whirl of white petals. Sedgely hovered just above the wicked-looking thorns, his wings quivering with strain.

Slowly, slowly, Lisandre bent over and reached out one hand for the branch, the knife glinting in the other. Pedrin held tightly to her waist.

"Too … far … away," Lisandre panted. "Closer, Sedgely … please…"

Sedgely beat his wings and rose high again, before swerving down and hovering once more just above the tree. The courtyard was now filled with soldiers but the river-roan was too high for them to reach him with their spears and the garrison leader was obviously reluctant to shoot the king's second cousin down from the sky with a fusillade of blue lightning.

Once again Lisandre leant over. Very carefully she seized the branch, placing her hand between two of the cruel, curving thorns.

At that very moment there was a great whoosh as a sisika bird plunged down from the battlements. All the children ducked, and Lisandre screamed. The rider had a long spear in his hand. He took careful aim, then flung the spear with deadly precision straight at Sedgely's breast. The old river-roan was already labouring to keep himself and the five children hovering so close to the starthorn tree. He did not have the strength to rise or swerve, and if he folded his wings and dropped, all six of them would be entangled in the venomous barbs of the starthorn tree.

It all happened so quickly the children had no time to do more than gasp and clutch their legs tighter to Sedgely's sides. He neighed and strained his wings, trying to swerve, but the spear was too swift and he was too heavily laden.

Then Snowflake darted between the spear and the river-roan, so that the spear plunged straight through her, emerging on the other side a mere handspan from Sedgely's heaving chest. She gave one plaintive bleat and then fell, crashing through the black barbs of the starthorn tree, tumbling and cartwheeling, her soft white coat torn to shreds. She landed with a sickening crunch on the cobblestones and lay still, the spear protruding from her side.

Pedrin gave a great shout and lunged forward, as if he meant to throw himself down beside her. Briony held him back with all the strength in her thin arms, though she was weeping herself, her mouth open and gasping with shock. All were trembling and dumbfounded, unable to do more than stare down at the crumpled figure of the goat.

The sisika bird screeched loudly in triumph and, despite all the attempts of his rider to drag his head around, glided down to crouch on Snowflake's body, tearing at her stomach with his beak and feasting gleefully on her entrails. Briony and Mags both hid their faces. Pedrin stared down numbly, watching a great red stain creep across the snow.

Thundercloud folded his wings and dived at the sisika's head, maddened with rage. The soldiers all readied their spears, glad to have a target they finally had a chance of impaling. Pedrin screamed for his billy-goat at the top of his voice. So high and shrill was his cry that it penetrated even Thundercloud's fury, causing the billy-goat to swerve and soar away again, even though he was bellowing with rage and anguish.

"Tell ... Sedgely ... to fly down ... to the tree again," Lisandre said in an odd voice.

Pedrin wrenched his attention away from the sight of the sisika bird crouched on Snowflake's body, his curved beak dripping with her blood, the nanny-goat's entrails spilling out of her torn flesh like loops of blue sausages.

"What?"

"Tell ... Sedgely ... fly down."

He realised with a sudden drop of his stomach that she was lying slack against him and that her voice sounded very strange indeed.

"What's wrong?" he asked, his voice ascending abruptly.

"I ... scratched myself," she answered and lifted her arm to show the skin from her wrist to her elbow gashed open and bleeding profusely.

Pedrin could not move, paralysed as he was with grief and horror.

"I have to ... cut the branch. Tell ... Sedgely ... quick!"

Numbly Pedrin obeyed. The old river-roan made a visible effort, heaving his weary body higher, his wings beating. They came so close to the starthorn tree, one hoof caught a branch, setting the whole tree swaying, but Lisandre leant forward and calmly seized the topmost branch with her bloody hand, slicing it off with a single slash of the silver knife. She then lay back limply against Pedrin's chest, the precious bough of flowers cradled against her.

"Ziggy ... now," she whispered.

"Up there, Sedgely," Briony pointed, her voice shaking with tears. "That room with the little balcony is the count's room. Can you be a-flying that high, you poor old dear?" She patted his blood-smeared shoulder affectionately.

His sides flecked with foam, Sedgely laboured to lift his heavy load higher into the air. They reached the casement of the count's bedroom and once again the big old horse hovered, his wings beating steadily.

Pedrin swallowed. With a great effort, he swam up out of the cold, dark depths of his grief, though he was trembling in every limb. He tried to think about what had to be done now, despite Snowflake's dreadful death, and the lifeblood now pumping out of

Lisandre's arm with every ragged breath she took. He had gone over their plan so many times in his head he was able to unhook the coil of rope at Sedgely's shoulder and drop one end down to the balcony despite all his movements being as clumsy and slow as a sleepwalker's.

Slowly he tried to ease Lisandre away from him, but she was limp and heavy. "Lise, I need you to sit up. Can you sit up?"

She nodded and sat up, casting him one wild, desperate glance out of eyes that were nearly black with pain and shock.

Pedrin slid off Sedgely's back, clinging tightly to the rope that was tied round Sedgely's belly like a saddle-strap. Quickly, not looking down, he slid down the rope and onto the balcony.

"Lisandre," he called. "Slide down. I'll catch you."

Lisandre risked a glance down, then shut her eyes and shook her head, wishing she had not. Pedrin looked down too, and saw the soldiers were all running into the castle, while the garrison leader pointed up at them, gesticulating urgently.

"Quick!" he cried. "We haven't much time!"

Lisandre nodded, her face very white and smeared with blood. She handed down her knife and the spray of blossom to Pedrin, then, with Briony's help, managed to swing down onto the rope. The goatherd reached out his arms, seized her about the waist and swung her in. She fell against him rather heavily, and he held her steady, her blood soaking his shirt.

Durrik leant down from the river-roan's back, saying rather shakily, "Keep safe, won't you? Look after milady."

"I will," Pedrin replied as confidently as he could.

"Will she be all right?" Mags asked anxiously.

Pedrin could only shrug and try to smile.

In a matter of heartbeats, Briony was beside them, swinging down as nimbly as any wood-sprite. As soon as her foot touched the balcony floor, Sedgely beat his wings strongly again and soared up towards the battlements, Thundercloud at his heels.

"Is the ... starthorn blossom ... safe?" Lisandre panted, holding her bleeding arm against her body.

Pedrin nodded, shielding it carefully from the gusty wind. Briony seized Lisandre's wrist and examined the wound anxiously, then pulled the pot of healing ointment from her sack and slathered it on generously. She then bound Lisandre's arm tightly with a strip torn from her own skirt. "That should stop it bleeding," she said reassuringly. "Keep breathing in the perfume of the starthorn blossom. Mebbe it'll heal your arm as well as wake your brother."

Lisandre nodded, though her face was white and pinched with despair. She bent her head over the spray of blossom, breathing in its sweet, faint scent. When she raised her face, she did look a little better, though the bandage was already seeping blood.

Somewhere an alarm bell was ringing.

"We shall have to be quick," Lisandre said, bending over and picking up her dagger. She had to stand still a minute to keep from fainting, and bent her head over the starthorn blossom again, breathing in its restorative scent. Pedrin put his arm about her shoulder anxiously and she gave him a wan smile and unlatched the window. The wind caught the white curtains and sent them billowing inside. One by one the three children scrambled over the windowsill.

Inside all was still and quiet and dark. Count Zygmunt slept peacefully under his white satin counterpane. Firelight flickered on the stone walls, illuminating his thin, pale face, his smooth fair hair.

A tall figure rose from the chair by his bedside.

"Ah, so you have arrived at last," Lady Donella said. "I have been expecting you."

35

She smiled sweetly at them, holding a long dagger in one hand. She looked so elegant in her sweeping robe of amethyst silk, her hair piled high within the silver filigree of her cornet, that the glittering dagger in her hand seemed somehow even more menacing.

Pedrin, Briony and Lisandre stood frozen in shock.

"What, nothing to say?" Lady Donella said. "Lisandre, my dear, that is not like you. Do not tell me you have learnt discretion during this madcap adventure of yours? That would be ironic, would it not?"

"You!" Lisandre hissed.

"Oh, my dear, how very melodramatic. Yes, it is I. Did you think I would not know of your coming?"

"But ... but how..."

"The crystal tower, of course," Lady Donella purred. "My dear Lord Zavion only thinks to use its far-seeing lens to scan the starry skies. I, however, could see a much more appropriate use for it. He may believe you to be devoured by wild beasts or drowned in the mire, but I knew we could not be rid of you so easily. So I ordered the guards to keep a close watch on the Perilous Forest and was justified in my caution when they called me to the tower this morning. I was most disappointed that you managed to evade the welcoming party I sent to greet you. But, my dear, dear Lisandre, what a shock when I saw you! What *have* you done to your hair?"

Lisandre's colour rose. She put one hand up to her halo of unevenly hacked, windswept hair.

"And the outfit! You look like a horrid little hearthkin brat."

"Thank you," Lisandre said defiantly, her cheeks burning. Although she was rather unsteady on her feet, she made an effort to stand up straight and proud, determined to show no weakness before this woman who had murdered her father.

"But come. Enough idle chit-chat. Why do you not hand me that very sharp-looking dagger you are carrying. Not at all an appropriate plaything for a lady of the Ziv. And you! Goat-boy. Throw down any weapons you might have. It will only take a moment to plunge this knife of mine into Count Zygmunt's breast, if you do not obey me exactly."

"Would you not find that rather difficult to explain away?" Lisandre said sweetly.

"Not at all. I would just blame the goat-boy. Lord Zavion has already charged him with treason and sedition, after he smashed the lens in the crystal tower. It cost a great deal to replace that, particularly since so many of the peasants have had to be confined

460

in gaol to prevent them mounting an insurrection. That dirty little boy caused a great deal of trouble and displeased my Lord Regent very much."

She cast Pedrin a look of distaste, as if he were something she had stepped on in the stable, but he could only stare back at her, sick with dismay.

"No one will find it hard to believe he murdered Zygmunt in some ill-judged attempt to overthrow the rule of the starkin," Lady Donella continued, smiling. "The whole castle saw you arrive in his company, on the back of a flying horse, of all things. It is clear you have fallen into the hands of witches and wildkin. They will just think you ensorcelled. The goat-boy will be drawn and quartered and you, my dear, will be locked away in a tower room for the rest of your life. Any accusations you make against me will be thought the babbling of a poor, deranged fool."

Pedrin swallowed with difficulty, his mind too full of visions of himself being drawn and quartered to think about obeying her command to discard his weapons. With one swift, graceful movement Lady Donella pressed the point of her knife into the hollow at the base of Count Zygmunt's collarbone. Lisandre threw a pleading glance at Pedrin and very reluctantly he threw down his slingshot and bag of stones, his hands clenched into fists.

Lady Donella laughed. "Very wise. Now what is that you carry there, in your other hand? Throw that down too."

Very carefully Pedrin laid the flowering branch on the floor. Lady Donella looked at it and a triumphant smile spread across her face. "I see. Starthorn blossom. So you know the truth about the dear count's unnatural sleep. Yes, such a shame. He must have only tasted the apple-ale I prepared so carefully. I had thought my little goad about him being too young would have driven him to drink as deeply as any of the men, but young Zygmunt was ever an unnatural boy, immune to such mockery."

She stepped forward gracefully and gathered up all their weapons, then ground the blossoms into the floor with her high-heeled shoe. Lisandre gave a little cry and started forward, but Lady Donella menaced her with the knife and she recoiled.

"Now what am I to do with you?" Lady Donella mused. "Your brother will die quietly now and your mother soon after, and no one will question their deaths. But you, Lisandre, and your lowborn friends pose a trickier conundrum. If only you had been more discreet in your arrival! I could have killed you all quietly and none would have been the wiser. Now I must dispose of you all without raising too much of a fuss. You, I think, shall die protecting me from your hot-headed goat-boy, who seeks to murder all those of starkin blood. Your little spinner friend can be killed in the struggle. But what about the others? There was another horrid hearthkin brat with you, and the boy that started all this trouble, the son of our one-time bell-crier, now rotting in prison where he belongs. Where are they?"

"They've gone to rescue the bell-crier and all t'others, me ma and sister too," Pedrin said defiantly.

"They will have set them free by now, and there's naught you can do to stop them!"

"Is that so?" Lady Donella said, frowning. She tapped her foot impatiently, then said, "I will deal with you later! First I must send the soldiers to prevent the prisoners being released. It would not suit me at all to have a crowd of angry hearthkin barging about, accusing me of murder! Quickly, sit down all three of you, back to back. I see you have a great deal of rope with you. Most thoughtful of you."

They obeyed, exhausted, enervated with a sense of failure and futility. Lisandre was so unsteady on her feet she almost fell, and only the supporting arms of the others helped her to sit upright. Lady Donella rapidly began to tie them up with Briony's rope, so tightly the circulation to their hands and feet was cut off. It was then that she noticed the bloodstained bandages binding Lisandre's arm from wrist to elbow, and the little involuntary jerks of Lisandre's limbs.

"What is this?" she asked softly, bending down and touching the red, sodden bandages with a gentle finger. "A cut that bleeds and bleeds and will not stop?" A laugh illuminated her beautiful face. "Do not tell me, my dear Lisandre, that you were foolish enough to pick the starthorn blossom yourself?" She gave a peal of silvery laughter. "I need not trouble myself in wondering how to dispose of you myself now. Do you not know the thorns are deadly? There is no cure for their poison."

Lisandre cast an involuntary glance at the mangled twig of starthorn blossom and Lady Donella laughed and kicked it under the bed. "Maybe a cordial distilled from bucket-loads of the flowers would help, but a few broken old flowers like that? I'm afraid not, my poor dear child. The poison is too virulent. It will not be long and you'll be sunk in as profound a coma as your beloved brother, though a lot less peaceful, I'm afraid. The only comfort I can offer you is that death will be swift thereafter."

A shudder ran all through Lisandre. Pressed tight against her, both Briony and Pedrin felt the involuntary trembling in her arms and legs. Lady Donella checked their bonds were pulled cruelly tight then, her skirts swishing, glided from the room, closing and locking the door behind her.

Pedrin bowed his head. He felt numb with defeat. They had come so far and suffered so much, yet only a pace or two away from the sleeping count, they would lose everything. He would have wept if he had any tears left in him but he was dry and empty as a seed husk.

Lisandre was feverish with desperation. "Briony, how long will your rope last? Will it turn back to thread soon?" She squirmed against the rope with all her strength.

"I don't know," Briony replied miserably. "Me magic seems to be a-getting stronger, and the rope's a-touching me. It could be hours."

"We do not ... have hours!" Lisandre panted. Her whole body jerked as if she had been stung by a bee. "Can you not ... unweave the rope? Please?"

"If me hands were free," Briony said. "But me

hands are a-tied so tightly I can't hardly move a finger."

The three children all struggled against the rope but
it was no use, Lady Donella had tied them all too
securely. At last they desisted, Lisandre sobbing in
pain and frustration.

"If only she had left the knives behind, we could've
found some way of cutting the bonds, we could've, I
know we could've," she cried. "And look what she
did to the starthorn blossom! Oh, we came so close to
saving Ziggy, I cannot believe we should fail now."
Her sobs grew more bitter.

"I have a little pair of scissors in me sewing kit.
Mebbe..." Briony said.

With a great effort, they shuffled sideways across
the floor, using their legs to propel their bottoms
along. Lisandre left a red smear behind her as blood
dribbled down her hand and onto the floor. Pedrin
could feel his sleeve growing sticky with it. She was
panting heavily now and muttering under her breath,
her movements growing more frenzied. Pedrin had no
confidence in their ability to cut themselves free, but
Lisandre was so hectic with hope and desperation that
he was willing to try anything to soothe her.

At last they reached the sack, which lay where
Briony had dropped it. It took more contortionism to
get the sack open and tip the contents out. Briony then
had to drag her boot off with the other foot, before
groping through their belongings with her toes. She
managed to extract the scissors but it was too difficult
to wield them with her hands tied behind her back

and they were too small and blunt to even shred a strand of the rope.

Defeated, they slumped back against each other. On the bed, the sleeping count lay as still as if he were dead. The firelight flickered over the satin canopy, picked out gleaming threads in the gilt embroidery, glimmered upon something that lay on the floor near Lisandre's foot.

She leant forward. "My mirror!"

With a burst of wild, unnatural energy, Lisandre brought both her boot heels smashing down upon the mirror so it shattered. Swift as an eel, she wriggled forward and seized a large piece of glass in her fingers, propping it up against her leg. With the others craning their necks to see, she pulled her wrists as far apart as she could and began urgently to rub the rope back and forth against the edge of the glass. Every now and again she winced as the glass cut into her skin, and once she drew in her breath in a long, shuddering sigh of pain and misery. At last the rope frayed and parted, and she could drag her chafed wrists free.

For a moment she slumped forward, her head resting on her arms, her body shaking with suppressed sobs. When she raised her face it was slick with perspiration, and her eyes were unfocused. Pedrin murmured some kind of reassurance but she did not seem to hear, moaning and letting her head drop down again.

Briony seized the jagged piece of broken mirror and began to quickly try to cut her own bonds, crying aloud as she sliced her fingers. When she was at last free, she shoved the glass at Pedrin and crawled hastily under the bed, seeking the twig of starthorn blossom. Snow howled against the window, and all was dark and quiet in the room.

Pedrin managed to free himself, though he had cut a couple of fingers almost to the bone in his haste. He sucked them tenderly, kneeling beside Lisandre and examining her arm with a sense of despair rising in him like bile. The bandage was wringing wet, her hand as red as if she had dipped it in a vat of blood, her fingernails black crescents. A pool of blood was slowly spreading out below her.

"Here!" Briony said, thrusting the starthorn twig at him. "Hold this under her nose. See if it rouses her. I'll try again t'ease the bleeding."

Pedrin obeyed. The faint scent of the blossoms roused Lisandre enough for her to lift her head and open her eyes blearily, though she looked at Pedrin without recognition. Her face was damp and fiery-red, and the involuntary twitch of her limbs had intensified so that she jerked every few seconds as if someone was sticking her with a pin.

Briony unbound her arm and looked at the gaping wound. Released from the bandage, it spurted blood that sprayed across Briony's face. Briony gave a little sob and pressed both hands over the wound. "I don't know how to stop it!"

She lifted her hands away and groped in her sack for the healing ointment. Pedrin gave a little cry. "Briony, look!"

Briony turned and looked. To her surprise the blood had stopped spraying. Briony frowned and tentatively laid both her bloodstained hands over the wound again. When she lifted them away, there was once again a perceptible lessening of the flow of blood.

Briony lifted both her hands and stared at them in bemusement. They were covered in blood, both Lisandre's and her own, pumping out of the cuts on her fingers.

"Pedrin, you try," she said in a strange, distant voice.

Pedrin obediently laid down the starthorn twig and pressed both his hands as hard as he could over Lisandre's wounds. When he lifted them away, the ragged lips of the gash seemed to have closed a little, and the blood was flowing only sluggishly. Lisandre murmured and opened her eyes, then tried to sit up. Although she shivered every now and again, the dreadful jerking of her limbs had stopped.

"Blood," Briony said. "'Tis our blood that's healing her."

"Our blood?" Pedrin said blankly, looking down at his bloodied fingers.

"'Tis the second riddle of the Erlrune's," Briony said. "To make whole what was torn, kith must be as kin. For kith to be as kin, what is whole must be torn." Slowly she repeated the first line. "'To make whole what was torn'. It meant Lisandre's arm all along. If we hadn't cut our fingers on the bit of glass … I had Sedgely's blood on me hands too, from when I patted his shoulder. I remember me hand came up all bloody."

"Our blood!" he cried and pressed his hands over the wound again. "Oh, we need Durrik and t'others! Where are they? We need them here!"

36

At that very moment, Durrik, Mags and Sedgely were hurrying down a dark spiral staircase. They were all dressed in the white and gold castle livery, having shed their fur-trimmed coats at the very first opportunity.

After the others had climbed down to the count's balcony, the river-roan had flown to the top of the square keep, the only tower not topped by a tall, pointed spire. The guards on duty there had been leaning over the battlement, watching the commotion in the courtyard below, and so had plenty of warning of their coming. Sedgely was able to knock one out with a well-timed kick of his hind hooves, however, and Mags banged the other over the head with the frying pan so that he crumpled where he stood.

As soon as the two children had slid down to the snow-encrusted pavement, Sedgely transformed back into an old man, his wings dissolving into nothing, like his mane and tail. He had looked over his shoulder at his bruised and bloodied bare back and said rather regretfully, as he gratefully huddled into Durrik's coat, "Well, I couldn't expect to keep them, I s'pose."

"Come on!" Durrik cried. Leaning heavily on his crutch, he limped over to the door and banged it open, an impatient Mags at his heels.

Sedgely had followed slowly, grumbling, "Hold your horses, young feller! You two have been sitting pretty while I've had to fly all this way, carrying all five of you great, heavy lumps on me back. Give a poor old man a chance to catch his breath."

"We haven't time," Durrik had responded, hobbling down the stairs as fast as he could, his crippled leg stiff and cramped after the long ride.

"Always in such a rush, you young things," the old man sighed, limping along behind.

With Thundercloud running at their heels, they had come to the end of the staircase, opening the door carefully and peeking out. A squire had been walking towards them, carrying a tray. They waited until he was right at the door, then swung it open, whacking him in the face. Durrik had seized him and dragged him in, while Mags banged him over the head with the frying pan. Despite his weariness and pain, Sedgely, somehow managed to catch the tray with its ceramic jug and two tankards, stopping it from crashing to the ground. While Durrik quickly changed into the squire's clothes, he had poured himself a tankard of apple-ale and drunk deeply.

Wiping his mouth, he said with satisfaction, "That's the stuff to warm you on such a wintry day!"

471

They had locked the door upon the unconscious squire then made their cautious way down the corridor, looking in all the doors. They found an outfit for Sedgely hanging over the bed-rail in one of the bedrooms, and another for Mags on the back of a serving-girl, leaving her tied and gagged in a cupboard. By now their confidence was rising and they hurried down the spiral staircase, Thundercloud bounding along before them. Although it was obvious Sedgely's injuries were bothering him, he made no complaint, limping on valiantly.

A great shout and clatter below gave them just enough warning to conceal themselves hastily behind the hanging tapestries. Peering out cautiously, Durrik saw Lord Zavion stride out of a door, Lady Donella smiling and simpering at his elbow.

"You must not allow the prisoners to be rescued!" the Regent commanded. "The hearthkin are sullen and angry as it is. All we need is one spark and the whole county could go up in flames! Make sure they are kept securely incarcerated and that those hearthkin brats are captured and held."

"Yes, my lord," the commander of the garrison said, bowing low.

Lord Zavion turned and glided up the stairs, his handsome face marred by a petulant scowl. Lady Donella rustled after him. "Oh, my lord, I am so glad we have such a strong, decisive Regent to protect us in these times of trouble and strife. Just imagine the turmoil the county would be in if you were not here! Those soldiers are weak and badly trained and

472

infected with my poor, dear, dead cousin-in-law's soft notions about the hearthkin serfs. I swear they would have done nothing to stamp out this insurrection if you were not here."

Durrik held back a quivering Thundercloud as the two starkin glided right past where they were hiding behind the tapestries. Lord Zavion murmured something in response, and then their voices faded away as they turned the corner.

Meanwhile, the commander of the garrison had gone back into the guardroom. They could hear him addressing the soldiers sternly. "You heard him, boys! Grab your weapons and let's get moving. Quadruple guard on the dungeons and the rest of you, search the castle! Those children have to be found."

Durrik and Mags looked at each other in dismay. "How did Lord Zavion know we mean to rescue the hearthkin?" the crippled boy whispered.

"Don't a-worry about that now, let's a-worry about stopping those soldiers!" Mags said. She pulled out the wallet of lock-picking tools from her pocket. "If I slam that door shut, are you strong enough to hold it shut while I lock it on them?"

"I don't know. I don't think so," Durrik replied.

"Well, you're a-going to have to!" Mags snapped. "Come on!"

She charged out from behind the tapestry, Thundercloud leaping ahead of her, and sped down the stairs. His heart sinking, Durrik followed with Sedgely right behind, shaking his head and pulling doubtfully at his beard. "So rash!" the old man said. "So impetuous!"

473

The tall soldier was standing right by the door, shouting instructions. His golden eyes glinting balefully, Thundercloud lowered his horns and charged. The soldier was knocked to the ground with a cry of surprise and pain. Before anyone could react, Thundercloud had spread his black wings and soared out of the guardroom, Mags slamming the door shut behind him. Durrik and Sedgely held the door shut with all their strength as the bandit-girl fumbled with her tools. They felt the handle being twisted and then fists began to beat on the door, the soldiers within shouting in anger. The door handle was tugged so hard Durrik thought his arms would be wrenched from their sockets. Just when it seemed the soldiers within would drag the door open, the lock snapped shut.

Mags gave a huge sigh and looked up at the others. "Thank Liah!" she breathed. "I knew me pa's tools would come in handy." Defiantly she scrubbed her eyes dry and wiped her nose on her sleeve. "Though I must say I've never *locked* a door with them before."

"Let's get a-moving before anyone hears them a-shouting," Durrik cried, breaking into an awkward run, his crutch swinging wildly. For once there was no protest from Sedgely, who led the way down the steps in a scrambling rush.

A few more turns and they began to find it hard to see their way, for there were no windows here, only the occasional lantern hanging on the wall. The air smelt foul, and the wall beneath their fingers was slimy.

474

They came to a thick oaken door, firmly locked. With a few deft manipulations of the tools Mags carried in her pocket, the lock clicked open. Slowly she swung the door open and they stepped cautiously inside.

Within was a square guardroom, its walls hung with weapons of all kinds. A wooden table stood in the centre of the room, its surface greatly pitted and scarred. There was a fire burning merrily on the hearth, a kettle whistling on the hob, and three tankards and a jug of apple-ale on the table.

"Don't like the look of that whistling kettle," Durrik began. Before he could finish his sentence, they heard heavy steps approaching, and then the door on the opposite side of the room swung open. A heavily armed man came in, saying cheerily over his shoulder, "Kettle's boiled, Darrion. How 'bout that hot toddy?"

He then saw the three intruders hesitating on the doorstep and his mouth dropped open. Then he was calling loudly, "Darrion, Raymond, to arms! To arms!"

A sword in his hand, he came charging across the room. Close behind him were two more guards, even bigger and uglier than the first. With a little shriek, Mags raised the frying pan and Durrik his crutch, but neither had much hope of keeping the guards off. It was more a gesture of defiance than anything else.

Calmly Sedgely stepped forward, breathing two long spumes of mist out his nose. Fog rolled forward, engulfing the men. Shivering with cold, Durrik and Mags huddled behind him, trying to see. For a long time, nothing happened, though it grew so cold

Durrik's fair skin turned blue and Mags's teeth were chattering. Then slowly the mist subsided. There the three men stood, frozen into immobility, encased in a thick sheath of ice.

"Another old river-roan trick," Sedgely said. He stepped past the three men and poured himself a cup of apple-ale. "Got a bit chilly in here," he explained before quaffing the cup with evident enjoyment.

Rubbing their goose-pimpled arms vigorously, Mags and Durrik rather gingerly stepped past the three blocks of ice. Inside the three men stood, their expressions frozen into grimaces of rage, their weapons still raised.

"How long will they stay frozen?"

"Hard to say," Sedgely said, wiping his straggly moustache.

"We'd best hurry then," Durrik said.

"For once I agree with you, young feller," Sedgely said. "If ever this was a time for being hasty…"

They hurried through the door and found themselves in a long, dank corridor, lit only by one lantern. Iron doors lined the corridor, each with a little flap at eye level and another near the floor. Mags pulled out her lock-picking tools with a flourish and began to work on the nearest door, while a rather nervous Durrik kept a close eye on the ice-bound guards and the door beyond.

Mags flung open the door and the prisoners within flinched back, holding up their hands against the dim glow of the lantern. There were fifteen or more crammed inside the small room, with nothing to sleep on but filthy looking straw. All looked thin and sick, with torn clothes and old bruises discolouring their faces and arms. The room stank horribly.

"Papa?" Durrik said incredulously.

A gaunt man with wild, straggling grey hair and a grimy frock-coat dropped his protective hand, peering at the figure in the doorway suspiciously. "Durrik? No, it can't be!"

"Papa!" Durrik cried and flung himself across the room.

Johan embraced him close, saying shakily, "Merciful Marithos! I thought you dead."

"Not I!" Durrik said with a forced grin. "I'm hard to kill. What about you? You look ghastly. Have they mistreated you?"

"Not unless you call a-starving us and a-beating us and a-depriving us of our freedom 'mistreatment'," the bell-crier said grimly. "My Lord Regent has a great deal to answer for! Does he think I don't know the laws of the land, just because I'm a hearthkin? Get me free of this stinking cesspool and I'll make sure the king hears of this! Lord Zavion had no right to throw the whole town into his dungeons, and the reeve and constable too when they complained!"

Mags had been busy unlocking the other cells while Durrik greeted his father, and now the corridor was filled with a great crowd of lean, angry prisoners, all muttering with resentment and indignation. Durrik's heart sank at the sight of them, however. There was not one who did not look as if their legs might collapse under them at any moment. He thought of the

477

tall, well-built starkin men-at-arms with their armour and fusilliers and knew a moment of black hopelessness.

A painfully thin hand seized his arm. "Pedrin? Where's me Pedrin? Is he alive too? Oh, Liah's eyes, let him be safe."

Durrik could only stare at her, dumbfounded. How could this wild-eyed, wild-haired woman be Maegeth? She was so thin her cheekbones stuck out like shelves and he could see the separate bones in her wrist. Her skin was grey and stretched so tight her big mouth was like a skeleton's grimace. By her side cowered a little girl.

Durrik whispered their names. The woman ignored him, sobbing aloud. "Oh, please, is me boy alive? Is he alive?"

"Yes," Durrik whispered. "He's here too." He jerked a thumb upwards. "He's a-waking the sleeping count. At least, I hope he is."

"Thank Imala!" Maegeth whispered. For a moment she crouched down, her hands over her face, then she stood up, some of her old fire and determination returning. "How do you come to be here?" Her gaze flickered over Mags and Sedgely in surprise and consternation. "Is this your rescue party, you and a little girl and an old man?"

"Merciful Marithos, surely not!" Johan cried.

"I'm afraid so," Durrik said. "But, please, we must get out of here. We locked the guards in their room but it won't be long before they break out and then they'll be a-heading straight down here. We need to get moving!"

"You mean … you have no one to help us fight free?" Johan cried. "I thought you must've stormed the castle, mebbe with Diamond Joe and his men."

"Diamond Joe is dead," Mags said stonily. "I'm his daughter. Would you stop your blathering and get a-moving like Durrik says? Else we'll be in the slam with yer!"

Dazed and confused, the prisoners all stumbled up the stairs into the guardroom. At the sight of the three guards entombed within their shrouds of ice, a murmur of amazement arose. Their initial surprise wearing off, the hearthkin busied themselves cramming food and apple-ale into their mouths and seizing weapons from the wall.

Suddenly there was a great shout of excitement. One of the men had pushed open another door at the end of the room, and found the armoury room. Here were shelves stacked high with fusilliers, both short-range and long-range, and tanks full of high-octane fuel, and brackets filled with long spears and curved daggers.

All the hearthkin men had always longed for a chance to examine the fusilliers and so they all crowded into the room, exclaiming with interest. Mags danced about in her impatience, unable to believe they would waste time running their hands over the gleaming blue weapons, lifting them to their eye so they could squint through the view-finder, arguing over the best way to attach the fuel-pump. The weight of the fusilliers in their hands gave all the hearthkin men a surprising animation. They began to growl with anticipation, saying things like, "Just let me get that dandyprat Regent in me view-finder and he'll soon know what it feels like to be blown to dust and ashes!"

With every one of them heavily armed, the hearthkin men felt a lot more cheerful and they followed Mags and Durrik with no further delay.

They heard the faint shouting and hammering of fists on the stout, oaken door of the guardroom as they came round the curve of the spiral stairwell. Mags and Durrik grinned at each other.

"Right, boyos," said the town constable, Galton of the Granite-Fist. "Six of you stay here and keep your weapons trained on that door. If they break through, shoot 'em!"

"No, no, you mustn't shoot them," said the town reeve, Aubin the Fair, named as much for his unusually pale hair as for his well-known integrity. "Just hold them at bay. We'll have to be a-taking our case to the king's courts and if we act with restraint, they'll commend us for it."

"All right then, hold 'em at bay unless they make a run for it, and then shoot 'em!" Galton said.

"Let's just hope they make a run for it," Burkett the field foreman said, setting up a fusillier so it pointed directly at the door. "All right, Galton, we've got this rat's nest covered. Good luck!"

As they climbed on up the spiral staircase, Pedrin's little sister Mina slipped her hand into Durrik's. "I knew you and Pedrin would come," she said happily. "I'm so glad you did."

480

"So am I," he said gently, knowing how upset Pedrin would be when he saw how thin and sick Mina was looking.

"Did Thundercloud and Snowflake come too?" she asked, looking up at him hopefully. "I've missed them so!"

Durrik hesitated, an image of the bloodied and gutted Snowflake flashing before his mind's eye. He was almost overwhelmed by grief, remembering all the times the little nanny-goat had run by his side so he could lean on her back, or comforted him with her warm, clover-scented presence. "Snowflake's dead," he said as gently as he could, though his voice rasped in his throat. "She saved us from a sisika bird."

Tears welled up in Mina's eyes. "Snowflake's dead? Oh, no!"

"But we're all alive because of it," Durrik said, his own eyes prickling. "She was a hero."

"Heroine," Mina corrected him, rather smartly.

"Yes, a heroine," he agreed, wiping his nose on his sleeve and clearing his throat.

"What about Thundercloud? Is he with Pedrin?"

Durrik looked about him, only then realising he had not seen the billy-goat in some time. His heart sank like lead. "I hope so," he said. "Though if Thundercloud's gone in search of Pedrin, 'tis because he thinks he's in trouble."

Mina gave a little sob of fear and Durrik remembered she was not yet seven. Silently he castigated himself, reassuring her with a smile and a pat on the shoulder, though his own stomach was twisted up with apprehension.

"Let's hurry!" he urged Sedgely, and the old man nodded and went up the stairs at a gallop.

"We have to get back to the count's bedroom," Durrik explained as they all hurried back towards the main building. "We're a-feared the Regent will try to harm the count once he realises he's awake. Also Pedrin and the girls are there all by themselves. They may need help!"

"Girls?" Maegeth asked, quickening her step. "What girls?"

"Briony and Lisandre," Durrik said.

"Lisandre? Not Lisandre ziv Estaria, the count's sister?"

"Yeah," Durrik said, getting a little short of breath.

"Jumping Jimjinny," Maegeth breathed. "That sounds like trouble ahead."

They hurried through a doorway and found themselves in a long hall, with a rough wooden table and benches running its length. Coming in through the door at the far end was the chief huntsman Adken and his men, all tall, wiry men with weather-beaten faces and hands greatly calloused from wielding spears and bows.

There was a long moment of tense silence, as the two groups of hearthkin men regarded each other down the length of the hall, weapons at the ready. Although the former prisoners were armed with fusilliers, they were all so thin and weak and sick that the huntsmen could have overpowered them if they had so desired. They made no move, however, looking to

Adken for instructions. The chief huntsman was fingering his beard, frowning at the ragged bunch of escaped prisoners from under heavy brows.

"Well met, fellers," he said at last, just as Johan was gathering together the courage to tell his followers to fire. "Looks like you're in a mighty big hurry to get somewhere?"

"Indeed we are," Johan responded. "There's a plot afoot to murder the young count and confirm Lord Zavion as ruler. We're rather keen to foil it."

"Is that so?" Adken murmured. "Lord Zavion seems to think that you lot are the plotters and he's your prey. We've been given orders to shoot you on sight."

"We do have a mighty big bone to pick with his preciousness," Galton Granite-Fist admitted. "First things first, though. It's the little count we be a-worrying about."

"We have no argument with the young count—" Aubin the Fair said.

"Yet," another of the men muttered.

"Nah, it's Lord Zavion we want to argue with!" cried another, with a low growl of agreement from the others.

Aubin continued as if there has been no interruption. "—His father treated us fair enough, for a starkin lord, and his young lordship seems like a nice enough boy. Whatever, he's our count and we can't be a-standing by and a-letting Lord Zavion have him murdered out of hand."

"So, Adken Hunter, whose side are you on?" the

foreman Burkitt said. "You planning to argue with these?" He raised his fusillier menacingly.

"Nah," Adken said. "Do I look like a tomfool? We're the count's men, same as you fellers. A suspicion of a plot to murder him? Obviously we're duty-bound to investigate before we go making any hasty decisions that might end up with someone a-getting hurt. Nah, nah, I think we'd best find out the truth of what you say, don't you agree, boyos?"

The huntsmen all nodded and murmured in agreement.

"So you won't try to stop us?" Johan said in relief.

"Stop you? I'll lead the way meself!" Adken said, his grin widening.

True to his word, the chief huntsman led the hearthkin swiftly through the bewildering maze of halls and corridors until they reached the main body of the castle. Even though they passed a number of servants and men-at-arms, no one challenged them, thinking they were all in the huntsmen's custody. At last they came to the entrance hall with its grand staircase leading up towards the solar and the ziv Estaria family's living quarters. Men-at-arms stood on guard on all sides.

"All right, men, let's try and keep this civilised," Johan said. "Remember what Aubin said – whatever happens we're a-going to have to face the king's justice one day and we want our account to have the power of right on its side."

The men grinned and one spat eloquently. They hefted their fusilliers, pumped them full of fuel, and charged out into the hall, firing at full speed. Blue lightning lashed out, blasting chairs, tables, tapestries, crystal bowls of fruit, china figurines, gilded candlesticks, musical boxes, and ornate silver and crystal lanterns to smithereens. The men-at-arms shrieked and dropped their weapons, cowering down to the ground as all the expensive follies of the starkin lords imploded into dust and drifted down to cover them in a soft, grey coating.

Silence fell. Smoke drifted away. One of the men-at-arms looked up through his fingers.

"Take us to your count," Johan said in his deep, slow, pleasant voice. "Please."

37

♦ ♦ ♦

Lisandre staggered to her feet, cradling her injured arm against her.

"Ziggy?" she cried. "Oh, is he … does he still live?"

She half-fell against the bed as Briony bent over the sleeping count, frowning. The wildkin girl could find no pulse and the young count's face was as still and cold as if carved from marble, with no twitch of the eyelid or flutter of breath to show if he still lived.

Lisandre sobbed and covered her face with her blood-drenched hands. She was very weak from the loss of blood, and the occasional tremor still shook her, though her eyes had lost that dreadful glaze of incomprehension.

Briony leant her cheek over the count's mouth for a long moment, before straightening with a tired smile of relief. "He breathes still – though only just! Pedrin, the starthorn blossom. Gather up as many of the petals as you can find. We may still be able to save him."

"Oh, please, please," Lisandre sobbed, laying her head down on her brother's chest.

Pedrin knelt, gathering up the broken starthorn branch and carefully picking up every bruised and crushed petal he could find. A sweet, faint scent rose to his nostrils and he breathed in deeply, finding new hope and courage filling him. He carried them to the bed and gently dropped them into Lisandre's waiting hands. She managed to smile, a very faint, wearied curve of her mouth, then slowly, almost fearfully, held the fistful of starthorn blossom under her sleeping brother's nose.

For a long moment it seemed as if the pitiful handful of mangled flowers would not be enough. Then, suddenly, his nostrils flared and his chest rose as he took in a deep breath. Again he breathed in deeply and then again, and slow colour crept up his ivory cheeks. His fingers flexed, then he yawned and stretched, opening his eyes.

"Lise!" he said with a tired smile. "What, have I overslept?"

Then he saw her cropped head, her blood-smeared face, the great red stain down her white dress. His smile died away. "Stars and moons, what has happened? What is wrong?"

Lisandre sobbed and laid her head down on his chest again. He hugged her tightly, his eyes widening in surprise as he saw Pedrin and Briony across her back, both as filthy and bloody as Lisandre.

"By the heavens! Lise, what is all this about?"

Lisandre did not move. Count Zygmunt tried to lift her away from him. She was too limp and heavy. He called her name in distress and lifted her face. It was

487

chalk-white under the smears of blood, and her eyes were closed. Below her was a great crimson stain as the blood again pumped steadily out of the ragged gash in her arm. Pedrin felt a sudden, sickening drop of his stomach. He had seen this before. He threw himself down by the bed, lifting Lisandre into his arms.

"Lise!" he cried.

He saw fresh tears well out of Lisandre's eyes and sat back, nauseous with relief.

"You're not dead," he said stupidly. "I thought you were dead."

"Of course I'm not dead, you asinine fool," Lisandre said in a muffled voice. She lifted her hand to scrub at her eyes. "Not yet anyway. I'm ... oh, it's just that I'm so happy!"

Suddenly she pushed her head into Pedrin's shoulder, both her arms tight about him. Pedrin put his arm about her, feeling rather weak and light-headed himself. He watched the blood pulse out of her arm, and wondered how it was that he could feel both wholly glad and utterly miserable at the same time.

"Please, will someone not explain to me what all this is about?" the count said haughtily, leaning on one elbow. "Who are you, sirrah, that you dare lay hands upon my sister? Do you not know she is of the Ziv?"

Lisandre laughed rather damply. "I think he's rather gathered that by now," she said, sitting up. "Oh, Ziggy, I am so glad to see you!"

The count's affronted look softened a little, but he

said with a dangerous crispness in his voice, "I'm glad to see you too, Lise, though I would very much like to know what that hearthkin boy is doing with his arm about you. May I suggest he removes it before I remove it for him?"

Pedrin rather selfconsciously took his arm from around Lisandre's shoulders and she blew her nose vigorously on her rather grimy handkerchief. "This is my friend Pedrin, Ziggy, and that is Briony. Oh, they are the very best friends anyone could want. They have helped me so much, and you too, Ziggy. You would not be alive now if it was not for them, and Durrik and Mags and Sedgely, and Thundercloud and poor little Snowflake too."

The count looked over her head to Pedrin. "Perhaps you would care to explain, boy, given that my sister seems to be delirious?"

Lisandre laughed, with an edge to her voice that made both Briony and Pedrin stare at her in grave concern. "I am delirious. You see, I'm dying. I scratched myself on the starthorn tree, picking the flowers to wake you. Look, that's my lifeblood you see on your counterpane. And here on my dress. And look! On Pedrin's shirt too. And all over the floor. Blood, blood, everywhere!" She laughed hysterically and suddenly gave a convulsive shudder, her eyes rolling back in her head. "Oh, I feel sick," she muttered. "Pedrin, Briony, are you there?"

Savagely Pedrin squeezed his fingers till fresh blood came welling out of his cuts and then he pressed his hands over her gaping wound again, smearing the wound with as much of his own blood as he could. "Briony!" he cried.

Briony followed suit, both of them rubbing their blood into Lisandre's wounds as if it was the most magical of unguents, which it was.

The count stared at them in horror. "Heavens above, what do you think you are doing?"

"Trying to save her life," Pedrin snapped. "Oh, Durrik, where are you?"

The count drew himself back against the headboard. "What foul witchcraft is this? Who are you and what have you done to my sister?"

It was a difficult tale to tell, particularly with Lisandre slowly sinking back into a restless, feverish sleep, muttering under her breath and occasionally calling out in terror. Although Pedrin and Briony constantly anointed her with their own blood or held the mangled starthorn blossoms under her nose to try to revive her, the poison was inexorably gaining ground.

Perhaps it was the sight of Lisandre sunk in fever, her eyes rolling, her limbs twitching, the stain of blood below her slowly creeping out. Or maybe it was the obvious love and anxiety in the faces of the two children who tried so desperately to tend her. Perhaps the story was so very strange that it seemed impossible it could be anything but the truth.

Whatever it was that convinced him, Count Zygmunt was at last persuaded to believe they were giving a true telling. He went through the whole gamut of emotions first, from incredulity to grief to anger, and back again. At last, though, he threw back his bedcovers, saying with a ring of command in his voice, "Help me get up! Where is Lord Zuma, my father's ... I mean, my cup-taster? And Lord Zustin, my spear-carrier? And the gentlemen of the chamber? Have I been left completely unattended?"

"I suppose they attend Lord Zavion ... he's Regent now, remember?"

"Not now that I am awake," Zygmunt said with determination. "Come, if it is the blood of your friends that will save Lisandre, then we must find your friends and quickly too!"

Just then there was a soft grating sound. Briony swung around with a cry of warning.

Lady Donella stood in the doorway, a corked jar hanging from her hand. At the sight of the four children crouched together on the bed, her eyes widened and then narrowed.

"What nuisances you are," she said, coming in and locking the door behind her. "How in heavens did you get yourselves free? And I see you have awoken my lord count. Greetings, my dear Zygmunt! I am afraid I would be less than truthful if I said I was glad to see you looking so well."

"Lady Donella!" Zygmunt said with a rush of blood to his face. "So it is true what they have told me. I can hardly believe it!"

Lady Donella sighed. "Alas, it is all true! And if it had not been for these meddling nuisances, you would be dead now and my dear, dear Lord Zavion would be count. I think I can say with some assurance that it would not have been long before I was

491

countess, a position much worthier of me than a mere lady-in-waiting. Of course, I would have preferred to have been countess of an estate closer to the king's court. However, I'm sure I shall have no difficulty in persuading my loving husband to spend most of his time – and money – in Zarissa."

As she spoke, Lady Donella had glided across the room to the table, where she set down the ceramic jar. She turned to survey them, standing so close they could have reached out and stroked the rich fabric of her dress. Instead they all instinctively cringed back.

"Now, what am I to do with you all? I have no desire to lose everything I have worked so hard to accomplish. I have made too many sacrifices to lose all now."

"Sacrifices? What sacrifices have you made?" Count Zygmunt cried bitterly. "It was my father and all his men that were sacrificed!"

Lady Donella waved her hand nonchalantly. "You must see what hindrances they were to me," she said reproachfully. "Lord Zavion may have been born of the Ziv, but he had no prospects of his own and was already out of favour at the court. Why do you think he was mouldering all the way out here? I could not marry a man with no estate of his own, no matter how nobly born. So what other choice did I have?"

"What other choice!" Count Zygmunt was suffused with colour, his hands clenched beside him. "You murdered my father and all his men, and you tried to murder me!"

"I may yet succeed," Lady Donella said, whipping

her knife out and holding it against his throat, gripping the young count by his long, smooth fair curls. Count Zygmunt yelped in pain and Lady Donella dragged his head back further.

"I see I need not concern myself any more with your troublesome little sister, which is most gratifying as she was always a horrid little brat, very much lacking in respect. You, however? It does not suit my plans at all to have you wake up at this point of time. Now, you have a choice, my dear Ziggy. Either you drink the delicious apple-ale I have prepared for you and die a happy, drunken death, or I slit your throat and you bleed to death beside your dear, sweet, departed sister."

Her voice was very light and agreeable and, as always, she was smiling. A watcher from afar would have thought her a loving and affectionate aunt, genuinely concerned with the count's health. Yet her words struck a chill of horror into them all. Pedrin's legs trembled. The whole room seemed to have suddenly swelled so it pressed hot and dark against his eyeballs, against his lungs, against his inner organs. He could hardly breathe. He could not have taken a step or spoken. His ears were filled with a roaring sound, like a raging fire. He turned his head and looked at Lisandre, who lay peacefully, her hand lax, her eyes nearly closed, only a thin white slit of eyeball showing within. Blood had ceased to pump from her arm.

"No!" Count Zygmunt cried, only to yelp again as Lady Donella pulled viciously at his hair. Lady Donella turned her wrist so the knife slid along his throat. A red line welled up in its wake.

"I must assure you, my dear count, that I shall have no hesitation at all in slitting your throat. I shall blame the goat-boy, of course. Really, the stars are smiling on me today, delivering you all into my hands in such a neat, tidy way. Lisandre would always have been a danger to me if she had lived, once she knew the truth, and you too, goat-boy. Really, I could not ask for things to end in a more satisfactory way!"

Her face was too perfect. It looked as if it must have been crafted from a piece of old ivory, the mouth carved in a perpetual curve. Even her eyes, as violet-blue as her gown, shone with the hard brilliance of a jewel rather than the changeable hues of a human eye. There was no doubt in any of their minds that Lady Donella would, without hesitation, slash her knife across the strained cords of the count's throat.

Count Zygmunt swallowed and said, very faintly, "Very well, give me the apple-ale to drink. If I must die, let me die dancing!"

A tiny grating sound caught Briony's ear. Very slowly she turned her head and glanced toward the door. As Lady Donella smiled and lifted away the knife, Briony saw the door silently open. An old man in the Estaria livery stood outside, his finger to his lips, a key held in his other hand. He pushed the door open a little more and Briony saw Thundercloud leaping forward, horns low.

In a swift, sudden move, Briony seized a pillow from the bed and swiped at Lady Donella. Startled, the lady-in-waiting spun, slashing out with her knife and ripping the pillow so feathers burst everywhere. The count flung himself down to the ground and Thundercloud soared over him, ramming into Lady Donella and knocking her flying.

"Milord!" Briony cried and dropped to her knees beside him. "Are you hurt?"

Ruefully Count Zygmunt rubbed his elbow. "Only my dignity," he answered with a grin. Feathers drifted down like a flurry of snowflakes. Coughing a little, Zygmunt waved his hand to clear the air. The feathers whirled and scudded, tickling their noses, but at last wafted down so that they could see. The old servant came running forward, wringing his hands and exclaiming in horror at the sight of Lisandre's limp, bloodied form. Close on his heels were Durrik and Mags, with Sedgely hobbling behind, his shaggy hair and beard wilder than ever.

"Durrik!" Suddenly Pedrin could not breathe. Sobs were tearing at his ribcage. "You're too late!" he accused. "She's dead, she's dead!"

Their grins of welcome faltered. "Milady?" Durrik cried. "Oh, no!"

"We could've saved her, we could've saved her," Pedrin said and laid his head down on Lisandre's body, shuddering with dry, hot sobs that seemed to shake him to his very foundations. He was weeping for Lisandre, for Snowflake, for his lost innocence, for all that had been ruined and changed.

Suddenly he sprang up, his eyes alight. "She breathed!"

Briony was beside him in an instant, groping for a

pulse, her hand on Lisandre's chest as she felt for any alteration in her ribcage. She looked up too, the dark stormy grey of her eyes changing in an instant to a bright, summery green. "She's alive! Quick, Pedrin! The dagger."

Pedrin seized the silver dagger that the Erlrune had given to Lisandre, and grabbed Durrik by the wrist, dragging him forward.

"What? What?" Durrik cried, not exactly fighting his friend but not exactly going willingly.

"Blood! I need your blood," Pedrin cried.

"The riddle, the second riddle," Briony cried.

Pedrin forced his friend's hand open and down came the knife with a quick slash across Durrik's palm. He screamed, as much in shock as pain, then watched uncomprehendingly as Pedrin pressed his bloody palm over Lisandre's gaping wound.

"Our blood will heal her," Briony said, hanging close. "'Tis the Erlrune's riddle, remember? 'To make whole what was torn, kith must be as kin. For kith to be as kin, what is whole must be torn.'"

"To heal Lisandre, we must cut ourselves," Pedrin said, lifting Durrik's hand away and then holding out his own gory hand imperatively to Mags. She came willingly, holding out her hand like a child asking for cake. The silver knife slashed down and Mags pressed her bleeding palm over the wound. Lisandre stirred and moaned. Then Sedgely stepped forward, shaking his shaggy white head mournfully, his hand stretched out. "The last cut was only just beginning to heal," he sighed. "But if blood is the answer..."

"Blood is the answer," Pedrin grinned, giddy with joy and relief.

As Sedgely closed his huge, hairy hand over Lisandre's arm, she sighed and opened her eyes, looking about her blankly. Then, unexpectedly, she began to laugh.

Pedrin and Briony hurried to soothe her, afraid she was still hysterical with fever, but she waved them away with an impatient flap of her free hand, saying with a catch of laughter in her voice, "Oh, look!"

38

♦ ♦ ♦

They all looked.

Lady Donella was lying on her back, a pair of black, curving horns only inches from her face. Her silk skirts were all scrunched up, showing a pair of very white and skinny legs ending in ridiculously high-heeled shoes. The knife lay half-concealed by feathers only a few inches from her hand but she dared not reach out for it with Thundercloud's slitted yellow eyes glaring at her so menacingly.

"Would ... someone ... call off ... the goat?" she said through stiff lips.

Zygmunt turned to Pedrin with a smile and a courtly bow. "Your goat, I presume? I must say, I have never been so glad to see a billy-goat in my life!"

"Me neither," Pedrin said. "And I'm always glad to see him!"

"You would not care to call him off?"

Pedrin eyed the lady-in-waiting, lying rigid on the floor, staring with trepidation at Thundercloud's horns which he was swinging back and forth, less than an inch from her fair, soft skin.

"I don't think so," he said with a grin. "He seems to be enjoying himself."

He sat down rather limply on the bed. Lisandre sat up next to him, rubbing her arm. Nothing was left of the wound but an ugly, red, jagged scar. "I'm healed?" she asked incredulously. "I'm not going to die?"

Pedrin shook his head. "Our blood healed you," he said rather blankly.

"Is it all over?" she asked. "Are we safe?"

"I think so," he replied.

Lisandre sighed. "I am glad!"

The servant was kneeling on the floor by Zygmunt, kissing his hand fervently. "I should never have left you, milord," he said brokenly. "I knew she warn't to be trusted, with her sweet smile and sly ways. But when she ordered me to go and attend to your mother, I could not refuse else she would have had me head."

"How did you happen to come back just then?" the young count asked, sitting down in the armchair with a sigh. "Another minute and I would have drunk her apple-ale, and I'd be dancing and singing my way to death."

"When I saw the goat a-flying past the door, a-heading towards your room, I thought I'd best come and see all was well. I've never seen a flying goat before!"

"I do not think any of us have," the count replied with a faint smile.

"I hope you will forgive me, milord, but when I found your door locked and the goat so agitated outside, I put me ear to the keyhole. Just to ascertain if all was well, milord."

"So did you hear everything Lady Donella said?"

"Yeah, milord, and me blood ran cold. Who could believe milady's own cousin capable of such wickedness?"

"We may need you to testify at the king's court, Iven. Would you be willing?"

"If you so desire it, milord, of course."

The count gave a weary smile. "Thank you."

"You think the king will listen to a doddering old man and a handful of grubby hearthkin brats?" Lady Donella sneered.

"Yes, I do," Zygmunt replied simply.

While the count and his faithful old servant had been talking, the hearthkin had been crowding around outside, not willing to interrupt those inside. At the sight of a dirty little face peering around the doorjamb, Pedrin was galvanised into sudden action. He raced across the room, calling, "Mina! Mina!"

Brother and sister embraced enthusiastically just inside the door, words spilling out from both but muffled in each other's filthy rags. "I'm so glad to see you!" Pedrin managed to say at last, breaking his little sister's clinging hold so he could see her pale, peaked face, all streaked with dirt and tears. "When did you get so skinny? Any skinnier and we'll be a-sweeping the floor with you! All that hair would come in mighty useful as a broom."

She laughed and pressed herself closer to him, and he rocked her in his arms, saying in a very thick voice,

"Where's Ma? Where's me ma?"

"Here I am, boyo," Maegeth said, her own voice almost suspended in tears. She knelt beside him and enfolded both her children in her arms, and Pedrin embraced her so hard he felt every narrow rib and bony protuberance of her spine. "Talk about skinny!" he said. "Haven't they been a-feeding you?"

"Not much," she answered, sitting back on her heels and grinding her fists into her eyes. "And what they did give us, I made sure Mina had. A growing girl needs her tucker. Oh, Pedrin! I'm mighty glad to see you. I thought you must be dead." Her voice broke in a wail, and she covered her face again, rocking a little as she wept.

"I almost was, about a hundred times," Pedrin answered. "Oh, Ma! Wait till you hear what we've been a-doing! You'll never believe it. We've fought off ghouls and gibgoblins, and got enchanted by the Erlrune, and a grogoyle saved us from the soldiers, and—"

"Nah, you're tomfooling!" Mina cried.

"You're a tale-teller now, are you, me boy?" Maegeth said, wiping her eyes and smiling. "I might believe you fought off a ghoul, but that a grogoyle saved you? I don't think so!"

"Oh, but 'tis true," Durrik said, dropping down on his haunches beside them and grinning. "Every word of it."

"And I'll believe you too, me little joke-teller," Maegeth said.

"Just wait till we tell you the whole tale. There's

501

much more for you to disbelieve," Durrik grinned. He yawned and stretched. "Liah's eyes, I'm a-weary!"

"Durrik was a-telling us that Snowflake was killed," Maegeth said, giving Pedrin's arm a little rub. "I'm so very sorry, me boy. I know how much you loved her."

Pedrin nodded, his face shadowing.

"Is that Thundercloud, a-holding that starkin lady down?" Maegeth said. "Pedrin, she looks mighty angry. Don't you think you'd best call him off?"

"Nah," Pedrin said. "Thundercloud can keep a-butting her back down as many times as he likes. She's a mighty bad lady, that one, Ma."

The billy-goat had looked up at the sound of his name and bleated in response. Suddenly Sedgely bounded forward, quick as any colt, and stamped his big bare foot down hard on Lady Donella's wrist, just as her fingers closed upon her knife. "Not a good idea, milady," he said respectfully. "A few too many angry fellers here. Would hate to see such a pretty lady hurt."

Lady Donella spat a foul curse at him and Sedgely shook his head regretfully. "Now, now, no need for language like that. Dear me, I have to wonder about the way the starkin raise their children. No respect, no respect at all."

Over the rumble of the hearthkin's deep voices came a shrill, angry voice. "This is an outrage! Unhand me, you oaf! I will have the skin flayed from your back for this impudence. Prison must have addled your brains. Do you not know I am the Count of Estelliana?"

"Not yet," Zygmunt said.

Lord Zavion had just been pushed into the room, trying without success to smooth his disordered curls and straighten his rumpled robe. At Zygmunt's words, he looked up sharply. The angry colour drained from his face, leaving him ashen.

"My dear Ziggy!" Lord Zavion said, his composure regained in an instant. "You have awoken at last."

"Yes, no thanks to you," Zygmunt said coldly.

Lord Zavion straightened his sleeve. "But whatever do you mean, my lord? I did everything within my powers to arouse you from your enchanted sleep. I even had them raise a crystal tower, at great trouble and expense—"

"Great trouble and expense for the people of my land," Zygmunt said scornfully. "I have heard what you did while I was asleep, my lord, and believe me, I shall make sure the king hears of it also."

"I hope so," Lord Zavion said smoothly. "Indeed, I have worked hard on your behalf, my lord. I have had to put down a most unruly insurrection, which could well have seen you lose your vacant throne, and I have gathered many unpaid taxes, so that your coffers are well filled again." He looked about him haughtily. "But I see the leaders of the late, unsuccessful insurgency are here, in your very room, with starkin weapons in their illegal possession. My lord! Do you speak under restraint? You need not fear to tell me the truth. They may have us at an impasse now but as soon as the king hears of their vile effrontery, troops will be dispatched and these impudent hearthkin shall die a traitor's death."

Count Zygmunt made an effort to bear himself with as much cold composure as the Regent. "If anyone is to die a traitor's death it shall be you, Lord Zavion…"

"Oh, I doubt that, my dear boy," he replied, smiling urbanely.

"…and your paramour, Lady Donella, who has admitted her guilt in the hearing of a number of witnesses."

For the first time Lord Zavion noticed Lady Donella, lying on the ground still, trying without success to smooth down her skirts with one hand. Sedgely's enormous foot was still clamped upon her other wrist, the knife dropped from her nerveless fingers.

His pupils dilated. For the first time he looked truly shaken. "My lady! What in heavens has happened? What is all this about?"

"Lady Donella poisoned my father and all his men, and tried to poison me," Zygmunt said coldly. "Are you trying to tell me you knew nothing of this?"

All the blood had drained from Lord Zavion's face, leaving him the colour of skimmed milk.

"My lord, I assure you I had no idea, no idea at all," he cried. "I can hardly believe … surely there is some mistake…"

"Lady Donella has admitted her guilt in the hearing of my man Iven, and all my sister's friends," Zygmunt said. "I assure you there is no mistake. She has told us she murdered my father so that you could inherit the throne and make her countess. You expect me to believe you were not a party to her evil schemes?"

Lord Zavion stood motionless, colour fluctuating in his face. Then he cast a look of acute dislike at Lady Donella. "Make *her* countess?" he said in a voice dripping with malice. "My dear Ziggy, I am of the Ziv, related in blood to the king himself. Do you think I would lower myself to marry a mere lady-in-waiting, born of one of the lowliest starkin families? I think not! She is not even in the first flush of her beauty. The king would never believe me capable of such romantic folly. She may well have committed all sorts of heinous crimes in the hope of ensnaring me, but that does not make me guilty by association."

"That may be true," Count Zygmunt said, "but you have abused your powers here in Estelliana and the king will be made aware of it. I have heard what state my lands are in, with the hearthkin starving and the fields all untilled, all because you imprisoned the men of the land on an egotistical whim."

"My dear boy—"

"Please address me by my title," Count Zygmunt said coldly. "I am the Count of Estelliana."

Lord Zavion ground his teeth. "My lord," he said coldly. "I do not know what foul lies these hearthkin serfs have been telling you but I—"

"I can see the truth of their tale in their very dress and bearing," Zygmunt cried, indicating the filthy, bruised, emaciated figures crowding close about, their faces set in grim lines. "And believe me, the king shall hear the truth also, if I have to go to Zarissa and convince him myself! These are not animals, to be beaten and starved and locked up in pens! These are people,

Lord Zavion. I would condemn you for treating a goat like this, let alone the people of my land who have worked hard and faithfully all their lives. Oh, I am sickened to my stomach at the very thought of what you have been doing while I have been asleep."

"My lord, I protest vociferously! I am of the Ziv. How dare you believe a pack of mangy, filthy, rebellious peasants over your own flesh and blood! I shall have you declared insane and these impudent dogs put to death!"

"The king will ascertain the truth." Zygmunt waved his hand. "Please, somebody, take him away! Take them both away! They weary me."

The bell-crier stepped forward and bowed deeply. "Milord, I am glad to see you awake and well!"

Zygmunt nodded rather warily. "I thank you."

"I'm afraid we had to rough up a few of your soldiers to get here," the bell-crier said.

Zygmunt grinned, suddenly looking like a boy of only fifteen instead of a tired and grief-stricken count. "Think nothing of it, my dear fellow. I'm sure they were in need of the practice."

"I am sure all of us here would be glad to rid you of these pus-filled pustules. The question is, what do you wish us to do with them? They're as dangerous as vipers in the grass, milord."

"Much as I would like to make her drink her own poison, I think we had best have Lady Donella sent to the city for the king's judgement," Zygmunt replied, his face sobering. "Lord Zavion too. Until then, I suppose the dungeon is the best place for them."

"Are there lots of rats and cockroaches there?" Lisandre said hopefully.

"Hundreds," the bell-crier answered with a twisted smile.

"Good," Lisandre smiled.

Lady Donella was hauled roughly to her feet and marched out of the count's bedroom by an escort of angry-faced hearthkin, Lord Zavion haughtily stalking along behind, fastidiously releasing his sleeve from the grasp of his hearthkin escort and dusting it clean. "You will be sorry for this, my lord," he hissed. "I am not without influence at court!"

"Which is why you were sent to Estelliana in disgrace," Zygmunt responded in a bored tone.

"How dare you touch me, you imbecilic peasants!" Lady Donella was screaming. "Take your filthy hands off me, I say. I will have you all flayed for this..." Her shrill voice faded away.

"Supercilious beast," Lisandre said. "Who does she think she is, talking like that?"

The others all laughed at her. She blushed and gave a rueful smile.

"What I want more than anything else on earth is a hot bath," Lisandre said, looking down at her blood-encrusted hands. "And some clean clothes. And maybe a nice bowl of hot bouillabaisse, because I'm starving. Then I want to see my mother! Oh, has anyone seen her? Is she very ill?"

The old servant Iven smiled at her reassuringly. "She is well, milady. Or at least she will be now that Lady Donella won't be a-forcing her foul drugs down her throat any more. I did my best to protect her, milady, but that viper was a-slithering everywhere, a-watching us all with her sly eyes and keeping us a-starting at shadows. I'm mighty glad to have you home again, and the count awoken, and everything right with the world."

"Me too," Lisandre sighed. "Though everything's not right in the world, Iven. I've seen a lot while I've been gone and I never knew..." She drew a deep, sighing breath. "Well, I know now and I'll make sure Ziggy knows too. There's a long way to go before we can even begin to think the world's a good place to be."

"Yeah, that's the truth, milady," Iven said, nodding his silver head. "But having you home is enough to begin with."

Lisandre smiled rather mistily. "I'm glad to be home too," she said simply.

"Well," Sedgely said cheerfully, his eyes brightening at the sight of the jar of apple-ale on the table. "I think a toast may now be in order!"

He uncorked the jar with an enthusiastic pop, and was just lifting it to his mouth when a chorus of voices cried, "No, Sedgely! Stop! 'Tis starthorn ale!"

Sedgely stopped with the mouth of the jar only an inch away from his bristling moustache. He put it back on the table, shaking his head sadly. "I should've known," he said miserably. "All together too much apple-ale left lying about in this castle. I should've known some of it would be poisoned! Remind me never to touch another drop of starkin brew."

"Very well, if you are sure," Lisandre said.

Sedgely tugged his beard despondently. "Yeah, I'm sure."

"It's rather a shame, though, for I was just about to ask my brother to grant you unlimited access to our kitchen and our cellars for the rest of your life, as a reward for your courage and loyalty. But since you are determined not to drink a drop of starkin brew…"

"Now, now, no need to be hasty," Sedgely said hurriedly. "Have to give an old horse time for reflection, you know. Mustn't be rash. I know you young things are always in a hurry, not taking the time for reflection or repose, but it doesn't pay, I promise you. Slowly does it, young miss, slowly does it."

"You are a very wise old horse," the starkin girl said, her blue eyes gleaming bright with laughter. "Ziggy, will you call for refreshments? I think Sedgely is right. A toast is definitely in order – and I'll bet a bag of silver crowns that Pedrin and Durrik are hungry!"

Lisandre had been bemusingly pretty even when grimy and matted with leaves, or with her face red and scrunched up with tears, or set hard with misery and determination. Now, with her whole being radiant with joy, her face alight with mischief, she was so entrancing that Pedrin could not take his eyes off her.

Suddenly he became aware that Briony was watching him, her eyes sombre and grey as the sky outside. Colour scorched up his face, right to the very tips of his ears. He gave her an anxious, pleading look and she smiled at him, the colour of her eyes suddenly lighting to moon-silver. He smiled back rather ruefully but, as if drawn by a magnet, his gaze returned once more to Lisandre, who was gleefully telling her brother some of their adventures.

Durrik nudged him in the ribs. "Shut your mouth, Pedrin, you're drooling," he whispered.

Pedrin cast him a furious, embarrassed look but Durrik only grinned and mimed wiping his mouth.

"You climbed down from the castle on a rope?" Ziggy cried, a little scandalised. "And stowed away on a barge? Lisandre!"

"Well, Ziggy, you'd still be fast asleep if I hadn't," Lisandre said rather impatiently. "Or dead."

"I suppose so, but Lise ... what if someone had seen you!" Zygmunt said. "And really, the clothes you are wearing ... and your hair!"

Lisandre rolled her eyes and looked towards her friends, expecting and receiving sympathetic grins. Then her eyes suddenly lit with impishness.

"Pedrin, Durrik, I've got one! Listen! What is the difference between Ziggy awake and Ziggy asleep?"

"What?" they asked obediently.

"The first, he's a sheepish count, and the second, he's counting sheep!"

Laughter pealed out.

"Bully beef!" Mags cried.

"Not bad," Durrik conceded. "We'll make a riddle-master out of you yet."

"You are such a tomfool, Lise," Pedrin grinned and gently punched her arm.